Praise

"Fans of C. S. Forester's Horatio Hornblower will delight in discovering Baker's Sikander North."
—*RT Book Reviews* (starred review)

"*Valiant Dust* is an excellent example of military SF at its best."
—Michael A. Stackpole,
bestselling author of *Rogue Squadron*

"In the finest tradition of Honor Harrington, Black Jack Geary, and Nicholas Seafort . . . an exciting new entry that fans of the genre won't want to miss."
—Dayton Ward,
bestselling author of *24: Trial by Fire*

"Intelligent space opera with lots of vivid action . . . A sociological novel [that] examines the problems (on both sides) of a Third World aristocrat in a First World navy whose hierarchies are equally rigid."
—David Drake,
author of the Hammer's Slammers series

"Intensely satisfying. Bravo! I look forward to more exploits of Sikander North!"
—Ed Greenwood,
creator of Forgotten Realms™

"An excellent mix of military action and political intrigue."
—Eric Flint, author of the 1632 series

RICHARD BAKER

RESTLESS LIGHTNING

A TOM DOHERTY ASSOCIATES BOOK
New York

This is a work of fiction. All of the characters, organizations, and events portrayed in this novel are either products of the author's imagination or are used fictitiously.

RESTLESS LIGHTNING

Copyright © 2018 by Richard Baker

All rights reserved.

A Tor Book
Published by Tom Doherty Associates
120 Broadway
New York, NY 10271

www.tor-forge.com

Tor® is a registered trademark of Macmillan Publishing Group, LLC.

ISBN 978-1-250-30386-8

Our books may be purchased in bulk for promotional, educational, or business use. Please contact your local bookseller or the Macmillan Corporate and Premium Sales Department at 1-800-221-7945, extension 5442, or by email at MacmillanSpecialMarkets@macmillan.com.

First Edition: October 2018
First Mass Market Edition: September 2019

Printed in the United States of America

0 9 8 7 6 5 4 3 2 1

FOR MOM.

*Thanks for taking us to places
where I could learn to appreciate history.*

So ye shall bide sure-guarded when the restless lightnings wake
In the womb of the blotting war-cloud, and the pallid nations quake.
So, at the haggard trumpets, instant your soul shall leap
Forthright, accoutred, accepting—alert from the wells of sleep.
So at the threat ye shall summon—so at the need ye shall send
Men, not children or servants, tempered and taught to the end;
Cleansed of servile panic, slow to dread or despise,
Humble because of knowledge, mighty by sacrifice.

—Rudyard Kipling, "The Islanders"

RESTLESS
LIGHTNING

1

Bagal-Dindir, Tamabuqq Prime

This is a damned peculiar way to travel," remarked Commodore William Abernathy in a sour tone. He waved one hand to indicate the open-sided carriage in which they rode, the elaborately dressed Tzoru driver with his—or her?—painted dermal patterns, and the *alliksisu* yoked to the boatlike prow. The Aquilan flag officer fidgeted in a vain effort to find a comfortable posture for his seat. Short and slight of frame, with iron-gray hair and a stiff terrier's mustache, Abernathy disliked sitting still, especially on a cold and damp day. "It'll take us half an hour to reach the embassy at this pace, and I'll be damned if it isn't snowing by the time we get there."

Lieutenant Commander Sikander Singh North, Commonwealth Navy, noted that his new commanding officer's favorite word appeared to be "damned" and carefully hid a smile. He found the cold, clammy weather uncomfortable too, but he had about thirty kilos on Abernathy, all of it muscle. Most people from his homeworld—Jaipur, in the Kashmir system—possessed the stocky, broad-shouldered frames common among natives of planets a little over standard gravity. If *he* felt the chill through his Navy overcoat, the commodore probably felt like he was sitting in a freezer.

"It's tradition, sir," he told the commodore. "At least the

ride is smooth." Maglev rails buried under the avenue powered every street in the Tzoru capital, providing a wheelless suspension for the carriage. The transportation network had been installed around the same time ancient humans had first figured out agriculture. Time and again during Sikander's tour of duty in the squadron posted on the Navy's Helix Station he'd started to believe he might actually understand something about the culture or psychology of the alien Tzoru—and time and again he'd been confronted by some new piece of evidence that humans didn't really understand the Tzoru at all. *For example, powering the roads but not the vehicles. Leave it to the Tzoru to come up with that one!*

"Tradition? A damned stupid one, I suppose," Abernathy muttered, confirming Sikander's suspicion about his favorite word.

"Powered ground cars would challenge the place held by the carriage-driver *sebetu,* sir," Captain Francine Reyes explained to Abernathy. Tall and poised in comparison to her wiry, energetic superior, she wore a more or less permanent frown of disapproval at the various idiosyncrasies of the Tzoru. Abernathy had taken command of the squadron patrolling Helix Station only a week ago, but she'd served as deputy commodore under his predecessor for more than a year. Like Sikander, she'd had plenty of time to experience the peculiarities of Tzoru customs.

"*Sebetu*—those are the Tzoru clans, right?"

"Something about halfway between a clan, a guild, and a caste, yes." Reyes had anticipated that the weather might be cold; she at least had dressed warmly for the carriage ride. She continued her explanation: "Taking away the role of the carriage-driver *sebetu* would upset the harmony of things. The Tzoru simply don't do that unless they must."

"Are you serious, D-Com?" said Abernathy. "In ten thousand years no one's convinced the taxi drivers to retire their ridiculous draft beasts? So why couldn't we just land at the embassy grounds and skip the whole thing?"

Sikander took that as his cue. "Sir, no one flies over Bagal-Dindir except for members of the aristocratic *sebetu* or their soldiers. If it's any consolation, the privilege of an official carriage is a sign of Tzoru deference to your rank. Otherwise we'd have to take the trolley or walk." He'd learned more than a few hard lessons about Tzoru inflexibility during nineteen months as Helix Squadron's intelligence officer, especially when it came to Tzoru military protocols. Sikander was a line officer by trade, but not even a career intelligence specialist could be expected to make sense of the contradictions and challenges every Commonwealth officer who rotated through Helix Squadron encountered. In fact, the Admiralty staggered relief assignments specifically to ensure that the squadron staff always included at least a few officers who'd been on Helix Station for some time.

"Walking might be warmer," Abernathy said with a snort. He shivered inside his overcoat, and leaned forward to address the driver. "You, there. Can we go a little faster? I want to beat the snowstorm." The translation device clipped to his collar emitted a string of guttural Tzoqabu a moment after he finished.

The driver turned to regard the small party reclining in the open carriage, twisting easily in a motion that would have tested a human contortionist. He (or so Sikander guessed, since humans could have a difficult time telling Tzoru of different sexes apart) replied to Abernathy in Tzoqabu; Sikander's own translation device fed the interpretation into his ears: "The *alliksisu* has no interest in hurrying, honored friends, but if you are cold I can activate the heating plates."

"There is a heater?" Abernathy asked in a flat tone.

"Yes, honored friend. I shall activate it." The Tzoru adjusted controls on a small panel near his left hand, then returned to the task of directing the *alliksisu*—a creature that looked like a blue, scaly rhinoceros with long legs and three wide toes on each foot. A moment later, a pleasant warmth enveloped Sikander's legs and began to well upward from the floor.

"Could've used that ten minutes ago," said Lieutenant Mason Barnes, leaving his translator off. The fourth in Abernathy's small party, Barnes—Sikander's roommate in their Academy days, and one of the closest friends he had in the Navy—served as Helix Squadron's communications officer. He had the pale complexion, red hair, and rural accent of a Hibernian. People who evinced characteristics of the old Terran races were somewhat unusual in the metropolitan worlds of the Aquilan Commonwealth, or any of the other great powers in the Coalition of Humanity. Noticeably distinct traits like the fair skin of the Hibernians, or the coppery complexion and wavy black hair common in Kashmir, indicated descent from populations that had been isolated at some point or other during humanity's expansion to the stars. Mason caught Sikander's eye and nodded at the driver's back as if to say, *A Tzoru being Tzoru, what can you do?*

Sikander answered with a small shrug. Humans had encountered only four other starfaring species and the long-dead ruins of a few others in nine centuries of interstellar travel. Of the living four species, Tzoru were perhaps the most humanlike, but despite bipedal morphology and technology comparable to human technology, Tzoru were indeed *alien*. They had evolved from semiaquatic pack hunters millions of years ago; a sort of stiff cartilage made up their skeletons, and they had tough rubbery crests with breathing apertures instead of noses. In place of skin, Tzoru had a gray, leathery dermis with patterns of scales—broad and thick on the back and shoulders, finer and more colorful around the face. Their eyes were large and dark and set almost on the sides of their bullet-shaped heads, and their wide, lipless mouths were filled with serrated teeth. Tzoru dressed themselves in kilts and sleeveless tunics for everyday wear, layered robes in cold weather, or elaborately ornate robes when they wished to demonstrate their social status . . . which was at every opportunity, in Sikander's experience.

Tzoru thought processes and emotions likewise ranged

from near-human to coldly pragmatic and uncompassion-ate. They had nothing like the human drives of romantic love, ambition, restlessness, or a craving for thrills, but they showed great affection for friends and relatives. And they had exactly zero empathy for strangers, which meant that a car-riage driver bundled up against the chill of a cold day would never even begin to imagine that his passengers might be cold if they didn't bring it to his attention.

"I knew it. Now it's snowing," Abernathy observed. Sikan-der glanced up; sure enough, wet, heavy flakes drifted down from the gray clouds overhead. The commodore drew his overcoat more snugly over his chest and settled back in his seat with a sigh of resignation.

"If you'll look over thataway, sir, you can see the Anshar's Palace," Mason said, perhaps hoping to distract Abernathy's attention from the cold, wet ride. "Just through that gap in the treeferns, there. Those're the monuments of the Royal Ward." Slender spires, mighty domes, and steep-sided zig-gurats loomed a kilometer or two from the boulevard down which they rode. Bagal-Dindir had the population of any large human city, but Tzoru built few high-rise buildings; as a result the capital sprawled over a vast area. In some neighborhoods one could hardly tell that one was in a city at all, but the Thousand Worlds ward—the city's "Embassy Row"—stood in an old temple district not far from the seat of the Dominion's government. The drive from the space-port to the Aquilan embassy offered some of the better views to be found in the city.

"That big ziggurat with all the gold on it?" Abernathy asked, craning for a better look.

"Yes, sir. They say that one building covers almost three square kilometers."

"Impressive," Abernathy admitted. "Have any of you been there?"

"No, sir," said Sikander. "Only a handful of humans have ever set foot in the palace."

Reyes gave a small snort of disgust. "The Anshar's attendants almost never permit non-Tzoru to sully the grounds with our presence. It's rather insulting, if you ask me."

"Hmmph." Abernathy grunted and looked away, turning his attention to their immediate surroundings. Private homes, workshops, and small businesses dotted both sides of the boulevard, interspersed with open spaces that allowed longer views. Tzoru dressed in the colors of many different *sebetu* hurried from one establishment to another or rode along in carriages and carts that cluttered the street. Quite terran in many ways, Tamabuqq Prime had breathable air, oceans filled with water, natural flora dominated by green plants, and more or less Earthlike seasons and weather. But even after a year and a half stationed in the heart of the Tzoru Dominion, Sikander still found it disconcertingly alien. The sounds and smells were all wrong: the avians hissed and clicked instead of singing, overpowering spice-like scents filled the air, and the sky on a sunny day was a pale green hue.

Five more months, Sikander told himself. His tour in Helix Squadron would soon be over. The Tzoru frontier lay more than a month from Aquila's core systems; it was the sort of place where ambitious officers went to make names for themselves without the oversight of their superiors, and superiors who didn't want to deal with troublesome subordinates could send them out of sight and out of mind. Sikander belonged to the latter group: Very few Kashmiris served in the Aquilan navy, fewer still came from families as pedigreed or powerful as the Norths of Jaipur, and exactly one had taken command of an Aquilan warship in the middle of a battle, fighting through to victory in the face of orders to withdraw. After the prominent role Sikander had played in the Gadira incident, half the Admiralty had wanted to commend him, and the other half had wanted to court-martial him. The compromise that had eventually won out was evidently to hide him in the most remote post they could think of. *But which side of the debate does Abernathy favor?* The new commodore hadn't bothered to tell Sikander whether he approved or disapproved of his actions at Gadira.

A snowflake slipped past the visor of his cap, narrowly missing his eye. Sikander brushed at his face, noting that the flurry seemed to be growing heavier. He hadn't seen snow in years, a simple accident of assignments to bases in temperate climes and periods of leave that never seemed to align with the cold season at home. Now that he thought of it, it had been snowing the first time he met William Abernathy. Fourteen years ago, back at the Academy, a day filled with heavy flurries—

—dancing outside the high windows of Powell Hall's formal hearing room. The afternoon is cold and gray; the furnishings are dark, old wood, massive as battlements. Sikander, a freshman, faces the Disciplinary Committee: five senior midshipmen with faces that might have been carved from stone. A dozen of Sikander's classmates and upperclassmen from his company sit behind him; he can't see them, but their silence is a tangible weight at his back. At the side of the room, Commander Abernathy, staff advisor to the committee, sits with his head leaning on his hand, watching the scene. His posture suggests he is falling asleep.

The committee chairperson, a senior named Adelaide Wallace, reads from a document: "Midshipman Fourth Class North, you have been placed on report for the infraction of striking a superior officer. Your company commander states that on the evening of February tenth, he found you engaged in a fistfight with Midshipman Second Class Gray. During this altercation he saw you throw several punches at Mr. Gray, and that you continued to do so even after you were ordered to stop. The purpose of this proceeding is to examine the facts of the report, provide you an opportunity to make answer, and then determine the appropriate punishment. This is an administrative proceeding and is not a hearing under the military justice code, but any statements you make here are considered to be in the public record and you are expected to be truthful under the Academy honor code. Do you understand?"

"I do, ma'am," Sikander answers.

"Midshipman Second Class Gray and your company commander have already stated that they agree with the facts as stated in the report. Do you dispute any part of the report?"

Sikander hesitates before he speaks. "No, ma'am. The report is correct."

Midshipman Wallace looks up at that. "You are admitting that you are guilty of striking Mr. Gray? The customary punishment is expulsion, Mr. North."

"Ma'am, Midshipman-Commander Farrell accurately reported what he observed when he arrived on the scene and what Mr. Gray said to him at that time. But the report says nothing about what happened before Mr. Farrell got there, or whether Mr. Gray was telling the truth."

"You dare to call me a liar, Snottie?" an angry voice snarls behind Sikander. A clatter of scraping chairs follows.

Sikander can't help it; he turns around. Midshipman Victor Gray, a junior in Sikander's own company, knocks his chair over as he springs to his feet. He is a tall, sandy-haired young man, stocky and strong for an Aquilan, and his face is twisted in fury.

Sikander looks him right in the eye. "Yes, sir. I do."

Gray takes a half step toward him and balls his fists. The midshipmen that make up the Disciplinary Committee look at each other in confusion. Several people start to speak at once. But Commander Abernathy sits up straight and slaps his open hand on the tabletop in front of him so loudly everybody in the room jumps. "Strike that from the record!" he snaps. "And Gray's remark too. We will have no such insinuations on the transcript, is that clear?"

Adelaide Wallace stares at Abernathy in surprise before nodding to the underclassman who serves as the committee clerk. "As Mr. Abernathy requests," she says to him. "Strike the last two remarks, please."

"Ms. Wallace, I suggest a brief recess," Abernathy continues. Without waiting for her reply, he stands and marches over to where Sikander stands. He's easily ten centimeters shorter than Sikander or any of the other midshipmen, but in that moment the only commissioned officer in the room seems to tower over everyone. It's all Sikander can do to stand his ground without flinching. "North, come with me. I need a word with you."

He spins on his heel and strides away as the midshipmen watch. Sikander stares after him for a moment, then hurries after him—

"What's going on here?" Abernathy asked suddenly, rousing Sikander from the old memories. The commodore had a little more gray in his hair and gold braid on his uniform than the officer Sikander remembered from his Academy days, but seemed otherwise unmarked by the passage of fourteen years.

Sikander turned to see what had caught the commodore's attention. Scores of agitated Tzoru crowded together in front of an open-sided shelter or hall a short distance up the street. Many wore green, double-pointed caps of a design he hadn't seen before, and one individual standing on a parked cart led a responsive chant. At each pause, the Tzoru in the crowd raised their hands in the air and shouted wildly in response: *"Ebneghirz! Ebneghirz!"*

"Some kind of religious procession," said Deputy Commodore Reyes with a scowl of disapproval. Like many Aquilans, Reyes had no use for religious beliefs of any sort, human or alien. "There's some such nonsense every day in Bagal-Dindir. That building behind the crowd is a shrine—they're all over the capital."

"They seem worked up about something," said Abernathy. The crowd slowly drifted into motion, streaming down the street toward the carriage. "Is this typical?"

"It's the first time I've seen something like it, sir," Sikander said. It didn't seem to be any kind of religious event;

Tzoru shrine processions were celebrations, not protests or rallies. Perhaps that distinction was lost on most Aquilans—secularists and rather smug about it—but as a Kashmiri he'd been raised in New Sikhism and surrounded by Hindu friends and acquaintances. That didn't make him an expert on Tzoru public displays, but it did mean that he was not as quick as his Aquilan comrades to assume that religious beliefs were at the root of any inexplicable or belligerent behavior. He looked up at the carriage driver, activating his translator. "Excuse me, driver—who are those Tzoru over there?"

"They are *warumzi agu*," the driver replied. "I did not know that there would be a gathering at this hour."

"What are they going on about?" Mason Barnes asked.

"They are praising Ebneghirz," the driver repeated. The name seemed familiar to Sikander. He thought he might have seen something about it in recent intel summaries—a passing mention, perhaps. The Tzoru Dominion simply didn't have any kind of media culture, and finding out what any large number of Tzoru thought about something was surprisingly difficult. The driver seemed annoyed rather than concerned, but of course that might mean anything. On the other hand, it only took Sikander a few moments of watching to decide that he didn't like the look of the crowd at all. He'd never seen a Tzoru mob in person, but he'd seen more than a few human ones, and something about this group shouted *danger!* at him.

"Driver, are they angry at us?" he asked directly. Sometimes that was necessary to get a Tzoru to consider a situation outside of his or her own narrow interests.

It worked—the driver glanced down at Sikander, back to the *warumzi agu* procession, and back to Sikander again before nodding. "They may be," he conceded. "Honored friends, it would be better if we went a different way." He made a clicking sound at the *alliksisu* and touched its flank with a long, reedlike goad, turning the creature toward a cross street before the crowd reached them. Driving an *al-*

liksisu carriage seemed to involve a good deal of suggestion and persuasion, and few actual controls.

The Tzoru leading the crowd caught sight of Sikander and his companions in the carriage, and suddenly raised their voices in excitement. "I think that's a good idea," Abernathy said. He and Reyes occupied the rear seat of the carriage, so they now had their backs to the crowd; the wiry commodore twisted in his seat, scowling at the approaching Tzoru. "Driver, get us out of here."

Francine Reyes glanced back as well, then keyed her comm device. "*Exeter* shuttle, this is Captain Reyes. Stand by for immediate retrieval of our party. We have a situation developing."

"Ma'am, the Tzoru authorities will never permit an overflight," Sikander said.

"I don't intend to ask them," said Reyes. "Better to—oh, *damn*."

Behind the carriage, the leading ranks of the *warumzi agu* broke into a run, bounding after the carriage in short, springy strides that swallowed up the distance with alarming speed. "Look out!" Sikander shouted. He rose from his seat and crouched upright in the carriage, ready to fend off anyone trying to climb aboard. He had no idea if unarmed combat against a Tzoru was a good idea or not, but he'd rather go down swinging if it came to it. Mason Barnes followed his lead, and got up to guard the other side of the carriage.

"*Exeter* shuttle, come get us!" Reyes shouted into her comm unit.

The carriage driver flicked his goad again, and the *al-liksisu* fell into a clumsy trot . . . but the mob continued to close the distance. Some of the *warumzi agu* drew close enough to pelt the humans with small stones, bottles, and even round, hard fruit of some sort, an angry hail that clattered against the metal sides of the carriage or bounced back into the street. Sikander ducked and raised a hand over his head to protect himself—and then a fist-sized bottle sailed out of the crowd, striking the driver in the back.

The driver gave a sort of whistling hiss and suddenly abandoned his post, leaping down to the street and scuttling away. "Do not hurt me!" he shouted before the translator lost his voice. Sikander caught a glimpse of the fellow scissoring his hands in front of him and bowing as he hurried off, a Tzoru gesture more or less equivalent to a human raising his hands over his head. The pursuing Tzoru swarmed around him; several began to tear at his robes and pummel him savagely.

Confused, the *alliksisu* began to slow again—and then something else was thrown into the carriage, a clawed creature about the size of a large rat. It had a spiky carapace and a barbed tail equipped with a jabbing sting, and it scrabbled about the floor of the carriage, clacking its mandibles. All four humans flinched away from the repulsive little monster.

"What is *that*?" Abernathy snarled.

Sikander had no idea, but when the creature darted after Reyes, he saw his opportunity. He stepped forward and swung his right foot through the creature in a magnificent soccer-style kick that punted the thing a good six meters through the air. It disappeared into the crowd. At the same time, Mason scrambled up over the passenger bench to the driver's position, seized the slender goad, and whacked the *alliksisu* across the rump with a blow so forceful that Sikander heard the *crack!* above the shouting and screams all around them. The draft beast let out a roar of pain and bolted away, throwing the passengers back into their seats and scattering the crowd surrounding the carriage. Sikander lost his balance completely and fell heavily onto Abernathy and Reyes.

By the time he extricated himself from his superiors, the mob of green-capped Tzoru had fallen far behind. Barnes stood in the driver's position, guiding the galloping beast with the goad. He managed to coax the *alliksisu* into turning down a cross street, and let it gallop on for a few hundred meters. Astonished Tzoru stopped in their tracks to goggle at the carriage and its human occupants racing past. Sikander ignored them and kept watch on the street behind the carriage, making sure the mob couldn't catch up to them.

"Mr. North, any sign of pursuit?" Abernathy said, raising his voice to be heard over the draft beast's bellows of protest and galloping footfalls. Sikander noticed that at some point in the encounter the commodore had lost his gold-braided cap.

"They gave up two or three hundred meters back. I think we're clear for now, sir."

"Very good. Mr. Barnes, see if you can slow this thing down before we flip the carriage or run over somebody. D-Com, cancel the shuttle, if you please."

"*Exeter* shuttle, belay your orders," Reyes said into her comm unit. "We are no longer in immediate danger."

"Yes, sir." Mason glanced around the driver's post, and carefully adjusted a lever. The carriage magnets changed their orientation, applying a smooth braking resistance to the *alliksisu*. The beast immediately responded to the signal, slowing to a walk.

"Well done," Abernathy said. "When in the world did you learn to drive one of these ridiculous things, anyway?"

"I'm Hibernian, sir. Not the first time I drove a horse-drawn carriage. Or whatever the Tzoru call their horses."

The commodore snorted. Hibernia had a reputation for being rural and backward, at least by Aquilan standards. "It would seem so. Now, where is our embassy again?"

"I know the way, sir," Mason replied. "We're not that far off. But shouldn't we go back for the driver?"

"Of course not," Abernathy said. "If he didn't want us to leave without him he shouldn't have abandoned his post in the face of danger. Mr. Barnes, the embassy, if you please."

"Yes, sir." Mason applied the goad again, gently this time. The draft beast picked up its pace; the lieutenant guided it onto another crossing avenue, and settled into the driver's position. He looked ridiculously out of place, but he seemed to have the draft animal under control.

"Very good. Now someone explain to me what just happened there. Who are these Warzi Gooey fellows? Why did they chase us? Mr. North?"

"I'm not sure, sir. I think it's some kind of popular movement—the Tzoru have a lot of them, but nothing that makes it onto our threat assessments." Sikander shrugged helplessly. "I'm afraid the only intelligence the squadron staff collects on local civilian matters is what the Tzoru report on their own broadcasts."

"That's not good enough," Deputy Commodore Reyes said to Sikander. "You should review local conditions with the embassy before we even set foot on the ground, Mr. North. An intelligence officer is supposed to anticipate trouble, especially when a flag officer's personal safety may be at risk."

Sikander bristled, and barely succeeded in fighting down a sharp retort. In the first place, it was not a fair criticism—local developments weren't really part of his job as squadron S-2. His team focused on the formations and capabilities of the Tzoru military *sebetu,* as well as the squadrons of half a dozen other human powers that maintained a presence in Tzoru space. Tzoru politics were *complicated,* and even the expert diplomats of Aquila's embassy had trouble interpreting events here. Secondly, he didn't care at all for Reyes making a point of criticizing him to their new commanding officer. She'd done enough of that with Commodore Morse; the last thing he needed was for her to continue that sort of harassment now that Commodore Abernathy had assumed command.

Unfortunately, arguing against a superior officer's criticism rarely improved matters. So instead he said the only thing he could in reply: "Yes, ma'am. I will touch base with our embassy staff."

Commodore Abernathy let the exchange pass without comment. Instead he made a show of studying the ancient walls surrounding the Thousand Worlds ward, now coming into view, and gave his stiff mustache a small tug. *A note of approval, or disapproval?* Sikander wondered. For a man who carried himself with such energy and wasn't shy about sharing his opinions, William Abernathy could be surprisingly hard to read at times.

Mason tapped the *alliksisu* on its flank and turned the creature and the carriage to the right, passing beneath the ceremonial gateway leading into the Thousand Worlds ward. The ancient fortifications rose up around them, then gave way to a crowded district of homes and workshops and mercantile establishments huddled together within the old walls. More floating *alliksisu*-drawn carriages crowded the narrow streets, but here human diplomats and businesspeople mingled with Tzoru servants, shopkeepers, and retainers in the service of one or another of the noble clans. No less than nine different human powers maintained embassies in the Thousand Worlds ward, not to mention a sprawling Nyeiran mission and a Velar consulate hidden in one of the back alleyways. In eight square kilometers of the old walled district, humans and nonhumans from almost all of civilized space met and interacted with each other in a disorderly, chaotic cauldron of activity.

"Here we are, Commodore," Mason announced. He guided their draft beast into a circular driveway in front of a sprawling building—recent human construction, not ancient Tzoru—that reminded Sikander of the governor's mansion on New Perth. Aquilan marines in dress uniforms stood watch by the main entrance; their crisply pressed uniforms were much the same as the ones their predecessors had worn for centuries, but the mag rifles at their sides were brand new and very, very functional.

"Very good," Abernathy grunted. He stood and hopped down from the seat without waiting; Sikander and Reyes followed, while Mason handed the goad to a Tzoru attendant who hurried up to relieve him. Sikander took a moment to check his uniform for any unsuspected tears or marks, and discovered a section of ripped seam along his side and a purple stain—probably from some foodstuff or other thrown at the carriage—on his left shin. The others in the party likewise took note of smudges or damaged uniforms with various scowls.

A short, broad-shouldered woman in the uniform of a marine major emerged from the embassy and marched out to meet them. She glanced once at the disheveled carriage, but said nothing before snapping a salute to Abernathy. "Commodore Abernathy, welcome to Bagal-Dindir. I'm Major Constanza Dalton, officer in charge of the protective detail. Ambassador Hart is waiting to see you; there have been some unusual developments today."

"The *warumzi agu,* we know," said Abernathy. He returned her salute. "Excitable fellows—they let us know that they didn't appreciate humans riding about in the capital."

"*Warumzi agu?*" Major Dalton frowned. "We've been getting reports about them in other cities, but this is the first I've heard about any in the capital. However, that's not what I referred to. I was speaking of the trouble in the Dominion High Council."

"Trouble? What trouble?" asked Sikander. After five visits to Bagal-Dindir in nineteen months, he'd come to know Constanza Dalton fairly well. She prided herself on maintaining a certain decorum as the commander of the embassy's marine detachment, and that meant a mild term such as "trouble" likely carried a great deal of understatement with it.

"The first councillor just announced that he's stepping down," Dalton replied. "The news broke an hour ago. It's all the buzz in the streets of the Thousand Worlds today."

Reyes shot another look at Sikander, but he ignored her. "Sapwu Zrinan is no longer in power? Who's in charge at the Anshar's court?"

"That's the question, isn't it?" Major Dalton returned

her attention to Abernathy, and gestured toward the embassy's front door. "Right this way, Commodore. Ambassador Hart said that you were to go on up as soon as you arrived."

2

Bagal-Dindir, Tamabuqq Prime

orman Hart, Aquilan ambassador to the Tzoru Dominion, met the Helix Squadron officers at the door to his office. He stood ten centimeters taller than Francine Reyes, the tallest in their group, and with his florid face, thick silver hair, and checkered Tzoru-made stole, he seemed to fill the room with his very presence. "Captain Reyes, Mr. North, Mr. Barnes, good to see you again," he said, his expression warm. Then he extended a hand to Abernathy. "Commodore Abernathy, it's a pleasure to meet you. Please, come in."

"Thank you," said Abernathy, taking the offered hand. "The pleasure's mine, Ambassador."

"I hear that your ride in from the landing field took an unpleasant turn. I'm sorry—nothing like that has happened in years." The ambassador shook his head as he ushered them toward the sitting area in the spacious office. "If we'd had any warning that trouble might be brewing we would have warned you to bring along some marines, or arranged for a detail to meet you at the landing field. Thank goodness no one was hurt."

Except our driver, Sikander added silently. He glanced at the bright row of windows looking out over the carefully manicured grounds of the embassy as if he could somehow catch a glimpse of how things had turned out a couple of kilometers behind them. The gardens held no answers, although they did boast an impressive variety of blooms from several different Commonwealth worlds. He'd always found the ambassador's garden peculiarly out of place beneath the greenish skies of Tamabuqq.

"Mr. Barnes deserves much of the credit for that. He had the good sense to seize the reins and drive us out of trouble when things turned ugly." Abernathy took the seat indicated by the ambassador as the other officers found places on the comfortable sofa, but he remained perched on the edge of the cushion. "You say that these *warumzi agu* aren't normally a problem?"

"Not remotely. The neighborhoods surrounding the Thousand Worlds ward are quite safe most of the time; many of the Tzoru nearby earn their living by providing services to the diplomatic missions here or operating establishments frequented by humans. The local business clans have no interest in chasing away customers."

"Then who attacked us?" Reyes asked.

"I suppose you'd call them activists. The *warumzi agu* like to go on about traditional folkways and what it means to be Tzoru, or some such thing." Seeing Abernathy's frown deepen, the ambassador shrugged and continued. "Tzoru popular movements are like fads. Today it's mysticism, tomorrow it's a religious revival, and it might be authoritarianism the day after that. Most of it is pure nonsense. To tell the truth, we don't pay much attention to the popular discourse of the lower *sebetu*—all the political power is concentrated in the aristocratic clans of the Anshar's court."

"Perhaps we should start," Abernathy said with a small snort. He reached for a carafe from a tray on the table, and poured himself a cup of coffee. "Speaking of the Anshar's court, your Major Dalton said that there was some surprising news today. What's happened?"

"The first councillor—a rather stuffy but more or less decent fellow named Sapwu Zrinan—abruptly resigned," Hart replied. "Well, technically Sapwu saw the need to commit himself to a life of monastic contemplation somewhere far from the capital. But that's how high figures in the Dominion government are pushed aside."

"The Anshar herself has almost nothing to do with the administration of the government, sir," Sikander told Abernathy. "For all intents and purposes, the first councillor is the Tzoru prime minister, wielding power in the Anshar's name."

Abernathy shrugged. "Ministers rise and fall in any government, human or nonhuman."

"Yes, but this is a bolt from the blue," said Hart. "Tzoru politics are a slow and stately dance. Major developments like this are telegraphed many months in advance, because the Tzoru abhor uncertainty and lack of harmony. I've been trying to reach officials close to the situation to find out what's going on, but I'm afraid they are all occupied with their own affairs at the moment."

"Any chance that might've set off the *warumzi agu* we ran into?" Mason Barnes asked.

Hart considered the question for a moment, then shook his head. "I doubt it. The average Tzoru on the street has no interest in the politics of the court—the rivalries of the noble *sebetu* simply have no relevance outside the palace walls. But I'll have my people look for a connection, just in case. God knows the Tzoru surprise us from time to time, usually just when we think we have them figured out."

Abernathy sipped at his coffee. "What's the significance of Sapwu Zrinan's resignation for us?"

"My best guess is that Sapwu is the tip of the iceberg, and the Manzanensi are now out of favor," said Hart. Abernathy gave him a blank look; the ambassador continued. "They're one of the court factions. Half a dozen or so major factions are constantly maneuvering for prestigious positions in the Dominion government. The Manzanensi are a rather moderate bloc led by the Sapwu *sebet*. You might think of them as Monarchists, mostly unconcerned with matters outside the interests of a few high-ranking clans. Relations with the great powers of human space are little more than a passing curiosity to them, hardly worth the attention of the Heavenly Monarch."

"I regard the friendship of the Aquilan Commonwealth as something more than a passing curiosity," Deputy Commodore Reyes sniffed.

"But *they* don't," said Hart. "Remember, their Dominion is bigger than our own Commonwealth. The Tzoru control one hundred and twenty-two planets with a combined population of nearly one hundred billion people. If they were human, they'd be the largest power in the Coalition of Humanity by a third or more. And they had interstellar travel before we had bronze or iron or alphabets." The ambassador rolled his eyes. "Trust me, Sapwu Zrinan made a point of sharing that observation every time we met."

"Be that as it may, they've got a fleet that's a hundred years out of date and an economy that is positively medieval," said Reyes. "And they think we're irrelevant? It's ridiculous."

Sikander couldn't disagree with the deputy commodore, although he had a little more sympathy for the Tzoru position. His own home system of Kashmir had likewise fallen behind the rapid expansion of the great powers over the last century, reduced to a colony system under de facto Aquilan control. It all came down to technology: The improved warp generators and advanced induction drives developed in the last few generations by the leading powers of human space had enabled the rise of true interstellar nations based on cheap, fast commerce between the stars. Polities such as the Commonwealth of Aquila or the Republic of Montréal had expanded nearly as far in a hundred years as the Tzoru Dominion had expanded in a hundred centuries. In fact, the Tzoru had even visited Earth early in human history, giving rise to the legends of "sages from the sea" recorded in Sumerian myth and influencing Sumerian language and agriculture. But the Tzoru hadn't seen much reason to continue what were at the time decades-long voyages to a distant planet of warlike primitives, and turned their attention to colonizing worlds within the practical limits of their drive technology. When the rising powers of the Coalition of Humanity had finally reached Tzoru space, they'd found a decrepit Tzoru stellar empire comprised of isolated systems that had little contact with each other.

"So Sapwu and his Monarchists are out, and we don't know who's in," said Abernathy. "What would be your guess, Ambassador? Where's your money?"

"Not on Tzoru court politics, that's for certain," Hart said with a smile. "It might be the Militarists—they're conservatives, led by the Hish clan—or perhaps the Mercantilists or the Kishpuzinir, whom we might think of as technocrats. There are a few other minor groups, but I don't see any of them getting ahead of one of the more important factions. We'll find out for certain once a new first councillor is named."

"How long will that take?"

"It could be months. Sapwu and his Monarchists have held the upper hand for almost forty years. Now each aristocratic *sebet* is reevaluating which faction it should back, and each faction is eyeing clans in other factions that might be persuaded to defect."

"Damn it all," Abernathy muttered. "I can see it's going to take me a while to learn who's who."

"Think of them as political parties in a parliamentary system," said Hart. "There are half a dozen that are worth paying attention to, and they form or break up governments by choosing to ally or oppose one another."

"And of course there are no popular elections, and membership in these parties is determined by one's *sebet* and religious affiliation," Sikander added. He saw a flicker of disapproval on the commodore's face; Aquila had its own patrician families, but the power of the Senate was balanced by the Commonwealth Assembly, whose members stood for election every three years. "No, it's not remotely democratic, but it works for the Tzoru."

"I'll have to take your word on that, Mr. North," said Commodore Abernathy. He looked back to Ambassador Hart. "In light of recent events, what's our schedule for the next few days?"

"It should be mostly unchanged from the itinerary I sent you, Commodore. Tzoru don't break appointments. You'll be joining me for a busy social schedule this week, starting with an engagement this evening at the palace of the Baltzu clan to commemorate the agreement by which we're acquiring exclusive trade rights to the Shimatum system."

"Congratulations on that, by the way," Abernathy said. "I understand you've been working toward a new treaty for a while."

"Almost six years—we finally persuaded the Baltzu to sign on the dotted line last month." Hart smiled broadly, pleased by the recognition. "We've been fighting ten other powers for elbow room in Kahnar-Sag since the Dominion opened to trade. The trade concession and basing rights at Shimatum are a game changer for securing Commonwealth interests in the Tzoru Dominion. Clayne Industries, Data-Mark, and half a dozen other Aquilan corporations are already planning major development projects. And by this time next year, you'll have a large, modern naval base strategically positioned in the heart of the Dominion's coreward systems for Helix Squadron."

"That's our next stop after Tamabuqq. I want to get a good look at the base site and check up on the construction plans."

"I think you'll be pleased. Anyway, you and I—and Captain Reyes—are scheduled to visit the Baltzu estates outside the capital." Hart nodded at Sikander and Mason. "I'm afraid your junior officers aren't invited, but we're on good terms with the other human embassies here in the Thousand Worlds neighborhood. Visitors from home are a bit of a novelty here—our social secretary can steer them toward some suitable events until you need them."

"Thank you, Ambassador," said Abernathy. He stood and

shook Hart's hand again; Sikander, Reyes, and Mason did likewise. "When will you need me and Francine?"

"Four P.M. should do. It will be a long evening, and then tomorrow we leave early for a two-day visit to the Parzillu clan estate in Bnu-Sandu."

The commodore nodded. "Very well, then. D-Com, Mr. North, Mr. Barnes, let's meet briefly at three, then I suppose you two"—he looked at Sikander and Mason—"can keep yourselves busy until Wednesday evening."

"Yes, sir," Sikander and Mason replied.

Ambassador Hart saw the foursome to the door of his office. "Major Dalton can show you to your rooms," he said. "Just let her know if there is anything you need."

Sikander hesitated as the other three filed out. "Mr. Hart, is Lara Dunstan in town? I didn't see her when we came in."

"Dr. Dunstan?" The ambassador raised an eyebrow. "She's up in Durzinzer this week—there is a scholars' gathering at the library there, and she didn't want to miss it. Is she a friend of yours?"

Sikander nodded. "She is. I heard she'd been posted here by the Foreign Ministry, and I was hoping to see her as long as we were in-system."

"I see. Well, there is regular airship service to Durzinzer, and the ride's only an hour or so. Very scenic, too, I might add. Perhaps you can surprise her."

Sikander smiled. "Thank you, sir. I think I might."

As an officer of middling rank, Sikander didn't rate one of the luxurious private suites in the embassy building itself, like Abernathy or Reyes. Instead, he and Mason were assigned a modest room in the embassy compound's marine quarters for the duration of their stay in Bagal-Dindir. It suited Sikander well enough, since he didn't intend to spend much time there. He changed into a clean uniform, and then, before he did anything else, he put a call through to the squadron staff offices aboard the heavy cruiser *Exeter,* orbiting six hundred kilometers above the Tzoru homeworld.

A dark-eyed woman with short-cropped hair and the comet-and-anchor insignia of a senior chief petty officer on the collar of her jumpsuit answered the comm call. "Squadron Intelligence, Senior Chief Lin speaking. Oh, hello, Mr. North."

"Good afternoon, Senior Chief," Sikander said. Senior Chief Intelligence Specialist Joanne Lin headed up the team of enlisted experts who served as Sikander's section of the Helix Squadron staff. "I need you to check up on something for me."

"Already? You only left an hour ago, sir. We've barely even started to goof off."

Sikander smiled to himself. Lin liked to pretend that she didn't do a thing unless he was around to supervise, but in the six months since she'd joined his team, he'd learned that he could count on her for anything. His assignment as an intelligence officer with a squadron staff represented a brief detour in his career track; any Aquilan officer eventually received an assignment or two in nonline billets such as intelligence, logistics, personnel, or construction. It served as a little cross-training and perspective-broadening for leaders who might one day command major stations or facilities devoted to those tasks. But while Sikander had spent a couple of months in Staff Intelligence School at Laguna in preparation for his assignment, Senior Chief Lin and the other specialists on his team devoted their whole careers to intel work. They understood their jobs better than he did.

"Can you see what we've got on a Tzoru group or movement called the *warumzi agu*?" he said. "Touch base with the embassy cultural experts, they might have some leads."

"*Warumzi agu,* got it," Lin replied. She glanced away from the screen, jotting down a note. The Intel Section might be running a little more informally than it would if Sikander were there, but that was a long way from any reasonable definition of "goofing off"; the senior chief would see to that. "What's up with them, sir?"

"We ran into some kind of demonstration on our way from the landing field to the embassy. Maybe it's nothing, but they were definitely not too happy to see us. They pelted us with bottles, rocks, rotten fruit, and nasty-looking insects."

"That's a nice 'welcome to Tamabuqq' for the commodore," Lin observed. "Okay, Mr. North, we're on it. Should I ask Chief Reza to join you?"

Sikander shook his head. "I don't think that's necessary. It's probably an isolated incident." Darvesh Reza, the Kashmiri veteran assigned by Nawab Dayan North to serve as Sikander's valet, bodyguard, and general minder, would almost certainly disagree with that assessment. By long-standing arrangement, Darvesh traveled with Sikander unless other military personnel accompanied him. Sikander could request a special shuttle trip to bring Darvesh down to the planet's surface, but he didn't want his new commanding officer to see him as anything other than a competent Aquilan officer. Perhaps Abernathy wouldn't care, but Sikander knew well enough that Francine Reyes disapproved of any so-called favoritism or exceptions associated with Sikander's family name. Besides, there wasn't a dangerous neighborhood to be found on a Tzoru planet; Tzoru society had no place for violent crime. *And if I wait for Darvesh to catch a shuttle, I might miss my chance to see Lara.* "Give me a call if you turn up anything interesting."

"Yes, sir," Lin acknowledged. "We're on it."

"Thanks, Senior Chief. North, out." Sikander cut the connection. He hated to retask his team, but Reyes would expect some kind of report as soon as possible. If she asked him about it, he'd better be able to tell her that the squadron intel specialists were working on it.

Mason Barnes looked up from his seat on the edge of his bunk, where he scrubbed at a stain on his overcoat. "Your folks got nothing on those *warumzi*?" he asked.

"Not yet. Diplomatic intelligence isn't really our thing.

We're more about counting ships than keeping track of civil unrest. Which, I should note, we haven't seen a hint of during the time I've been on station."

Mason snorted. "Good luck selling that to Reyes. Pretty sure she'll pin it all on you anyway."

"Oh, so you've noticed that, have you?"

"Hard to miss, Sikay. She looks at you like you just crawled out from under a rock."

Sikander snorted. "She wants to make an impression on our new commodore."

"Maybe." Mason held up his overcoat, examining his handiwork. "But now that I think on it some, Reyes has been on your case as long as I've been on station. What'd you ever do to her?"

Sikander hesitated before answering; he didn't like to offer excuses, even to a good friend. His father hadn't raised him to blame others for his problems . . . but in this case, the information seemed relevant. "She runs in the same circles as Peter Chatburn," he said. "And it turns out that Victor Gray is her cousin—Commodore Morse told me right before he was relieved. She's held a grudge against me since I was a snottie, and I never even knew it. After all, this is the first time we've served together."

Mason winced. "Well, shit. I guess that explains a lot. What're you going to do about it?"

"Not a thing. Making staff officers like you and me miserable is a deputy commodore's job, after all." Sikander allowed himself a wry smile. "Captain Reyes just has a special reason to enjoy her work in my case."

"Document everything. You might need some ammunition if she keeps on like this."

"I'm not that worried about it." Sikander stood and checked his small overnight duffel. "But I am going to avail myself of the opportunity to put Francine Reyes out of mind and take a little liberty. I'm heading up to Durzinzer for a day or so."

"Got it," said Mason. "Have fun. And stay out of riots."

* * *

Three hours later, Sikander landed at the Durzinzer airship platform. He debarked from the vessel's cabin amid a small crowd of Tzoru travelers who appeared completely uninterested in him, as well as a handful of humans—a Dremish banker, an Aquilan manufacturing rep, and a Californian couple dressed for a backpacking trip. The platform stood a good forty meters high, offering a commanding view of Durzinzer and the picturesque mix of verdant forest vales and craggy uplands surrounding the town. Sikander paused to take in the view and spotted the domes of the ancient library buildings only a kilometer or two away, nestled amid natural rock spires now glowing golden green in the late-afternoon sunlight. *Ambassador Hart was right,* he decided. *It is scenic here.*

Sikander examined his dataslate to verify his directions, then descended the wide spiraling ramp that led down to ground level; Tzoru used elevators only for heavy freight. It felt good to stretch out his legs, and he set a good pace as he struck out along one of the ancient town's winding roads. He found the travelers' hostel only two hundred meters from the airship platform, and made a note of its location; he'd reserved a room there in case there were no better accommodations available closer to the scholars' conference. Besides, he didn't know what sort of reception to expect from Lara Dunstan. Four years ago they'd been just at the beginning of a very promising relationship . . . and then Sikander's ship had been sent off to the Gadira system, where he'd found himself in a different romantic entanglement. During the months after his return from Gadira, he and Lara had started seeing each other again, but something had changed. A bit of Sikander had stayed behind with Amira Ranya el-Nasir, and things hadn't quite gotten back on track with Lara. She'd gone on to her work with the Foreign Ministry, and then he'd received orders to a new ship based at the other end of the Commonwealth. *God, it's been two years since*

I've seen or spoken to her, he suddenly realized. *And we've exchanged maybe three messages in all that time? What am I doing, dropping in without at least calling to ask first?*

"Brilliant plan, Sikay," he murmured aloud. Well, he was committed now. He sighed and shifted his duffel to his other shoulder, turning one way and then another to check his bearings once again.

Three Tzoru stood on a footbridge over the roadway, watching him intently.

Sikander looked up at them, a little taken aback to find himself under observation. Tzoru considered staring to be bad manners, and generally avoided meeting one another's eyes. Then he noticed that they wore odd, double-pointed caps of a deep green hue—the same headwear he'd seen adorning the *warumzi agu* when they swarmed the commodore's carriage.

Who are *these people?* he thought. He watched them watching him for a long moment, waiting to see if they meant to seek a confrontation of some kind, but the three Tzoru did not move. Sikander turned and continued on his way, picking up his pace and paying a good deal more attention to his immediate surroundings, watching doorways and the shadows of narrow lanes as he passed by. *Perhaps I shouldn't have been so quick to head off without Darvesh.* He could feel their eyes on his back until the path took him around a bend and out of their sight.

Ten more minutes brought him to the Durzinzer library complex without any more unsettling encounters. Treeferns planted in curving rows and elegant statuary lined the paths winding through the grounds of the ancient institution; Tzoru disliked straight lines in their architecture and landscaping. Tzoru dressed in scholarly robes strolled slowly from one building to another. The simple serenity of the place was almost enough to make Sikander doubt whether he'd had any real cause for alarm in the unusual encounter along the road between the airship platform and the library. *Certainly there's nothing alarming about this place!*

He checked the embassy's notes on the conference schedule, and confirmed that the last presentation of the day had just concluded in the library's western dome. He made his way there, and stationed himself on a bench outside the door as a crowd of robed Tzoru, a couple of humans he didn't know, and even a Nyeiran in an elegantly painted carapace emerged and began to disperse across the plaza in small knots of conversation.

At first he didn't see Lara, but then he caught sight of a glimmer of golden hair amid several Tzoru. Lara was quite petite for a native of New Perth, and crowds tended to swallow her up. Sikander watched as she laughed and explained something to the alien scholars with whom she conversed in natural-sounding Tzoqabu. He had no idea what she was saying; his translation device couldn't pick up her speech from across the small plaza. But she had the attention of the Tzoru around her, several of them nodding in quite human fashion as she spoke.

He stood to go greet her as she drew closer, but she suddenly excused herself from the Tzoru she'd been speaking with and took a few steps to one side, raising a hand to her ear. "This is Dr. Dunstan," she said, answering a personal call. "Oh, hello, Milo. What's up?"

Sikander paused a few meters behind her, giving her space to take her call. Lara listened intently for a moment. "The Ingurra port project?" she said, speaking to the other party. "I sorted that out with the Maruz yesterday, they're ready to proceed. Tell Mr. Yeager that the report is already in the ambassador's inbox. Now what's this about a new Shimatum provision?" She opened a message or file on her dataslate and studied the display intently.

Bemused, Sikander watched her. He'd never actually observed Lara at work, but he was struck by how direct and confident she seemed. She finished her assessment of the dataslate's contents. "No, this isn't going to work," she told her caller firmly. "We just got the Baltzu to agree to the Shimatum timeline—it's too late to move the goalposts now.

Clayne Industries is just going to have to wait. No, no, the ambassador's wrong—I'll explain it to him. . . . He won't like it, but I'll let him down easy. . . . Thanks, Milo. I'll be back tomorrow evening, but call me if we get a meeting with the Sapwu! . . . Okay, see you then."

Lara slipped her dataslate back into her suit pocket and turned to rejoin the Tzoru nearby. Sikander took that as his opportunity to announce his presence. "Hello, Lara," he said.

"Sikander?" Lara stared in surprise; then she beamed and hurried up to hug him. She held him close for just a moment but squeezed him with all her strength before she let him go again. "What in the world are you doing here?"

"Looking for you, of course," he replied. "Ambassador Hart said you were here in Durzinzer, so I decided to catch an airship and see you as long as we were on the same planet."

"It's about time. I've been on Tamabuqq Prime for half a year now, and I was beginning to wonder if your squadron was ever going to pass this way again."

"We're late. Commodore Morse was due for relief, so we delayed the customary cruise a few weeks until Commodore Abernathy arrived to take over." Aquila's Helix Squadron was actually based at Kahnar-Sag, a Tzoru world located sixty light-years or so closer to the border. Aquilan warships visited the Tzoru capital system every couple of months, although the flagship made some visits and skipped others. This was Sikander's fifth visit to Tamabuqq Prime, but only the first since he'd learned that Lara had been sent here by the Foreign Ministry.

"The Navy has a terrible sense of timing. When I found out I'd be posted to the Dominion, I thought I'd see you a couple of times a month."

"I'm sorry that it hasn't turned out that way," he told her. He noticed the scholars she'd been speaking with watching the two of them with patient expressions. "I hope I'm not interrupting anything, by the way."

"No, I'm finished for the day." Lara followed his gaze, glancing back at the Tzoru. "Oh, forgive me. I should make some introductions."

She put her arm through his, and led him toward the waiting scholars. "Honored friends, this is Lieutenant Commander Sikander Singh North of the Aquilan Commonwealth Navy," she said. His translator device picked up her fluent Tzoqabu and repeated it in a soft, neutral tone. "He's also the Nawabzada of Ishar, which is an aristocratic title from the system of Kashmir. Sikander, this is Radi Sabub, a scholar of the second rank, and his assistant Maruz Uditzu, a scholar of the third rank."

"It is a pleasure to meet you, sir," Radi Sabub said in good Anglic. He spread his hands and bowed; Tzoru as a rule did not shake hands, embrace, or otherwise initiate physical contact except when greeting a child or lifelong friend.

Sikander returned the gesture. "And you, Scholar Radi." He turned to Maruz and bowed. "Scholar Maruz, a pleasure."

Maruz returned his bow and spoke in her native tongue. "Forgive my inability in your language. A friend of Lara Dunstan is a friend of ours, Sikander North."

"Have you eaten dinner yet?" Scholar Radi asked. "My home is not far and my *sebet* has a meal prepared."

"I don't want to impose," said Sikander. He glanced at Lara, looking for guidance. He was not entirely sure about the etiquette of the situation, but more important, Tzoru cuisine ranged from fair by human standards to almost completely inedible; many dishes were fermented or pickled to a borderline toxicity. She smiled at his concern and gave him a subtle nod, so he continued. "But if you're sure it's no trouble, then I'd be honored to visit your home."

The Tzoru scholar let his mouth fall open in the equivalent of a toothy human smile. "Excellent! Follow me."

The foursome set off more or less in the direction from which Sikander had come, but when they left the library grounds, they turned toward the south and headed into a part of Durzinzer that consisted of courtyard-style dwellings and small shops surrounded by large park spaces. Sikander fell in easily beside Lara as the two Tzoru led the way. "I'm a little surprised to find you engaged in a Tzoru academic gathering," he said. "I thought your background was international relations."

"It is," she replied. "But I chose to work on the rise of the Tzoru Dominion and the centralization of power under the Anshars as my thesis. A lot of people think that Tzoru history is a huge expanse of not much happening, but appearances can be deceptive."

"The *Helix Daily Post* article described the conference as a review of poetry from the Third Ninazzu Dynasty. What's that have to do with the rise of the Dominion?"

"Calling it poetry is a bit of an exaggeration. Tzoru historical documents are commissioned by the Anshar's ministers to be written in a particular style that's a sort of literary form. The poetic language isn't really my interest, but the dynastic wars that followed the age of Ninazzu rule are."

"Ah. Rather like reading the *Iliad* to get a sense of the Trojan War."

"Or *War and Peace* to understand the Napoleonic Wars. Exactly."

Sikander shook his head. Napoleon he'd heard of, but not the story Lara mentioned. However, her familiarity with Tzoru culture suggested something to him. "Speaking of Tzoru traditions, what do you know about the *warumzi agu*?"

"It's a popular movement," she answered. "The words don't translate exactly, but the name means something like 'servants of royal honor.' They're followers of the philosopher Ebneghirz, who stands for traditional ways."

Sikander raised an eyebrow. It figured that Lara would know something like that off the top of her head when his own intelligence specialists hadn't even heard the name before. She was as sharp as anyone he'd ever met, and she had the work ethic to drive herself fiercely if she felt she had ground to make up. *I should have just called her first to ask about the fellows in the green caps,* he decided. "Are they Monarchists?"

"No, you're confusing the political factions at the Anshar's court with the social movements of the common *sebetu*. Ordinary Tzoru follow public thinkers the way we follow our favorite sports team. All their political, religious, and family affiliations are more or less determined for them at birth, so Tzoru invest a good deal of individual expression in choosing their social philosophies." Lara glanced up at him. "Where did you say you read about them?"

"I didn't read about them. I *saw* them—a large protest in the streets outside the Thousand Worlds ward, and several surly-looking fellows right here in Durzinzer."

"Really?" Lara frowned in thought. "That's unusual. I've been thinking for a while now that we don't pay enough attention to Tzoru popular movements. All our diplomatic attention is focused on the aristocratic *sebetu* since they're pretty much the entirety of the government and the military, but ordinary *sebetu* outnumber the nobles ten to one."

"What do you think we're overlooking? We have to work with the noble clans to gain access to the planets they control, don't we?"

"Yes, but we're only engaging a small part of the Dominion." Lara nodded at the Tzoru walking ahead of them. "That's why I'm here, really. I think the Tzoru have a lot more to offer us than new markets and strategic resources, if we'd only take advantage of the opportunity to learn from them while we're here. And that means getting out of the Thousand Worlds ward and meeting ordinary Tzoru as well as the Tzoru who rule planets."

"Here is my home, honored friends," said Radi Sabub. He turned and indicated a gateway in an old wall covered in growing vines and intricate relief carvings. "Sebet Radi is happy to welcome you, Mr. North."

"Thank you," said Sikander. "Your home is beautiful."

Sabub gave a small fluttering motion of his hands. "I am

fortunate." He opened the gate and led the way into a large courtyard-style dwelling of two stories. A dozen Tzoru bustled out to greet him, including a number of children. The younger Tzoru struck Sikander as oddly quiet and serious; human children that size would have filled the house with squeals and laughter. *Just one more difference between us, I guess.*

A dizzying array of introductions and polite bows followed; Sikander gathered that the Radi home in Durzinzer consisted of about fifteen or so adults and their children. Tzoru didn't build their homes around the nuclear family; adults from different clans made agreements to mate, and then one parent or the other brought the offspring back to their own *sebet* to be raised as part of the next generation. He knew little about how the Tzoru picked out their mates or decided which children would be raised by which family, but he decided it would be best to keep his questions to himself and perhaps look it up later. This was the first time he'd been invited into a Tzoru home and he wanted to make sure he didn't give offense.

He glanced over to Lara for guidance on one or two occasions to follow her lead, and noticed that none of the Tzoru were introducing themselves to her. Instead, she watched him with a small smile. "I take it you've met everyone already?" he asked her.

"I've been staying here all week," she replied. "It's quite a bit closer to the Library than the traveler's hostel, and I couldn't pass up the opportunity to meet Sabub's family. He's been a good friend and guide to me ever since I arrived on Tamabuqq Prime."

"That is true," said Radi Sabub. "My field of study is human culture. As a result, I often work with the Aquilan embassy to help newly arrived human diplomats learn about our ways. Will you be in Durzinzer long, Mr. North?"

"Only a day or so. I'll need to return to the capital the day after tomorrow."

"Then you are welcome to stay here if you like."

"Thank you," said Sikander. He glanced at Lara, who gave him another subtle nod. "I am honored."

"Will you stay with friend Lara, or will you require a separate room?" Radi asked.

Sikander blinked, taken aback by the directness of the question. Tzoru had a lot in common with humans, but an appreciation for the delicacy of sleeping arrangements didn't seem to be one of them. "Ah—I don't—I mean—" he stuttered.

Lara came to his rescue. "A separate room for Sikander would be fine, Sabub," she said firmly.

"I shall prepare it," the scholar said. "One moment, please." He bowed and withdrew, leaving the two humans surrounded by the rest of the family and the shy, curious children.

"Sorry. That caught me off guard," Sikander said to her.

Lara smiled. "Tzoru can be very frank about sex. It's not something they get very emotional about, so you shouldn't read anything into the question. I'm afraid our dating customs are pretty confusing to them."

He smiled. "They're confusing to us, too."

"It's good to see you, Sikander." Lara stood on her tiptoes and kissed him on the cheek. "Now excuse me while I go wash up for dinner. I hope you can handle spicy food—Tzoru have almost no sense of taste."

3

Kadingir, Tamabuqq Prime

In the first light of the dawn, General Hish Mubirrum climbed the two hundred and twenty-nine steps of the Kadingir Temple to stand in the holy gateway of the mountaintop. It was a difficult ascent; he was no longer young, his armor weighed on him, and he was massively proportioned for his people, towering two and a half meters in height with cords of dense muscle knotting his torso and bare arms. For ten thousand years Sebet Hish had selected their mates with an eye toward physical prowess, and Mubirrum represented the apex of a hundred generations of painstaking work. In his youth he could have bounded up the steep stairs at a dead sprint, armor or no armor. Now he found himself compelled to ascend one deliberate step at a time, replacing reckless energy with a measured inevitability. *At least the stairs provide one with the opportunity to think along the way,* he reflected. A Tzoru who stood only one step from the Anshar herself and ruled over the fate of billions enjoyed few opportunities for solitude.

The warriors standing guard by the gateway known as the Eningurra stood by in silence as Mubirrum completed his ascent and performed the ancient ritual of greeting the sun, speaking the words of prayers dating back fifty millennia. Mubirrum doubted whether the gods cared about his obeisance, but he wasn't trying to impress them. To pass through the Eningurra and set foot within Kadingir one had to climb the steps and speak the prayers, and like many of his people's traditions, the ritual endured simply because one observed traditions.

Whether some blessing of the divine had indeed come down to him or he'd simply been invigorated by the early-morning exercise, Mubirrum felt keenly awake and alert by the time he finished. He loved the silence and the dignity of the homeworld's old temples more than anything in the world. In its natural beauty, its carefully preserved history, and its unchanging ritual Kadingir embodied the best of his people. For fifty millennia pilgrims had come from all over Tamabuqq Prime to greet the sunrise at Kadingir. Repeating the ancient words and rites renewed his connection to those who had come before him, reminding Mubirrum of what it was to be Tzoru.

So few places like this are left, he reflected. When he'd first visited Kadingir—a hundred years ago now?—scores of Tzoru had thronged the plaza around the Eningurra for sunrise. But now he stood alone, except for a few old priests and the warriors posted to guard Kadingir's special guest. He surveyed the familiar grounds, and his eye fell on a large coffee cart standing in an alcove on one side of the ancient plaza. Angular human writing marked its metal sides, along with garish illustrations of some human beverage or an-other. *This is what we have come to?* he thought in despair. *Our shrines stand empty, except for the occasional alien who comes to gawk at them?*

He turned from the offensive sight and strode over to the pavilion where the Anshar's soldiers stood guard. "I need to speak with Tzem Ebneghirz," he said.

"As you wish, General," the guard commander replied.

"And have *that* removed," Mubirrum added, pointing at the cart. "It does not belong here."

"Yes, General." The guard bowed. "Ebneghirz is in the south gallery. I will take you to him."

Mubirrum followed the younger warrior into the old temple building. Delicate tilework so old that its original colors had faded to different shades of brown and gray finished the interior; great bronze drums held scrolls of metal foils on which were inscribed the Sixty-Four Prophecies. Priests in plain robes tended the holy scrolls, gently rotating one or another to reveal writings that hadn't seen the daylight in years and applying preservative oils to the delicate foil. Mubirrum envied them; he wished he could devote himself to the study of the sacred texts, too. Visiting this place always humbled him, reminding him that he was only one small light in a great constellation that stretched back a thousand centuries. *And yet I am fated to live in the time when all of this comes to its end,* he thought bitterly. *Why in the name of the Sixty-Four was I not born in an earlier time?*

Mubirrum's steps faltered as the familiar grief dug its talons into his heart. He'd wrestled with his secret despair for half his life; he no longer knew who he would be without it. His escort paused and waited silently for him, until the old warrior gestured for the younger guard to continue.

They came to an open gallery that looked out over the mountaintops to the south. The morning chill lingered in the air, but bright sunlight filled the space. Here a bent and weary male sat on a simple stool, gazing at the view with a sleepy expression. Tzem Ebneghirz was smaller than Mubirrum expected, well into his middle years, and he had the rounded shoulders and dull dermal markings of one born among the common rural *sebetu*. He was, in fact, the most ordinary-looking individual Mubirrum could have imagined as the founder of a movement that had spread to a hundred worlds, and for a moment he wondered if perhaps the guards of Kadingir Temple conspired to deceive him with an impostor. "This is Ebneghirz?" he asked his escort.

"This is," Ebneghirz answered before the guard spoke. The philosopher glanced over his shoulder and made a small gesture of welcome. "And you are General Hish Mubirrum, if I am not mistaken. Come and sit by my side, General. I am curious what brings a mighty councillor in the service of the Heavenly Monarch to see me."

Mubirrum nodded once in acknowledgment, and took the seat Ebneghirz indicated. "I wished to meet you," he said.

Ebneghirz looked up at Mubirrum then, and the general was struck by the hazy silver-green intensity of the small male's eyes. He'd seen images of the philosopher a hundred times, the light plates or artistic engravings anyone might be expected to accumulate over a long and public life, but the representations simply didn't capture those eyes. Something fierce blazed there, and for a moment Mubirrum's resolve wavered. *There is genius in him,* he decided. *And there is danger in that genius.* Tzem Ebneghirz might have been born to a simple weaver *sebet,* but destiny had chosen him to be something extraordinary.

Seeking a moment to collect himself, Mubirrum gestured at the temple around them. "How are you being treated? Are you comfortable?"

Ebneghirz drew a deep breath, and thumped his chest with his hands. "The morning air is bracing," he said. "The view from my prison is excellent, your guards are polite to me, and I must admit that I am rediscovering an appreciation for the subtleties of the Sixty-Four Prophecies in the absence of any other reading material. I would rather enjoy it if I did not know that I am needed elsewhere."

Mubirrum eyed Ebneghirz. "One cannot publicly criticize the Anshar without consequences. You are fortunate that you were given the opportunity to seek religious seclusion."

"Hmm, I suppose so." Ebneghirz gave a small shrug, and turned to face Mubirrum directly. "I doubt you climbed two hundred and twenty-nine steps merely to assure yourself that I am comfortable in my exile. Shall we speak of why you are really here, General?"

"Your followers are quite agitated by your arrest," Mubirrum told him. "There have even been some demonstrations. They want to know that you are well. I think it would be wise to transcribe a message explaining how you expect them to conduct themselves in your absence."

"If you expect me to tell my brothers and sisters to acquiesce in the face of injustice, you do not know me very well," said Ebneghirz. "It is clear to all that the Anshar is surrounded by greedy fools, selling off our ancient Dominion to barbaric foreigners one world at a time. I will not say otherwise for your convenience!"

Mubirrum hissed softly at that. He was, after all, one of the high advisors to the Anshar that Ebneghirz slandered. Reckless speech such as that had led the Baltzu and their allies among the Litum-Kibabbar—the Mercantilists—to demand the philosopher's arrest a month ago. With an effort, the general controlled his temper; he was not here to argue with Ebneghirz.

"You misunderstand me, Philosopher," he replied. "Of course the Baltzu and the Kaspum and the Maruz are as complicit as you say; you would not be here otherwise. But other *sebetu* at court frankly share your concern over the ways in which our Dominion is changing. You are a powerful voice reminding our people of what it is to be Tzoru and rallying them to the defense of our ancient traditions. We think it is important that you continue to be heard."

"You wish me to continue my missives?" The philosopher stood abruptly and paced over to the window, taking a moment to digest Mubirrum's words. "Hmm, now I see. This is about the Hish! It serves your purposes to encourage even more popular discontent. You mean to free me in the hope that my protests will weaken the Baltzu and the other *sebetu* opposed to you."

"Yes, and no," said Mubirrum. "Yes, this is an opportunity for me to confront my rivals at court. For years you have taught that those of us who believe in the Dominion must choose to fight back or choose to surrender; your arrest has made it clear to some *sebetu* at court that now is the time to make that choice. But no, I would not say that I mean to free you." Whether Ebneghirz had intended it or not, his criticism of the noble clans that favored engagement and trade with foreign powers had provoked an overreaction. By demanding the philosopher's silencing, the Baltzu and their allies had alienated clans more sympathetic to Ebneghirz's message and inadvertently brought down the neutral first councillor. Sapwu Zrinan and his Manzanensi had kept the peace between mercantile and conservative factions at court for forty years, but with the sly old first councillor now out of the way, a long-delayed reckoning was at hand.

"No? Ah, of course. I am more valuable to you in my forced seclusion. My situation is a cause that stirs anger among my *warumzi agu*."

Mubirrum nodded. "As you say."

Ebneghirz paced from side to side, eyes narrowed as he considered Mubirrum's words. "The Anshar's officials may free me anyway in an attempt to restore harmony, you know."

At which point we may be served just as well by a martyr, Hish reflected. He hated to consider the idea; if nothing else, he recognized that Tzem Ebneghirz loved the Anshar and sought to protect the Dominion just as he himself did. But sometimes a Tzoru of high standing had an obligation to take distasteful actions for the good of the Dominion. "It may be so," he admitted, keeping his reflections to himself. "But our work should be well along by that point."

"Indeed." The philosopher paused as a new thought struck him. "A suspicious Tzoru might wonder if your intention is to encourage my *warumzi agu* to do something rash, just so you'd have the opportunity to quell our movement decisively."

"Did it never occur to you that your movement might find favor with high *sebetu* who value the traditions of our people and worry about the fate of the Dominion?" Mubirrum answered. "We are not all human lackeys. The Hish have been forced to stand by for decades while one human state after another has humiliated the Dominion. We've watched the greedy and foolish among our people throw aside a hundred millennia of honor, of *purpose,* to embrace foreign values and alien ways. We've argued before the Anshar again and again that this path leads to the end of our Dominion. Now we learn that the Baltzu mean to sell a billion more Tzoru on Shimatum into foreign rule. I tell you, Ebneghirz, I cannot let it stand. I mean to act in the Anshar's interests whether she wants me to or not."

"Spoken like one of my *warumzi agu*," Ebneghirz said.

"Our roads run side by side, Ebneghirz. We both recognize that our Dominion is dying, and we both want to save it. I have an opportunity to turn the High Council in a new direction and reaffirm our traditions and our sovereignty in the face of those who do not value those things. Your followers would be a great help to me in that work."

"How so?" The philosopher turned his back on the wide window with its view of the mountains, and folded his arms. "We are not an army, General Hish. We have no weapons, no command structure, no training. We cannot conquer the citadels of the Baltzu or the Zag."

"I do not need an army. I need a *revolution*. Your *warumzi agu* have numbers, and you have resolve. I want you to paralyze the Dominion with strikes, protests, marches, acts of sabotage. Provoke confrontation with *sebetu* both low and high who profit by their association with offworlders. Your followers are primed for this work—they're already in the streets, demanding action. Let your words loose them. As for weapons, well, I expect that some of the soldiers responsible for guarding a Hish armory or two will find themselves carried away by sympathy for your cause. We can see to it that some small arms and light artillery fall into your hands—not enough to directly challenge the *sebetu* of the court, of course, but certainly sufficient for the *warumzi agu* to withstand any effort to brush away their complaints."

"You are asking me to strike a spark in a very dry forest," said Ebneghirz. "Neither you nor I can know in which direction that fire will burn, General. Tzoru will die—*my* Tzoru will die."

"I know it," Mubirrum said. "I know it. But when the

Litum-Kibabbar and the business interests attempt to suppress your *warumzi agu,* I will have the pretext I need to act. My sacred duty is to protect the Tzoru people against their enemies. The Anshar cannot permit *sebetu* supported by humans to turn their guns against common Tzoru fighting only to preserve the Dominion—that would bring down the dynasty itself. No, she will be forced to take a stand against those who have forgotten what it means to be Tzoru."

The philosopher fell silent, his face fixed in a frown of disapproval as he weighed Mubirrum's proposal. "Very well, General Hish, I am convinced of your sincerity," he finally said. "What is our next move?"

"In a few hours your guards will be replaced by troops who answer to me, not the High Council. They will provide you with the things you need to speak to your disciples, and protect you against any efforts by the Baltzu or their allies to silence you." Mubirrum stood, and shrugged his armor back into place. He towered over the slight philosopher when they stood side by side. "Your first message is to call your *warumzi agu* to the streets and strike that spark. I will see to it that the troops of *sebetu* friendly to our cause stand aside and leave some of the local armories unguarded."

"And what will be your response to the demonstrations I incite?"

"Nothing," said Mubirrum.

"Nothing?" Ebneghirz asked.

"Nothing. The Anshar's court is broken, Philosopher Ebneghirz, and now I must break it further. I take my leave."

"I thank you, General," said Ebneghirz. "This has been an enlightening conversation."

"Enlightenment is the purpose of seclusion at Kadingir, is it not?" Mubirrum let his mouth fall open in a smile, then bowed in parting. He left the philosopher where he found him.

The morning sun shone brightly through the Eningurra as Mubirrum turned his attention to the two hundred twenty-nine steps, still deeply shadowed by the hillside behind him.

He wondered when he would visit the Kadingir Temple again, and what the Dominion would look like on the day he did. *Will the Hish be seen as the saviors of the Dominion then?* he wondered. No Hish in the ten-thousand-year history of the clan had ever skirted so close to treason as Mubirrum meant to go, but what choice had been left to him? His *sebet* was sworn to defend the Dominion; they were a sword in the hands of the Anshars that had struck true against a hundred threats down through the centuries. *The Fifteenth Prophecy says that a sword that rusts in its scabbard is no sword at all. All I ask is a chance to serve just one more time. If a lowborn rabble-rouser like Tzem Ebneghirz can confront the danger with nothing but words, what greater obligation befalls me?*

In the broad stone plaza at the bottom of the ancient steps, Mubirrum's clan-cousin Hish Pazril waited with Mubirrum's skybarge and retinue. The younger male served as Mubirrum's herald, chief assistant, and bodyguard commander. Even taller than Mubirrum himself, if not quite so massively built, he had the intelligence and decisiveness needed for high command; Mubirrum already knew that when the time came to step down, Pazril would be his successor.

"Did you see Ebneghirz, General?" Pazril asked.

"I did," Mubirrum replied. "I think we understand each other. Pass the order for the Peerless Swords of Scarlet to proceed with assuming garrison duties here, and instruct them to allow Ebneghirz unrestricted access to his *warumzi agu*."

The younger warrior frowned. "Is it safe to let Ebneghirz speak as he wishes, my lord?"

"Not in the least." Mubirrum believed that the ideas of Ebneghirz were in fact much more dangerous than all the warriors and weaponry of a powerful clan. "But I need a forest fire, and I am willing to accept the consequences if the wind shifts against me."

"As you wish, General." Pazril drew a communication scepter from its sheath at his hip, and spoke softly into its transmitter. The herald had made preparations to have Hish soldiers set Ebneghirz free, to keep him secluded, or to arrange for his death depending on the outcome of the conversation; it only took a moment to set the appropriate measures in motion. "The Peerless Swords acknowledge the order. They are on their way."

"Good. Let us return to the palace."

Pazril motioned to the guards of Mubirrum's personal detail. The two high-ranking Tzoru climbed up into the luxurious cabin of the skybarge while the guards took their positions at the controls and weapons mounts. The vessel rose gracefully into the air, its drive plates humming softly, and turned south toward the distant sprawl of Bagal-Dindir; the spire-like crags of the mountain ridges surrounding the Kadingir temple complex drifted serenely past the wide windows and fell astern.

"Any word from the chamberlain's office?" Mubirrum asked Pazril once they were airborne.

"Yes, General. They called while you were in the temple. Your presence is desired for a meeting of the High Council at midday. I believe they intend to discuss the matter of appointing a new first councillor."

"I am not surprised," Mubirrum said. He gazed absently at the mountain peaks slipping behind the skybarge, his mind busy calculating the next steps of the dance. The vacancy of such a high post represented an egregious disorder in the customary business of the court, and the Anshar's officials dreaded disorder. Under the best of circumstances, it would take months for the *sebetu* of the High Council to agree on a successor. But with the collapse of the Monarchists, no faction existed that could forge a consensus between the clans enriched by trade with the aliens and the clans fighting to protect Tzoru sovereignty. If Mubirrum merely stood his ground, he'd easily stymie any effort to name a moderate successor to Sapwu Zrinan . . . or any successor at all, for that matter.

Now that *is an interesting thought,* Mubirrum reflected.

Pazril started to speak again, but Mubirrum made a gesture of dismissal; he needed to consider this new idea. The younger warrior nodded and left him to his thoughts for the rest of the flight.

4

Durzinzer, Tamabuqq Prime

Since Lara had a full schedule with the Tzoru scholars' gathering in the morning, Sikander spent a few hours exploring the Library of Durzinzer. Two young members of the Radi clan served as his guides: a serious whip-thin male named Shuhad, and a boundlessly energetic female named Damiq. Like all Tzoru, they aspired to follow their elder relations into the profession of their *sebet*—scholarship, in the case of the Radi. Shuhad struck Sikander as well-suited to the family business, but he soon developed his doubts about Damiq. She was simply too restless to spend hours upon hours poring over musty old tomes or listening to the learned discourse of her elders. More than once he found himself wondering how Tzoru handled teenage rebellion or how Tzoru *sebetu* went about disowning their misfits, and resolved to ask Lara about it when they could speak privately.

The first thing he learned about the Library was that the word "library" didn't quite capture the purpose of the place. Millions of works—most of them large volumes with leaves of stamped metal foil, durable enough to last for thousands of years—were carefully preserved at Durzinzer, of course. But many of the dome-like buildings protected immense collections of historical artifacts, specimens reflecting Tamabuqq Prime's natural history, and examples of industrial technology. Dormitories housed hundreds of scholars who studied the archives and tended the collections, plus young students pursuing their educations. The Tzoru didn't really have universities or public schools of any kind, since *sebetu* looked after their own children's educations, but Sikander quickly came to realize that Durzinzer and the other great libraries scattered throughout the Dominion served as a close analogue to human institutions of higher learning.

They wandered through hall after hall filled with the fossilized remnants of extinct animals, which Radi Damiq described to Sikander in breathless detail; the natural sciences especially interested her, and the collection was her favorite part of the Library. Then they moved on to a collection of ancient arms and armor. Why the Tzoru had organized their collections in such a way that fossils millions of years old were displayed next to medieval-looking weaponry Sikander couldn't begin to imagine, but it offered a welcome change of pace from Damiq's enthusiasm for her own specialty.

"How old are these weapons?" he asked his Tzoru guides.

Shuhad gave a small shrug. "They represent artifacts from the early ages of the Dominion, about sixty thousand years ago."

Sikander shook his head in disbelief. "These are *sixty thousand* years old? Incredible." That was ten times older than the pyramids of Egypt! Nine hundred light-years lay between Tamabuqq and Old Terra, but an even more startling gulf of *time* separated the ancient Dominion from the new starfaring nations that made up the fractious Coalition of Humanity. At a time when humans could barely manage stone arrowheads, the Tzoru produced exquisitely decorated steel blades with advanced metallurgy and wrote epics and religious texts still preserved today. *But six hundred centuries later, we expanded into their space—they never managed to expand into ours. Despite all their learning and philosophy and artistic genius, time simply passed the Tzoru by.*

"I am sorry, I was not clear," Shuhad said. "These are only replicas, not the original artifacts. Those are now missing."

"Missing?"

"Someone removed them several years ago. We believe they were sold to offworld collectors."

"You mean humans?" Sikander asked.

Shuhad gave a small flutter of his hands, a Tzoru gesture of apology or consternation. "I am afraid so, friend Sikander. Many valuable artifacts have vanished in recent years— renegade Tzoru have learned that some humans are eager to buy objects of historical or artistic interest."

"Not the scholar *sebetu*!" Damiq added. "We try to keep them safe."

"As best we can," Shuhad said. "The authorities have had little luck in deterring the practice. It is a new problem."

Sikander grimaced. *We've taught the Tzoru how to be art thieves?* He'd seen plenty of Tzoru relics for sale in the shops of human art dealers based in Kahnar-Sag, but he'd assumed those were purchased legally from *sebetu* willing to part with old knickknacks. The idea that some Tzoru might be tempted to pilfer the displays of museums such as Durzinzer and pocket the proceeds had never even crossed his mind. Then again, something similar had taken place when Aquila first established contact with Kashmir, hadn't it? One of the few things an advanced, wealthy society found valuable in more isolated systems or peoples was their artwork. *One more benefit of interstellar commerce, I suppose.*

He shook his head and resumed his wanderings, studying the ancient military equipment in its glass cabinets. In a way, it reminded him of the Greene Hall Collection at the Academy, a dusty relic that held little relevance to the students of the current day. The midshipmen of the sprawling Aquilan Commonwealth Naval Academy rarely found reason to visit the fading uniforms and scratchy holovid displays sleeping in the east wing of Greene Hall . . . except when some upperclassman needed an excuse to harass a snottie. Sikander stood before the old Tzoru displays, watching the play of dust motes—

—drifting aimlessly in the slanting light that fills the old museum room. The place is silent as a tomb when Sikander lets himself in with the borrowed passkey. It's Sunday afternoon, a time when fourth-class midshipmen—simply "snotties" to their older classmates—are left alone to catch up on their academic work or wander into town for a few hours away from the crushing pressure of the Academy's first year. Unfortunately those options are not open to him today. Midshipman Second Class Gray informed him that the display case for the Starburst of Valor needed cleaning, so Sikander is here during what should be his free time with a can of spray cleaner and a pocketful of rags. He can guess how this will go: Gray will think of things that need cleaning all day long, and he's expected to take the harassment without complaint.

He sighs and trudges over to the display case, but then a sudden clatter catches his attention. Sikander peeks around a corner, and sees another snottie working hard to polish the brass hinges on a cabinet. The other freshman—a stocky, redheaded fellow—looks up at him, and shakes his head. "Nice to know I'm not the only one on the shit list today," he says in a reedy Hibernian accent. "What're you in for, buddy?"

"Failure to maintain a sufficiently respectful demeanor in the presence of a superior officer," Sikander replies. "In other words, I gave a second-class a dirty look."

The Hibernian midshipman grins. "Well, there you go. Don't give the upperclassmen dirty looks. I'm Mason, by the way. Mason Barnes."

"Sikander North, but my friends call me Sikay."

"Nice to meet you, Sikay. Help yourself to my rags if you need 'em." Barnes smiles and returns his attention to his brass hinges.

Sikander grins back, then heads to the Starburst of Valor

display case. It's spotless, of course, but he sprays the cleaner on the glass anyway; Gray is just the kind of tin-pot tyrant who might check Sikander's cleaning rags to see if they're damp or not. Then his eye falls on the shining silver medal in the center of the case, and the placard describing who won it and why. It's labeled VADM ALBERTO REYES, CLASS OF 2873, SECOND BATTLE OF JAIPUR.

"Son of a bitch!" Sikander growls. Now he understands the depth of Gray's contempt. The upperclassman has sent him to clean the award case of the man who smashed the last independent Kashmiri fleet, establishing Aquilan power over Sikander's homeworld. Sikander has rarely given much thought to the hundred-year-old history of how Aquila came to dominate Kashmir. In fact, up until a moment ago he wouldn't have harbored any special resentment toward the long-dead Admiral Reyes. But it's the fact that Victor Gray intends it to be humiliating that infuriates him.

"What? What is it?" Barnes asks. He looks over at Sikander, then looks at the case. Barnes isn't dumb; he figures it out in only a moment. "Oh. Damn. Sorry, Sikay. That's a shitty thing to do."

Sikander stands and stares at the case, not trusting himself to speak. His first inclination is to put his fist through the glass . . . but that's what Gray is hoping for, isn't it? He can feel Barnes watching him, waiting to see what he will do. And he remembers something his father told him: An insult has only the power you choose to give it.

Deliberately, he raises the cloth in his hand and begins to polish the case.

Before he finishes the first panel, he hears the museum room door open. He glances back to see what other snottie has drawn cleaning duty, but it's not another underclassman. It's Victor Gray, with three of his fellow upperclassmen. And they have very ugly looks on their faces—

"Are you interested in the armor of the Second Margidda Dynasty?" Shuhad said to Sikander.

"I'm sorry?" Sikander shook himself out of his reverie, and realized that he'd been staring at one of the old display cases while lost in the memory of his encounter with Victor Gray in Greene Hall's museum. "Er, no, I'm not. I'm afraid I became lost in thought for a moment."

"Lost in thought?" Damiq and Shuhad looked at each other; then Damiq laughed silently. "Oh, we call that 'listening to memory.' We do it too sometimes."

"I didn't know that about Tzoru," said Sikander. Did all sentients mentally wander from time to time, or only some species? "I wonder if Nyeirans or Velarans are the same? I'll have to ask one sometime."

"The morning session of the conference is about to let out," Shuhad said. "Did you wish to rejoin friend Lara?"

"Yes, please." Sikander realized he was hungry. Breakfast at the Radi clan home had been some sort of pickled fish that he'd found difficult to stomach first thing in the morning. "I'd like to see if she is available for lunch."

"I know the way!" Damiq said, and hurried off through the ancient halls.

Sikander shrugged, and followed after the young Tzoru. A few minutes' stroll through the Library brought them to a doorway leading to the plaza where he'd met Lara yesterday evening. It took Sikander's eyes a moment to adjust to the cold, clear daylight after the dimly lit halls of the Library. The conference had already let out by the time Sikander and his guides reached the place; he spotted Lara speaking with several Tzoru he didn't recognize.

"Radi Shuhad, Radi Damiq, thank you for the tour," he told the young scholars. "If you're available later on, I'd like to resume it. I feel like I only saw a small portion of the Library."

"It was our pleasure, friend Sikander," Shuhad said seriously. "You need only ask any Library attendant, and they will send for us. We take our leave."

Sikander exchanged bows with the two Radis, and then made his way through the small crowd to Lara. He waited a moment until she finished her conversation, then approached her. "Dr. Dunstan, are you by any chance free for lunch?"

"So formal, Mr. North!" Lara laughed at him. "It's only me. Yes, I can go to lunch, although I need to be back in good time—I'm the first presenter after the break. What did you have in mind?"

"I did a little research and learned that there's a sort of tavern in town that maintains a human-friendly menu. Apparently enough sightseers and businesspeople come to Durzinzer to make it worth their while." Sikander tapped his dataslate. "It's maybe a ten-minute walk, if it's not too chilly for you."

"I'll put up with the weather for a chance at a decent lunch. Sabub and his family are wonderful hosts, but I'm afraid that fish this morning was not for me."

"Me neither," Sikander agreed. He set out in the direction of the town, and Lara fell in beside him. It was a clear if cold day by the standards of Tamabuqq Prime. Most of the Tzoru they passed by bundled themselves up in heavy winter robes and hurried from place to place, but the sunshine glinted brightly on the gold filigree decorating the Library's ancient buildings. They chatted amiably about the weather and gossiped about mutual friends as they walked; Lara was close to Sikander's cousin Amarleen, and they knew many of the same people.

They found the Tzoru tavern with only one missed turn. It wasn't anything like a human restaurant or drinking establishment, of course. The Tzoru *sebet* who ran the establishment made a living by preparing food and brewing fermented fruit ales for the special celebrations of other clans, and during the workday they simply opened the kitchen to sell takeout snacks to Tzoru whose work kept them from returning home to prepare their own midday meals. The human menu consisted of skewers of spicy grilled meat and safe but bland vegetables. Sikander realized that he'd been spoiled by his previous visits to the Thousand Worlds ward—the establishments of the capital's offworlder district had a much better understanding of the human palate, it seemed.

They took their plates to a low wall in a park across the street, and settled as best they could. "A little chilly for dining alfresco," Lara remarked. "Forgive me if I keep my coat on. How did you find this place again?"

"It was the only eatery listed in *Baum's Excursions,*" Sikander said with a smile. At least the food was tolerable; he devoted himself to his skewer while Lara attacked her own. "So how have you been?" he asked between mouthfuls.

"I'm well. I like my work—the Foreign Ministry is fascinating and it's good to find a use for all that education. The travel's interesting, and I get the chance to help shape important decisions and make a difference, as they say." Lara dabbed at her mouth with a handkerchief. "What about you? I remember that you were assigned to *Mackenzie* after the board of inquiry, but I lost track of your postings after that."

"I served on *Mackenzie* for two years. Good ship, good crew, and Captain Brandt never let any of the dark clouds from my board of inquiry color his judgment of my work. After that I had a nine-month shore posting at Fleet Base Operations in New Perth, followed by Intel School at Laguna and my posting to Helix Squadron staff as intelligence officer. I've been here a year and a half now, and I'm due to rotate out in a few months."

"They don't keep you in one place very long, do they?"

"That's the Navy. Although the Gadira business definitely confused my career track." Most junior officers didn't survive the sort of charges Acting Captain Peter Chatburn of CSS *Hector* had leveled against Sikander immediately after the battle against the Dremish forces attempting to seize control of the Gadira system. Months of hearings, the Dremish disavowal of their local commanders' actions, and the preservation of the status quo in Gadira had eventually vindicated Sikander . . . but there'd been no way he could continue in his billet aboard *Hector.* Few captains wanted anything to do with an officer who'd earned such notoriety under a previous CO, to say the least.

"I imagine so," said Lara. "Did you find the occasion to sweep any more princesses off their feet?"

Sikander winced, but Lara's easy smile suggested that she only teased him. Gadira had thrown other things in his life into confusion too, including the question of what kind of relationship he had with Lara Dunstan. "No, I'm afraid not. And before you ask, no, I'm not seeing anyone right now. Helix Station offers few opportunities for meeting people outside your own chain of command—humans, anyway. It's a rare occasion when I manage to find a date in the off-worlder district at Kahnar-Sag. Yourself?"

"I haven't swept any princesses off their feet, either," she said. She stuck her tongue out at him when he shot her a sharp look, then shrugged. "I was seeing someone in my Foreign Ministry training group for a while, but then he went to the California Union and I was posted here, and, well . . . we decided to go our own ways."

"I'm sorry, Lara."

"You don't need to be. It wasn't the sort of thing you would make plans around, so I suppose I was happy to let the Foreign Ministry settle it for me." Lara tidied up her plate and folded her handkerchief. "We probably should head back. Tzoru are bizarrely punctual for people who don't bother to make clocks."

"Of course," Sikander said. They disposed of their platters in a nearby waste receptacle; then he turned back to the wall where they'd been sitting to see if they'd left anything behind.

A small group of Tzoru wearing green caps and green tunics stared at them from fifty meters down the street.

Sikander frowned, and watched them for a long moment. They did not seem agitated, and it could certainly be difficult to read Tzoru expressions; the immobile features and wide, unblinking eyes simply didn't convey nuances humans had evolved to pick up from other human faces. But even so, he didn't like the way they were looking at him and Lara. He'd spent enough time in the Dominion to become used to having conversations with Tzoru studiously looking at something over his shoulder or down at their feet. On the rare occasions when one made accidental eye contact, Tzoru quickly averted their gaze. He could *feel* the challenge and resentment in those cold stares.

"What is it?" Lara asked, noticing that he had not yet moved.

"*Warumzi agu,*" Sikander replied. "Come on, let's get you back for your presentation." So far he hadn't seen any of the disciples or protesters or whatever they were around the Library grounds—perhaps Durzinzer's scholars didn't think much of what Ebneghirz had to say. But just in case, he stayed close beside Lara the whole way back and kept an eye on the winding streets behind them. No more green-clad Tzoru appeared.

When they returned to the Library grounds, Lara reached up to give Sikander a kiss on the cheek. "Thank you for lunch," she said. "I really am glad that you came up here to visit me. Do you want to sit in on my presentation?"

"Is that allowed?" he asked.

"I don't think anybody here today will mind if you take a seat in the back."

"All right, then." Sikander smiled. "My father always says that you learn something new every day. Break a leg—I'll be in shortly."

Lara took a deep breath and strode confidently into the hall where the conference representatives were gathering again. Sikander waited until she was out of earshot. None of the Tzoru in sight seemed to be paying any special attention to him, but he couldn't shake the unease that had settled over him. The way those Tzoru near the eatery had simply stared at him . . . cold, emotionless, almost predatory in a way, like being watched by a shark. *I really need to find out more about these* warumzi *fellows,* he decided. *Maybe Lin has something more on them by now.*

He glanced up at the sky, wondering where *Exeter* was in her orbit, and keyed his comm unit. "*Exeter,* this is Lieutenant Commander North. Put me through to the squadron S-2 desk, please."

The ship's info assistant beeped once in acknowledgment. A moment later the channel clicked over to the flag spaces. "Intel Section, Senior Chief Lin speaking."

"Senior Chief, this is Mr. North. I thought I'd check in and see what's new."

"I was just about to call you, sir." Lin's tone grew crisp; a rustle of movement came over the connection. Sikander had worked with her long enough to recognize a hint of concern in her voice. When Lin put on her professional face—well, voice, anyway—it meant that she didn't like what she was looking at. "Where are you right now?"

"I'm in a town called Durzinzer, a couple hundred kilometers north of the capital."

"Durzinzer? . . . Okay, I see it on the map display. What are you doing all the way up there?"

"Taking in some of the local culture. There's a big scholars' conference at the library here." Sikander decided that his enlisted people didn't need to know he was using his free time to look up an old flame—he'd hear about that for the rest of his tour. "You said you were about to call?"

"Yes, sir. Things have been getting strange over the last twelve hours or so. Tzoru courier traffic departing the system is spiking, and we're seeing large demonstrations or marches forming up in major population centers. We're also monitoring increased military activity from the high clans: more flyer patrols, troops staging to new bases, a big uptick in coded comm traffic. All of the sudden everybody's talking to everybody."

"Really?" Sikander frowned at his comm unit. As a general rule of thumb, if Lin wasn't worried then he wasn't worried . . . but the converse of that was also true. "I haven't seen anything like that since I've been on station. Watching the strongholds of the high *sebetu* is about as exciting as watching grass grow."

"This is my third tour on Helix Station, sir. I haven't ever seen anything like this, either. Have you noticed anything unusual on the ground?"

"Nothing like military activity, but then again, I'm not in Bagal-Dindir." Sikander glanced around the serene grounds of the Library, looking for ominous groups of Tzoru in green caps; none were in sight. "What do you make of all this, Senior Chief?"

Lin hesitated. He knew that she disliked speculating, and naturally focused her attention on things she could measure or prove. It was one of the things that made the two of them an effective team, since he was inclined to build and discard narratives to explain the data. "Beats me, sir," she finally said. "I really don't like those courier ships leaving Tamabuqq—that looks like bad news spreading, and we don't have a clue what the news is. If I didn't know the Tzoru better, I'd say this whole business with the first councillor stepping down has triggered a succession struggle."

But Tzoru don't fight Tzoru, Sikander told himself. The *sebetu* that ruled over the Dominion certainly had their rivalries, but the whole reason they existed was to protect the realm from outside forces; the Tzoru hadn't had anything like a war in thousands of years.

"Acknowledged," he said. "It sounds like it's time for me to get back to work. I'll finish up here and return to the capital. Is there anything else I should know?"

"The embassy's preparing a travel warning for later this afternoon—they recommend that Aquilan citizens return to designated offworld trade districts in major cities and remain there until things settle down. Oh, and I've got Macklin working on background research for the *warumzi agu* movement. We should have something for you by the end of the day."

"Very well," Sikander said. "Call me if anything new comes up. North, out."

He stood in the plaza for a moment, thinking about Senior Chief Lin's report. It seemed unlikely that unprecedented events such as the abrupt departure of Sapwu Zrinan, the appearance of violent demonstrations, and the sudden alarm of the powerful Tzoru clans would all spontaneously occur in the same week. His training in intelligence analysis was fairly basic compared to that of the dedicated specialists in the squadron's Intel Section, but even so Sikander had learned that there were few coincidences in the intel business. *This is all connected, but how?* he wondered. Perhaps the Radis could shed more light on things . . . he could ask Lara to bring it up with Sabub after her presentation. *Assuming, of course, that we're not recalled to Bagal-Dindir immediately.*

He tucked his comm unit back into his pocket and headed into the auditorium. Lara stood on a small dais at one end of the room, speaking in front of a vidscreen that showed images from her presentation. She glanced once at him as he slipped in and gave him a quick smile before returning to her topic—human myths that touched on demigod figures historians now correlated with Tzoru visits at the dawn of civilization. It had always struck Sikander as a little ironic and amusing that the ancient astronaut theories so derided before the First Expansion had been confirmed by alien contact a few centuries later. He soon found himself caught up in her subject; Lara was a natural lecturer, with a great sense of pacing and well-placed dramatic pauses.

Clever of her to emphasize Terran history, he decided. There wasn't much she could tell a gathering of Tzoru scholars about their own history, so she instead shared the Mesopotamian myths that seemed to document the first human-Tzoru contact, something that the Tzoru scholars probably hadn't heard before. It wasn't exactly her field, since Lara was not an archaeologist, but—

"Excuse me, friend Sikander?" Radi Damiq quietly took the seat next to him and whispered in his ear.

He glanced over in surprise; he hadn't even heard her enter the room. "Yes, Damiq? What is it?"

She looked about as uncomfortable as he'd ever seen a Tzoru look. "There is trouble," she admitted. "A demonstration is gathering a short distance from here. The leaders are calling for humans to leave the Dominion. They know that you and friend Lara are here in the Library."

"Demonstration?" Sikander frowned. "The *warumzi agu* are coming here?"

"Yes, friend Sikander. I think it would be wise if you and friend Lara left soon."

"Who are these people?" Sikander wondered aloud. "Why are they angry with us?"

"The followers of Ebneghirz dislike *sebetu* who welcome non-Tzoru to our worlds. My friend Kabbi observed as the *warumzi agu* gathered. She hurried here to warn me."

"Thanks, Damiq." Sikander glanced around the hall, thinking. He didn't even have a sidearm, not that it would help if an antihuman mob came for him and Lara. The safety of the Thousand Worlds district and the marine detachment guarding the embassy was two hundred kilometers away, a distance that now seemed much farther than it had just a moment ago. He quickly checked the airship schedule on his dataslate. The next flight for the capital departed in half an hour . . . could they make it?

He returned his attention to Lara, and saw that she had just finished her remarks. The Tzoru scholars signaled their approval by nodding vigorously and slapping their knees as they sat, which made it look as if they'd just heard her tell a sidesplitting joke. Lara bowed to the assembly, then descended from the dais to gather her things. Several Tzoru rose and crowded around her, ready to question her about her presentation.

This might not be the best time for that, Sikander decided. He made his way to where Lara stood and shouldered his way to her side, ignoring the looks from the scholars around her, then lowered his voice. "Lara, we have to go. Radi Damiq just warned me that a large band of *warumzi agu* is gathering not far away. They're not happy that we're here."

Lara gave him a puzzled look. "The conference? What do they have against scholars?"

"No," said Sikander. "*Humans.* We need to get out of Durzinzer at once."

"Sikander, I can't! It took me four months to arrange this invitation!"

"I ran into these fellows outside the Ward of a Thousand Worlds early yesterday. Trust me, we don't want to be anywhere near them if a mob is forming." Sikander saw that she was still dubious, and searched for a moment to find a persuasive argument. "Besides, if we stay, all these Tzoru may be in danger on our account."

"I have some things at the Radi home—" Lara began.

"We'll send for them later," Sikander told her. "Now, please, we need to go."

Lara grimaced, but she allowed Sikander to lead her out to where Radi Damiq waited. The young Tzoru wasted no time; she tugged at Sikander's sleeve and pointed. "This way, friends! I think we can still reach the airship platform."

"Lead on, Damiq," Sikander replied. She set off at once in a sort of bounding trot, guiding them past a building that marked the edge of the Library grounds and heading back into the town. Sikander and Lara were obliged to break into a jog to keep up. He wondered if running might draw more attention than keeping to an unconcerned walking pace, but he decided not to second-guess Damiq.

Lara paused for a moment to button her coat before falling in beside Sikander. "Is this really necessary?" she asked.

"Damiq seems to think so," said Sikander.

"Damiq is *nine years old,*" Lara said. "She's as excitable as Tzoru get."

Nine? Sikander looked again at the young Tzoru leading them along the treefern-shaded streets, and shook his head. He'd assumed she was the equivalent of a Tzoru college student . . . but Tzoru children matured very differently from humans. He resolved to ask an expert how one could tell a Tzoru's age as soon as he found a chance. *Besides, that doesn't mean she isn't right to be worried for us.*

Five meters ahead of him, Damiq turned a corner. Sikander and Lara followed her and nearly ran her down when she came to a sudden stop.

A hundred meters down the cross street, a mass of green-clad Tzoru stood chanting with fists raised in the air. Damiq hesitated; Sikander pointed to the shaded path across the street. "Keep moving!" he urged her. "Don't stop now!"

Damiq scuttled across the open space—but as Sikander and Lara crossed, Sikander saw heads turning in their direction. The chanting broke up in confusion. He risked one more look back, and saw Tzoru beginning to stream down the street after them.

That is not good, he decided. "Damiq, run! They're after us!"

"How many?" Lara asked. She slowed to take a look for herself.

Sikander caught her arm and hurried her along. "Enough," he told her. The two humans redoubled their pace, which was necessary because Radi Damiq began to pull away from them. Sikander realized that Tzoru might actually be a little faster than humans . . . *which means our pursuers could very well overtake us if we don't move it.* For a minute, then two, he concentrated on keeping up with the young scholar as she bounded on ahead of them, twisting and turning through the narrow streets and shaded lanes of the ancient town. More Tzoru stared and pointed as they ran past, or scattered out of their path. Lara kicked off her heels and sprinted alongside Sikander in her bare feet. Fortunately she took her fitness seriously and kept up with his longer strides.

He caught sight of the airship platform rising up out of the treeferns ahead of them, and allowed himself a quick grin, which faded just as fast as it appeared. Mooring lines still tethered the Tzoru airship to the platform—but even as he watched, the first line slipped free. "Hurry!" he called.

They sprinted across the last plaza and pelted up the ramp spiraling to the top of the platform. But when the three of them reached the top, the airship already drifted a good thirty meters off the platform, climbing sedately up and away from them. "Hey!" shouted Lara. "Come back! Come back!"

"They do not hear you, friend Lara," said Damiq.

Damn! Sikander snarled at himself. He hurried over to the platform edge, and looked back in the direction they'd come from. Scores of green-clad Tzoru poured down the street, hurrying toward the platform. There was no way they could get back down to the street level before the *warumzi agu* reached the bottom of the access ramp. *We just trapped ourselves up here.*

Lara realized their predicament, too. She scowled, but she didn't panic. "What now?" she asked Sikander.

"We call for help," said Sikander. He tapped his comm unit. "*Exeter* Flight Ops, this is Lieutenant Commander North. I'm on the airship platform in Durzinzer and I'm caught in a riot with civilians. We urgently require retrieval, over."

No one answered for a long moment, but then the comm unit crackled to life. "Mr. North, this is *Exeter* Flight Ops. What's the nature of your trouble, over?"

"*Exeter,* I'm with Dr. Dunstan from the embassy. We have a mob of angry Tzoru chasing us, and we're trapped on top of the airship platform in Durzinzer. If you've got a shuttle on the ground in Bagal-Dindir, we could really use it here, the sooner the better."

"Stand by," the watch officer in the ship's flight operations center replied. The line clicked over into a hold tone.

"Not helpful," Sikander said to himself. He risked another quick look over the platform rail; the Tzoru fanatics gathered around the base of the access ramp, pushing and jostling to climb up. If only he had his sidearm . . . but everyone knew Tamabuqq was *peaceful,* so nobody carried arms planetside except for the marine guards at the embassy grounds. He looked around for some way to barricade the top of the ramp, and spotted a large waste bin not far from the top of the ramp. *Good enough,* he decided. He hurried over, tipped it on its side, and sent it down the spiraling ramp with one mighty heave. The round metal bin banged and clattered from side to side as it barreled down the ramp, and then a chorus of high-pitched Tzoru squeals erupted from below.

"Now you've made them angry!" Lara said. "How long until your shuttle reaches us?"

"Fifteen minutes, I hope," Sikander said.

"You're going to run out of things to roll down the ramp long before then." Lara looked around, then pointed at a weather shelter near the center of the platform. "There. Can we get on top of that? They'll have a harder time reaching us up there."

That struck him as better than any of his own ideas. He tossed a small bench down the ramp, then ran over to make a stirrup of his hands by the side of the shelter. It was hardly any protection at all—not more than four meters square and about three meters high—but as long as the mob couldn't pull it down bodily, it might last long enough. Lara set her foot in his hands, and he lifted her easily up to where she could scramble over the edge.

"Radi Damiq, your turn," he told the young Tzoru.

"I step on your hands?" she said, eyeing Sikander dubiously.

"It's okay," he told her. *Do Tzoru not use the make-a-step move?* He could hear angry voices rising now from the platform's opposite corner, where a second ramp ascended. "And please hurry!"

Damiq approached and tentatively set her foot in Sikander's hands. "Now lean forward a bit and set a hand on my shoulder," he told her, and boosted her up to where Lara could reach down and catch her free hand. She was surprisingly light, probably not much more than thirty kilos. Then Sikander tensed and jumped for the shelter edge. He chinned himself up until he could throw an elbow and a foot over, then pulled himself over the edge with a little help from Lara and Damiq.

He paused for a moment, panting. "Please tell me that Tzoru can't just jump up here."

"No better than you, friend Sikander," Damiq said.

"Good." He rolled to his hands and knees and stood up, moving away from the edge of the roof. The shelter seemed pretty sturdy—he didn't think a mob could easily tip it over. But if the *warumzi agu* had any kind of weapons at all, then the three of them had nowhere to hide.

The first of the *warumzi agu* burst out from the top of the ramp onto the platform, followed by dozens more. The fanatics shouted in anger and quickly surrounded the shelter. Sikander picked up a few imprecations and shouted words—"Offworlders! Defilers! Human scum!"—but his translator couldn't keep up with so many individuals roaring and hurling insults all at once.

"Why are you angry at us?" Lara called down at the Tzoru below them. "We've done you no harm!"

"We are not your slaves!" one Tzoru shouted back loud enough for Sikander to hear. "Take your silver and go, aliens!" Another Tzoru threw a shoe at Lara, just missing her; Sikander pulled her back from the edge. A barrage of shoes followed; then several of the Tzoru jumped up to catch hold of the shelter edge and pull themselves onto the roof.

Sikander darted over to stomp on the hand of the first, then kicked a second in the face and sent him back into the crowd. But the third Tzoru managed to pull herself upright before Sikander got back over to her. The *warumzi* charged at Sikander, hands open to clutch and grapple, so Sikander stepped forward and threw a hard right jab at the broad space between the Tzoru's wide-set eyes. The thick dermis and springy cartilage of the Tzoru's flexible skeleton cushioned the blow; it felt like he'd punched a leather pad. But something crunched under Sikander's fist anyway, and the Tzoru staggered back hissing in pain before she toppled over the edge.

"*Sikander!*" Behind him, Lara faced another Tzoru, who'd scrambled up while Sikander cleared the opposite side of the shelter roof. The demonstrator grabbed her by the arms and tried to drag her back to the roof edge, perhaps with the idea of throwing her down to the waiting crowd below. Lara twisted an arm underneath the Tzoru's and executed a neat hip throw with a quick half turn. Against a human, it would have worked beautifully . . . but Tzoru were too springy for that. Lara managed to wrap her attacker around herself and spin in a circle, until she simply went limp to drop through his arms and get free.

Sikander headed over to help her, only to be confronted by two more demonstrators scrambling over the side. He found himself in a sudden flurry of hard Tzoru slaps and clutching hands, and lashed back with elbow strikes, hard punches, and more quick foot stomps. For a moment he thought he was going to be overwhelmed, but then he heard a sudden roaring sound overhead, followed by the *chirp-chirp-chirp* of an autorifle firing low-v mag rounds at close range. The Tzoru crowd erupted in shrieks of panic and pain, and abruptly broke as its members scattered for the ramps leading away from the platform.

Above the platform hovered one of *Exeter*'s orbital shuttles, a VO-8 Cormorant. The pilot slewed the craft in a slow circle to cover the elevated platform while the door gunner raked the mob stragglers with nonlethal rounds to hurry them on their way. A marine—Sergeant Wall from the ship's company, if Sikander had his name right—balanced in the open side door next to the gunner. "Mr. North!" Wall shouted. "Are you okay, sir?"

"We're glad to see you, Sergeant!" Sikander shouted back. He moved close to Radi Damiq and threw an arm over her shoulder just to make sure that no one in the shuttle mistook her for hostile. "Your timing is impeccable!"

"That's what they pay us for, sir." The sergeant scanned the rooftop and then motioned to the pilot, who carefully brought the Cormorant's open door level with the shelter rooftop. The drive plates hummed and crackled, but produced no prop wash or jet blast to speak of; the pilot steadied the shuttle just a meter away. "Mind your step!"

Lara turned to Damiq. "Would you like a ride? We can set you down somewhere away from the *warumzi agu*."

"No, I will stay here, friend Lara," Damiq replied.

"Are you sure?" Sikander asked her. "They must have seen you helping us, Damiq."

"I am sure. They were angry at humans, not Tzoru."

Sikander and Lara exchanged looks. "I hope she's right," Lara murmured.

"Ma'am, sir, if you're ready?" Sergeant Wall asked. The man was aptly named; in his combat gear he must have been a meter wide at the shoulders. "We're getting all kinds of protests from Tzoru authorities about cutting through their traffic patterns."

"Of course," said Sikander. He provided Lara a supporting arm she didn't need as she stepped across to the marine at the open hatch, then followed with one easy stride a moment later.

"Thank you, Damiq!" Lara called as the shuttle pulled away. "And thank your *sebet* for us! I'll be in touch with Sabub soon!" Damiq waved once, then scrambled down from the shelter roof.

Sergeant Wall motioned for Sikander and Lara to take seats in the passenger compartment. "Better strap in, sir, ma'am," he told them. "We've got to get Dr. Dunstan to the embassy and then hightail it back into orbit. The commodore wants to get under way as soon as possible."

5

W hat in the hell were you *thinking*, Mr. North?" Deputy Commodore Francine Reyes demanded. "Wandering off into the backcountry to see the sights! Do you realize that we had to fly *Exeter*'s shuttle through hostile-controlled airspace to save your sorry ass? The Hish threatened to open fire on our marines—you put the lives of five servicemen and women at risk with this little stunt of yours. I hope you're proud of yourself!"

Sikander stood at a stiff parade rest: hands folded behind his back, cap clasped in his hands, eyes fixed on the opposite bulkhead. The cruiser's flag cabin was finished in rich wooden paneling, and the carpet upon which he'd been called was a deep, seamless blue pile. Behind the commodore's desk, a large vidscreen showed the actual hull-camera view of the Tzoru capital system; distant lights moved slowly against the starfield, a myriad of ships and small craft maneuvering in the approaches to Tamabuqq Prime. The planet itself, an emerald orb with a haze of olive-colored cloud, slowly fell astern as *Exeter* climbed up and away from orbit. "No, ma'am, I am not," he answered.

Reyes glowered at him. She stood a meter away and just far enough to one side so that he couldn't easily see more of her expression. "Do you have some special entitlement to ignore liberty bounds and go where you like? Or did you think we were just too stupid to notice?"

Sikander clamped his mouth shut and stared intently at the vidscreen. Reyes had the right to be irked; he'd almost missed a ship's movement, after all, and he shouldn't have ever been caught in the situation at Durzinzer. *But if I hadn't been there, would anyone have called in the shuttle to retrieve Lara?* Either *Exeter* would have had to intervene to protect a civilian anyway, or they'd now be dealing with the fact that a high-ranking agent of the Foreign Ministry from an important senatorial family had been captured, injured, or maybe even killed by the mob at the airship platform. He didn't deserve to be chewed out like a first-year midshipman, and he didn't like the fact that he had to stand there and take it without pointing out what might have happened if he *hadn't* gone to Durzinzer . . . but he swallowed his anger, at least for the moment.

"Well? What's your excuse?" Reyes pressed.

I'll be damned if I give her anything else to yell at me about, he resolved. Serving officers in the fleet generally weren't dressed down like midshipmen. He found himself remembering the last time a Reyes—well, a Gray—had physically gotten in his face to chew him out: the Greene Hall museum room, Alberto Reyes's Starburst of Valor. Well, if Francine Reyes wanted to treat him like a snottie, then he'd give her a snottie's answer: "No excuse, ma'am."

Reyes bridled, but Commodore Abernathy—seated on the corner of his desk, and so far silent in the discussion—chose that moment to step in. "That's enough for now, D-Com," he said. "Mr. North, at ease. If you'd be so kind as to drop the Academy bullshit and tell me why you were in Durzinzer and how you wound up with a mob at your heels, I'd sincerely appreciate it."

Sikander glanced at Abernathy, and relaxed his pose. "Yes, sir," he replied. "Since you and Captain Reyes were going to be busy for a couple of days, I thought I had time to visit a friend. Ambassador Hart mentioned that she was attending a conference in Durzinzer, so I decided to go on up and surprise her. As for the mob, there was no sign of trouble at the Library. I couldn't say what set them off."

"Maybe you could if you'd done what I asked you to," Reyes snapped. "I distinctly recall telling you to look into those Tzoru fanatics we encountered and find out why we were attacked."

"I did, ma'am. I instructed Intel Section to check into the *warumzi agu* and pull together a threat assessment."

"Then where's my report?"

"I'm meeting with Senior Chief Lin as soon as we're finished here, ma'am," said Sikander.

Reyes subsided. Abernathy folded his arms and studied Sikander for a moment. "I assume Dr. Dunstan from the embassy was the friend you went to visit?" he asked.

"Yes, sir." Sikander met his gaze evenly. "In all honesty, I didn't see that a quick trip out to Durzinzer could pose a problem. The town has regular airship service from Bagal-Dindir, and it's only a ninety-minute flight. In fact, under normal circumstances the embassy recommends it highly as a sightseeing destination. The D-Com might remember that some of us went to see the temple at Kadingir the last time *Exeter* called at Tamabuqq Prime. The Durzinzer Library's only a little farther out."

"Circumstances do not appear to be normal," said Abernathy.

"No, sir. It's clear now that they're not." Sikander glanced at the vidscreen again, and decided to test out the waters a bit. "May I ask why we got under way ahead of schedule? I thought we had a full slate of visits and events for the next week."

"The Tzoru withdrew their invitation," Abernathy said with a snort. "The Dominion High Council couched it in a bunch of flowery language, but it basically came down to *we don't want you here right now,* so we're headed back to Kahnar-Sag."

"Really?" Sikander frowned. "That's something else we

haven't seen before." Human ships from any of the Coalition powers visited the Dominion's capital system only by invitation; the nearby star system of Kahnar-Sag served as the Dominion's primary port of call for human vessels. Over the course of many years, invitations to visit Tamabuqq Prime had become little more than a formality. Commonwealth warships made the short transit from Kahnar-Sag several times a year, and the Tzoru hadn't ever seemed to mind. *Everybody knows the Tzoru are as predictable as the sunrise,* he wondered. But the chaos in the Dominion government and the sudden appearance of the *warumzi agu* suggested that "everybody" knew a little less about the Tzoru than they thought.

"So I gather." Abernathy glanced at Reyes, then fixed his eyes on Sikander again. "All right, Mr. North. I think you took some liberties with your liberty and you knew damned well that I wouldn't have wanted you to leave town after our incident on the way to the embassy. I'm placing a letter of admonition in your service jacket. But it's an admonition, not a reprimand, so it will be removed when your tour concludes . . . as long as you don't try to play me for a fool again. Am I clear?"

Sikander grimaced. "Yes, sir."

"Get me that report," Abernathy said. "I need to know why the Tzoru Dominion decided to blow up the week I arrived. Dismissed."

Sikander straightened, set his cap on his head, and saluted. Then he turned and marched out of the commodore's cabin, making sure he closed the hatch behind him. *That could have been worse, I suppose.* A letter of reprimand was a permanent black mark that tended to end careers. He didn't think an admonition was warranted—after all, his actions wouldn't have been controversial in the least if not for local developments no Commonwealth diplomat or officer saw coming—but at least it would stay between him and his immediate superiors. Still, he hated the idea of handing Francine Reyes any more arrows for her quiver. He'd known for months that she wanted to add his head to her trophy case, and skipping town to go visit Lara played right into her hands.

He headed down to his cabin, two decks below the commodore's, to change out of his whites into shipboard working uniform. *Exeter* was older than he was and no longer suited to front-line service in the Commonwealth's main battle fleet, but at least she had plenty of space; most cruisers with flag accommodations had few staterooms to spare for staff officers.

He found Darvesh Reza carefully arranging his uniforms in the small closet when he let himself in. "Welcome back, Nawabzada," the tall Kashmiri said. He glanced at Sikander, then reached into the closet to pull out a buff-colored jumpsuit. "Your working uniform."

"Thank you, Darvesh." Sikander stripped off his whites, noting that he'd managed to tear the uniform at the knee and split a seam along the right side of the shirt. "I'm afraid this will need some mending."

"So I see." Darvesh served as Sikander's valet, secretary, and general minder. Formerly a senior sergeant in the Jaipur Dragoons, the elite guards protecting the household of the Nawab of Ishar, he now wore the uniform of a chief petty officer in the Commonwealth Navy with a simple green pakul for his head covering. As a rule, only flag officers had personal stewards, but Sikander was a special case; his father Dayan was an important prince in Kashmir, so under instructions from the Foreign Ministry the Navy allowed him an exception. Fourteen years ago Darvesh had accompanied Sikander to the Academy at High Albion, and he'd followed Sikander to his assignments aboard *Adept, Triton, Hector, Mackenzie,* and all the shore billets and schools in between. Darvesh picked up the shirt Sikander discarded, and ran a finger along the damaged seam. "You were fortunate, sir. This might have been a knife slash or a bullet hole—I saw the vid imagery from *Exeter*'s shuttle."

"It wasn't supposed to be that exciting, believe me."

Darvesh frowned at him. "That is why I am here, Nawabzada—to be on hand for trouble no one can foresee. Your father expects me to make sure you remain as safe as you can be while living aboard a warship and serving in the Commonwealth Navy. He expects *you* to avoid making my job difficult or taking senseless risks. You know perfectly well that you are not to travel unaccompanied, especially in dangerous areas."

Sikander pulled on his jumpsuit, and sat down on the edge of the bunk to slip on the boots. "I was with the commodore," he said.

"Until you chose to leave the embassy alone. Do I need to remind your commanding officer of the arrangements between the Nawab's Office and the Aquilan Foreign Ministry?"

"That won't be necessary," Sikander said, fighting vainly to conceal his irritation. The last thing he needed was for Abernathy or Reyes to receive a pointed message from the Admiralty about making sure Sikander's security detail, small as it might be, was not impeded in its duties. Once or twice Darvesh had carried through on those threats earlier in Sikander's career before they'd eventually settled into their current working relationship. *Darvesh is only trying to do his job,* he reminded himself. *And you knew that you were bending the rules by heading off to Durzinzer without him. If there's anyone to be angry with, it's yourself.*

Darvesh gave him a long look, but acceded with a nod. "Very good, sir. I will see what I can do with the torn seam."

"Right. I'm off, then." Sikander stood and picked up his dataslate. "Captain Reyes expects a report, so I'd better give her one."

As a department head aboard *Hector* and *Mackenzie,* Sikander had been in charge of more than fifty enlisted personnel and a handful of junior officers. As the staff intelligence officer for Helix Squadron, Sikander had only five enlisted personnel in his section . . . and two of those were back at the squadron headquarters in Kahnar-Sag. His domain on board *Exeter* consisted of four cubicles and one tiny conference room within the ship's flag spaces. That wasn't unusual for staff tours; Helix Squadron's entire staff consisted of only thirty-three personnel, including officers.

"I'm back," Sikander announced, taking his place at the conference table in his section in *Exeter*'s flag spaces. He could feel the deck plates trembling softly under his feet as the big cruiser accelerated along its course for Kahnar-Sag. The greater a ship's real-space velocity at the moment the warp generators activated, the quicker the warp transit, so ships spent hours accelerating before a standard transit. "Gather around, everybody. The commodore and the d-com would like to know why the Tzoru have all lost their minds this week, and they expect us to come up with some answers."

"Good to see you, Mr. North," said Senior Chief Intelligence Specialist Joanne Lin. A native of the high-g mining world of Orcades II, she was noticeably shorter and stockier than Sikander, which meant that she looked rather like a fireplug in the company of the Caledonians or Albionans who composed much of Aquila's naval personnel. She grinned easily as she took her customary seat at the small conference table, but her smile didn't erase the measuring look in her eyes. "Are you okay, sir? It looked like things got pretty exciting at the airship station."

"A few bumps and bruises, nothing serious," he told her. "You saw all that, did you?"

"We trained one of the hull cams on Durzinzer when you called for the orbiter, sir," said Petty Officer Macklin, taking the seat across from Lin. He was an intel specialist first class, the second-most-experienced hand in Sikander's team. A native of the sun-drenched tropics of New Andalusia, he had skin of a deep brown shade almost as rare among the common Aquilan genotypes as Sikander's own copper-bronze hue. "Nice punch on that one guy, by the way. You dropped him like a bad habit."

"I thought the goal of making port visits to friendly worlds was to *avoid* punching your hosts, sir," said Petty Officer Ortiz, an IS second class and the most junior member of Sikander's team. A native of New Seville, dark-haired and dark-eyed, he sometimes struck Sikander as a little too clever for his own good. But he was good at what he did—comm-traffic analysis—and he could dig in on tasks that interested him with an absolutely fierce tenacity. Lin and Macklin grinned at his remark.

"It seemed like a good idea at the time," Sikander admitted grudgingly. "Once they trapped us on the platform, I was out of better options. Speaking of which, did anybody see if the Tzoru with me got away after we left? She was the small one in the brown tunic and dun-colored robes. She said she'd be fine, but I'd like to know that she got home safely."

"Yes, sir, she did," Lin told him. "Once the shuttle opened up with crowd-control rounds no one on the platform stuck around to see what happened next."

"Good," said Sikander. He would have hated to hear that the crowd had turned on Radi Damiq. *I suppose Lara and I attracted the bulk of their attention.* "Okay, then, enough about my misadventures. Tell me about the military movements in the system."

"Yes, sir," said Lin. She activated the conference table and brought up a vid display of the Tamabuqq system. "Here's what we've seen over the last twenty-four hours or so. Pretty much all the major clans have dispatched courier ships to their nearest strongpoints—the Baltzu to Shimatum, the Sapwu to Latzari, the Hish to Badibira and Isk-Aranu, and so on. The local squadrons are otherwise holding station, but then again, the high clans don't keep a lot of combat power in Tamabuqq."

Sikander nodded. Most of the aristocratic *sebetu* maintained token squadrons in Tamabuqq, but the real naval strength of clans such as the Hish or the Baltzu or the Ninazzu lay in various provincial or frontier fleets they controlled.

Tzoru starships relied on the same sort of warp technology as human ships, so if you paid attention to the course a ship accelerated along before generating its warp field and vanishing into its own little pocket universe, you could determine its destination easily enough.

"What about the Golden Banner Fleet?" he asked. That was the Tzoru home fleet, commanded by the Zabar clan. In theory, the powerful Golden Banner Fleet served under the direct control of the Anshar, and the privilege of crewing its ornately decorated battleships was a high honor for the Zabar. In practice, it was so poorly maintained that Sikander hadn't seen a single one of its warships under way since he'd been assigned to Helix Squadron.

"*Baraqqu* shifted to the repair dock yesterday, but no work's started on her yet. We haven't seen any other activity."

"Business as usual, then. I suppose that's a relief—go on."

Lin reset the display to show the Tzoru capital world in detail. Bright red icons flashed at a dozen spots around the globe. "This animation summarizes our observations of events on the ground. Forces under the control of the Zag, Baltzu, and Maruz clans have deployed to these points, taking up defensive positions around civic buildings or commercial centers. Those are hot spots where civil unrest is particularly bad." She pointed to two more indicators. "Here and here, demonstrators managed to break into the armories of minor clans. We observed those events from orbit—it looked like the guards just walked away from their posts and let the mobs in."

"Wait a moment—the soldier clans just *gave* these demonstrators weapons?" Sikander didn't like that idea at all. He'd gained all too much experience with that sort of trouble when dealing with the Caidists in Gadira four years ago, or the Palarist movement in Kashmir before he'd been sent offworld to the Aquilan naval academy. Of course, there wasn't much *Exeter* could do about the armed demonstrators even if Commodore Abernathy wanted to intervene. In an hour or so they'd be in transit for Kahnar-Sag, and events in Tamabuqq would just have to look after themselves for a bit. "Please tell me that we passed that information to Major Dalton at the embassy before we broke orbit!"

"We did, sir. But we don't think the mobs got their hands on any heavy stuff."

"I wouldn't make that assumption; the fact that we didn't see it doesn't mean it didn't happen." Sikander chewed it over for a moment, wondering what common-clan Tzoru would do with an armory's contents. Virtually all military power in Tzoru society belonged to the high *sebetu;* Tzoru of the working classes simply didn't own any guns or serve in the armed forces. He set that question aside and moved on to the principal purpose for the meeting. "What did you find out about the *warumzi agu* and Ebneghirz? Are all these demonstrations tied to them?"

"We think so, sir. Macklin ran that down this morning," said Lin. She nodded to the IS first class. "Tell Mr. North what you found out."

"It's sort of a Tzoru nationalist movement, sir," said Petty Officer Macklin. "The Tzoru have lots of pet movements, of course—socialists, religionists, nihilists, whatever. Tzem Ebneghirz is a political theorist who calls for a restoration of Tzoru sovereignty, a ban on imports from foreign powers, and more accountability from the high clans of the Anshar's court. In short, the *warumzi agu* want the good old days back, and they're sick and tired of nobles and merchants who are getting ahead by expanding trade with human powers like us."

"Like the Baltzu and the Shimatum deal."

"Exactly, sir. Although there are plenty of other high clans they're sore at."

Damn. Sikander frowned, considering Macklin's words. *So this Ebneghirz is basically in direct opposition to anyone we're friendly with.* "Why has he turned up now?"

"He's been around for quite some time, sir. I found essays of his dating back thirty years or more. What's new is that he was arrested a couple of months ago, and sent off into religious seclusion. That fired up his supporters and brought them out into open protest. And just in the last day or so new missives from Ebneghirz have suddenly appeared, calling for an outright revolution. Not against the Anshar, of course, but against her so-called false advisors."

"For a Tzoru traditionalist, Ebneghirz seems to have studied some human history," Sikander observed. "Do we have any idea how much popular support the *warumzi agu* really have? Is the general populace sympathetic to their aims, or do they support the mercantile interests?"

"We can't tell yet," Senior Chief Lin answered. "It's the same old problem with the Tzoru. They just aren't chatting about the situation anywhere we can listen in."

"I was afraid of that." A human world would have thousands of media channels to monitor—vid programming, social media, bulletin boards. Tzoru, on the other hand, didn't get their entertainment from vid channels and didn't seem interested in news unless it obviously affected them personally. The Dominion government and all the major *sebetu* made use of modern communication channels for administration and reports, but analysis of current events or political speculations simply didn't exist in Tzoru public life. After all, a Tzoru knew his or her *sebet*'s place in the world and had few interactions outside of it; what was there to speculate about? Tamabuqq Prime, the hub of the entire Dominion, got by with only half a dozen public broadcast channels, and those carried little more than weather forecasts and the occasional public service announcement. Sikander's intel specialists rarely gleaned anything useful from Tzoru broadcasts or reportage.

He sighed and stood up, absently rubbing his knuckles. He didn't think he'd bruised his hands in the brawl on top of the airship platform, but he definitely had some abrasions from striking Tzoru dermis. "Good work, everybody," he told his small team. "While we're in transit, let's dive in more on Ebneghirz's writings and see if we can identify any other prominent figures in the *warumzi agu*. I suspect we'll find that he's explicit about his intentions if we take him at his word."

"Yes, sir," the enlisted hands replied.

"Senior Chief, send me a copy of the brief on Ebneghirz and your notes for the animation with all the incident locations plotted." Sikander nodded at the green globe hovering in the conference table's display, and the icons dotting its surface. "I want to take an hour and work through these one by one, so that I can brief the commodore on exactly what kind of mess we're leaving behind today."

Five days after leaving Tamabuqq, *Exeter* arrived at the Tzoru system of Kahnar-Sag. Sikander watched the end of the transit from his station on the cruiser's flag bridge. In all of his previous shipboard assignments he'd been directly responsible for some element of the ship's handling or readiness, but as part of an embarked staff on a flagship with no other vessels in company, he was really little more than a passenger with a good view. A countdown timer in one corner of the main display slowly ticked down to 0:00:00, at which point *Exeter*'s warp generator cut off. The ship's displays gave a small flicker and reset themselves to use live feed from the external sensors instead of a computer-generated simulation of what might be outside the bounds of the warp bubble.

"Good navigation," Deputy Commodore Reyes observed, checking her displays. "Captain Howard's nav team only missed their mark by three light-seconds."

Sikander smiled at the idea that emerging from a warp bubble nearly a million kilometers from where you planned to constituted good navigation, but it was true. Ships in warp transit couldn't see where they were going or make any kind of course correction; any maneuvering they did took place during their initial boost to the designated transit course and speed, at which point the warp generators kicked in and surrounded the ship in its own microuniverse until the time came to cut off the generators and see where the ship was. Deviations of a fraction of a percent in course, speed, or warp duration routinely resulted in arrival miscalculations of millions of kilometers. As a result, captains aimed for the wide-open outer reaches of a star system to make sure that a bad bit of navigation didn't put them on course for a planet or busy shipping lanes. A miss of three light-seconds was better than most transits managed.

He swept his eyes across the U-shaped main display that ringed the flag bridge, looking for anything out of the ordinary. Icons representing scores of merchant ships under way or parked in high orbit populated the screen as the ship caught up with its now-live feed, and the bright orange-and-blue eye of the Helix Nebula—only a few light-years away here, a spectacular sight in the darkness—gleamed on the starboard side of the cruiser. Decades ago Aquilan sailors assigned to ships patrolling the Tzoru frontier had nicknamed Kahnar-Sag "Helix Station" in honor of the local landmark, and the mismatched collection of old cruisers and escorts that served here naturally became known as Helix Squadron.

"Who's in town today, Mr. North?" Commodore Abernathy asked. He slouched in the admiral's battle couch, glancing through reports on his dataslate without looking up at the main display.

Sikander checked the tactical readouts at his own station. "The Nyeirans, Dremish, Californians, Montréalais, and Cygnans, sir. No sign of the Bolívarans or Taurans." Most of the human great powers with significant commercial interests in the Tzoru worlds maintained small squadrons in various systems along the frontier, each protecting its own favored ports and investments, but Kahnar-Sag served as the crossroads for trade. It was more heavily populated and more heavily industrialized than even the capital system of Tamabuqq, a bustling hub of commerce home to tens of thousands of human businesspeople. The Empire of Dremark, the California Union, the Republic of Montréal, and of course the Commonwealth of Aquila all maintained a more or less permanent naval presence at Kahnar-Sag, while warships from the Kingdom of Cygnus, the Principality of Bolívar, and the Tauran Hegemony visited less frequently.

"Is it the same Nyeiran squadron?" Abernathy said.

"Yes, sir—the Mountain-class battle cruiser, the Hero-class light cruiser, four destroyers, and the replenishment ship."

"They like showing off, don't they?" Reyes said with a frown. The Nyeiran squadron actually outgunned any of the human squadrons based at Helix Station. Aquilans were accustomed to being the biggest fleet in space; it always seemed somewhat out of place when a smaller power sent more ships to a system than the Commonwealth did. Then again, the Nyeiran Star Empire bordered directly on the Tzoru Dominion, while the Commonwealth of Aquila lay hundreds of light-years distant. "Assigning a battle cruiser to a gunboat's duties seems a little amateurish to me."

"Are you suggesting the *Exie*'s a glorified gunboat?" said Abernathy. "I wouldn't share that opinion with Captain Howard if I were you."

"I'm only saying that I don't care for the idea of Nyeirans showing off their new toys, sir," Reyes replied. "It makes me wonder if their ambitions in this sector are similarly out-sized."

Sikander finished counting the warship icons on his display. After a year and a half on Helix Station, he'd come to know the detachments of the rival powers quite well. Each navy had long ago made arrangements to lease its own docking areas on the massive Tzoru orbital station known as Magan Kahnar, a tethered asteroid connected to the sprawling city of Alhalsu by a space elevator that had been built around the same time as the cathedral of Notre Dame on Old Terra. The Commonwealth Navy rented out one whole branch of the spaceport; the light cruisers *Hawkins* and *Burton* occupied their customary berths, as did the destroyers *Jackal*, *Mongoose*, and *Fox* as well as the corvette *Venda-*

val. Brigadoon, sister ship to *Exeter,* was absent, engaged on a long patrol to the farther reaches of the Tzoru Dominion. Then Sikander noticed that the warships belonging to the Empire of Dremark had rearranged themselves to accommodate a new addition.

"Excuse me, Commodore," he said. "There's a new arrival of note—a Dremish cruiser, the *Prinz Oskar.* We haven't seen her on Helix Station before." Sikander had reason to pay special attention to the arrival of a powerful Dremish cruiser in an out-of-the-way spot like the Tzoru frontier; he remembered all too well the deadly encounter with Captain Georg Harper and his *Panther* at Gadira four years ago. He hadn't run into any more trouble with Dremish aggressiveness since then, but his first reaction to just about any Dremish activity was simply, *What are they up to now?* Too many good officers and crewhands had died aboard *Hector* for him to feel any other way.

"I wonder if the Dremish heard some rumblings about trouble in the Dominion and decided to step up her deployment," Reyes mused.

"If they did they've got better sources than we do," said Abernathy. "As far as I can tell we've been caught completely flat-footed by events."

The commodore's remark suggested an idea to Sikander. He couldn't very well speak to the Dremish about their information—relations between the Commonwealth and the Empire remained cool even four years after the Gadira incident, and many Dremish officers were naturally familiar with his own prominent role in the encounter—but the intelligence services of friendlier powers might be willing to trade a little news. He made a note to place a call or two as soon as *Exeter* docked.

"Anything else out of place?" the commodore asked.

"One moment, sir." Sikander brought up a snapshot of the tactical displays he'd taken the day they departed Kahnar-Sag for Tamabuqq and had the ship's info assistant compare it to current data as a quick way to check for less noticeable changes. Sure enough, several green icons popped up in low orbit—a pair of ancient Tzoru warships that comprised the naval strength of the Tzoru clan that governed the port facilities at Kahnar-Sag, along with a handful of smaller cutters normally employed in customs inspections. "Sebet Gisumi's monitors aren't moored in their normal spots. They're maintaining semistationary orbits above Alhalsu. I think they might be keeping an eye on events on the ground."

"Events? What events?" said Reyes. "Be more specific, Mr. North."

"Nothing we can see from here, ma'am," Sikander replied evenly. They were nearly four light-minutes from the planet, after all, much too far to get any direct imagery of anything smaller than a city block. "I'm merely pointing out that the Gisumi ships are maneuvering in orbit, and we haven't seen them leave their berths in years. I don't think they would do that unless they had a reason to."

"Mr. Barnes, contact *Hawkins* and ask them to bring us up to date," Abernathy said to his communications officer. "They've got a ringside seat on Magan Kahnar, I think we can assume they can tell us what's going on planetside."

"Yes, sir," said Barnes. He turned to his console.

"Mr. North, let me know if anything changes." Abernathy tapped his comm controls. "Bridge, Captain Howard please."

Quentin Howard's image appeared in the small display reserved for the commodore's personal use. "Yes, Commodore?" he answered. The captain of CSS *Exeter* was bald as an egg, a humorless man with a narrow face, deep-set eyes, and a gravelly voice. While both Howard and Reyes held the rank of captain, Howard was *Exeter*'s commanding officer; naval etiquette allowed only one officer on the ship to be addressed as captain. Other officers of similar rank defaulted to their billet titles, so Reyes went by deputy commodore, or d-com, while on board.

"What's our time to berth?" Abernathy asked.

"About seven hours, sir," Captain Howard replied. "We can shave that by an hour or so if you're in a hurry."

"Please do," Abernathy told him. "I feel that we've got some catching up to do."

6

Bagal-Dindir, Tamabuqq Prime

The embassy's watch center buzzed Lara Dunstan two hours before dawn. "Dr. Dunstan, I'm sorry to disturb you at this hour," the marine at the watch desk said. "But there's a Tzoru gentleman here to see you, and he says it's very urgent."

Lara sat up, and tried to shake the grogginess out of her head as she fumbled with the comm unit on the nightstand. Some people had the power to wake up from a deep sleep and be instantly functional, but she was not one of them. "Who the devil wants to see me at four in the morning?" she muttered aloud.

She didn't mean the question literally, but the marine comm specialist on the other end of the audio link took it that way. "He says he's Scholar Radi Sabub, ma'am. Should I tell him to come back when the embassy opens in the morning?"

"No, no. Tell him to stay there. I'll be down in just a minute," Lara replied. She cut the line, and slipped out of her bed. As the embassy's political affairs officer, she served as one of Ambassador Hart's chief advisors and enjoyed a spacious suite second only to the ambassador's own quarters. Larger and more comfortable than anything she could have rented in the Thousand Worlds ward, the suite had only one disadvantage: she never really managed to leave work for the day. *What in the world brings Sabub down here from Durzinzer?* she wondered as she dressed and pulled her long hair back into a ponytail.

She found Sabub waiting in the embassy foyer, dressed in a nondescript laborer's garb. He looked cold and miserable, but his expression brightened when he caught sight of her. "Friend Lara!" he said. "I am sorry for waking you, but I have news that cannot wait. Can we speak?"

"Of course," she said. She took him by the arm and steered him into a conference room just off the foyer. "Would you like some warm *dimu*? I can have the kitchen send up a carafe." Humans couldn't tolerate *dimu,* but for Tzoru the beverage served much the same purpose as strong coffee fortified with a shot of cream liqueur.

"Yes, thank you," Sabub said. "I have been traveling all night, and I am very cold."

"Consider it done." Lara tapped a kitchen service request into her dataslate, and added some coffee for herself before she set the device down on the table. "What do you need to see me about, Sabub?"

"The *warumzi agu* plan to storm the Thousand Worlds ward in a matter of hours. Many are gathering in the nearby districts, and I think they may be armed."

"Wait, what?" said Lara. She shook her head, not sure if she'd heard the scholar correctly. "What do you mean they're going to storm the district? How do you know this?"

"Earlier tonight the *warumzi agu* held a rally in Gishpun—that is a town not far from Durzinzer. I went because I wanted to hear for myself what they were saying, or even argue against them if it seemed wise to do so. Many others showed up simply to see if anything would happen. The *warumzi agu* leaders called for action against humans and those who do business with them. Then they led a march to the armory of the Muzuq, where they broke in and seized weapons."

"Who are the Muzuq?"

"A soldier *sebet* in the service of Sebet Hish. Some of

the Muzuq joined the demonstrators and let them into the armory. After they emptied the armory, more *warumzi agu* arrived with power wagons and loaded most of the arms into them. I was close enough to hear the soldiers and the *warumzi agu* leader instructing the drivers about the destination and calling for volunteers to go with them. They said that many thousands were gathering in Bagal-Dindir and that the weapons would be needed to seize control of the Thousand Worlds ward today."

"I see." Cold dread served as a better stimulant than the coffee on its way from the embassy kitchen; Lara discovered that she was suddenly wide awake. She'd seen reports of *warumzi agu* mobs getting into armories, but she hadn't heard of any incidents so close to Bagal-Dindir. And she hadn't ever heard of militant clans sharing their weapons with the common artisan or laborer clans—or, for that matter, a situation in which the common-born Tzoru might even *want* weapons in the first place. "Why didn't you just call?"

"I tried. The *warumzi agu* took control of the communications centers. I could not get through, so I borrowed a friend's power wagon and drove from Durzinzer." Lara winced for Sabub; a Tzoru power wagon was little more than a big maglev flatbed with no protection from the elements, and she would have been surprised if one could manage fifty kilometers per hour on the winding rural roadways outside the capital. No wonder Sabub was cold; he must have driven half the night in wet snow flurries. "When I reached the outskirts of the capital, a band of *warumzi agu* stopped me. I tried to fight them off, but they confiscated the power wagon. I had to walk the rest of the way."

There was a soft knock at the door, and one of the embassy's Tzoru kitchen attendants carried in a tray with two carafes and mugs. "You asked for coffee and *dimu*, Dr. Dunstan?"

"I did, thank you." Lara gave him a grateful smile as he poured a cup of each stimulant; Sabub seized his *dimu* and drank deeply, huddled over the steaming mug. She waited for the attendant to leave before resuming the conversation; after Sabub's story it seemed like a good idea to be a little more careful about what she said in front of Tzoru she didn't know well. "Sabub, did you hear anything about exactly when or where the attack would take place?"

"Later today, friend Lara. I know that *warumzi agu* are gathering in the outer districts of the city—I saw that much for myself."

She nodded. The next question she had to ask might seem suspicious, but she had to make certain she understood Radi Sabub's motives. "Why did you decide to warn us?"

"When the *warumzi agu* attack I fear that many humans and innocent Tzoru will be killed," said Sabub. "These are difficult times for my people. Many of our old traditions are being forgotten, but we need to learn from your people, not shun them. If the *warumzi agu* get what they want our Dominion will be set back a thousand years. And also I worried about you, friend Lara."

"I thank you for that, Sabub—you're a good friend." Tzoru never failed to surprise Lara. How many humans would risk their lives by mingling in a hostile crowd, then race off through foul weather to carry a warning to someone of a completely different species? She would like to think she would have shown the same courage and determination in Radi Sabub's place, but she'd never been put to such a test. She took a swallow from her coffee, thinking about what to do with the scholar's warning, then stood. "I can see there's no time to waste. Wait here and warm yourself—I need to wake some people up."

Twenty minutes later, Radi Sabub repeated his story for Ambassador Norman Hart and Major Constanza Dalton in the same conference room. As one might expect of a marine officer, Dalton showed no sign that she'd been awakened long before dawn; she'd answered Lara's call on the first ring, and made her appearance dressed in her spotless uniform in a matter of minutes. Hart woke less easily and had settled for belting a robe over his slippers and pajamas, but to his credit he hadn't questioned Lara's judgment in summoning him. He greeted Sabub courteously and heard him out, asking the same questions Lara did.

When Sabub finished, Hart stood and spread his hands in a Tzoru-style bow. "I thank you for your warning, Scholar Radi. I know you must be exhausted. We'll have the staff show you to a room where you can rest while we discuss what to do. I may have more questions for you later."

"I am happy to have been of service, honored friends," said Sabub, blinking slowly in a sign of fatigue that was not very different from the human mannerism. "I will sleep now, if I may."

"Of course." Hart motioned to one of the marines standing nearby, who showed the scholar out.

The ambassador waited until Sabub and his escort disappeared down the corridor outside, then turned back to Lara and Major Dalton. "It's clear that you find the threat credible, Lara, or we wouldn't be here at this indecent hour," he said. "Major Dalton, what do you make of it?"

"Dr. Dunstan's friend seems sincere, and it corroborates some of the reports we received from *Exeter* before she left orbit. As to whether we're correctly interpreting what we think we've seen . . ." The marine shrugged. "I've never heard of anything like it anywhere in the Tzoru Dominion. With your permission, I'll have my marines send up a couple of Dragonfly drones and scout the nearby districts. Those are technically against the rules for Bagal-Dindir, but if there are any dangerous crowds massing, we should be able to spot them easily enough."

"Go ahead," Hart told the major. The Dragonflies were not much bigger than a human thumb, but they mounted a good vidcam and they could fly, hover, perch, or crawl as the operator needed. In the darkness and the poor weather they would be virtually invisible. "I'll get dressed and contact the civil authorities to see what they have to say. Let's reconvene in the operations center once we know what we're dealing with."

"Yes, sir," said Major Dalton. While the ambassador went back to his residence to change, Dalton headed for the embassy's nerve center, already issuing orders to her detachment via her comm device. Lara followed her.

The op center served as the security headquarters and secure communications facility for the embassy, just one flight of stairs beneath the ambassador's personal suite. While the Bagal-Dindir embassy was by no means a military command post, the operations center offered state-of-the-art comms and surveillance equipment. Dalton picked up a remote and clicked through feed options for a display screen until a grainy color-enhanced image appeared. "Ah, here we go," she said. "That's the first Dragonfly. Let's get the second on-line and see what we can see."

Lara settled on a padded stool to watch the feed from the tiny drone. She recognized the ancient stone walls ringing the Thousand Worlds ward passing underneath the camera, and the broad boulevards outside the walls. It seemed quiet enough; the streets were empty, and few lights showed in any of the businesses or homes close by. Tzoru, like humans, liked to sleep through the hours of darkness, although they tended to break up a night's rest into three or four sleep periods punctuated by short stretches of wakefulness. As the drone continued to move out over the city, the streets remained quiet. *Could Sabub have been mistaken?* she wondered. The ambassador and the major would not criticize her for an excess of caution, but she hated the idea of contributing to a false alarm—

"Oh, that doesn't look good," Major Dalton said. The feed from the second drone suddenly revealed a street full of Tzoru who surged and flowed around several parked power wagons. Even from the drone's distant view Lara could see the Tzoru standing on the wagon beds opening crate after crate, handing slender rifles down to their comrades. "No, that's not good at all."

"Where is that?" Lara asked.

"That's the Weavers' ward, ma'am," one of the marines

manning the center answered. "About three kilometers east of here."

"Looks like the first drone picked up something too," said Dalton. She nodded at the feed Lara had been watching, which now revealed another large crowd of Tzoru. Few of this group seemed to carry any firearms, but there were a *lot* of them, and Lara could make out quite a few cudgels and daggers brandished by their owners. She recognized the spot—a large plaza in front of a well-known temple a few kilometers to the north.

"Let's start a city-scale tactical display and map this," Dalton told her techs. She activated the conference table in the center of the room, and brought up a map of Bagal-Dindir. A moment later the Tzoru mobs appeared as shapeless red blobs, half surrounding the Thousand Worlds ward.

"Good Lord," Ambassador Hart murmured. Lara glanced over—she hadn't heard him come in. He'd changed into slacks and a sweater, his favored working clothes. "There must be thousands of them! How many are armed?"

"We're still working on that, sir," said Dalton. "I can see hundreds of rifles in that crowd to the east, though."

"What happens if they march on us?" Hart asked Dalton. "Can you defend the embassy?"

"Sir, I have thirty marines with no heavy weapons. We can protect the compound against three or four times our number of armed troops, or a mob of several hundred. But if we have a couple of thousand hostiles to deal with, we *will* be overrun." Major Dalton studied the footage again, and shook her head. "This is the sort of threat the armed forces of the host nation are supposed to protect embassies against. The Anshar's government should be dealing with this."

"No one at the Anshar's court is willing to admit those people are even here," said Hart. "I can't fathom it. An armed popular movement of the lower *sebetu* is a direct threat to the authority of the high clans. Are they really so out of touch?"

"I doubt it," Lara said slowly. She studied the imagery too, the surging crowds and the angry speakers, but her mind was elsewhere. She'd spent years studying political movements in both human and Tzoru history, and that included occasions when movements became violent. She'd never thought she would witness such a thing in person, but here it was anyway. "It's usually smart to bet on people acting in what they perceive as their own self-interest. The Anshar's officials might be ignorant of what's happening in the streets this morning, but I guarantee you that the high *sebetu* are watching. If they aren't intervening, it's because they think they can't stop this, or they don't *want* to stop this."

"To be fair, it's possible they just might not have any idea of what to do about it," Dalton pointed out. "We haven't seen something like this here in Tamabuqq before. It's probably been a long time for the Tzoru, too."

"Should we consider evacuation?" Ambassador Hart asked.

"Assuming we could get through the mobs surrounding the Thousand Worlds district, where would we go, sir?" Dalton replied. "We'd have to get out of Bagal-Dindir to be safe, and we simply have no transportation assets for the job. There are thirty marines and eighty diplomatic personnel in the compound, hundreds of Aquilan citizens in local lodgings, and a thousand or so friendly Tzoru who are also at risk. And that's just the Commonwealth citizens and interests. If you add in all the other embassies and their Tzoru employees here in the Thousand Worlds, it's more like fifteen or twenty thousand people to evacuate. You're talking about moving a small city in a matter of hours, with no powered transportation to speak of. We'd be better off to fort up and hope for the best."

"We can send for the fleet at Kahnar-Sag," said Hart.

"It's five days there and five days back," said Dalton. "We'd have to stand a siege of ten days at the bare minimum, and that assumes we can send word to the Navy immediately. I'm not sure we'll be able to get a courier away before this all comes down on us."

Lara gazed at the display of the Tzoru capital. Angry red blobs marked the approximate locations of *warumzi agu* mobs massing in the streets; the outline of the Thousand Worlds ward looked like a dark jigsaw-puzzle piece in the middle of the holographic map, bordered by its ancient walls. She found herself thinking about what Constanza Dalton had just said about a siege of ten days. *The whole ward is an ancient fortification. It's a city within a city, protected by the old walls. Maybe we* could *stand a siege here if the Militarist clans stay out of it.*

"Major, what about defending the entire ward?" she asked, interrupting Hart and Dalton as they argued about calling for help. "Most of the Thousand Worlds district is surrounded by a ten-meter wall, and there are only a handful of ways in or out. Can't we just stop the *warumzi agu* at the gates?"

"It's far too big," Dalton replied immediately, but a furrow creased her brow, and she shifted her attention to the part of the display showing the Thousand Worlds ward. "Maybe . . . maybe with a thousand troops we could do it, provided the attackers didn't have any artillery or aerial transport."

"How many soldiers do the other embassies have?" Lara asked her. "I bet that if you added the security detachments of all the embassies in the Thousand Worlds ward together, you'd have three or four hundred regular troops."

"And we could draft some of the diplomatic personnel or civilian volunteers if it's just a matter of numbers," Ambassador Hart said, nodding slowly. "We've got a dozen or so ex-military types and reservists on our staff, and plenty more in our expat community. We might not have a thousand troops, but if all the embassies pull together, we might be able to get you enough, Major."

Major Dalton drew in a deep breath. "I'll reach out to my counterparts in the other embassies. There are some dusty old plans about cooperating in case of emergency, but it would help if you convince the ambassadors to deploy their security details at once. Especially the Nyeirans—they have something like a hundred and fifty soldiers stationed at their mission."

"I think I can persuade most of my colleagues that we are all in grave danger. As the old saying goes, the prospect of hanging concentrates the mind wonderfully." Hart looked over to Lara. "You and I need to warn the other embassies immediately and get them to commit to a collective defense. We'll divide them up between us: You begin with the Californians and the Montréalais, I'll start with the Nyeirans and the Dremish."

"I'm on it," Lara told him. *And I hope to God they listen to me,* she added silently. At least Hart had handed her two of the friendlier embassies to start with; the California Union and the Republic of Montréal were inclined to follow the Commonwealth's lead in dealing with the Anshar's court and shared similar interests.

"Major Dalton, copy this drone feed if you please," Hart continued. "We may need the imagery to convince some of the more stubborn ambassadors. And while Dr. Dunstan and I are talking to the other embassies, go ahead and post guard detachments at each of the ward gates."

"That'll only be four or five marines at each post," Dalton protested. "They'd be run over by any one of these mobs!"

"You'll be reinforced soon enough with soldiers from other embassies. Right now we need to make sure that everyone can see that armed guards are in place. It might deter the *warumzi agu* from any sudden attack and buy us some time." Hart allowed himself a cheerless smile. "Besides, it will certainly demonstrate to my colleagues that we are taking the situation seriously."

The marine looked a little dubious, but she nodded. "Very good, sir. I'll set pickets immediately." She turned away and tapped her comm device, issuing orders to her noncoms.

Hart set a hand on Lara's shoulder. "Let's make some calls, Dr. Dunstan."

Lara retreated to her office to get away from the increasingly noisy and crowded operations center, and began making comm calls as sunrise painted the windows in golden-green hues. The Californian embassy put her through to their ambassador without delay; the Montréalais blocked her with a midranking assistant who informed her he wouldn't wake his own ambassador unless it was important enough for Mr. Hart to call in person. She notified Hart of the delay, and moved on to call the Cygnans and then the Taurans with varying levels of success.

To her surprise, not one delegation ignored the warning after Ambassador Hart straightened out the Republic functionary. By 8:00 A.M., men and women in the uniforms from half a dozen different great powers filled the embassy's operations center, including four Nyeiran warriors with mottled black-and-brown carapaces and scarlet sashes over their segmented battle armor.

For the first time in hours, Lara found herself with nothing that needed doing. She decided to go see for herself what was going on outside. She stopped by her suite to get a heavy coat. Then, on a sudden inspiration, she went to Radi Sabub's guest room and knocked on the door. "Sabub? Are you awake?" she called.

Sabub answered the knock a moment later, dressed and alert. "Yes, friend Lara. I have rested now. How can I help you?"

"I'm going to take a walk to see what's going on. Would you like to come?"

"Yes, please. I am very anxious about what the *warumzi agu* intend." The Tzoru scholar picked up the heavy robes he'd been wearing when he came in, and draped them over his scaly shoulders. The overgarment hung down to his ankles and surrounded his neck and head with a thick, puffy collar. Tzoru who had to work outside in cold weather wore garments designed for work; those who just had to endure the elements spared not the slightest bit of attention for what they might look like when they bundled up.

Lara found that the marine guards at the entrance to the embassy had changed from their dress uniforms to gray-green battle armor. Vehicular barricades stood in the drive-way, blocking access from the street. Outside the embassy, the Thousand Worlds district swarmed with Tzoru loading carts or carrying their possessions on their backs as they fled the ward, human merchants boarding up their businesses or residences, and groups of human soldiers or embassy offi-cials standing watch at every street corner. She stopped in midstride, astounded by the scene; inside the embassy build-ing she'd been sheltered from the chaos erupting outside.

"This is a disaster," she said aloud, staring at the scene.

"I agree," Sabub said, and shivered.

Lara turned to the left and made her way down the street toward the nearest of the gates leading into the ward. She expected to find Commonwealth marines garrisoning the gate, but no Aquilans were in sight. Instead, the troopers sta-tioned here wore the gray and black field armor of the Em-pire of Dremark. They had the gate three-quarters blocked with Tzoru wagons grounded on the street and reinforced by sandbags; a work crew of Tzoru laborers filled more sand-bags and carried them to the improvised fortifications un-der the supervision of a Dremish sergeant. Tzoru civilians fleeing the district lined up to slip out the gate, but another wagon to one side stood ready to be moved into place when the time came to block it altogether.

A young officer in Dremish colors noticed Lara watching the scene. "Please move along," he said in thickly accented Anglic. "We have no place for sightseers here."

"Oh, sorry," Lara replied. She spied a flight of stone steps leading up to the wall top, and faced the Dremish officer with a smile. "I work for the Aquilan ambassador. He asked me to take a quick look and report back. Can I go up there for just a minute?"

The officer frowned, but gave in. "Just a minute! It may not be safe." He turned and spoke to one of his troops in Ne-beldeutsch, pointing at Lara and Sabub. The young woman saluted, and trotted over to stand close to Lara. Whether she'd been ordered to stay close for Lara's protection or to make sure Lara and Sabub didn't linger too long was not entirely clear.

Lara shrugged, and climbed up the stairs leading to the wall top with Sabub and her Dremish guardian in tow. Four meters wide, the top of the ancient wall featured a high parapet on its outward face, looking out over the wide, treefern-lined boulevards of the districts surrounding the Thousand Worlds ward. She knew the wall top fairly well, since she occasionally used it as a scenic jogging path. Every five meters or so stone firing steps provided the short-statured with an easier look over the edge; she hurried to the first one in sight, and stepped up to take a good look at what was going on in the surrounding streets.

Mobs of angry Tzoru milled along the avenue, chanting in unison while waving their hands in the air. The cacophony of their voices echoed from the stone walls, rolling over her like the sound of distant thunder. Several hundred Tzoru crowded the street end immediately opposite the gate held by the Dremish troops; like their human counterparts inside the Thousand Worlds ward, they had dragged heavy wagons and carts into place as makeshift barricades, blocking the road only a hundred meters or so from the gate. Many wore the double-peaked green caps she'd seen in Durzinzer, but others wore green cloaks, tunics, or even armbands of green cloth over the heavy winter robes if they didn't have the right kind of cap. More ominously, a double-line of Tzoru carrying slender firearms of some kind stood in front of the barricade, glaring in the direction of the Dremish troops. Most of the armed Tzoru wore mismatched civilian tunics. *Militia of some kind?* she wondered. *They don't look much like soldiers.*

The Dremish soldier accompanying Lara studied the scene, and shook her head. "*Das ist verrückt,*" she muttered under her breath. "*Jemand wird erschossen werden.*"

"I don't know what you said, but I think I agree with you," Lara said. She shook her head. "I can't tell if we're fencing them out or they're fencing us in."

"What does it mean, friend Lara?" asked Radi Sabub. "What will happen next?"

"I think it means that we're not going anywhere for a while," said Lara. She hopped down from the old firing step, and motioned to the Dremish trooper that they were ready to leave. "As far as what happens next, your guess is as good as mine."

1

The main passageways of Magan Kahnar reminded Sikander of run-down city streets at night. The dim lighting and jostling crowds lent a claustrophobic feel to the spaceport, while the garish advertisements and thumping music of bars and dance clubs offering the visiting human sailor or businessman the opportunity to dispose of some of his or her hard-earned pay continued more or less around the clock. By station time it was late morning, but that meant little to anyone who ran a business in Magan Kahnar's busy passageways—one never knew when a tramp freighter might arrive in-system with a crew anxious for a chance to blow off some steam.

"Did you learn anything new from the Californians, sir?" Darvesh asked Sikander. The tall Kashmiri followed just a half pace behind Sikander as the two headed back toward the Commonwealth Navy's section of the Tzoru spaceport. They'd spent half the morning in a visit to the Californian Fifth Fleet Depot, the Union navy's equivalent of Helix Station.

"Not much, I'm afraid," Sikander admitted. "They've assembled a good dossier on Ebneghirz, which they kindly shared with me. It turns out the Baltzu were behind his arrest. His *warumzi agu* were engaged in a campaign of organizing local guilds and traditionalist societies against Baltzu business ventures." The California Union—named after the California Nebula, not the scenic Terran region—maintained only one old light cruiser and a handful of modern frigates on the Tzoru frontier, but Californian corporations invested heavily in trade with a number of Tzoru worlds. Even if they were not a first-rate military power in the sector, they were certainly a commercial presence to be reckoned with, and they had a talent for staying on almost everybody's good side.

"Organizing?" Darvesh asked. "To do what?"

"Pickets, product boycotts, sabotage, intimidation of Baltzu workers, that sort of thing." Sikander had offered his Union counterparts his own eyewitness account of *warumzi agu* agitation on Tamabuqq Prime in exchange for a briefing on what they'd observed here in Kahnar-Sag. He'd hoped their business contacts might help to shed some light on the sorry state of Tzoru politics at the moment, but as it turned out the Californian intelligence specialists knew—or at least cared to share—little more than he and his own team had already pieced together. *I'll check in with Sebastien Boyer over on* Dupleix *this afternoon,* he decided. The Montréalais squadron's flag lieutenant was a decent fellow, and had access to some good sources from other parts of the Dominion.

"The tool set of radicals everywhere, it would seem."

"Exactly," said Sikander. He paused at a busy intersection to check his bearings—Magan Kahnar was the size of a small city, and he didn't know the districts surrounding the Californians' naval depot very well. Thousands of people, both Tzoru and human, lived within the tunneled passageways and domed chambers of the asteroid that anchored the higher end of the ancient space elevator. Scores of import-export companies maintained offices and transshipment facilities on Magan Kahnar, profiting from the ever-growing trade between the Dominion and the various human powers. Banks, currency exchanges, dealers in luxury goods, and even a handful of adventure-tourism outfits could be found within the asteroid city, along with scores of restaurants, bars, and boardinghouses catering to the itinerant population of human businesspeople and spacehands. With humans from so many different nations visiting the gateway to the Tzoru Dominion, there was a demand for a wide variety of specialty cuisines and entertainments. In fact, Sikander could see a stir-fry place, a Dremish beer hall, a pita and kebob vendor, and a pizza parlor all within thirty meters of where he stood. More to the point, he could smell the savory aromas, and his stomach rumbled.

"Say, I'm a little hungry," he told Darvesh. "Let's find something to eat before we go back."

"As you wish, sir."

Sikander settled on the stir-fry restaurant as the best prospect in sight. It was somewhat off-hours, so the place was mostly empty. He and Darvesh ordered at the counter, and sat down to wait for their food. He occupied himself with reviewing more of the files the California Union Navy had shared, looking for anything important he might have missed. Darvesh shifted his seat so that he could easily watch the restaurant's entrance, and settled in to keep an eye on the people passing by in the crowded corridor.

This is interesting, he decided as he read. Tzem Ebneghirz had been an academic of some note before he became known as a Tzoru nationalist leader. In fact, he'd made a name for himself as a Tzoru student of human history. Some of his earlier speeches and writings suggested that he'd made a conscious effort to adapt the language and tactics of human populists to the challenge of awakening Tzoru patriotism and turning it against the human-friendly Tzoru progressives. *A Tzoru reactionary using the lessons of human demagogues to rouse his own people against the dangers of human contact? I suppose that's fighting fire with fire, as they say. Do the* warumzi agu *know where Ebneghirz borrowed his rhetoric from? Would they care?*

Darvesh shifted uncomfortably on the other side of the

table. Sikander looked up, and saw his bodyguard's attention fixed on something happening down the passageway. He turned to look for himself. Fifty meters away, a dozen Tzoru wearing green armbands stood in a close group, speaking quietly among themselves.

"That looks like trouble," Darvesh said to Sikander. "The *warumzi agu* wear green, do they not?"

"They do," Sikander confirmed. "I didn't think we would see any in Kahnar-Sag, let alone right here in the spaceport. What are they up to?"

"I do not know, but we should go, sir."

Sikander hesitated. He wanted to see if the *warumzi agu* intended to start any trouble . . . but he'd already been caught in two Tzoru nationalist riots. Darvesh only meant to carry out his duty, and he hadn't been making things any easier for the Kashmiri bodyguard recently. He owed Darvesh the courtesy of acting on his advice for once. "Very well. Let's get out of here."

He stood and counted out a handful of credits for the meal they'd ordered—and just then a sudden crash and the sound of breaking glass echoed down the corridor. Humans cried out or gasped in alarm; Tzoru passersby hissed like teakettles. Sikander whirled, and saw the group of *warumzi agu* Darvesh had been watching suddenly surge across the corridor to attack a pair of high-clan Tzoru with a small entourage following in their wake. Cudgels and knives hidden beneath their robes suddenly appeared in their hands as they swarmed over the nobles and their retainers. In a matter of seconds nearly twenty Tzoru were engaged in a furious melee in the middle of the crowded passageway.

Sikander started toward the fighting with some idea of going to the aid of the Tzoru who had been ambushed by the *warumzi agu,* but Darvesh caught him by the arm before he'd taken two steps. "I advise against that, Nawabzada," he said. "This is no fight of ours."

"Someone needs to help!" Sikander protested. "Those are Clan Gisumi colors. We're supposed to be their allies!" But just then he heard the sharp crackle and saw the bright flash of a Tzoru shock pistol as one of the noble Tzoru shot down an attacker. The pistol wielder turned to fire at another target, but a *warumzi* armed with a cleaver-like knife hacked him down from behind. More shock-pistol fire crackled in the hallway, and a stray bolt blasted the vidscreen menu suspended over the door to the restaurant. It burst in a shower of sparks.

The two Kashmiris ducked away from the doorway, and Darvesh simply looked at Sikander. "All right, you win," Sikander told him. They retreated back through the restaurant to a kitchen entrance that opened up on a service corridor. A number of people from other establishments near the fighting apparently had the same idea; the corridor filled up with humans and Tzoru hurrying in the opposite direction. Sikander saw no Tzoru dressed in green and no sign of weapons in hand, so he joined the flow of the crowd and followed them until they reached another main corridor. He was by now thoroughly turned around, but he spotted a tube station—one stop in the network of maglev trams crisscrossing the Tzoru spaceport—across the passageway, and made his way inside. He had to consult his dataslate to figure out which tram to catch, but in a matter of minutes he and Darvesh were on their way back toward the Commonwealth naval station.

Sikander settled in for the ride, still not entirely sure that he'd done the right thing by heading away from trouble. *That's three times now that I've run away from* warumzi agu, he realized. Perhaps it wasn't his fight, but he had an obligation to act when civilians were threatened; any honorable officer did. Of course, it would have been the height of folly to get mixed up in a knife and pistol fight while unarmed, but that could be amended in the future. He resolved not to leave *Exeter* again without carrying a sidearm, not while things seemed to be falling to pieces in the Tzoru worlds.

His comm device chirped at him; he tapped it and answered. "Lieutenant Commander North."

"Sir, this is Senior Chief Lin. We've just received word of some major developments in Tamabuqq. You'd better finish up your business ashore and return to the ship."

Sikander glanced around, making sure none of the other passengers paid too much attention to the audio. "What's going on?" he asked Lin.

"A civilian news-service courier just arrived from the Tzoru capital, sir. The *Helix Daily Post* reports major fighting in Bagal-Dindir near the Thousand Worlds ward. All the human embassies are blockaded inside the district by a large number of armed Tzoru protesters. There's some kind of siege in place."

"What do you mean, siege?" Sikander demanded. "Are you telling me that Tzoru and humans are shooting at each other in the Dominion capital?"

"It looks pretty complicated, Mr. North, but they're certainly pointing their guns at our people and our people are pointing their guns back." Lin paused. "Um, it looks like the d-com just showed up. Can I tell her you're on your way?"

Sikander glanced at the route map in the tram car. "Tell the d-com I'll be there in ten minutes. And see if you can verify that report from any other sources—check Kahnar-Sag traffic control to see if any other ships have arrived from Tamabuqq recently."

"We're on it, sir," Lin replied. "Lin, out."

A siege in Bagal-Dindir? Sikander shook his head. *Is Lara in the embassy, or is she somewhere else on Tamabuqq? And is she safe?*

Darvesh tapped him on the shoulder and pointed at a vidscreen in the tram compartment that carried local news coverage. "The news, sir," he said to Sikander. The screen flashed brightly as a breaking-news alert suddenly replaced the normal programming; aerial vid feed from a low-flying drone camera came on the screen, showing streets crowded with surging mobs of Tzoru and human soldiers manning posts atop the old walls surrounding the Thousand Worlds ward.

"So I see." Sikander frowned. If the *warumzi agu* were willing to launch attacks in Kahnar-Sag before, what might they do once they heard about events in the Tzoru capital? He looked again at the route map, and willed the lift tram to go faster.

An hour later, Sikander watched the same footage for the third time in the wardroom of CSS *Exeter.* The cruiser's flag conference room simply couldn't accommodate the entire Helix Squadron staff along with the commanding officers of the seven Aquilan warships currently in Kahnar-Sag and the various seconds they'd brought with them in answer to Commodore Abernathy's summons, so the officers' mess had been pressed into service instead. After nineteen months on Helix Station, Sikander had come to know each of the twenty-five men and women in the room fairly well; the squadron was a tight-knit community a long way from home. Some were good friends and old shipmates, in fact: Lieutenant Karsen Reno, operations officer of the destroyer *Fox,* had served as Sikander's assistant gunnery officer on board *Hector,* and Commander Magdalena Juarez, now captain of the corvette *Vendaval,* was another *Hector* shipmate.

Unfortunately, the sight of a few friendly faces didn't make up for the fact that Sikander had to present an intel briefing on a developing crisis with less than an hour of preparation. He rarely felt much anxiety about being the center of attention, but then again, he usually knew that he knew what he was talking about. This was not one of those times. The worsening situation in the Tzoru Dominion presented far more questions than answers at this point, but the rest of the squadron officers naturally expected the intelligence officer to be on top of current events.

Given the paucity of concrete observations, Sikander had

opted for simply showing the squadron's officers an edited version of the *Daily Post* footage and allowing them to draw their own conclusions. When the footage ended, he switched the vidscreen to a city map of Bagal-Dindir that showed his specialists' best guess about the *warumzi agu* positions around the Ward of a Thousand Worlds, and brought up the lights in the wardroom.

"That is pretty much all we know as of this moment," Sikander said by way of a conclusion. "At the risk of stating the obvious, this footage is five days old. We don't know anything about how the situation has progressed since the *Helix Daily Post* courier left Tamabuqq, although I expect that over the next few hours or days we may receive additional updates as more merchant traffic arrives from the capital."

"How many marines do we have at our embassy?" asked Quentin Howard of *Exeter*. "How long can they hold off a mob of that size?"

"Thirty, sir," said Sikander. "And no, that's not nearly enough to defend the embassy compound against a mob. It looks like some or all of the other diplomatic missions in Bagal-Dindir are cooperating in a collective defense of the district. We think they have a few hundred trained soldiers between them, and they may also have some help from human civilians or friendly Tzoru trapped within the walls."

"What are the high clans doing?" asked Magdalena Juarez. "They've got tens of thousands of soldiers on or around Tamabuqq Prime with heavy weapons and air support, don't they? I know their formations are obsolete by Coalition standards, but I have to imagine they could scatter any number of poorly armed revolutionaries if they wanted to."

"We don't know what's going on at the Anshar's court," Sikander admitted. "When we left Tamabuqq there was quite a bit of confusion with the political alignments of the Tzoru high *sebetu*. Sapwu Zrinan and his Monarchist faction are no longer in power, and it remains to be seen who's going to step up. Our best guess is that the court's knotted up between clans that support the *warumzi agu* and clans that want to suppress them, so no one can figure out what to do."

"That's a hell of a thing to have to guess about," Captain Howard grumbled.

"Indeed," Francine Reyes added. She fixed her cool gaze on Sikander. "It's not an overstatement to say that we've experienced a colossal intelligence failure here. Heads should roll for this at the Foreign Ministry . . . if you ask me."

Sikander had no doubt whose head Reyes wanted to collect, and he suspected that most of the other officers in the room understood what she meant, too. He clamped his jaw shut with an effort of will, determined to resist being baited into defending himself.

"There will be plenty of time to sort out who missed what later," Commodore Abernathy said. He nodded at the drone-cam footage on the screen. "The important question is right there. We have something like a hundred diplomats and marines in our embassy on Tamabuqq Prime, plus hundreds of Aquilan citizens living and working in the Thousand Worlds ward. There's a damned mob of ten thousand angry Tzoru outside their walls. It seems to me that we need to get our squadron under way and go protect our people. If someone can tell me why that's a bad idea, now's the time to say so."

No one spoke for a long moment. Then Mason Barnes cleared his throat. "It's another five days back to Tamabuqq, sir. By the time we get there this whole mess'll be ten days old. The mob might give up, they might overrun the Thousands Worlds district, or the Anshar's court might get its act together and do something about this. We don't know what we might be running into."

"We could scout Tamabuqq first," said Lieutenant Commander Giselle Dacey. A native High Albionan who held the title of Senator Kilgore, she owned a sharp and incisive mind as well as vid-star looks. She served as Helix Squadron's S-3, or operations officer. "Or move the squadron closer and then send in a scout so that we don't waste ten full days to get a five-day-old assessment of the situation."

Abernathy nodded. "That's not a bad idea. Keep going, people."

"The Tzoru suspended our free-passage agreement, sir," Sikander pointed out. "If we go back to Tamabuqq, especially in any kind of force, they may regard it as a hostile act."

"I regard ten thousand revolutionaries encamped outside our embassy as a hostile act," Abernathy replied. "I'm not going to lose sleep over bruised Tzoru feelings while our people are under their guns."

"Nor will any of us, Commodore," said Magdalena Juarez. She was only four years Sikander's senior, and the corvette *Vendaval* was her first command. "But I think Mr. North has a point. Right now the Tzoru military clans and fleets are sitting on the sidelines. How will they react when we send in a squadron of warships?"

"Their ships are a hundred years out of date," Captain Howard said. "The Hish and the other clans have plenty of ground troops, sure, but there isn't much they can do to stop us from occupying the planet's approaches and threatening their capital with orbital fire."

"Sir, I don't believe that is true," Sikander said to *Exeter*'s commanding officer. "Yes, the Golden Banner Fleet is obsolete. But they've got eight battleships and twenty-six lighter vessels to protect their capital. They have at least ten times our tonnage, and that assumes no reinforcements from the provincial or frontier fleets show up before we get there. Given the situation on Tamabuqq Prime, I think we'd better count on the noble clans stepping up their readiness or calling for help."

Reyes glanced over at Abernathy. "What about the other squadrons here at Kahnar-Sag?" she asked him. "The Dremish and the Montréalais and all the rest must be in the middle of meetings just like this one. If we combined our forces, we'd probably match the Tzoru in sheer numbers if not in tonnage, and I am confident that any modern warship can outfight a Tzoru rust bucket three times its size."

"Again, I worry that might play into the hands of these *warumzi agu*," said Magda Juarez. "The best information we have is that they're largely motivated by xenophobia. If we drop in on their capital with a powerful human fleet to threaten them, we'll show the high clans the revolutionaries were right about us."

"Or the show of force might convince the Anshar's court to clean up its own mess before we have to do it for them," said Howard.

Commodore Abernathy drummed his fingers on the table, thinking over the arguments. He glanced up at Sikander, still standing near the vidscreen. "What's the Intel Section estimate, Mr. North? Would we push the Tzoru into a situation where they would feel they have to close ranks against humans, or would they try to keep us out of it by handling things themselves?"

Sikander hated to duck the question, but he didn't see any way around it. "I'd have to put that to my team, sir," he said. "Until last week I would have told you that Tzoru reactions were pretty predictable. Today, I simply don't know. But I think we'd be better off by aligning ourselves with friendly Tzoru elements such as the Baltzu or Gisumi, so that we have a clear invitation to move into Tamabuqq and Tzoru in authority to speak for us when we get there. A combined human-Tzoru fleet would seem to be a lot less provocative."

"I don't know if I would trust any Tzoru at the moment," said Reyes. "If the high clans can allow this"—she waved a hand at the siege lines shown on the display—"who's to say which side they might come down on?"

"If that's the case, ma'am, then it seems we ought to be careful about giving them a push," Barnes said.

"Maybe, but it's pretty clear to me that we need to give them a *lesson*." The deputy commodore's voice took on an icy tone. "There are maybe a million humans in Tzoru space, surrounded by more than a hundred billion Tzoru.

We're outnumbered a hundred thousand to one! The only reason this backwards Dominion of theirs is a safe place for us to do business is that the Tzoru *know* they can't challenge our military power. If we don't respond to the attack on the Thousand Worlds ward with immediate and overwhelming force, that one essential truth is going to be exposed as a sham. Every Tzoru governor or fleet commander or merchant clan that might see an advantage in renegotiating an agreement with us is going to turn their own malcontents loose against our people. Everything the Commonwealth has worked for in this sector for generations is now at risk. We don't *dare* give the Tzoru reason to believe that we are not absolutely resolute in our determination. In fact, an opportunity to demonstrate our superior power now might go a long way toward keeping this sector peaceful for many years to come."

If the firepower of our fleets is the only thing that keeps the Tzoru from our throats we might be going about this in the wrong way, Sikander thought. He found himself wondering if Aquilan admirals such as Alberto Reyes had entertained similar discussions in response to challenges arising from Kashmir's restless independence movements, and which side he'd want to be on during such a debate. In the long term, intimidation served as a poor foundation for building enduring relationships . . . but in the short term, the aggressive response Reyes advocated might be effective. *And it's not clear that the* warumzi agu *are going to give us the time to explore other options.* He remained silent, and waited to see how Abernathy would respond.

The commodore frowned at the vidscreen for a long moment, and then made his decision. "We have to assume that time is of the essence. I think that means that our best course of action is a joint response with all concerned powers that maintain squadrons here in Kahnar-Sag. Mr. North, have your team work up an estimate on Tzoru reactions to a combined human squadron moving on Tamabuqq, but I don't think we can wait until we're confident we know which way the high clans will jump before we take action. Ms. Dacey, work up a simple organization scheme for creating a joint task force from half a dozen squadrons that haven't operated together before." He glanced over to Mason Barnes. "And Mr. Barnes, get me a conference with the senior officer of every other nation present in this system, highest priority."

"Yes, sir," Barnes replied. He started tapping orders into his dataslate.

"Captains, have your ships ready for departure within three hours," Abernathy continued. "With or without our Dremish and Californian and Montréalais friends I mean for the squadron to be under way by the end of the day . . . except for *Vendaval*. Commander Juarez, I want your ship in Kahnar-Sag to look after our installations here."

"Yes, sir," Magdalena Juarez answered. If she was upset about being left out, she did not show it.

Abernathy stood, and the other officers in the room rose as well. "We have a lot to do, so let's get to work," he said. "Dismissed."

The end of the day proved to be wildly optimistic. The small Californian squadron—three Decatur-class frigates—was ready enough to follow Abernathy's lead, but Capitano Emilio Durante of the Cygnan cruiser *Cagliari* demanded hours of planning and projections far out of proportion to the dubious contribution his obsolete ship made to the task force's overall combat power, and Acting Contre-Amiral Sabine Verger of the Montréalais navy became embroiled in a comparison of relative seniority with Commodore Abernathy over which of the two flag officers should exercise overall command. The commanding officer of the powerful Nyeiran squadron politely declined to participate in any potentially aggressive actions without seeking the guidance of hisher government, and expected the courier heshe had dispatched to return in twelve days or so with the necessary instructions. And the senior captain of the Dremish squadron insisted on an in-person conference before committing his forces to a joint operation.

As a result, Sikander found himself waiting on *Exeter*'s quarterdeck a little before 2100 hours ship's time to greet Kapitan zur Stern Reinhold Zimmer and his executive officer. The midships belly airlock served as the ceremonial reception area while the ship was secured in a docking cradle; a short access passage to the spaceport stood open, although a detachment of Commonwealth marines guarded the station end of the passageway as a precaution against any serious outbreak of violence on Magan Kahnar. He tried not to allow his impatience to show; he had dozens of things that needed doing at the moment, but the rest of the squadron staff was even busier with operational planning and teleconferences with their counterparts.

The intercom to the marine post at the foot of the passage crackled. "*Prinz Oskar,* Imperial Navy of Dremark, arriving," the marine sentry reported. By ancient tradition, captains were announced by the name of the ship they commanded.

The young ensign standing the quarterdeck watch nodded to Sergeant Wall, on duty as the petty officer—well, noncom—of the watch. "Four bells," she said.

"Aye, ma'am," Wall replied. He positioned himself by the watchstander's console and sounded the ship's announcing bells while she waited to greet the arriving Dremish captain.

Two officers emerged from the passage, dressed in the blue and black of the Imperial Navy: a sturdy, fair-skinned man with silver-streaked hair and a matching goatee, and a tall, stern-faced woman with short-cropped hair of rust brown and a bladelike nose. *Helena Aldrich!* Sikander stared in surprise. He had no idea that he might know anyone in the Dremish squadron. He'd only met Aldrich one time, under circumstances very different from those of the current day: a dinner party aboard SMS *Panther,* in orbit around Gadira II. More than a few of those present in *Panther*'s wardroom that evening had died in the battle that followed less than a week after the social occasion.

The two Dremish officers executed the time-honored boarding ritual, pivoting to salute the Commonwealth flag that stood by the quarterdeck's aft bulkhead. "Permission to come aboard?" Captain Zimmer asked. His Standard Anglic was flawless, without a hint of a foreign accent.

"Permission granted," said the ensign on watch, returning their salute.

The Dremish officers stepped over the sill of the airlock, and turned to face Sikander expectantly. He shook himself and stepped forward to greet them. "Senior Captain Zimmer?" he said to the first officer. "Welcome aboard, sir. I am Lieutenant Commander North, squadron intelligence officer."

Zimmer offered his hand. "Mr. North, a pleasure to meet you. May I introduce my executive officer, Kapitan-Leutnant Helena Aldrich?"

"I have already had the privilege," Sikander said. He carefully offered his hand to Aldrich. "Ms. Aldrich, I hope you are well?"

Aldrich took his hand after a momentary hesitation. "Mr. North. I am surprised to find you here."

Captain Zimmer raised an eyebrow. "You know each other?"

"We do, but I'm afraid we last met under difficult circumstances." Sikander faced the Dremish captain. "I served as gunnery officer aboard CSS *Hector* at Gadira."

"I see," Zimmer said, his expression tightening. Sikander certainly hadn't sought out any opportunities to discuss the Gadira incident with his counterparts in the Dremish navy, but he'd heard that many of Dremark's naval officers felt that Captain Elise Markham had engaged in an unprovoked attack when she'd ordered *Hector* to open fire on *Panther*. The Imperial Navy had been outraged and humiliated by the results of the battle; Kapitan zur Stern Georg Harper had been court-martialed and drummed out of the service.

"I cannot say I am pleased to see you, Mr. North," Aldrich said slowly. "Many of my friends died that day, and

I was seriously wounded. I have wondered for years what I would say to you or your shipmates if ever we met again."

"Many of my friends died too," said Sikander. He realized that Helena Aldrich had, in fact, most likely fired the K-cannon salvo that killed Captain Markham—she'd been *Panther*'s gunnery officer, after all. Then again, if she had blood on her hands, so did he. He'd left *Panther* to his fire-control officer, but he'd fired the salvo that wrecked the destroyer *Streitaxt*. Elise Markham had been one of the finest officers he'd ever known . . . but it wasn't Helena Aldrich's fault that Markham was dead. He made himself meet Aldrich's eyes. "I regret that so many were hurt or killed on both sides, Helena. We had our orders, and you had yours. I sincerely hope that our governments do not put us in that position again."

She returned his gaze, and nodded after a moment. "On that we can agree."

"Perhaps we should proceed to the developments of the day?" said Zimmer.

"Of course," said Sikander. "Please, follow me."

It took two hours of discussion with Commodore Abernathy and Deputy Commodore Reyes plus another lengthy intel presentation from Sikander, but eventually Kapitan zur Stern Zimmer agreed to commit *Prinz Oskar* to the relief expedition, as well as the light cruiser *Kassel* and a pair of destroyers. Under normal circumstances a flag officer commanded the Imperial Navy's Kahnar-Sag flotilla, but the sudden crisis in Tamabuqq had caught the Dremish in the middle of a squadron reorganization; the new admiral wouldn't arrive for another four or five weeks. In the absence of a flag officer, Reinhold Zimmer was the senior Dremish officer present and had the authority to take the necessary action.

After the Dremish officers returned to their ship, Sikander caught a few hours' sleep. He rose again before 0600 to continue updating the assessment of Tzoru military capabilities and likely reactions from each of the aristocratic clans. Delays in provisioning some of the ships in the allied flotilla, finishing maintenance tasks, and improvising command arrangements took up most of the day, but late in the afternoon, Commodore Abernathy called for an in-port tactical exercise with all the ships joining the relief force to test out communications channels and command signals. Captain Howard and *Exeter*'s tactical team manned their general quarters stations on the cruiser's bridge, while the Helix Squadron staff took up their posts on the flag bridge and brought the Californians, Cygnans, Dremish, and Montréalais into their command circuit one by one.

An hour into the frustrating exercise, an alert signal flashed on Sikander's console. He glanced down expecting yet another delay from one squadron or another, and instead barely swallowed an oath of surprise. "Commodore, the bridge reports new arrival signatures," he reported to Abernathy. "It's a large formation in loose order, distance nine light-minutes, bearing zero-three-zero relative. We read nine . . . no, make that ten, eleven contacts."

"Someone skipped a few pages of their script," said Abernathy. "We're not supposed to start the exercise engagement for an hour yet, are we?"

"Sir, it's not part of the exercise," Lieutenant Commander Dacey told him, studying her own displays. "This is an actual system arrival by an unidentified force."

Abernathy got up from his battle couch and moved to look over Dacey's shoulder, studying the squadron-ops tactical display. "That's a big squadron," he muttered aloud. "None of our fleets are close by and the Montréalais and Dremish don't have that many ships in the sector."

"Maybe the Nyeirans?" Reyes guessed. "They're a lot closer to home than we are here. Perhaps they put us off yesterday because they knew they had help coming."

Sikander studied his display, trying to correlate the sensor data. At this range, a target's acceleration and a rough guess at its size were all that could be readily observed. "It's not the Nyeirans, ma'am. The acceleration and mass figures are all wrong unless they're deliberately holding back on decelerating from their transit emergence."

"All right then, Mr. North, who the devil are they?" the commodore asked.

The distant fleet seemed to be turning toward Kahnar-Sag, but it would be a number of hours before they arrived. On the other hand, Sikander could now pick up their electronic emissions as the arriving ships activated their navigational radars and routine communications—nine minutes ago, at any rate. He blinked in surprise. "We've got their identification codes, sir," he told Abernathy. "They're Tzoru warships at full military acceleration."

8

Tzoru fleet?" Commodore Abernathy scowled beneath his bristly mustache. "I thought all the Dominion warships were assigned to the provincial fleets or frontier patrols. What are these fellows doing in Kahnar-Sag?"

"I'm not sure, but I don't care for the aggressive posture they seem to be taking," said Reyes. She met Abernathy's eyes. "Commodore, I know you're new here. You should know that in the year I've served in Helix Squadron, I have never seen a Tzoru fleet under way *anywhere*. Even their most modern formations spend all their time in parking orbits."

"You think they're hostile?" Abernathy asked her. Reyes gave a small shrug; the wiry Aquilan commodore frowned, and turned to the rest of the staff. "Cancel the current exercise, Ms. Dacey. Mr. Barnes, pass the order to all ships—Aquilan and participating allies—to make preparations to get under way. I won't have my squadron tied down in docking cradles if trouble starts."

"Aye, sir," Mason Barnes and Giselle Dacey replied together. They busied themselves with carrying out the commodore's orders.

"Which fleet are we looking at?" Reyes asked Sikander.

Sikander had in fact been working on that very question, trading quick messages with Senior Chief Lin and checking the squadron's ship-recognition database. "We believe that's the Shining Resolve Fleet from Alaktasa, ma'am. They're a provincial fleet under the control of the Karsu clan."

Abernathy's scowl deepened. "Remind me, Mr. North, who the damned Karsu are and what they might be doing here."

"They're one of the Monarchist-faction clans, sir, or at least they were before Sapwu Zrinan's fall. They have substantial holdings at Alaktasa, which is where the Shining Resolve Fleet is based." Sikander checked the Shining Resolve's record of movement, and as he expected he found almost no previous activity. "As the d-com says, we haven't seen them leave Alaktasa before, so I'm afraid I couldn't tell you why they are here."

"What's their strength?" Reyes asked.

"Normally four battleships, two to six cruisers, and about twenty escorts." Sikander nodded at the tactical display. "It looks like this group is only part of the Alaktasa fleet. We've confirmed two battleships, two armored cruisers, and a mix of torpedo cutters and corvettes for the rest of the force."

"Only half the provincial fleet?" Abernathy asked.

"That might have been all they could get under way," Reyes told the commodore. "A lot of the Tzoru fleets are in an appalling state of disrepair."

"So noted, but battleships are battleships, D-Com. I'd like to know what they're doing here."

"Incoming transmission," Mason Barnes reported from his station by the comm console. The lieutenant listened to his audio feed, and winced. "Sir, you're going to want to hear this."

"Go ahead, Mr. Barnes," said Abernathy.

The screen nearest to the commodore flickered as he keyed it to play the message. An old, corpulent Tzoru in ornate space armor appeared on the screen. He began speaking in harsh Tzoqabu; the ship's info assistant played the translation. "Attention, foreign warships," the Tzoru male said. "I am Karsu

Herum, in command of the Shining Resolve Fleet. All previous agreements regarding the presence of non-Dominion military forces in Kahnar-Sag are hereby suspended. You are to remove your warships and your soldiers from this system at once. I give you one local day to comply, and then I will destroy any vessels not in compliance with this requirement. Do not return to Tzoru space." Then Karsu Herum cut his connection, leaving a blank screen.

The commodore's face reddened, and he glared at the empty screen. "Why, that arrogant, puffed-up, big-bellied buffoon!" he snarled, surging to his feet. "Who does he think he is, ordering Aquilan warships about?"

"Sir, the Dremish captain would like to speak to you," Barnes reported. His display lighted up with incoming communications. "Er, so would the Montréalais commander. And the Cygnans."

Sikander just managed to conceal a snort of amusement with a hasty coughing fit. It wasn't funny, but he imagined that every human commanding officer in Kahnar-Sag—and probably the Nyeiran, too—was at this very minute spluttering in shock and anger, shaking their fists in the air, or demanding explanations from blank screens. Aquilans were not accustomed to high-handed treatment from any "second-rate" power, and the Kashmiri in him couldn't help but savor their response for a moment. No doubt the Dremish, Montréalais, and all the rest felt the same way, which meant that whether he intended to or not, Karsu Herum had just managed to unite the quarrelsome commanders of the human fleet in shared outrage. Sikander hadn't yet developed much of a feel for William Abernathy's command style, but he would have bet his right arm that Abernathy wouldn't respond well to threats.

Abernathy muttered under his breath, and slowly returned to his seat. "Mr. Barnes, hold the calls for a moment," he said. "Ms. Dacey, tactical analysis. How long until the Shining Resolve Fleet gets here?"

"About nine hours for a zero-zero intercept, sir," the ops

officer replied. Of course, an attacking fleet didn't need to physically dock at Magan Kahnar, so a zero-distance zero-speed calculation did not tell the whole story, a fact that did not escape Giselle Dacey. "That assumes they keep their formation together and that the Baraqqu-class battleships top out around sixty g's of acceleration. They're probably a bit slower than that. If they intend to make a high-speed firing pass and they're willing to divide the force, their lighter ships could engage in about three hours."

"They'll make it a near zero-zero and take up a position within their firing range so that they'll be ready to attack when the deadline elapses," Reyes suggested. "No point in issuing the warning otherwise."

"Most likely, but I think we should be careful about assuming Tzoru are going to do what we expect them to right now. I'm not inclined to stay tied up to this station and provide that Karum Harum character with easy targets in case he forgets about his deadline." Abernathy nodded to himself, perhaps reviewing the analysis again. "All right, it seems we're going to have to respond to this situation before we can take care of our people in Tamabuqq. Mr. Barnes, conference in all the squadron commanders. I'll take the calls at the same time."

Lieutenant Barnes nodded and set to work with the comm specialists in his corner of the flag bridge. It only took a few moments to arrange the conference. Half a dozen of the vid displays ringing the compartment flickered and switched over to show the faces of high-ranking officers from the human squadrons at Kahnar Sag: Kapitan zur Stern Zimmer, Contre-Amiral Verger, Capitano Durante, the Californian squadron commander, and Captain Howard of *Exeter*.

"Commodore Abernathy," said Verger, a rail-thin woman with a severe face and hair of iron-gray. Her Anglic was heavily accented. "I assume you heard Admiral Karsu's threat. I must inform you that the Republic has no intention of removing its military personnel and warships in response to such a demand."

"Nor will the Empire of Dremark," Reinhold Zimmer added.

"I assure you the Commonwealth of Aquila feels the same way," Abernathy told the other commanders. "I frankly refuse to have the movements of my squadron dictated by some local panjandrum with a fleet of museum ships. I'm certain that the Tzoru is bluffing . . . but just in case, I intend to ready the combined squadrons for action. Have your ships ready to get under way in an hour; we'll take station a hundred thousand kilometers above Magan Kahnar and show Admiral Karsu that we are ready to deal harshly with him if he insists on continuing."

The other commanders nodded in agreement, but Reinhold Zimmer frowned and tugged at his small beard. "Commodore Abernathy, it occurs to me that the Shining Resolve Fleet dictates our movements whether we like it or not. We can't proceed to Tamabuqq and leave Kahnar-Sag uncovered as long as the Karsu are here. We all have many more citizens and investments in Kahnar-Sag than we do in the Thousand Worlds ward. What will you do if Karsu Herum decides to wait for us to leave?"

Abernathy's scowl deepened; Sikander wondered if the commodore had realized that before the Dremish commander brought it up. "I need to consider our options," he finally said. "At some point a fleet that prevents us from leaving Kahnar-Sag is just as hostile as one actively blocking a relief force in Tamabuqq. If I have to make that clear to this Karsu fellow, I will. Abernathy, out."

As it turned out, Admiral Karsu Herum was not interested in explaining himself to Commodore Abernathy or any other human officers or officials. When nearly two hours passed with no response from the Tzoru commander, Abernathy ordered the combined squadrons to sortie and take up a defensive position protecting the orbital station. By that point, the Shining Resolve's course and acceleration clearly indicated the near-zero intercept Reyes had predicted, heading for a point from which the Tzoru battleships could bring the human-controlled docks and facilities of Magan Kahnar under their guns.

Throughout the afternoon and evening, repeated strategy conferences with the commanders of the combined squadrons failed to produce any clear consensus on the question of when an attack against the Shining Resolve Fleet might be justified, while further attempts to negotiate with Karsu Herum were met with silence. The Tzoru fleet took up a position about fifty thousand kilometers from the human warships, and settled in to wait. Sikander found an opportunity to get a few hours' sleep as the standoff wore on, but he made sure he was back at his post before Karsu's announced deadline.

Commodore Abernathy arranged the human cruisers into a simple line formation, serving as the combined task force's main body. All the lighter ships he deployed into a screen under the command of the Montréalais rear admiral Verger. The destroyers and frigates patrolled slowly in the no-man's-land between the two fleets as the countdown ticked down to zero . . . and nothing happened. The two fleets continued to drift in space; no new messages from Karsu Herum appeared.

"Damn it all," Abernathy observed. "Zimmer was right. We've got somewhere to be, but we're stuck here as long as that Karsu fleet wants to stare us down." The commodore fixed his gaze on the tactical display, his chin on his hand. "How long do we wait?"

"We could detach a smaller squadron to proceed to Tamabuqq, sir," Barnes suggested. "A cruiser and a couple of escorts won't do much against serious Tzoru opposition, but even a token force could influence events if the Tzoru are as disorganized as we think they are. And it might show the Karsu that we're not going to let 'em hold us here."

"Better to move in force, or not at all," Reyes said in answer. "Isolated formations are defeats in detail just waiting to happen."

"Sir, I suggest we reach out to Sebet Gisumi and have

them serve as intermediaries," Sikander said. "The last thing the Gisumi want is to lose our business. They might persuade the Karsu to—"

"Sir, the Shining Resolve Fleet is maneuvering!" Lieutenant Commander Dacey suddenly announced. "They're turning toward Kahnar-Sag and accelerating. EM blooms from the Tzoru battleships!"

"They're *firing* on us?" Abernathy's astonishment lasted no more than a second or two, and then he swung into action. "Comms, general signal to all friendly units: Engage the enemy as directed in your firing plan!"

The ship's action alarm sounded. Sikander adjusted his battle-station armor: torso armor, helmet, gauntlets, and magnetic boots that turned his shipboard working uniform into effective vacuum protection. At Captain Howard's orders *Exeter* had set general quarters before the Karsu deadline expired, so all the watchstanders already wore their battle gear. He left the visor open—the helmet's sensors would slam it shut in the event of a compartment breach, but until then it was easier to keep on top of events if he could hear what was going on around him—and fixed his eyes on the tactical display. It looked like each of the four Tzoru heavy ships had picked out its counterpart in the human formation, opening up with extreme-range fire. The even ranks of the human fleet fell into sudden disorder as the ships under fire detected the incoming K-shot and took evasive maneuvers; *Exeter*'s deck tilted, and acceleration pushed Sikander back into his restraints as the big cruiser reacted to the attack.

"Not a word of warning first?" Reyes snarled. "Did Karsu Herum think he'd catch us off-guard?"

"They did warn us, ma'am," Sikander told Reyes. "They gave us a deadline yesterday. Tzoru aren't in the habit of repeating themselves or stating the obvious. Karsu Herum allowed a few minutes just in case our clock was running a little behind his, and then he did what he said he was going to do."

"In other words, Tzoru don't bluff," Abernathy growled. "Nobody here thought that might be worth mentioning to me before now?"

Sikander grimaced. *Brilliant, Sikay,* he told himself. Well, at least the initial Tzoru salvos seemed to have inflicted little damage; modern warships could easily dodge fire from a single attacker, provided the flight time of the kinetic rounds offered an opportunity to react. It was strangely unnerving to find himself aboard a ship going into battle with no immediate combat responsibilities. The job of maneuvering *Exeter* and firing on enemy targets belonged to the cruiser's bridge crew, not the squadron officers. At least he'd been in battle before and knew what to expect. The vast majority of Commonwealth officers and crewhands—and, by extension, the officers and crew serving on the warships of other nations—had never been in actual combat.

"Ms. Dacey, let's keep this simple since we haven't had a chance to integrate our allies into our command links," Abernathy said. "All cruisers, form a single column ahead on *Exeter* and engage the Tzoru heavies. Mr. Barnes, notify Contre-Amiral Verger that she is in command of the screen; I want her to handle the Tzoru light stuff while we're busy with the big ones."

"Sir, Captain Durante of the *Cagliari* is signaling," said Barnes. "He's requesting instructions."

"Pass my orders along and he'll have them," Abernathy replied. He tapped his internal comm screen, calling *Exeter*'s commanding officer. "Captain Howard, we're forming a column with the cruisers from the combined task force. *Exeter* is in the van. Give me military acceleration on course . . . two-eight-zero, down twenty. That should get us out in front of their formation."

"Aye, Commodore," said Howard. "Sir, shall I return fire?"

"Hold fire until we establish assignments," Abernathy said. "I'll turn you loose soon enough, Quentin."

Crossing the T, Sikander noted. The tactic dated back to

the days of steamships fighting on the seas of Old Terra, but it survived because it served as an excellent way to concentrate the full firepower of a number of ships on a smaller number of enemy targets. Karsu Herum wasn't quite co-operating, since the Tzoru were arranged in a sloppy line abreast rather than a well-ordered line ahead, but at least Abernathy ought to succeed in employing his cruisers' broadsides against the forward-facing mounts of the Shining Resolve Fleet. *If Admiral Karsu is on the ball, he'll execute a simultaneous turn to starboard and shift to an open-order column paralleling the allied task force.* But as the minutes crept by, the Tzoru warships turned together to keep their bows toward the human ships, trying to close the range as quickly as possible. More electromagnetic blooms crackled across the tactical displays—the Tzoru warships firing wildly with their kinetic cannons at extreme range. Some of the allied ships replied, in spite of Abernathy's effort to coordinate fire. *Cagliari* blasted randomly at the nearest Tzoru torpedo cutter, a light vessel half the size of a destroyer, while the Californian frigates seemed unable to resist the temptation to try their luck with some ranging shots.

"What part of 'hold your fire' does Captain Durante not understand?" Francine Reyes observed. "This is pure chaos."

"We can't expect every squadron to be up to Aquilan standards," said Abernathy. "I appreciate their offensive spirit, anyway."

Sikander kept his eyes on his own display. In combat, Intel Section made sure all enemy forces were identified and tracked, and provided the best battle-damage analysis they could on enemy units. Trying to manage the battle for the commodore or the Operations Section would win him no friends today . . . although there was nothing wrong with noting an opportunity when he saw it.

He waited for Abernathy to finish a set of hasty instructions for Contre-Amiral Verger about organizing the task force's screen of destroyers and frigates before speaking.

"Commodore, the Tzoru don't seem to be reacting to your maneuver," he said. "They're certainly intelligent enough to recognize the advantage of crossing the T, but they're still coming straight on for our formation. I'm only guessing, but I suspect their command-and-control challenges are even worse than ours."

Abernathy glanced back at Sikander and raised an eyebrow. "You think they're debating what to do next?"

"Or they don't have the ability to coordinate formation maneuvers because they don't have the tool set for it. They might not have clear lines of communication, or they might not have a set of recognized tactical commands to fall back on."

"Hmmph. Well, Mr. North, you just made me feel a little bit better about this three-ring circus I'm in charge of on our side." The commodore returned his attention to the tactical displays. The icons for the mismatched task force at his command appeared in various shades of blue, while the ships of the hostile Tzoru fleet glowed red and the handful of Gisumi warships in orbit around Kahnar-Sag were assigned the light gray of neutral warships.

Minutes crawled by as the human task force settled into Abernathy's simple battle formation: heavy cruisers in the front, light cruisers following, lighter warships forming into three- and four-ship elements to screen the main column. *Exeter* led the way, followed by *Prinz Oskar, Dupleix, Hawkins, Burton, Kassel,* and last of all *Cagliari,* which seemed to have a hard time keeping up with the acceleration of the more modern cruisers. Standard Aquilan doctrine frowned on the idea of placing the flagship at the head of the column; it was the most exposed position, after all, and dead admirals made for poor fleet commanders. But as the multinational force sluggishly sorted itself out, Sikander began to see Abernathy's wisdom in taking the lead. The commodore could be certain of the movements of exactly one ship, and given the doubts expressed about Aquila's command of the combined force, setting a firm example of personal leadership was probably for the best. *Still, he could have directed* Hawkins *or* Burton *to serve as the formation guide,* Sikander thought. Either of the Aquilan light cruisers would have served to carry out Abernathy's orders without confusion or delay.

"Captain Howard reports that we're well within effective range, Commodore," Lieutenant Commander Dacey said from the squadron tactical console. "He requests permission to open fire on the Baraqqu-class battleship in the center of the Tzoru formation."

Abernathy studied the display for a moment, then nodded. "Commence fire," he said calmly.

The instant Dacey sent the signal to engage, *Exeter*'s kinetic cannons whined and bucked. The cruiser's bridge and flag bridge were sheltered in the center of the hull far from the weapons mounts, but even so the deck plates under Sikander's feet shivered each time the big cannons fired. Each weapon was a potent coil gun accelerating a hardened dart of tungsten alloy to tremendous velocity through the application of massive power charges: in the case of *Exeter*'s Laguna Mark III medium kinetic cannon, something close to thirty-five hundred kilometers per second. Since even the most agile target needed a few seconds to plot the incoming round's trajectory and initiate enough acceleration or deceleration to get out of the way, the cruiser's guns had an effective range of about thirty thousand kilometers—a little more against large, slow targets, or significantly less against small and nimble ones.

Behind *Exeter,* each of the cruisers in the main column joined in, concentrating their fire on the first Tzoru battleship. It was a long shot for the ships at the rear of the column, but that mattered a good deal less when a target already faced multiple enemy broadsides. When seven ships all chose the same target, there was simply no evasive maneuver that could avoid every incoming shot. Even so, the great majority of the combined barrage missed. Tiny inaccuracies in firing solutions or minuscule power fluctuations in the capacitors introduced a natural spread to any K-cannon salvos, and a K-cannon shot that missed the target's hull by just a centimeter or two might as well have missed by million kilometers . . . but half a dozen projectiles from the cruisers' opening salvo *did* hit, scoring direct impacts on the battleship's massive bow. Dense steel alloy boiled and vaporized in an instant before erupting in streamers of white-hot metallic gas and plasma; the sheer force of exploding armor and venting atmosphere hammered the Tzoru battleship first one way and then another, sending it staggering like a prizefighter under a devastating combination.

The crew manning the flag bridge whooped as they watched the effect of the first combined salvo. "Multiple hits on the primary target!" Giselle Dacey announced. William Abernathy allowed himself a fierce grin and Mason Barnes clenched his fist by his armored chest, but Sikander winced and looked away from the screens on his console. The telescopic cams mounted on *Exeter*'s hull captured the destruction in all its hellish glory; a sensation of sick horror knotted his stomach. He remembered all too well what it was like to be on the receiving end of K-cannon fire: the shattering impact, blasts of molten steel, alarms wailing as systems failed, the wounded screaming for help . . . no, he couldn't bring himself to cheer.

God, let this be over soon, he prayed. *Tzoru or human, spare all the lives You can today.* Then he forced himself to study his screen again and do his job, since the fastest and surest way to bring this tragic confrontation to an end would be to win decisively.

A ragged second volley from the allied column crashed into the crippled Tzoru battleship, igniting more explosions. More K-shot struck this time, since she could barely maneuver after the first salvos. And they inflicted more damage, too, hammering into a structure badly weakened by the first devastating hits. Battleships, even century-old relics like the Baraqqu-class ships, were tough targets, designed to stand up to the hits of cruiser-weight weapons, but even if the human fire couldn't punch completely through the wounded ship's vitals, dozens of hits sufficed to peel away appalling masses of armor, savage the weapons mounts, shatter drive plates, and riddle the interior with spalling fragments. The Tzoru battleship's power output dropped to zero and it lost attitude control, falling into a slow tumbling spin as it streamed vapor and gobbets of molten steel.

"She's dead," announced Commodore Abernathy. "All ships, shift fire to next primary target. Mr. Barnes, damage reports from our ships?"

"One moment, sir," Barnes replied. He checked his screen. "*Hawkins* lost her after turret to a battleship-caliber hit. *Prinz Oskar* reports a partial power outage from a light hit. *Cagliari* has taken several nonpenetrating hits from the Tzoru corvettes and also reports a failure in her main power system—most likely an engineering casualty, not battle damage. Our destroyer screen has also taken some light hits, nothing major reported so far."

Sikander turned his attention to the task force's lighter ships, skirmishing now with the Tzoru cutters and corvettes. Admiral Verger had organized her screen into several small squadrons. The Aquilan destroyers operated in one group, the Dremish and Montréalais combined to form a second, and the Californian frigates made up a third element. The Tzoru light ships were outnumbered by significantly larger and more capable human warships, but they seemed to be giving a better account of themselves than the Tzoru capital ships, wheeling together in loose formation and dodging quite a bit of allied fire.

Sikander frowned, and keyed his comms to speak with the rest of his small team; the squadron's intelligence specialists manned the flag office at general quarters. "Senior Chief, what do we have on those Ziltu-class cutters? They seem a good deal more nimble than the other Tzoru ships."

"One moment, Mr. North, we're pulling up the records now," Lin replied—crisp and professional, now that the fleet was engaged in an actual battle situation. "Okay, sir, we've got them. They're new Montréalais-built ships, manufactured in the STK Arsenal of Dwight IV. The Shining Resolve Fleet took delivery of a squadron of eight units just four years ago."

"These are *human*-built ships?"

"Yes, sir. It looks like the Republic marketed Ziltus aggressively to several of the high clans over the last ten or fifteen years."

"No wonder they're handling themselves better than the ancient Tzoru cruisers and battleships," Sikander muttered under his breath. The great powers of the Coalition of Humanity often competed with each other for the favor of less advanced nations through arms sales; he'd known that some of the powerful *sebetu* had ordered warships from Cygnan, Montréalais, or even Aquilan builders eager to find new customers. The Aquilan Foreign Ministry at least took care to make sure that top-line weapons and sensors weren't delivered to potential adversaries, but perhaps the Montréalais hadn't been quite as careful. Regardless, the tactical display clearly showed that the Ziltus had more capable systems than the older ships in the Shining Resolve Fleet. "Senior Chief, make a note: We'll want to catalog all human-built warship deliveries to any Tzoru clans over the last twenty or thirty years and make sure we know exactly where those ships are. Those at least won't be museum pieces."

"Got it, sir," said Lin.

"Sir, that's not all," Petty Officer Macklin added. "We should expect to see those ships in the hands of younger and more aggressive commanders. Battleships and cruisers are prestigious commands—they go to Tzoru with the most seniority and the best patronage networks, regardless of ability. Small, foreign-built ships tend to be under the command of officers who don't have the connections to win more impressive assignments—"

"—which means they earned their commands with personal ability instead of a good pedigree," said Sikander, finishing the intel specialist's observation.

"Exactly, sir," said Macklin.

"Good to know. Thanks, Macklin. We'd better start collecting dossiers on Tzoru ship commanders."

"We have some already, sir—at least, we have some for the fleets we know well, like the Golden Banner or the Baltzu formations at Shimatum." The specialist paused. "We just don't see much of the Shining Resolve because we don't visit Alaktasa very often."

Sikander's frown deepened. "Very well," he said, acknowledging the report. Maybe one of his counterparts in the other human squadrons knew more about the Karsu formations; he'd have to ask around after the K-shot and torpedoes stopped flying.

Another chorus of whoops caught his attention. He looked up and saw a huge explosion rock the second Tzoru battleship—a capacitor containment failure, most likely. Her forward battery fell silent immediately, power dead in the forward part of the ship. "Shift fire to the armored cruiser, the big one," Abernathy ordered.

"Aye, sir!" Giselle Dacey replied. She switched the squadron targeting systems to the next-largest warship in the Shining Resolve Fleet. The Tzoru main body finally showed signs of reacting to the allied squadron's crossing of their T, turning starboard in a loose mob and increasing their acceleration in an attempt to form a parallel column . . . but the maneuver was late and poorly executed. The old Tzoru ships simply didn't have the acceleration to match even the slow-footed *Cagliari* at the tail end of Abernathy's force, and the badly damaged battleships were little better than drifting wrecks.

Exeter suddenly gave a sharp lurch and quarter roll, a teeth-jarring impact that caused the tactical displays to flicker and jump. A terrible *wham!* shook the ship, echoing from somewhere below and behind the flag bridge. "Hit on the aft ventral turret!" Reyes called, repeating the information from the ship-status displays. "It sounds like the mount's knocked out, Commodore. Any instructions for the flagship?"

"They were certainly throwing enough K-shot in our direction, I suppose we shouldn't be surprised they got lucky." Abernathy grimaced. "Let me know if Captain Howard reports any loss of maneuverability or communications. Otherwise let's leave him alone and let him fight his ship."

"Minor hit on *Jackal,* sir," Sikander reported, keeping an eye on the dueling escorts. "It looks like three of the Tzoru torpedo cutters are incapacitated—wait, make that four, the Dremish destroyer just landed a torpedo hit on the Tzoru element leader." The Ziltus might have been capable little ships, but they were outnumbered and badly outgunned by the destroyers and frigates of the combined squadrons; the difference in firepower began to tell. *How much more of this is Karsu Herum going to take?* he wondered. Any rational commander in the Shining Resolve's position had to give thought to preserving what was left of his command.

William Abernathy apparently had the same thought Sikander did. "Mr. Barnes, signal the Tzoru flagship, message as follows: Admiral Karsu, you have shown great courage, but your fleet is overmatched," he said. "I urge you to think of your crews and cease hostilities. You can accomplish nothing more today except additional loss of life. Abernathy, out."

"Message sent, Commodore, but I can't guarantee that Karsu got it," Barnes said. "Their flagship is dead in space and I doubt they've got working comms. Or Admiral Karsu might be dead."

"We have to give it a try, Mr. Barnes," said Abernathy. *Exeter* punctuated his remark with another thrumming salvo from her heavy K-cannons.

"Sir, it looks like the Shining Resolve Fleet is turning away," Dacey said. "Yes, they're definitely moving to disengage."

"General pursuit, Commodore?" Reyes asked. "I don't think we want to leave a Tzoru fleet in Kahnar-Sag, no matter how beat up they are."

Abernathy shook his head. "It would be shooting fish in

a barrel, Francine. I think we've demonstrated to Admiral Karsu or whoever's left in command over there that we have overwhelming superiority. I'm going to let them go." He looked up from the tactical display in the center of the compartment. "Ms. Dacey, disengage. Signal all ships to cease fire immediately."

"Aye, sir," the operations officer acknowledged. She began relaying orders.

"Assuming no one's shooting at us, direct Admiral Verger's destroyers to commence aid and rescue operations for any Tzoru ships unable to leave the area under their own power—with care, of course. Keep them under our guns in case somebody decides to take a shot while we're trying to help them." Abernathy swiveled in his command couch, looking over to the comm station. "Mr. Barnes, any response from the Tzoru yet?"

"No, Commodore. But it sure looks like they've had enough for today."

"I'd say so too," said Abernathy. He studied the tactical display, now filled with the blinking red icons of crippled and destroyed Tzoru ships, and shook his head. "What a waste. What a damned waste."

9

Bagal-Dindir, Tamabuqq Prime

Winter held Bagal-Dindir firmly in its grip. Clear new sheets of ice crackled and groaned on the countless lakes and canals of the capital, but the only snow that fell came in the form of small dry flakes that danced in the wind without ever seeming to reach the ground. Not for the first time, General Hish Mubirrum found himself wondering why the Anshars of old had decided to choose such a northerly city for the seat of their dominion. His species had evolved in the tropics of Tamabuqq Prime, after all, arising from nomadic bands of pack hunters who spent nearly as much time in the warm shallows of the sea as they did in the humid jungles and marshlands. Some scholars believed that Bagal-Dindir had grown into the planetary capital because the rich mines and fossil-fuel deposits of the surrounding region had helped the powerful Margiddas to become the first Tzoru clan to industrialize. But Mubirrum had also heard other scholars insist that natural climate variation caused Bagal-Dindir's notoriously unfriendly winters; the capital had been founded more than fifty thousand years ago, after all, more than enough time for a new glacial interlude to impose a nearly subarctic climate on a city that had been founded in a more temperate age. *In which case we might improve the capital's winters by simply waiting a few thousand years for the next temperate interval to come along,* he told himself, and shivered.

"This cold is difficult for the militia," said Hish Pazril, as if reading Mubirrum's thoughts. "Few of them have the winter clothing necessary to remain outside for long, and that means they can't properly man their positions. The physicians expect serious cold injuries over the next few nights."

The two Hish officers stood beneath a row of frozen tree-ferns tightly curled against the cold temperatures, a short distance behind the improvised barricade blocking the end of an avenue that met the road encircling the Thousand Worlds ward. The ancient walls glowered at them, only three hundred meters distant. A few dozen armed *warumzi agu* hunkered down in fighting positions behind the barricade, part of a twelve-kilometer ring surrounding the old fortifications, while hundreds more militia sheltered in the nearby buildings. The distant crackle of Tzoru shock rifles and the chirping whine of human-built mag weapons punctuated the stillness of the afternoon, a pattern of desultory sniping that accomplished little other than ensuring that both sides showed themselves as little as possible. This sector seemed quiet enough for the moment; otherwise Mubirrum's bodyguards would not have allowed him to visit the line at all.

"The Seventeeth Prophecy tells us that disorder chooses its own season," said Mubirrum. He nodded at the walls of the offworlder district. "At least the defiant elements inside the ward are in an even more difficult situation than the *warumzi agu.* Our misguided allies have warm homes to shelter in and hot meals to revive them after their watches, but I doubt that the aliens can hold out for long without the city's power or water."

"Most of the embassies have their own power supplies," Pazril noted glumly. "And humans stand up to cold better than we do, damn them."

"But not hunger. Or running out of ammunition." No Tzoru armies had taken the field in centuries, but Mubirrum had read enough to know that in the days when such things happened, campaigns had generally come to a complete halt during northern winters. Given that, he was not dissatisfied with the siege of the Thousand Worlds ward. Yes, it would have been much easier and quicker to bring the professional soldiers of the Militarist *sebetu* to bear on the problem of the offworlder district; a few hours of fighting would settle the whole business. But tens of thousands of commoners fired with revolutionary zeal certainly sufficed to box the humans, the Nyeirans, and their Tzoru collaborators into one crowded city district where, by all reports, conditions worsened every day. While the mixed force holding the Thousand Worlds had managed to repel several poorly planned assaults by the revolutionary militias, *warumzi agu* sympathizers inside the walls reported that food was becoming scarce after three weeks of the siege.

"Perhaps if we allowed some skybarges to participate in the next assault . . ." Pazril suggested.

"No, not yet," Mubirrum told his younger cousin. As long as the Dominion High Council dawdled and debated, no soldiers sworn to the Anshar's service could participate in any kind of open attack on the humans and their allies, but the current standoff served Mubirrum just as well. It kept Bagal-Dindir's *warumzi agu* busy, it embarrassed his rivals at the Anshar's court, and each failed attempt to storm the gates or scale the walls raised the stakes of the game. "The situation progresses to our advantage as things now stand, but if we take a more active role we invite the censure of the High Council."

"Does that really matter?"

"The only way the Hish can lose this war that is not a war is if the other high clans unite against us," Mubirrum told Pazril. "Of course they all know we are sympathetic to the *warumzi agu,* but as long as we maintain an appearance of containing rather than inciting the revolutionaries, the Baltzu and the Maruz and their friends can't rally the neutral *sebetu* against us. So yes, Pazril, the Dominion High Council matters, at least for a little longer. It is not yet time for us to move openly."

The younger warrior frowned, but nodded in understanding. Pazril was one of the very few Tzoru privy to Mubirrum's true plans, but he was young; he naturally longed for decisive action, and cared less for the subtleties of the high-clan politics Mubirrum had wrestled with for decades.

"Come, Pazril. I am too old to enjoy the rigors of a day like this." Mubirrum turned his back on the barricade and strode away beneath the shrunken treeferns, not allowing the cold to rush his steps; hurrying for shelter was beneath the dignity of a Dominion councillor and powerful general, after all. Three blocks behind the revolutionaries' positions his skybarge waited, screened from direct observation by the humans in the Thousand Worlds ward by the tall domes of a sprawling conservatory.

A fifteen-minute flight brought Mubirrum back to the Hish estate on the outskirts of Bagal-Dindir. He returned to his private office to review the news of the day from other systems of the Dominion. Word of the siege in Bagal-Dindir appeared to be spreading swiftly to worlds such as Alaktasa, Kahnar-Sag, Shimatum, and more, sparking protests, acts of sabotage, even the occupation of governmental centers in some cases. Mubirrum wrestled with his reactions to the reports. On the one hand, he understood intellectually that the *warumzi agu* were a necessary evil at this point—a wildfire burning out of control, as he'd described them in Kadingir. But on the other hand, he could not deny the stirrings of dismay in his heart. He was an old warrior who had devoted his life to the preservation of the Anshar's authority and the rule of harmony throughout the Dominion, and he could not bring himself to embrace the idea of allowing disorder to spread throughout the realm even as he recognized its necessity. It seemed . . . dishonorable.

Shortly after midday, Mubirrum's chief scribe interrupted his studies. "Pardon the interruption, my lord," the old female said, bowing from his doorway. "Admiral Hish Sudi requests an audience."

"Sudi is here?" Mubirrum straightened from the stack of documents that cluttered his working space. "Send her in."

Admiral Hish Sudi paused to bow from the door, then approached. Mubirrum noted her troubled expression at once. The oldest of his dozen or so offspring, Hish Sudi had compiled a record of competence and achievement with little help from him. Her accomplishments reflected well on the Hish, not him personally, but he took a certain pride in them nonetheless. He did not dote on his offspring's successes—no Tzoru did, really—but he was gratified that she had turned out to be a leader in her own right. "Welcome, Admiral," he said, rising to return her bow. "I did not expect to see you today."

"Nor I you, Lord Mubirrum," Sudi replied. She bowed and spread her hands. "I have just received news from Kahnar-Sag, and it is not good. I regret to report that the Shining Resolve Fleet suffered a great defeat at the hands of the human warships in Kahnar-Sag. Admiral Karsu was killed in battle."

"What?" Mubirrum demanded. "Karsu Herum was not supposed to attack the human squadrons unless he possessed an overwhelming advantage! Why did he accept battle if he was overmatched?"

"That I could not say, but I can tell you that Karsu Herum led only about half of the Shining Resolve Fleet to Kahnar-Sag." She reached into a pocket of her tunic and withdrew a recording cube. "This is a battle summary based on recordings captured by one of our courier ships observing at a safe distance. It provides a good overview of the action."

Mubirrum took the cube and activated the report for himself. The recording included tactical records from several of the ships on the fringes of the engagement, compressed for time and augmented by graphics to show which ships had fired on one another. Terse annotations described the key events of the battle. He was no expert in naval tactics—planetary combat was his specialty—but one could not come to command the military power of an important *sebet* such as the Hish without acquiring a basic understanding of the relative strength of warships and how they fought one another. What he saw in the recording cube appalled him.

Two of our best battleships crippled by a few salvos from a mixed force of cruisers! Thousands of dead Tzoru and eight ships destroyed with hardly a hit scored against their adversaries! He'd certainly been aware of the fact that human warships were much more modern than the Dominion's own antiquated war fleets, but still . . . battleships were supposed to be able to handle three or four times their number in cruisers. If the human ships enjoyed that much of a qualitative edge against Tzoru vessels, then a lot of what he thought he knew about the relative strength of the Dominion and its rivals was simply not true. "Where is the rest of the Shining Resolve Fleet?" he asked the admiral.

"As far as I can determine it is still at Alaktasa. I would guess that Karsu Herum left them behind because maintenance requirements or inadequate crew training meant that they were not able to get under way in time to join his force."

"Are those widespread problems in our fleets?"

"Yes." Sudi made an apologetic gesture. "Among the formations our *sebet* controls, somewhere around a third of our warships are not available for operations at any given time. It's substantially worse in fleets under the command of less diligent *sebetu*."

"Such as the Karsu."

"Such as the Karsu," Sudi agreed. She hesitated for a long moment, evidently deciding whether or not to go on. "I feel that I must point out that Karsu Herum's decision to proceed with only part of the Shining Resolve Fleet is not the only reason for his defeat. All our simulations suggested that our warships would give a better showing against foreign classes. We evidently have a substantial inferiority to the human warships in maneuverability and fire control. And

Karsu Herum showed little ability to respond to the tactical maneuvers of the human fleet."

"Can we remedy those deficiencies?"

"There is nothing we can do about inferior drives, Lord Mubirrum. But with time we can devise better fire doctrines to make the most of our fire-control systems, and see to it that our commanders practice modern tactics and formation handling."

Time which we may or may not have, Mubirrum reflected. "Begin immediately," he told his offspring. "And see to it that Hish-commanded formations are rotated to critical worlds. I do not want to have to count on the Karsu or the Ninazzu or some other clan of half-wits to defend the Dominion against alien aggression."

"It will be done."

"What are the human squadrons doing to follow up their victory?"

"Our sources in Magan Kahnar—and the humans' own news channels, I should add—are confident that the Aquilan admiral Abernathy is preparing to move on Tamabuqq in an effort to intervene in the situation at the Ward of a Thousand Worlds. But as of the courier's departure five days ago he hadn't yet departed and did not seem likely to depart for at least a few days. I suspect that he is unsure whether it is safe to leave Kahnar-Sag uncovered, since there are other provincial fleets beside the Shining Resolve that might threaten the human holdings there."

Mubirrum rubbed a hand over the rough dermis at the back of his neck, thinking. If he were Abernathy, he knew that he would want to take advantage of an easy victory to press toward his goal while his enemy was in disarray. "So the human fleet is coming, but we likely have a few days to prepare for their arrival. Thank you, Sudi. I must bring this to the High Council."

"Of course, honored parent. I wish I had better news for you." Hish Sudi recognized the dismissal; she bowed and withdrew.

After she left, Mubirrum watched the recording cube's battle summary several more times in the hope that he might spot some weakness in the conduct of the human squadrons, but his mind was already elsewhere. Kahnar-Sag was a battle lost; no amount of second-guessing or fault-finding would change that, and there were Tzoru better equipped than he—Hish Sudi, for instance—to analyze the results and determine what lessons could be learned. No, the real significance of Kahnar-Sag was that there'd been a battle in the first place, and what that meant for the turbulent currents now swirling around the Anshar's seat.

It is unfortunate that our fleets are not as ready as we thought, he reflected as he watched the tiny blossoming explosions recorded in the cube. *The humans worked together— something we have never seen them do—and easily defeated a force the same size as their own. We can meet the human Abernathy with a force five times greater if he is rash enough to challenge us here. And if I find the right differences to exploit, perhaps I can turn their nation-clans against one another.* If he succeeded . . . if he managed to bring about the defeat of the human fleet and saved the very seat of the Dominion from the indignity of alien aggression . . . then he finally would be in position to dictate the Dominion's reaction to the outrageous encroachment of the lesser powers that surrounded it and perhaps usher the Tzoru into a new and glorious era.

But first I must bring the human fleet to Tamabuqq and destroy it. The first step was simple enough: Whether Ebneghirz and his followers knew it or not, they had provided him with the perfect bait for that task by threatening the human diplomats and merchants in Bagal-Dindir. As for the second step, that posed a more difficult challenge. Mubirrum considered the problem for a time, staring at the ceiling of his chamber. Then he called in Pazril to dictate messages for key commanders of the Hish and those *sebetu* allied with them. In the face of a threat that could materialize at almost any moment, he needed to ensure that the right officers and officials took charge of preparing a defense—and that others would take no action at all until he told them to. Only after he was satisfied that his instructions were in place did he turn his attention to forwarding duplicates of the recording cube to each of the other high *sebetu,* as would be expected of him after the report from Kahnar-Sag.

Shortly before sundown, he called for his skybarge again, and made the short flight from the sprawling Hish palace to the towering ziggurat of the Anshar's Palace. He paused only to don his court dress in a robing room, layer upon layer of ornate robes in crimson and gold—the colors favored by the *sebetu* counted among the militarists of the Emuqq-Mamit faction—and then he allowed his retainers to affix his sword of office in its jeweled scabbard to the wide bronze-plate girdle around his hips. The court costume had not changed significantly since the rise of the Dominion, thousands of years before his people had mastered space travel; Mubirrum always felt that donning the trappings of his office took him back to a simpler time, a better time.

"I was born in the wrong age," he murmured aloud, adjusting the scabbard at his waist.

"Did you speak, Lord Mubirrum?" Pazril asked.

"It is nothing," Mubirrum replied. "A pointless regret."

Pazril shrugged. For all the younger male's intelligence and reliability, he lacked the imagination to see things other than as they were; Mubirrum envied him that sometimes. "The council awaits you, Lord Mubirrum," he said.

"Then let us proceed." Mubirrum allowed Pazril and the rest of his retinue to escort him into the council's chamber. Even after twenty years as a high councillor, he was still moved by the Hall of Auspicious Judgment. It was not quite as large as the Anshar's actual throne room, but the Anshar presided in public so rarely that the throne room was little more than a museum. On the other hand, the business of a Dominion that sprawled across one hundred and twenty-two worlds took shape every day in the Hall of Auspicious Judgment. Great glowing orbs fashioned in the likeness of each of the Tzoru worlds hovered beneath the soaring ceiling. Sixty-four beautiful reliefs covered in finely hammered copper leaf ringed the walls, each depicting the central narrative of one of the Sixty-Four Prophecies. The martial imagery of the Fifty-Third Prophecy's Faithless Advisor and the True Guardian who persevered to victory had always stirred Mubirrum's soul . . . and seemed particularly apt today, now that he thought on it. *Which will I be remembered as?* he wondered. He knew down to the marrow of his bones the part that belonged to him in that ancient tale, but then again, how many years had the True Guardian endured dishonor before he'd been justified at last?

He noted that he was the last of the high councillors to arrive. The rest of his peers had already taken their seats, while the lesser councillors arranged themselves in the lower, outer ring of the concentric council table. Scores of guards, attendants, and scribes cluttered the great room's galleries, waiting quietly for Mubirrum to take his place. He did not even have the opportunity to seat himself before the court chamberlain—Ebabbar Simtum, a hale, big-bellied noble of an old royal *sebet*—raised his scepter of office and rapped it sharply on the stone floor. "The Heavenly Monarch graciously permits her servants to attend their duties!" he said loudly.

With all the others in the chamber, Mubirrum bowed deeply. Then the chamberlain tapped the floor once again, and the assembled officials straightened and seated themselves. The monarch herself did not attend, but that wasn't out of the ordinary; by tradition even the most urgent business of the Dominion High Council was considered beneath her attention. The session began with the customary preliminaries, which Mubirrum observed with care. Court proceedings were bound up in tedious tradition that could easily consume hours, but they provided a necessary demonstration of continuity—the promise that what had come before still mattered today. But to Mubirrum's surprise, Chamberlain Ebabbar quickly concluded the ancient rites and allowed the councillors to begin the business of the day, taking his seat once he had finished his ceremonial duties.

Since the post of first councillor currently stood vacant after Sapwu Zrinan's resignation, it fell to the second councillor—Baltzu Sidr, leader of the powerful Sebet Baltzu and the court's Mercantilist faction—to conduct the business of the High Council. A male of fabulous personal wealth, Sidr made a point of wearing scandalously modern garb and even painted his dermis in intricate designs of gold flake, a common custom among the aristocratic ranks of Shimatum. He bowed once in the direction of the screened balcony representing the absent Anshar's throne, then faced the rest of the councillors. "This council is convened for one purpose today," he began. "We must decide how we will respond to the terrible news that arrived from Kahnar-Sag. I call upon the attendants to play for the council the message from Gisumi Veddab, planetary governor of Kahnar-Sag."

Mubirrum waited patiently as the attendants activated a display and played the message from the governor. The courier ship that had brought Admiral Hish Sudi her recording cube had carried dozens more messages from the various officials and prominent *sebetu* of Kahnar-Sag, none adding any significant new details to the account. No doubt every one of the councillors present had already seen at least two or three versions of the report by this point, but the governor's, coming from the highest-ranking official in Kahnar-Sag, carried the most importance. A very worried-looking Gisumi Veddab concluded by urging the High Council to take no hasty action, blaming Admiral Karsu Herum's rash and inflexible demands for the entire unfortunate episode.

"This report is five days old," Maruz Ningi observed when the governor's message concluded. Fourth councillor and leader of the Kishpuzinir technocrat faction at the court, she was a lean old female who generally gave her support to whatever faction was strongest. "The human fleet could already be on its way to Tamabuqq, correct?"

"Yes," Baltzu Sidr said in reply. "That is why we should prepare a response."

"What in all the heavens possessed Karsu Herum to issue such an inflammatory demand?" asked Ninazzu Gi, the seventh councillor. The *sebetu* of her faction held many high positions among the temples and the courts of law. "By whose authority did he presume to abrogate dozens of treaties?"

"Ask the Karsu," Baltzu Sidr said, waving a hand in disgust.

Karsu Amraq, the fifth councillor, grimaced in embarrassment. Up until a month ago he'd been a staunch supporter of the Sapwu and their Monarchist faction; now he had no other friends on the High Council. "It was not by any resolution of ours," he said. "We received a message from Karsu Herum just a few hours ago that made it clear he regarded the situation at the Thousand Worlds ward as an act of alien defiance against Tzoru requirements. Evidently he decided to employ the Shining Resolve Fleet to prevent the humans and the others from dispatching any military forces to Tamabuqq."

"Then your clan-cousin was an idiot," said Ninazzu Gi. "His rashness has virtually guaranteed that outcome now."

"Blame Tzem Ebneghirz and his foolish pronouncements for creating this situation in the first place," said Baltzu Sidr. He stood again, and raised his hands to signal a formal proposal. "The difficulty at the Thousand Worlds ward must be resolved before more misunderstandings occur. It is clear that we must suppress the revolutionaries so that we can take control of this situation. I therefore propose that we authorize action of the Magnificent Victory Army to disarm and disperse the *warumzi agu,* while we open negotiations with the diplomatic missions within the Thousand Worlds ward to bring this crisis to an end. The human powers are interested in trade, not war."

"I concur," said Maruz Ningi.

"I too concur," said Ninazzu Gi, although she scowled.

"I do *not* concur," Mubirrum said firmly.

Shocked silence fell over the Hall of Auspicious Judgment. All in attendance understood that high councillors *never* voted against a proposal once it was clear that it had the support of at least half the council factions, instead joining the consensus. In all the years Mubirrum had been a part of the Dominion High Council, he had never before voted against a majority proposal.

"This is madness," Maruz Ningi snapped. "Half the cities on Tamabuqq Prime are embroiled in daily protests, and the unrest is spreading to nearby worlds. A response is required! How do you suggest we quell the disorder if we cannot act in harmony?"

"I suggest that we do nothing at all," Mubirrum replied. "The *warumzi agu* are rightly aggrieved by those *sebetu* who have sold out our worlds for the silver of alien peddlers. It is not the place of the Hish to stand between the *warumzi agu* and the justice they seek."

Baltzu Sidr stared at him in confusion, uncertain whether to continue the now-pointless declaration of concurrence. "But your concurrence is required!" he finally managed to say. "The High Council cannot function without it!"

"Better a nonfunctional council than a council that is complicit in the Dominion's dissolution, Baltzu," said Mubirrum. "Talk all you like, go and beg mercy from the offworlders bottled up in the Ward of a Thousand Worlds. For my own part, I intend to lead the Hish and all *sebetu* loyal to the Anshar in the defense of our homeworld against alien aggression. I do not need anyone's concurrence to defend our Dominion against its enemies." Then, with great deliberation, he turned and strode out of the room, a breach of decorum that no one living had ever seen in the Anshar's Palace.

The Hall of Auspicious Judgment erupted in chaos behind him.

10

On the last morning of *Exeter*'s warp transit back to Tamabuqq, Sikander woke tired and yawning from a restless sleep. A glance at the clock display on the bulkhead confirmed his suspicions: early morning, a few minutes before the alarm was scheduled to wake him anyway. "Get up, Sikay," he told himself, sitting up and swinging his feet out of his bunk. "Time to go to work."

He yawned again, fighting off the last of his weariness. It was harder than it should have been—in his ten years of active duty aboard Aquilan warships, Sikander had never worked so hard during a transit as he had over the last five days. Warp transits traditionally served as downtime; officers and crew spent the time catching up on routine tasks, working out, studying up for their next rating examinations or promotion boards, and sleeping close to eight hours a night. But after leaving Kahnar-Sag, the Helix Squadron staff had settled in for an intense cycle of after-action analysis and operational planning. Sikander's Intel Section had spent hundreds of man-hours examining every scrap of sensor information recorded during the battle against the Shining Resolve Fleet, while at the same time plotting out dozens of possible threat assessments of what the squadron might find waiting in Tamabuqq. Naturally, Francine Reyes had challenged Sikander's work at virtually every step of the process. He actually found himself looking forward to their arrival in a Tzoru home system that might be full of warships ready for a fight, just so Reyes would have something else to think about for a time.

A neatly pressed shipboard jumpsuit hung by the closet, with a well-shined pair of boots below—Darvesh Reza's handiwork, of course. He dressed, ran a comb through his hair, and then headed to the cruiser's wardroom to find some breakfast. Crewhands hurried by him, busy with their own errands as the ship prepared for arrival in Tamabuqq.

He found Mason Barnes, Giselle Dacey, and Francine Reyes seated at one of the wardroom tables. While he rarely had much taste for Reyes's company, he could hardly avoid her table without being conspicuous about it, so he carried his plate over. "Good morning, ma'am," he said. "May I join you?"

"Please do," said Reyes warmly, and nodded at an empty seat. The deputy commodore harbored a small smile, and for once she seemed pleased to see Sikander, or at least pleased enough with the general state of affairs in the wider universe that she didn't mind his presence. She surveyed his plate—a small omelet and a couple of pieces of rye toast—with approval. "I see that you're not afraid to have a good breakfast before a fight."

"It's my strategy for settling my stomach. Better to have a little something for ballast than to let my nervousness work on an empty belly."

"I had the same idea, but it's not working for me this morning," said Giselle Dacey. She looked as tired as Sikander felt; as the squadron's operations officer and Commodore Abernathy's principal tactical action coordinator, she had been engaged in nonstop battle simulations with her team since leaving Kahnar-Sag. She'd pulled her raven-dark hair back into a simple ponytail, and her eyes—a dazzling light blue—showed small dark circles. Under normal circumstances, Giselle demonstrated nothing but complete self-possession and poise; she wore her aristocratic title and Aquilan self-assurance well. Today her breakfast sat more or less untouched in front of her, and she gripped a steaming mug of coffee as if she clung to a life preserver. "I don't even know why I'm trying to eat."

"There's no reason for anxiety," Reyes told her. "Our experience at Kahnar-Sag certainly reassured *me* that we can handle anything the Tzoru might throw at us. Our ships are a hundred years ahead of theirs, but we've got an even bigger edge in doctrine, training, and personnel. I'm sure that everybody will perform splendidly today."

"I know that we have all the advantages, ma'am," said Giselle. "But I simply have no idea whether we'll be able to maneuver a force composed of so many commanders who all have their own ideas about what we ought to be doing." The ops officer gave a helpless shrug. "There's a lot that can go wrong with our command-and-control arrangements."

"If there's anybody who can settle that mess, it's you," Mason said to her. "Me, I'm not worried about doing my job—it's the prospect of sailing into an even bigger battle than the one we just fought that scares the shit out of me. Now that I've been in one battle, I'm not looking forward to another."

Reyes raised an eyebrow. "You might have picked the wrong line of work, Mr. Barnes. Nothing polishes up an officer's résumé like seeing action. Selection boards see thousands of candidates who are perfectly competent, but actual battle experience in your service jacket can do wonders for your career. Just ask Mr. North here; he was fortunate to have had the opportunity to distinguish himself at Gadira."

"I'm afraid it didn't seem that way at the time," said Sikander, careful to keep a neutral expression on his face. While he was proud of what he'd done to at Gadira, the deputy commodore's remarks didn't sit well with him. He found himself remembering the jarring impact of Dremish K-cannon fire raking *Hector,* and being whipped against the restraints of his battle couch while damage alarms screeched in the smoke-filled bridge. "I was fortunate to have merely *survived*. Anything else that happened was incidental to that."

"Your modesty is admirable, if not strictly necessary," Reyes said to him, and raised her coffee mug in salute. "Let's hope that today we all earn the right to tell stories with a similar amount of understatement in years to come."

Good God, she means what she is saying. Sikander found that he wasn't as hungry as he'd thought, and he set down his fork with a bite of omelet still on it. No wonder the deputy commodore enjoyed such an expansive mood—she hoped for a battle, maybe even a war, and she was likely to get exactly what she wanted today. He'd assumed that Reyes's earlier belligerence stemmed from an outraged sense of Aquilan superiority or a certain contempt for less advanced civilizations, but it seemed that professional ambition and a hunger for glory contributed to her zeal. *How many other officers in the squadron feel the same way?*

He started to excuse himself, but Reyes rose before he could speak. "On that note, I think I'll be on my way," she said, and nodded at a transit clock displayed in one corner of the wardroom's main vid display. "We're an hour out, and I still have a million things to do. Ms. Dacey, Mr. Barnes, Mr. North: Good hunting today." She smoothed the front of her tunic, and left the wardroom with a confident stride.

"Well, the d-com's starting her shift," Mason observed. "I guess it's time for the rest of us to get to work."

"It seems so," Sikander agreed. He took one more bite of his breakfast, and then pushed the plate away. Reyes would be expecting the rest of the staff officers at their stations within a matter of minutes, or so he imagined. "I sincerely hope that today turns out to be much less interesting than we're all expecting it to be, but in case it isn't . . . good luck, everybody."

"You too, Sikay," said Mason.

"Likewise," Giselle added. The three staff officers exchanged nervous smiles, then headed off to their duties.

Sikander stopped by the Intel Section to make sure he had the latest version of his team's projections in hand before making his way up to his battle station. He spent the remaining minutes of the transit arranging intelligence estimates of the static defenses around the Tzoru homeworld on his console and trying not to watch the clock. *Exeter*'s sensor techs had naturally recorded the positions of all military assets during the cruiser's short visit of three weeks past; Senior Chief Lin and the rest of the team had worked hard to update target lists and threat assessments based on the most recent data. Of course, anything mobile—warships in parking orbits, ground formations, minefields, even some of the lighter facilities of Tamabuqq's orbital infrastructure—might have been moved since *Exeter* had departed. But he didn't think the Tzoru would have seen the need to begin any such efforts before news of the fleet encounter at Kahnar-Sag had reached the Anshar's court, which meant they'd only had two or three days to rearrange their defenses.

"Commodore on the flag bridge," a petty officer near the compartment's hatch announced.

"Carry on," William Abernathy said as he took his place near the tactical display. "D-Com, what's our status?"

Reyes checked her console. "All squadron stations report manned and ready, sir. Captain Howard reports that *Exeter* is secured for action and all systems are ready for arrival."

"Very well," said Abernathy. "I'll bet you twenty credits *Cagliari* misses her designated emergence point by ten million kilometers or more."

"Make it twelve million and you're on, Commodore," said Reyes.

"Done," Abernathy replied.

The countdown clock in the main screen ticked down to 0:00:00. *Exeter* cut her warp generators exactly on cue, and the displays all around Sikander flickered and updated with live data again. Nothing seemed to be nearby the cruiser, which of course was the intention; the consequences of returning to normal space at ten percent of light speed only to discover an impending collision were too horrible to contemplate. Warp bubbles also shed a tremendous amount of lethal radiation in the instant that the generators cut out, making it dangerous to end a warp transit too near inhabited planets or stations, or even other ships traveling in company. Before they'd left Kahnar-Sag, the ships of the combined squadrons had spread out over several light-minutes of space to ensure that one vessel's terminal cascade didn't damage another nearby ship in the moment of arrival in a potentially hostile system. But, as planned, no other ships appeared within a million kilometers of *Exeter* or each other, even as flashes of brilliance rippled across the displays, marking the task force's arrival.

"Well, everybody knows we're here, or they will in a few minutes," Abernathy observed. "Ms. Dacey, how did we do?"

The squadron ops officer studied her display. "Normal fleet scatter, sir. No impingements on arrival, no other traffic nearby."

"And *Cagliari*?"

"She missed her target point by eleven million kilometers, sir."

Abernathy grimaced. "It seems I owe you twenty credits, Francine. Ms. Dacey, direct the fleet to head for the assembly point and assume cruising formation." In accordance with the usual procedure for a fleet movement, Abernathy had designated an assembly point so that ships dispersed for safe transit—or scattered by tiny variations in course or timing—could resume formation before any defending force reacted to the arrival signatures. Then the commodore turned to face Sikander. "Mr. North, what's waiting for us here?"

"Nothing nearby, sir," Sikander reported. That was not unexpected, since once you traveled more than ten or fifteen light-minutes from the primary, even the most built-up star systems were lonely and desolate places. *Exeter*'s passive sensors—mostly gravitics, EM receivers, and external cams with high magnification—already scanned the inner reaches of the system, comparing new contacts with the expected positions of older ones. "Light system traffic, fairly typical for Tamabuqq. But it looks like part of the Golden Banner Fleet has moved. There's a formation of fifteen heavy ships about a million kilometers above Tamabuqq's north pole."

"I thought those ships never got under way."

"First time I've seen them anywhere outside their parking orbit, sir," Sikander confirmed.

Abernathy nodded. The Tzoru fleet was still many millions of kilometers away; at this distance, it would take an hour for simple greetings or challenges to be exchanged, let alone any more pointed interactions. "They're expecting trouble of some kind, then," said the commodore. "Anything from the Thousand Worlds ward?"

"I'm afraid we can't tell much from this distance, sir. Maybe in an hour or two we'll be able to make out details with our camera systems."

"Then we'll proceed as planned." Abernathy looked over to Mason. "Mr. Barnes, message for the embassy: Ambassador Hart, this is Commodore Abernathy. I am in command of a force of seventeen Commonwealth, Dremish, Montréalais, Californian, and Cygnan warships assembled from the picket squadrons at Kahnar-Sag. It is my intention to direct the Dominion authorities to end hostilities against the Thousand Worlds immediately. I expect to reach Tamabuqq Prime in . . . six hours. Please advise. Abernathy, out."

"Message transmitted, sir. It'll be a while before we get a reply."

"So noted. Next message, this one for the Golden Banner formation that is currently under way: To the commander of the Golden Banner Fleet, my compliments. This is Commodore William Abernathy of the Aquilan Commonwealth Navy. I am in command of the multinational task force which has just arrived in Tamabuqq. We are gravely concerned by the developments at the Thousand Worlds district in Bagal-Dindir and we intend to protect our diplomats and civilians, through military force if necessary. To avoid any unfortunate misunderstandings, I require the Golden Banner Fleet to hold its current position while this fleet proceeds to Tamabuqq Prime and takes station in high orbit. Please signal your intention to comply. Abernathy, out."

Sikander took a deep breath, but kept silent. Tzoru of high *sebetu* had a great deal of self-regard, and any officer in command of a portion of the Golden Banner Fleet would be a highborn Tzoru indeed. He or she wouldn't like being ordered around by Abernathy or any human commander. He'd warned the commodore in meetings over the last few days that dealing with high officials of the Dominion or important clan leaders might be tricky, but Abernathy didn't hold much sympathy for Tzoru sensibilities—at least, not while Aquilan diplomats and civilians were in danger. *Hard words, perhaps, but easy to understand,* he decided. *Perhaps being very clear about what we want is better than sparing some aristocrat's feelings . . . especially if they've watched the recordings of the Kahnar-Sag fight.*

"That's certainly clear," Reyes murmured, echoing Sikander's thoughts. "I guess we'll find out what they make of that in an hour or so."

Slowly the ships of the allied task force decelerated from their transit-emergence speeds, maneuvering toward the designated assembly point. Abernathy arranged his cruisers in two mixed elements, each with its own small screen of lighter units; a few extra hours of practice in Kahnar-Sag allowed him to attempt more advanced tactical commands than the simple column he'd hastily arranged to confront the Shining Resolve Fleet. This time, *Cagliari* quickly pulled away from the rest of the force, unable to match the deceleration of the more modern ships. Abernathy muttered under his breath and adjusted the formation to accommodate the old Cygnan cruiser. By the time the Tzoru response to Abernathy's message arrived, the allied squadrons had assumed something close to an efficient battle formation.

"Transmission from the Golden Banner Fleet, sir," Mason Barnes announced.

"Very good, Mr. Barnes," Abernathy replied. He set down his coffee mug and swiveled to face the nearest comm display. "Let's see it."

The screen revealed a Tzoru male in the ornate armor of a high-ranking officer. His dermis was stippled with marks of high birth. "I am Admiral Zabar Kedhrum," he said in Tzoqabu, translated by the ship's info assistant. "You are interfering in the internal affairs of the Tzoru Dominion, Commodore Abernathy. The presence of an uninvited war fleet in Tamabuqq is an intolerable affront. You will therefore depart immediately and return to Kahnar-Sag to await instructions. Any non-Tzoru warships that approach Tamabuqq Prime will be met with force."

"We seem to be at an impasse," Abernathy muttered. "What's the Golden Banner Fleet doing?"

"Holding in place for now, sir," Giselle Dacey said. "If we continue on our current course, we'll be in contact in five hours."

"Very well." The commodore glanced over to Reyes. "Tell Captain Howard to stand his people down in shifts over the next four hours. Same for the squadron staff—I want everybody rested and fed before we try to pass the Golden Banner Fleet."

Sikander remained at his station during the first shift, continuing to update and correlate the potential threats present in the Tzoru home system while the allied force continued in toward Tamabuqq Prime. For an hour or more, nothing new came up other than more warnings from Tzoru authorities and Commodore Abernathy's terse responses. Then Petty Officer Macklin buzzed him from the Intel Section in the flag office. "Mr. North? We're getting some good imagery from Bagal-Dindir, sir," said the intel specialist. "I'm sending it up to your console."

"Already?" Sikander asked. "I thought we were still out of range."

"The power of multiple platforms, sir," Macklin explained. "We're linking vid feed with other ships and using some powerful processing software to make the squadron into one big vidcam. Here you go, sir."

Sikander studied the imagery that appeared on his console. Bagal-Dindir now passed slowly through Tamabuqq Prime's nightside. From space, the Thousand Worlds ward appeared as a prominent dark splotch in the middle of the city, illuminated only by a handful of lights. "Dear God. Is there anything still standing there, or has the whole district been leveled?"

"We thought that too, sir. But if you select the infrared filters you can see that the Thousand Worlds neighborhood is pretty intact. The power's been cut off, but some of the embassies have backup generators—although they're probably blacking those out to make sure they don't provide easy targets for the *warumzi agu*."

"Ah, I see. You're right." Sikander adjusted the imagery filters, bringing more of the district into view. Now he could see makeshift barricades blocking all the streets that led to the old district, but the resolution still didn't allow him to make out individual troops on either side. "Thanks, Macklin."

He set up one of the displays in the flag bridge to show the steadily improving imagery of the Thousand Worlds ward. Then he took a short break while Senior Chief Lin relieved him at the duty intelligence officer's post, eating a quick meal and doing his best to rest while he could. He returned to the flag bridge twenty minutes early, relieved Lin, and resumed his watch. Commodore Abernathy had never left.

As the allied fleet neared Tamabuqq Prime, the squadron's comm techs managed to establish a link to the Thousand Worlds ward. "Sir, I've got contact with the embassy in Bagal-Dindir," Mason reported to the commodore. "Ambassador Hart is on the line, but we may lose the link at any time—the embassy's having a hard time transmitting through local interference on their end."

"Put him through, then," Abernathy said. He faced the comm screen by his battle couch as Norman Hart's image appeared. The ambassador seemed thinner and grayer than he'd been the last time Sikander had seen him, although it was difficult to be certain with the lines of static hissing across the screen. "Ambassador, I'm glad to see you're still there," said the commodore. "We're less than an hour from taking up position over Bagal-Dindir. What's your situation?"

"Relieved to see you, Commodore," said the ambassador after a brief transmission delay. The audio crackled noticeably as he spoke. "The *warumzi agu* have pulled back to their barricades for now—Major Dalton thinks they're waiting to see what happens when your fleet arrives. But just yesterday our troops repelled a fairly determined attack on the ward's northeast wall. The casualties were light, thank goodness."

"How much longer can you hold out?" Abernathy asked.

"Four or five weeks. It's cold, but we've got plenty of water and we can stretch out the food stores if we have to. It all depends on the *sebetu* of the court—if they commit their troops and heavy weaponry to an assault, they'll overwhelm us."

"Not while we're here, Ambassador. That I promise you."

Hart's image flickered out before reappearing. "No, I suppose not. But that brings me to something important, Commodore. You must avoid firing on Tzoru formations as much as you can without risking your fleet. Many of the high clans are sitting on the sidelines at the moment, but indiscriminate attacks could bring them in against us. If Tzoru forces offer resistance to your advance, it's vital that you only fire on Tzoru who are firing on you."

The commodore grimaced beneath his stiff mustache. "I'll do what I can. But if my ships are threatened, I'm going to have to take steps to preserve my fleet regardless of the political fallout."

"Nevertheless, I must ask you to show as much restraint

as possible," said Hart. "Our best chance to resolve this crisis is to allow the high clans of the Anshar's court time to repair their consensus and see the necessity of dealing with the *warumzi agu* themselves."

"That may expose our force to considerable risks, sir," Deputy Commodore Reyes said to Abernathy. She kept her voice quiet so that the comm panel wouldn't share her remark with the ambassador. "It's not a good idea to offer an enemy the first shot, even if your enemy's as incompetent as these Tzoru fleet commanders seem to be. In fact, passivity might invite an attack."

Abernathy's frown deepened as he weighed Reyes's advice against Hart's request. Sikander watched him carefully, considering the commodore's dilemma and the advice he'd offer if asked. Reyes made a good point that a display of hesitation might be misread as weakness. *Then again, there are times that your enemy wants you to throw the first punch . . . like that day in Greene Hall with Victor Gray.* He remembered the ugly sneer on Midshipman Gray's face—

—as the four upperclassmen swagger into the museum, grinning with anticipation for whatever sport they're planning: Victor Gray, Miles Marshall, Ada Fonseca, and Thomas Burke, native-born Aquilans from the best families. They count admirals, senators, industrialists, and high government ministers among their relations. Generations of Grays have held court over Academy rites for as long as anyone can remember; in fact, Victor's cousin Francine Reyes commanded one of the midshipmen battalions when Victor himself was a snottie, and another Gray cousin is expected in next year's class.

"You call that cleaning, Snottie?" Gray says to Sikander. He seems to be the instigator of this little gathering. After all, he's the one who sent Sikander down to dust the display cases in the collection, and he's shown many times over the last few months that he regards it as his special duty to torment the fourth-class midshipmen. "I suppose I shouldn't

expect anything better from a damned dirty Kashmiri. It's not like your people have any sense of cleanliness, is it?"

Sikander clenches his fists, but he manages to hold himself still. No one would speak like that to a North on Jaipur unless he meant to start a fight, but that's the stupid little game that Gray and others like him play with first-year midshipmen. They see if they can get someone to lose his temper or just quit to get away from it. You are not going to get the better of me, you bastard, *Sikander tells himself, and he clamps his mouth shut.*

Miles Marshall—tall, gangly, and sharp-featured—notices Barnes standing at a brace on the other side of the room. Marshall simply tugs on Gray's jacket and points; Gray glances at Barnes in irritation. "You, Snottie. Get lost," he says.

Barnes glances at Sikander and hesitates, sensing trouble. Gray glares at him. "Are you fucking stupid?" he demands. "I said, get lost! And close the door behind you."

"Sir, yes, sir!" Barnes replies. He squares his shoulders and marches out of the room, but not without one more look at Sikander.

Gray and his friends watch Barnes leave, then round on Sikander again. "I think you've got an attitude problem, North," the upperclassman says. "I think you think you're better than us, and you know what? I find it hysterical that a jumped-up piece of shit like you thinks he belongs in the Commonwealth Academy. You're taking up a slot that someone else actually deserves, *Snottie."*

Sikander fixes his eyes on a ship model across the room, looking over Gray's shoulder. He says nothing. He knows he loses if he lets the upperclassmen know they can intimidate him or get him angry.

"Didn't you understand me, Snottie? Maybe your Anglic isn't good enough." Gray looks him in the eye, then deliberately spits on the glass case. "How come that display case is dirty? Are you telling me you're too fucking stupid to know how to clean a case?" Sikander says nothing, simply

looking ahead until Victor Gray's face grows red. The upper-classman steps up and snarls into Sikander's face. "Answer me, you little turd!"

"Sir: What is the question, sir?" Sikander snaps out.

"You think that's funny?" Gray storms. "DO YOU THINK THAT'S FUNNY?"

Sikander fights to keep from laughing in Gray's face or baring his teeth in a snarl of anger. You know, I think I do, you sick sadist, *he silently tells the upperclassman. But he doesn't trust himself to* say *anything at all in that moment—*

"Sir, the Golden Banner Fleet is maneuvering!" Giselle Dacey called out.

Sikander shook his head, bringing himself back to the present. He focused his attention on the tactical display in the center of the compartment. The force of Tzoru battle-ships hovering above the planet began to accelerate, the red icons gaining thin arrow-headed vectors as they got under way.

"Where are they going?" Reyes demanded.

"They're moving to block our approach to Tamabuqq Prime, ma'am," Giselle replied.

"My apologies, Mr. Hart, but it looks like the Golden Banner Fleet intends to offer battle," Abernathy told the ambassador. "I'll do what I can to avoid engaging any other forces in the area, and call you back when the situation allows. Abernathy, out."

"They have to know we can stand off at long range and hammer them to pieces after Kahnar-Sag," said Reyes. "Don't they?"

"I'm trying not to make any assumptions about what Tzoru might or might not know," the commodore said, frowning as he studied the movements of the Golden Banner Fleet. It was a substantially larger force than the Shining Resolve squadron they'd faced in Kahnar-Sag, but there wasn't a modern Tzoru warship in sight. Giselle Dacey's Operations Section had spent much of the last five days gaming out the challenges of engaging the old Tzoru battleships. Against such large, sluggish targets the modern cruisers of the Coalition powers could stand off at ranges of fifty thousand kilometers or more and deliver punishing blows with impunity, while the Tzoru warships would have to close within ten or fifteen thousand klicks to pose a threat—a difficult proposition considering the significant maneuverability advantage Abernathy possessed.

"Sir, the Tzoru commander may believe we'll have to come to them if we want to approach the planet," Sikander said.

"He may, but then why come out to meet us?" Abernathy shifted in his command couch, eyes fixed on the master display. "Ms. Dacey, let's use a little more deceleration and keep the range open. Give me a low-speed firing pass at . . . forty thousand kilometers, Battle Formation Bravo. Make sure everyone holds their fire until I give the command."

"Aye, sir," Giselle replied. She and her ops specialists began revising the combined fleet's approach, issuing maneuvering orders to the various squadrons under Abernathy's command.

Sikander studied the tactical situation, frowning. Something was not quite right, but he couldn't put his finger on whatever troubled him. The hazy green disk of Tamabuqq Prime hovered in the center of the display; merchant ships slowly began to clear out of the way, climbing up out of orbit as the warships took up their stations. *They certainly took their time,* he noted. Perhaps the freighter captains intended to continue their lighterage transfers until the last possible moment, or held their orbits in the hope that no actual shooting would break out.

"Ask Captain Howard to set general quarters," Abernathy ordered. He reached for the battle armor stowed in his station; Sikander followed his example and suited up as the alarm sounded throughout *Exeter.*

The range narrowed as the ships of the allied force approached Tamabuqq Prime, now boosting hard with their bows pointed almost behind them to slow down and change a zero-zero orbital insertion into a pass tens of thousands of kilometers above the planet. The Tzoru line sluggishly responded, shifting course to try to cut the intercept distance. The fleets were close enough now that *Exeter*'s external cams could easily resolve the Golden Banner warships: ornately decorated hulls covered in dazzling gold leaf, elegant weapons mounts fashioned in the shape of mythical creatures, drive plates glowing in delicate curved fairings. *These are not just warships,* Sikander decided. *They're cathedrals— more works of art than machines of war. Firing on them would be an act of vandalism.*

"Now that's a sight," Abernathy murmured softly, echoing Sikander's sentiments. "Not terribly practical, but I suppose practical isn't what they wanted."

A hush fell over the flag bridge as the rest of the watchstanders waited to see whether Zabar Kedhrum or William Abernathy would open fire first; even though he'd been through two space battles now, Sikander felt the uneasy ache in his stomach growing tauter with each passing moment.

"Forty thousand kilometers, Commodore," Giselle Dacey murmured softly.

"Very well." Abernathy leaned back in his seat. One foot tapped nervously on the deck—the only sign that he felt the tension too.

"Captain Zimmer of *Prinz Oskar* is asking if he should open fire, sir," Mason Barnes reported from the comm station. "Captain Durante, too."

"Hold fire," said Abernathy. He glanced over at Francine Reyes. "Mr. Hart reminded me that there is a diplomatic element to this whole business. If Zabar feels the need to fire first when we're still out of his reach, I mean to let him."

"How much closer do you intend to cut it?" Reyes asked him.

"Not close enough to give him an even chance." Abernathy returned his attention to the display.

"EM blooms!" Giselle Dacey called. "They're firing, sir!

Concentrated volley, target *Hawkins*!" The Aquilan light cruiser led the first division of cruisers today, so naturally she'd come under fire first.

Sikander watched the tactical display adding tracers to show which ships had fired on which. At first glance, it seemed that *Hawkins* was doomed, pinned at the apex of scores of lethal trajectories . . . but appearances could be deceiving. The Tzoru gunners had to hit a 230-meter target at a distance of just under forty thousand kilometers, and the target could adjust acceleration or course to not be in her projected position when the salvo arrived. Boxing fire to create spots a target ship couldn't dodge into helped to change the odds, and with a dozen heavy ships all boxing their fire at once, the defensive challenge became daunting indeed. But with a flight time of nearly ten seconds, *Hawkins* had plenty of time to evade by a few hundred meters. She took a grazing hit that cracked an attitude-control drive plate, and watched sixty more K-shots streak by without effect.

"Well, so much for leaving the Golden Banner Fleet out of this," Abernathy said. "Ms. Dacey, pass the signal: Fire Plan Bravo. All units, open fire!"

11

Exeter's K-cannons opened up with shrill electric whines and the heavy thumps of recoil mechanisms bucking against their stops a few decks from the ship's command compartments. The cruiser was millions of times more massive than the ten-kilo projectile of the Laguna Mark III cannon, but even so *Exeter* shuddered with every broadside she hurled at the enemy fleet. At the same time, each of the other cruisers in *Exeter*'s column massed their fire against the same Tzoru battleship the flagship attacked, while the cruisers of the second column targeted the next-closest battleship.

"Here we go," Mason Barnes muttered under his breath. The comm officer's duty station stood next to Sikander's intel console; Mason's remark was meant for his ears alone.

Sikander tightened his seat restraints in response, focusing on his job. "Multiple hits on Targets Bravo-One and Bravo-Two," he reported, studying the data provided by his team. "Fluctuating power levels and acceleration. They're hurt, sir."

"Thank you, Mr. North," said Abernathy. The flag bridge bounced and rumbled with another salvo of *Exeter*'s K-cannons. As at Kahnar-Sag, the heavy and unmaneuverable Tzoru battleships proved easy targets for more modern warships. Cruisers that normally expected to fight at ranges of twenty thousand kilometers or less easily scored hits at twice that range. Long-range K-cannon fire might have been easy to dodge, but it lost no velocity or hitting power in the vacuum of space; tungsten penetrators hit just as hard at forty thousand klicks as they did at four if the target couldn't get out of the way. "Prepare to shift fire, Ms. Dacey. I'd rather cripple a lot of them fast than destroy a few outright, it might make it easier for Zabar to give up."

"Aye, sir," the ops officer said. She spoke into her comm unit and began entering new commands in her console.

"It's like shooting fish in a barrel," Barnes murmured. "God, I hope someone over there develops a sudden case of common sense and calls this whole thing off."

"People rarely react to displays of superior force with common sense," Sikander replied quietly. He found himself thinking of Alberto Reyes's Starburst of Valor in Greene Hall's dusty museum. The Kashmiris who'd pitted their outclassed warships against the Aquilan fleet in the Battle of Jaipur had known that the fight could only have one outcome, but they'd stood their ground anyway. "Not immediately, anyway. Aristocratic Tzoru are *proud,* Mason. And they're not afraid to die over a point of pride, when it comes down to it."

"You're saying that they're going to make us kill them?"

"I'm saying that they feel humiliated and threatened, so they're going to fight as long as they can before they give up. Wouldn't you do the same?" Sikander watched impact after impact raining down on the Tzoru line of battle in his vid feed. The ancient battleships charged ahead, a magnificent sight as sunlight glinted from their golden hulls and ribbons of fiery plasma streamed from their flanks. *How can they not understand that it's futile to offer battle to an enemy who can outmaneuver them and strike from outside their range?* he wondered . . . and then he realized that the Tzoru crewing the Golden Banner battleships understood it perfectly well. He was a witness to the last defiant act of a warrior ethos passing into history.

"Mr. North!" Sikander's intercom blinked for attention; the armored head and shoulders of Senior Chief Lin appeared on his private screen. "Sir, there's something funny going on with the merchant traffic nearby."

"The merchant traffic?" Sikander asked. He adjusted his console, looking for the icons that represented the noncombatant ships trying to leave the area. "It looks like they're scattering. What's the problem?"

Lin met his eyes through the screen. "A lot of them are scattering toward *us,* sir. And they're redlining their power output to get here as fast as they can."

Sikander studied his display, then he saw it too. A handful of merchant ships certainly fled in the other direction, but now that he looked carefully, he could see that the distribution was far from random; a thick cluster of fifteen mismatched Tzoru freighters and bulk carriers clung together on a course leading them *past* the allied warships, not *away* from them. *There's no good reason for those merchant captains to choose a course so close to a battle zone,* he decided. But even if they were armed in some way, none of them seemed like they'd approach within a reasonable attack range for Tzoru fire control. . . .

"Thank you, Senior Chief," he told Lin, then raised his voice to address Abernathy. "Commodore, that group of merchantmen at bearing zero-seven-zero is up to something. They're trying to skirt close to our formation without quite coming right at us."

"Warships in disguise?" Abernathy asked sharply.

"I don't think so, sir. Power and acceleration look nonmilitary from here."

"Some kind of bomb ships?" Reyes suggested. "I can't see how they'd expect to get close enough—"

"New contacts, new contacts!" Giselle Dacey shouted. "Bearing zero-seven-zero, fifteen—eighteen, no twenty-five, twenty-six, thirty-three . . . multiple new small contacts! They were hiding behind the freighters!"

"What are they?" Reyes demanded.

"Mixed group, ma'am, mostly torpedo cutters and corvettes. Range thirty to thirty-five thousand kilometers and closing fast!"

"The Golden Banner Fleet doesn't *have* any cutters or corvettes!"

"Whoever they are, they're right on our flank," Abernathy growled. "Those bastards foxed me. We're going to carry right through their engagement envelope unless we change course and get too close to that line of battleships, or break off altogether."

"Commodore, we've got half a dozen captains requesting instructions," Barnes announced from the comm console.

Abernathy hesitated for a long moment, eyes flicking from one spot to another on the tactical display. *Exeter* continued to shudder and buck, her heavy K-cannon launching new salvos at the distant battleships. "Shift fire to the new enemy group and turn us away from Tamabuqq Prime," he ordered. "All units, stand by to repel torpedo attack!"

"Aye, sir!" Dacey replied. She signaled for an immediate formation turn; *Exeter*'s deck canted and the displays reeled as the cruiser spun sharply to a new orientation. Sikander's weight tugged against his battle couch's restraints until the ship's inertial compensation caught up to the movement. The allied fleet accelerated hard, seeking to open the distance from the oncoming battleships . . . which brought them closer to the mass of light Tzoru warships attacking from the starboard flank.

The three Californian frigates—*Decatur*, *Galvin*, and *Hara*—met the Tzoru surprise attack first. Leading the screen of the starboard-side column, they happened to be the ships closest to the new threat, and they turned at once to deal with the Tzoru torpedo cutters. Their light K-cannons posed little danger to capital ships, but almost any hit from a K-cannon sufficed to cripple or destroy a small combatant, and the Californian squadron added reckless amounts of fire from their point-defense lasers. Half a dozen of the ambushing Tzoru ships staggered or burned, crippled in the first exchange of fire. But the Californians were outnumbered ten to one at close range, and the new attack ships smothered them with fire from every side. The three frigates disappeared in a furious point-blank battle of sheer survival against a dozen or so of the Tzoru cutters, while the rest of the force swept on past the screen to come to grips with the Allied cruiser column.

"There are too many of them," Reyes said to Commodore Abernathy. "They're getting through our screen!"

"Ms. Dacey, detach the trailing units in the port-side screen," Abernathy ordered. "Let's see if we can give Contre-Amiral Verger some help over on the other side of the formation." That would leave the first cruiser column short on escorts, of course, but the only threat in sight on that side of the formation was the Golden Banner battleships, and they had little ability to press an attack now that the human task force had turned away. "And Mr. North, I'd dearly like to know where these damned torpedo boats came from."

"Aye, sir!" Sikander keyed the Intel Section intercom. "Senior Chief, this new formation doesn't match anything on my database for the Golden Banner. Who are we dealing with?" *Exeter*'s deck shifted again as she threw herself into high-acceleration evasive maneuvers. Great booming discharges rocked the flag bridge as the cruiser's heavy K-cannon threw out more tungsten penetrators, now targeting the lighter Tzoru ships to starboard.

"We're working on it, sir," Lin said. Sikander suppressed the urge to tell her to hurry; she could certainly understand the tactical situation without his help. *Exeter* continued to roll and twist as her K-cannon thundered away. The range was shorter, but the smaller, more modern Montréal-built torpedo cutters were far more elusive targets than the old Golden Banner battleships. Great volleys of K-shot streaked past the attackers, scoring a meager handful of hits. Sikander made himself block out the distraction of the flagship's participation in the battle as the seconds crawled by and the specialists worked to correlate the mix of classes and identifying marks with known Tzoru fleets in the ship's database. "Okay, we've got it, Mr. North. This is the Monarch Sword Fleet from Badibira. It's under the control of the Hish clan."

"Damn," Sikander muttered. He should have figured on the Hish making a stand; after all, they'd arranged for their minor allies to help arm the *warumzi agu,* hadn't they? So far none of their ground forces seemed to be taking a direct hand in the siege of the Thousand Worlds ward, but how long would that remain true if combat continued in the space above Bagal-Dindir? Would a victory embolden the Militarists to move directly against the embassy district? Would a defeat make them desperate enough to attack for the sake of seizing hostages? "Very good, Senior Chief. Check and see if there are any major elements of the Monarch Sword we can't account for at the moment—the Hish might have another surprise waiting for us."

"Yes, sir," Lin replied. "But I can tell you right now there are a dozen or so capital ships missing. We don't see them here." She turned back to the other intelligence specialists, now busy counting and identifying warships.

Sikander looked over his console at William Abernathy. "Commodore, we have an identification on this new force," he said. "This is part of the Monarch Sword Fleet from Badibira. It's a formation under the control of the Hish clan."

"So the Tzoru managed to sneak in a whole new fleet to reinforce Tamabuqq?" Abernathy gave Sikander a sharp look. "I'm getting tired of seeing things no one has seen before on Helix Station, Mr. North. I've got half the Dominion navy here today and they're all shooting at me. Are there any other unpleasant developments I should be expecting?"

"The Monarch Sword heavy units are nowhere in sight, sir. They're some of the best and most modern capital ships the Tzoru have, so there must be a reason they're not showing themselves."

"Then I suggest you locate them at your earliest convenience, Mr. North," Reyes snapped.

Sikander chose not to dignify the barb with a response. Instead he focused his attention on the sensor picture generated by the radars, lidars, mass detectors, and other systems dotting *Exeter*'s hull. The ship's data-management systems automatically shared information with other Aquilan ships nearby, greatly expanding *Exeter*'s sensor inputs. Unfortunately, the links of different navies didn't mesh; they had no way to add the Dremish or Montréalais networks into their own. Even so, what Sikander could see alarmed him. Fire from the destroyers and frigates in the formation screen raked the oncoming wave of Tzoru torpedo cutters while heavy salvos from the Allied cruisers blew one enemy cutter after another into wreckage, but the Hish commanders pushed forward with reckless bravery, racing forward to bring their torpedoes into range.

Not your concern, Sikay, he told himself. *Exeter* had her own tactical crew and weapons officers to handle her part of the fight. His job was to provide William Abernathy with the information he needed to make good decisions. At the moment, that meant figuring out whether another dozen or twenty major warships lurked somewhere nearby, waiting to join the battle. He was not an expert sensor operator, but technical expertise wasn't needed for this job; heat radiation and mass signatures meant that ships had a very hard time hiding without the help of some kind of sensor shadow, like the group of "fleeing" merchant ships had provided for the Hish torpedo craft. *So what nearby is big enough to hide battleships?* he asked himself. The classic answers were planets, moons, careful positioning with the sun at one's back, orbital infrastructure, or even ground clutter . . .

"Torpedoes incoming!" Giselle Dacey cried in alarm. Six thousand kilometers distant, two of the Ziltu-class torpedo cutters spun to align their bow tubes on *Exeter* and launch their warp torpedoes. The small ships only carried two tubes each, but warp torpedoes carried powerful fusion-bomb warheads that posed a deadly threat to even the largest targets. Within a few kilometers of launch the missiles disappeared into their own tiny warp bubbles, evading defensive fire through the simple expedient of leaving normal space during their run. Captain Howard threw *Exeter* into a radical evasive maneuver, slamming Sikander and everyone else on board back against the restraints of their battle stations—and then the Tzoru torpedoes reappeared, twisting through terminal attack maneuvers as they plotted new interceptions for the dodging cruiser and tried to avoid her point defenses. *Exeter*'s lasers slagged two torpedoes within seconds of their reappearance; the third detonated twenty kilometers behind the cruiser, too far back to inflict any real damage. But the last Tzoru torpedo got within five kilometers before its warhead exploded.

The flash burned out half the vidcams and radar arrays on one side of the ship, and boiled off a thin layer of *Exeter*'s armored hull. The cruiser shuddered, kicked to one side by its own hull expanding into white-hot vapor . . . but the armor held, a few millimeters of its thickness seared away as it soaked up the lethal radiation of the blast. Displays around the flag bridge went dark as their sensor inputs vanished, but one by one replacement systems came back on-line.

Abernathy grimaced. "That was damned close," he observed. "I think we dodged a bullet there."

"I'm afraid *Kassel* didn't, sir," Giselle reported. That was the smaller of the two Dremish cruisers in the combined force. "She took a bad torpedo hit forward. *Burton* and *Cagliari* are also reporting serious damage from torpedo strikes."

"Very well," the commodore said. "Ms. Dacey, adjust formation acceleration as needed to make sure we don't leave the Cygnans behind. Better to stay together and maximize our defensive firepower, I think."

"Aye, sir!" The operations officer quickly relayed his orders. "Sir, the Tzoru torpedo boats are passing through our formation. Should we turn to pursue?"

"Chase 'em down, Ms. Dacey. I'm not going to let them re-form for another coordinated attack pass."

Sikander grimaced. *For adversaries with outclassed ships and little experience in fleet handling, the Tzoru are showing a lot of fight.* The presence of the Monarch Sword fleet probably had something to do with that; the Hish clan prided themselves on their martial tradition. The threat assessments his team compiled consistently ranked the Hish formations as the most competent and prepared of the Tzoru fleets. *So think like a Hish,* he told himself. *You came up with a battle plan to get your torpedo cutters in close to the attacking fleet. You don't expect torpedo attacks to wipe out Helix Squadron . . . but maybe you hope that they can cripple enough ships to slow down the formation, so that Abernathy can't avoid action against your heavy forces. So where's your main battle line?*

Tamabuqq had two moons, Zalasa and Duga. At fourteen hundred kilometers in diameter, Zalasa, the closer one—an airless, cratered rock—provided a perfect sensor shadow for hiding a fleet, but the maneuvers of the international task force had already cleared its area. Duga, the second moon, was tiny, a captured asteroid only two hundred kilometers wide that orbited significantly farther out . . . but old mining and manufacturing structures cluttered its surface. Sikander took control of one of the ship's vidcams and zoomed in for a close inspection of the old industrial structures. He scanned Duga's surface once, then scanned it again—and spotted the blunt-nosed outline and black hull of a Tzoru battleship lurking in the shadows of a kilometer-deep excavation. Now that he knew what to look for, he quickly spotted several more large warships in the old excavations. And naturally, the remaining torpedo cutters now fled in that direction. *Clever bastards,* he conceded. *Zalasa was too obvious, but the second moon provided exactly the sort of ground clutter and residual power emissions to hide warships lying on its surface. The torpedo cutters want us to chase them right into the battleships.*

"Sir, I've got the Monarch Sword capital ships," he announced, forwarding the imagery to the tactical team. "They're on the second moon, grounded in the old industrial structures."

"Right where those damned torpedo cutters want us to go," said Abernathy. "Ms. Dacey, belay the pursuit order. They've already caught us napping once today."

"Belay the pursuit, aye," Dacey acknowledged. She immediately set to work canceling out the movement orders she'd just sent. "Commodore, what are your instructions?"

"Sir, Contre-Amiral Verger wants to speak with you," Mason reported.

Abernathy's scowl deepened. Sikander suspected that he didn't want to open up the conduct of the battle to debate, but Verger was the only other officer of flag rank in the international force, even if she was only an acting rear admiral. "Very well, put her through. Ms. Dacey, original course for now."

The Montréalais admiral's image appeared in the display by Abernathy's command seat. Sabine Verger studied Abernathy, her face a mask of steel. "Commodore, may I assume you have detected the Tzoru warships on Duga?" she asked.

"You may," Abernathy replied. "We are changing course to stay out of their range."

"What are your intentions for continuing this engagement?"

The commodore studied his tactical display before answering. "We'll continue on past Tamabuqq Prime and regroup here, fifty thousand kilometers from the planet. My intention is to stand off and neutralize or drive away the defending fleets with long-range fire, now that we know where they are."

Verger remained expressionless. "I feel that I must point out that we are substantially outnumbered and we now have hostile forces on three sides of us. We are facing twice as many warships as we anticipated, and it's clear that they are well led and prepared for a fight. My instructions require me to avoid battle unless I am certain of victory. At this time I feel no such certainty."

Abernathy's foot stopped tapping. In fact, he fell completely motionless for the first time in Sikander's experience, although his jaw clenched once. "What exactly do you propose, Amiral Verger?"

"The Republic forces under my command will not reengage under these circumstances." Verger's expression finally softened infinitesimally. "We can do no more here. This is not the fight we expected, William, and if we win it will come only at enormous expense. And we cannot allow ourselves to be crippled or destroyed in Tamabuqq. Kahnar-Sag is vulnerable in our absence."

"But our people—!" Reyes protested over the commodore's shoulder.

"Must hold out until we find a better solution," Verger said firmly. She shifted her gaze back to Abernathy.

Commodore Abernathy sat in rigid silence for a long moment, then grimaced and sat back in his seat. "Break off the action," he said in disgust. "Ms. Dacey, set formation course for a warp transit to Kahnar-Sag and begin acceleration."

In Sikander's limited previous experience, space battles ended with unmistakable finality. The engagement at Tamabuqq, however, did not. The Monarch Sword's lighter vessels harried and skirmished with the trailing elements of the international force's screen as they covered the retreat of the more damaged ships. The battle squadrons waiting at Tamabuqq Prime's second moon broke out of its feeble gravity well and accelerated after the human fleet in a long, futile pursuit that went on for hours, firing long-range K-cannon salvos that accomplished little other than forcing the retreating ships to occasionally evade. There was a bad moment two hours into the retreat when the Aquilan scout cruiser *Burton* lost power to her primary drive plates due to battle damage; the Tzoru ships in pursuit made up a lot of ground before emergency repairs restored *Burton*'s acceleration and the combined squadrons were able to pull away again.

Surprisingly, the only international ships lost outright were the Californian frigate *Hara* and the old Montréalais destroyer *Albatros*. On the other hand, it looked like the Californian *Decatur* would never fight again, and several other ships—among them *Burton, Jackal, Cagliari,* and the Dremish cruiser *Kassel*—had sustained serious damage that would require weeks or months of work to fully repair. *Exeter*'s damage was fairly minor, fortunately. She'd have to make do with some damaged armor and replacement sensors on her starboard side from the torpedo blast, but she was still combat-effective.

Six hours after breaking off the action, Commodore Abernathy composed a final message for Ambassador Hart. The conversation had become increasingly one-sided after hours of steady acceleration away from Tamabuqq Prime. At a distance of six light-minutes from the planet, communications stretched out with a twelve-minute delay between statement and response, and the interference in Bagal-Dindir—some form of Militarist clan jamming, it seemed—had effectively silenced the embassy anyway. Sikander watched the commodore record his words, his iron fury barely in check.

"Mr. Hart, I regret to inform you that we cannot reach you at this time. We are withdrawing to Kahnar-Sag," Abernathy began. "We simply don't have the numbers to deal with the Monarch Sword fleet and the Golden Banner Fleet at the same time, not without making repairs and gathering reinforcements. You told me before that you thought you could hold out for another five weeks. I'll need you to do exactly that. I will return in thirty days to break the siege of the Thousand Worlds ward by whatever means are necessary. The Hish surprised us today, but I promise you, it won't happen again. So, hold on! We are coming back. Abernathy, out."

"Got it, sir," Mason said. "Transmitting now."

"Will they hear us at this range?" Abernathy asked him.

"Our transmitter's a lot more powerful than the comm gear at the embassy, sir. They'll get your message."

"That gives us three weeks in Kahnar-Sag," Deputy Commodore Reyes said to Abernathy. "What do you expect to change in that time, sir?"

"*Efficiency*," Abernathy snarled. "When we come back we're going to leave that damned *Cagliari* behind so we can maneuver at standard battle acceleration. We're going to straighten out our command arrangements so that we aren't going to have to worry about the Montréalais vetoing our operations. And we are *not* going to be surprised again. Detach *Fox* to establish an outer-system picket on Tamabuqq for now, and observe Tzoru fleet movements."

"Yes, sir. We'll need to write up some reporting instructions for her before we go."

"She's to return and report if any significant Tzoru force arrives or departs. Have her remain on station five days, then proceed to Kahnar-Sag. If we need to update her instructions, we'll send a courier ship or relieve her."

"Understood," said Reyes. "Anything else, sir?"

"Make transit as planned." Commodore William Abernathy stood and glanced once again at the tactical display, now showing the task force dispersed for acceleration to the warp-transit initiation point—fifteen warships from five different powers, limping away from the Tzoru homeworld. Then he gave a small slashing motion of his hand and turned away. "I'll be in my stateroom."

The mood on *Exeter* was greatly subdued during the warp transit back to Kahnar-Sag. For the first two days of the transit, hardly anyone spoke to anyone else; the crew moved through their normal maintenance tasks in silence. The Helix Squadron staff quietly watched and rewatched the tactical recordings of the battle, noting the key decisions and developments without offering recommendations or drawing conclusions, but Commodore Abernathy did not show his face for a full forty-eight hours. Then, on the third day of the transit, Sikander received a summons to a senior staff meeting an hour after noon in the ship's wardroom.

He took his customary place at the table as the rest of the squadron officers arrived: Giselle Dacey and Mason Barnes plus a handful of senior enlisted personnel from the squadron's operating sections, as well as *Exeter*'s Captain Howard and his XO. The glum expressions and muted conversation were hard to miss; for his own part, Sikander studied his dataslate, looking over the latest battle-damage assessments prepared by his intelligence specialists after careful replay of the available sensor data. The Tzoru fleets hadn't gotten away scot-free—Intel Section assessed one Golden Banner battleship as a total loss and three others as seriously damaged, while the Monarch Sword had lost eight torpedo cutters with at least five more damaged during their aggressive attack. Perhaps more importantly, they'd launched forty or so Montréalais-manufactured warp torpedoes during their attack, and Petty Officer Macklin believed that the Hish and the Zabar clans had badly depleted their stock of the weapons in doing so.

We can only hope, Sikander reflected. Tacticians throughout the fleets of the great powers that made up the quarrelsome Coalition of Humanity had argued for a generation or more that a massed torpedo attack by lighter combatants could easily wipe out a conventional formation of heavier warships. Helix Squadron and the rest of the international task force had inadvertently put that claim to the test and survived, more or less . . . but that didn't mean he was anxious to repeat the experiment.

"Attention on deck!"

Sikander stood, along with everyone else in the room. Commodore Abernathy and Deputy Commodore Reyes stepped into *Exeter*'s wardroom, and made their way to the head of the table. "As you were," said Abernathy, taking his seat. In unison, the assembled officers sat, turning to await his instructions.

The commodore studied the staff for a long moment before he spoke. "I want to make sure we're all clear about what happened at Tamabuqq," he began. "We allowed an inexperienced opponent employing obsolete or second-rate ships to *humiliate* us. We fled the battlefield with a hundred dead on our damaged ships; the Californians and Montréalais fared even worse than we did and lost a ship apiece. And we left thousands of our diplomats, citizens, and local allies to the mercy of the radicals and xenophobes who are currently running amok in the Tzoru Dominion. We achieved exactly nothing, except giving our adversaries in this sector reason to believe they can meet and defeat us in the systems of their choosing. Any hope we had of overawing the Tzoru military commanders and bringing the Thousand Worlds situation to an acceptable conclusion without the wholesale destruction of our enemies' ability to make war against us is now *dead*. Does anybody care to disagree?"

None of the other officers spoke. Sikander didn't even glance around to see if anyone would.

"We may be tempted at this juncture to make some excuses for what happened," Abernathy continued after the pause. "Admiral Verger chose not to further hazard her ships when the situation deteriorated. *Cagliari* slowed us down. We were confident that the Anshar's court wouldn't allow any provincial units to reinforce the Golden Banner in the defense of Tamabuqq. Ladies and gentlemen, none of those excuses matters. The only reason we lost is that we underestimated our foes—our failure, and ours alone. I do not mean to make that mistake again. When we return, we are going to systematically eliminate the ability of any Tzoru force to prevent us from breaking the siege in the Thousand Worlds district . . . and then we're going to make sure our citizens are never threatened here again."

The commodore paused again, sweeping the room with his eyes in search of disagreement or doubt. Sikander did in fact have some doubts about the long-term consequences of an effort to punish the Tzoru military and intimidate the

Dominion. Kashmiris were all too familiar with the military and economic coercion practiced by a colonial power and the resentments that treatment stirred up, even if Aquila was a more enlightened master than some of the other great powers. But this was clearly not the moment to raise those objections, and Abernathy was probably right about what would be needed to break the siege at the Thousand Worlds ward. He held his peace.

Abernathy nodded to Reyes, and the d-com leaned forward. "We are now in preparation for the return to Tamabuqq," she said. "The commodore and I have come up with the overall operational scheme, which is now being forwarded to your dataslates. We're going to give you three hours to carefully study the new plan of attack and identify the major tasks and challenges facing your sections. We will reconvene at 1600 hours for further discussion. Are there any questions?"

"Ma'am, may we share the operational scheme with our sections?" Dacey asked.

"Key personnel only, Ms. Dacey," Reyes replied. "You can show it to your senior enlisted people to find out what they're going to need more detail on, but this is not a final ops plan, and we're not soliciting approvals."

"Yes, ma'am," said Dacey.

"That is all for now," Abernathy said to the rest of the squadron officers. "You're all dismissed until 1600 hours. Mr. North, you stay a moment."

Sikander stood aside and watched the other Helix Squadron officers file out of the wardroom. He didn't like the carefully neutral look on the commodore's face, or the fact that Francine Reyes remained behind as well. *This is not good,* he decided, but he adopted a pose of polite interest and waited. Mason Barnes gave him a sympathetic glance as he passed by, and closed the hatch behind him.

"Yes, sir?" Sikander asked the commodore when the room was empty.

"Over the last month or so we've suffered unprecedented

intelligence failures," said Abernathy. "No one saw the shake-up in the Dominion government or the radicalization of the *warumzi agu* or the siege of the Thousand Worlds ward coming. We were caught flat-footed by the sudden appearance of the Shining Resolve Fleet at Kahnar-Sag . . . and while we dealt with that situation handily enough, it's unacceptable that we didn't know they might move against Magan Kahnar until they showed up in the system. And it is absolutely unacceptable that we so badly misgauged the intentions and capabilities of the Hish and their Monarch Sword Fleet. I understand that our ability to collect and correctly analyze intelligence is limited by the quality of our sources, and that events now taking place in the Tzoru Dominion fit no previous patterns we have observed here. But the fact remains that the Militarists caught us unprepared, and lives were lost as a result."

Sikander seethed inwardly, but managed to keep his emotions from showing. He felt more than a little guilty about those failures, too, but he didn't think that *any* intelligence officer could have anticipated the events of the last month given the confusing and contradictory data he had to work with. "Yes, sir," he said. "We will not be caught off-guard again."

"I think you misunderstand the commodore," Francine Reyes said. "We no longer have confidence in your ability to execute the duties of squadron intelligence officer. A change must be made."

This time Sikander could not completely check his response. "What change?" he asked sharply.

"Effective immediately, you are relieved of your position as Helix Squadron S-2," Abernathy said. "Deputy Commodore Reyes will oversee Intel Section herself. I expect you to make available to her all notes, materials, or working documents she requires to assume those responsibilities." The commodore kept his voice level, but Reyes, on the other hand, almost glowed with fierce satisfaction.

"Sir, this is outrageous!" Sikander protested. "No one

foresaw these events—not us, not the other powers, and not even our friends among the Tzoru! And with all due respect to Captain Reyes, I have been on Helix Station longer than either of you, and I've developed a deeper working knowledge of conditions in the Dominion. You will need the Intel Section at its best when you return to Tamabuqq!"

"Outrageous or not, Mr. North, I feel that I have little choice but to make the change." Abernathy's eyes flashed dangerously. "You are temporarily assigned to Admin Section to assist with their work. When we unbubble in Kahnar-Sag I expect we'll find that casualties aboard *Burton* or one of our other damaged ships make it necessary to transfer you as a replacement. I'm going to have to shuffle officers around, and you served competently in previous assignments as a department head. But that all depends on whether you add insubordination or an inability to manage your emotions to my concerns about your work with Intel Section. Do I make myself clear?"

Sikander's fists tightened at his side, but he stopped himself from arguing further. This was not the sort of decision to be reversed by pleading his case. "Yes, sir. You are clear."

"Good," Abernathy said. He nodded at the hatch. "In that case, Mr. North, you are dismissed."

12

Bagal-Dindir, Tamabuqq Prime

General Hish Mubirrum delivered terms of surrender to the Thousand Worlds ward three days after the international relief expedition retreated from Tamabuqq. The document was not structured as an outright capitulation, of course; Tzoru decorum did not allow any official recognition of conflict in the capital. Instead the demand was couched as an offer of safe conduct to Kahnar-Sag in a time of civil unrest, to be accompanied by certain apologies and concessions on the part of the diplomatic missions bottled up in Bagal-Dindir's offworlder district. But Lara Dunstan could read the meaning as plainly as if the court's Militarist faction had arranged for skywriters to spell out threats in the olive-hued clouds: End all resistance, or face an all-out assault by Tzoru soldiers.

She reread the message to make sure she hadn't missed a subtle construction or turn of phrase that might alter the meaning, and settled back to think. She was bundled up in a thick sweater over two undershirts, and she wore insulated boots lined with faux fur on her feet. The heat in Ambassador Hart's office, as in every other room in the Aquilan embassy building, had been turned down to fifteen degrees C or so, and for someone of her size, that seemed like the next best thing to a slow death by exposure. Still, it was better than the conditions in most of the private homes and businesses throughout the ward, let alone what the troops posted along the perimeter faced outside. For a week or more the temperature had hovered below freezing, virtually paralyzing besiegers and besieged alike.

"I have represented the Empire in Bagal-Dindir for ten years now, and I have never seen a more sternly worded communication from a Tzoru," said Erika Popov. She served as the Dremish ambassador to the Tzoru Dominion and was known as a woman who concealed a legendarily sour disposition beneath a matronly appearance. She studied her dataslate with distaste, absorbing the contents of the note. Ambassador Hart had invited Popov to the Commonwealth compound to discuss General Hish's terms, along with Minister Jerome Hamel of the Montréalais Republic and Honored Speaker Chau-Drak-Zeid of the Nyeiran Star Empire. The four of them comprised the leaders of the diplomatic community in Tamabuqq Prime—the three humans because their respective nations were heavily engaged in trade with the Dominion and maintained century-long diplomatic presences in the Tzoru capital, and the Nyeiran because hisher people made up forty percent of the district's defenders. "These terms are appalling!"

"Indeed," Minister Hamel added. "But what can we do? We are hardly in a position to reject them out of hand. Capitulation may not be to our liking, but it is inevitable, is it not? The terms General Hish offers now may be better than those we receive later."

"It is difficult to see how they could be worse," Speaker Chau rumbled. While the humans sat in the leather chairs of Hart's office, the Nyeiran locked hisher four stubby legs into a resting pose and stood in place. Hisher barrel-shaped torso and stiff carapace weren't made for folding into human chairs, but a Nyeiran could stand all day without tiring. "I must tell you, respected colleagues, that it is beyond my authority to submit to such terms."

Popov nodded in agreement. "I think it is safe to say that

none of us are eager to put our names on this document," she said to Chau. "And what guarantee do we have that the terms will be observed once we order our troops to lay down their arms? General Hish is asking quite a lot from us."

"My thoughts exactly," said Norman Hart. A distant explosion rumbled outside, punctuating his words. He winced and glanced at the vid displays arranged along the wall of his office; the wide windows overlooking the embassy gardens had been sandbagged and boarded up as protection against shrapnel from mortar fire. The revolutionaries had little artillery, but they'd secured a few ancient tubes from some museum and they lobbed a dozen or two rounds each day into the walled district. The bombs fell at random, but over the last couple of weeks they'd killed or wounded a hundred people within the Thousand Worlds ward, mostly noncombatants. The vid feed on one of the displays flickered through several different cameras until it steadied on a slow-moving aerial view, showing a freshly damaged building amid a cloud of dust and smoke.

"It looks like that one fell in your carriage house, Erika," Hart said to the Dremish ambassador. "I don't think anyone was hurt, but your coach may not be in such good shape."

Popov pursed her lips and sniffed. "Ignorant savages," she muttered. "If *Prinz Oskar* were here, we'd show them a thing or two about bombardments."

Hart let Popov's remark pass without reply, and turned to Lara. "Dr. Dunstan, what do you make of it?" he asked her.

Lara considered the question for a moment. Her study of Tzoru history and politics gave her a better feel for what the aristocratic *sebetu* were capable of than most other diplomats in the Aquilan compound possessed. That was why the ambassador had invited her to sit in on his meeting with his peers; she was the best analyst he had available in the current climate. "The note came directly from Hish Mubirrum, not the Dominion High Council," she observed. "That's significant. He's speaking for the Emuqq-Mamit, not the council as a whole. I would guess that the high *sebetu* are still unable to agree on what to do about the *warumzi agu* and this whole situation, so he's taking matters into his own hands."

"I didn't know that Tzoru were even capable of such independent action," said Hamel.

"Nor I," Hart agreed. He glanced back to Lara. "Can we trust General Hish and the Militarists to honor their word and provide safe conduct for our people?"

"With all due respect to Mrs. Popov, yes, I think we can. I'm not aware of any incidents of bad-faith surrender offers in past eras of clan warfare. It's just not in the Tzoru makeup to extend an offer and then go back on the deal by imprisoning or massacring the people who voluntarily give up. And, more important, the Hish forces are strong enough to intimidate or brush aside the *warumzi agu* and make them let us go." Lara shrugged. "But can we accept the loss of face associated with agreeing to the terms Hish Mubirrum requires from us?"

"I'm afraid that's actually beside the point, Lara." The Aquilan ambassador grimaced. "Of course we can't capitulate without irremediable damage to our interests throughout the Dominion. No, the real question is whether General Hish is bluffing. And, if he is, whether we can hold off the *warumzi agu* until Commodore Abernathy returns."

Lara shivered inside her sweater, thinking hard about what she'd learned about Tzoru during years of academic study and Foreign Ministry training. Tzoru, especially aristocratic Tzoru, rarely lied outright, nor did they issue threats lightly. They placed too much importance on conducting themselves honorably and avoiding unnecessary confrontations. But they also appreciated a certain amount of guile and intimidation in the conduct of hostilities. "Tzoru of high clans don't say things that aren't true, but they are very good at leaving things unsaid," she admitted. "It would save Hish Mubirrum a great deal of trouble if we just gave up and begged him to protect us from the *warumzi agu*."

"Hah!" Popov snorted. "So it would, at that."

A crackle of distant small-arms fire echoed from somewhere outside. Lara and the four ambassadors couldn't stop themselves from glancing over to the vid displays on the wall. Stationary cameras and recon drones showed a dozen different views of the troop positions and the surrounding neighborhoods of Bagal-Dindir. "Looks like another effort to gain a foothold on the north wall," Minister Hamel noted.

Good luck with that, Lara thought. That was the Nyei-ran sector, and the Thousand Worlds siege had proven the toughness and discipline of Nyeiran troops over and over.

"The *warumzi agu* are pressing harder," Speaker Chau observed.

"So it seems." Hart studied the monitors for a long moment; armored Nyeiran troopers took turns popping up over the stone battlements to snap off shots at Tzoru revolution-aries scrambling over the broad, empty boulevard ringing the old fortress walls. The attack faltered almost at once—a probe, Lara guessed, designed to harry the defenders and see if they could be lured into exposing themselves. But probe or not, the recon drone's merciless vidcam captured half a dozen fallen *warumzi agu* on the open street, Tzoru who'd just given their lives to the cause of driving off-worlders out of their Dominion. "Dr. Dunstan, what did you mean by saving General Hish trouble? I have a feeling you were driving at something there."

"We know that important *sebetu* such as the Baltzu and the Sapwu have no interest in seeing the Militarists drag them into an all-out war against the Coalition of Humanity, the Nyeirans, and anybody else doing business in the Do-minion. The Hish have held off on committing their troops to an assault on the Thousand Worlds ward so far. I think that's because they still have reason to fear the other court factions disavowing their actions, or even taking up arms against them."

"Even after the battle against Abernathy's fleet?" Popov asked. "Hish Mubirrum's star has never been higher in the Anshar's court!"

"A battle in which the Hish and their allies in the Militarist faction acted *on their own* to prevent foreign powers from interfering in the Dominion's internal troubles, Madam Ambassador," Lara replied. "Taking it upon themselves to fight that battle was audacious, even reckless, for the Hish—I don't deny that. But resisting what they perceive as foreign aggression is very different from active support of a revolutionary movement. Helping the *warumzi agu* to overrun us here may be a line even the Hish are unwilling to cross."

"You're saying that they'd rather start an interstellar war than a civil war," said Hart.

"Tzoru hate discord," Lara said. "They'd rather be united in a mistake than conflicted over what might be the right course of action."

"Are you willing to hazard twenty thousand lives on that assessment, Dr. Dunstan?" Minister Hamel asked sharply. "Let us not forget the consequences of guessing wrong today."

"For months now we've seen one unexpected development after another from the Tzoru. They've broken just about every rule we thought they had. But even so they haven't taken the relatively simple step of committing heavy forces to the task of bringing this siege to an end." Lara gave a small shrug. "There must be a reason why General Hish and his Emuqq-Mamit are unwilling to do that."

"One might wish that reason was more apparent to us," Speaker Chau observed. "Still, I find myself in agreement with Dr. Dunstan. The high *sebetu* would not wish to confer legitimacy upon the *warumzi agu* by directly supporting them. I propose that we reject Hish Mubirrum's offer, and await developments."

"I disagree," Hamel said. "We should accept the terms for the sake of sparing lives. Then, when our fleets darken the skies above the Anshar's Palace in a few months, we can reopen the negotiations under more favorable circumstances. I am confident that a Republic battle division or two will succeed where Commodore Abernathy's hodgepodge multinational force failed."

"Or an Imperial assault group," said Popov. "However, that day is at least four or five months off. News of the current crisis won't even reach home for another five weeks."

"So you support accepting the terms?" Hamel asked her.

"I did not say that," Popov replied. "We have a communication channel of sorts with Kahnar-Sag. I have received word from Kapitan zur Stern Zimmer; he advises holding out for now. I say we should reject General Hish's note."

Lara glanced at the Dremish diplomat. *What kind of channel?* she wondered. The Aquilan embassy so far had only managed intermittent correspondence with other systems, smuggled out via friendly Tzoru traders.

If Norman Hart was surprised by Popov's admission, he hid it well. He simply nodded in agreement. "That's my position as well. Commodore Abernathy is coming back in four weeks. I think we can hold out that long, and I trust him to fight through now that he knows what he's up against. Jerome, do we have your support?"

The Montréalais diplomat gave a small shrug. "I can hardly agree to the Tzoru terms by myself if the rest of you are committed to fighting on. But I hope you all are correct in your assessment of General Hish's limitations, and Commodore Abernathy's ability to mount a rescue mission."

"As do I." Hart took a heavy breath, and stood. The others followed suit, although in Speaker Chau's case *unlocked* or *unfolded* might have been a better description of the change in posture. "Very well, then. I'll draft a polite refusal and circulate it for your approval. Keep your heads down, my friends."

For days after the ambassadors' rejection of General Hish's terms, Lara expected to hear the beginning of a fatal bombardment or the shrieking roar of Tzoru air strikes at any moment. But the siege continued with little change; the Hish assault troops, their heavy artillery, and their warplanes made no move to reinforce the *warumzi agu*. She could not make herself completely forget the grim possibility that the humans and their Tzoru allies within the Ward of a Thousand Worlds might be erased at almost any time by the armies of the Militarist *sebetu*, but somehow she managed to become accustomed to the idea and carry on with her duties anyway. Unfortunately diplomacy was at a standstill, and she had no insights or advice to offer the ambassador in response to the trickle of news from outside the walls. No one in the Thousand Worlds knew what was going on at the Anshar's court or whether there were any new developments from elsewhere in the Tzoru Dominion.

Simply to give herself something to do, Lara started volunteering in the field kitchens that had been set up to distribute the ward's dwindling food stores to the civilian population trapped within the walls. The meals were meager at best—simple bread, thin broth, a ladle of stew made from the stores being expended that day. She had no special talent for food preparation, but she spoke Tzoqabu and she could follow directions. And she also discovered that she had a knack for persuading embassy kitchens, human expatriates, and local Tzoru businessmen to coordinate and ration out their use of the food supplies on hand. Fortunately most of the diplomatic missions had a good deal of human foodstuffs at the start of the siege, simply because over decades of hard-won experience in Tamabuqq the diplomats of the human polities had figured out that it was not wise to rely on Tzoru groceries when produce palatable to humans might not be not available in some seasons. Several of the larger businesses in the ward were well-stocked grocers and restaurateurs, and there was even a Tzoru commercial bakery that had happened to have a ten-week supply of flour on hand when the siege began . . . although the *sebet* that owned it had to be persuaded to contribute to the collective effort by squads of Dremish and Nyeiran soldiers.

Nearly a week after the meeting of the four ambassadors, Lara found herself working in one of the field kitchens set up near Lake Gishtil. The hilly lakeshore was the only portion of the Thousand Worlds ward unprotected by the ancient city wall, but the two-kilometer lake served as an effective moat, especially since it was partially frozen over. Many Tzoru from other districts or cities who'd been caught inside the Ward of a Thousand Worlds by the *warumzi agu* protests were housed in a temporary encampment in Gishtil Park; a good deal of Lara's volunteer work went toward feeding and sheltering hundreds of stranded Tzoru who didn't actually live in the ward. While the people housed in the camp could hardly be called comfortable, the forest covering much of the lakeshore park offered a ready source of firewood, and the *warumzi agu* artillery showed no interest in shelling tents and park shelters hidden beneath the trees—at least, not on purpose.

She had just finished helping a half-dozen Tzoru from one of the local clans to stow the field kitchen's cookware after the midday meal when Radi Sabub appeared at the entrance to the shelter. Like many other Tzoru, the scholar had been stranded in Bagal-Dindir by the *warumzi agu* unrest before he could return home. "There you are, friend Lara," he said with an expression of relief. "I have been looking all over the Ward of a Thousand Worlds for you!"

"Hello, Sabub," she said. Never an imposing figure even at the best of times, Radi looked positively gaunt after a couple of weeks of strict rationing, and the cold weather was hard on him—he'd taken to going about with a blanket draped over his thin shoulders. She'd begged him to take shelter with one of the local clans who'd opened up their homes, but Sabub had insisted that there were others more in need. He spent much of his time helping in the improvised hospital, tending to people wounded in the fighting or suffering from the difficult conditions of the siege. "What's going on? Is everything all right?"

"All right? No, I would not say that," said Sabub. "Today I think I would say that everything is . . . unexpected, disquieting, perhaps even shockingly unexpected."

Lara frowned. "What is it?"

Radi Sabub glanced around in an excellent approximation of the human gesture for *others might be listening*. "That question would be best answered if I simply showed you. Can you come with me?"

"Of course," she replied, now thoroughly puzzled. "Lead the way."

Sabub turned at once and hurried off. They left the camp by Lake Gishtil, threading their way through the winding streets in the eastern portion of the Thousand Worlds ward. It was cold and clear, with little wind; most people in the ward sheltered inside, leaving the streets unusually empty. For once, the *warumzi agu* artillery stood silent. Lara guessed that the revolutionaries had no more desire to be out and about in the chill than the people trapped inside the walls did.

They came to an old carriage maker's workshop that had been converted into a hospital ward. Heavy curtains had been tacked up over a large hole in the second floor where a shell had recently struck the building, and a spray of rubble littered the ground beneath the damaged section. Sabub picked his way through the debris without hesitation, and entered the building. Inside, Lara found scores of patients occupying low, folding beds in the futon-like design preferred by Tzoru. Several Tzoru moved around the room, tending to the sick or injured.

"This is one of our temporary clinics," Sabub told her. "Our *sebet* leaders worried that the main hospital was becoming too crowded and feared that it might be at risk in a heavy bombardment, so we have been moving many of the sick and injured to smaller facilities such as this one. I helped to set up this one yesterday."

"I see," Lara murmured. The building itself was not in great shape, but the beds were clean, few of the patients appeared to be in much pain, and the medical staff appeared calm and professional. So far it seemed the Tzoru had managed to avoid horrible spectacles such as bodies frozen in the street or wards reeking of infection and death. "That would seem to make good sense. What's the trouble?"

Radi Sabub nodded toward a hallway partitioned off by a

heavy curtain. "Many of these people are strangers here," he said. "They were swept up in the violence when the *warumzi agu* protests took over the streets and revolutionary bands attacked the businesses or homes of *sebetu* supporting human presence in Tamabuqq. The male we are about to meet is one such person. He was caught in a riot right before the *warumzi agu* surrounded the Thousand Worlds ward, and he sustained serious injuries. No one knew him, but he managed to reach the ward before he collapsed, so he was taken to the hospital."

"And then here. Who is he?"

Sabub simply held aside the curtain and allowed Lara inside the darkened hallway. In a small storeroom stood a single bed, on which lay a rather plain-looking Tzoru with a brownish-gold pattern of fine scales along the cheekbones and the back of the neck—the markings of a common craftsman or laborer. Fading bruises marked one side of his face, and a bandage still covered part of the head. The fellow sat partially propped up with one arm in a sling; he looked over at Lara as she entered. She didn't recognize him.

"Lara Dunstan, is it not?" he said. The elegant tones and stilted pronunciation of the injured male's Tzoqabu instantly marked him as a Tzoru of high clan, perhaps even an official of the Anshar's Palace, despite his common appearance. "I am pleased to see that you are well."

Lara peered more closely at the Tzoru . . . and suddenly recognized the voice, if not the face. She'd met him once, in very different circumstances, and at that time he'd proudly carried himself with the markings of his high clan. "*Sapwu Zrinan?*" she said, blinking in astonishment. "What are you doing here? Everyone thinks you retreated into religious seclusion!"

Radi Sabub clutched Lara's arm and hissed softly. "Quietly, friend Lara! No one else knows he is here right now, but there are *warumzi agu* sympathizers—and possibly Hish spies—everywhere."

"Of course," Lara said, lowering her voice. She did her best to set aside her surprise and make her mind start working again. It seemed nothing short of incredible that the former first councillor had gone unnoticed in an itinerants' sickroom in the Ward of a Thousand Worlds. But he'd disguised himself by modifying his dermal patterns, and clearly he'd been beaten around the face and head, severely enough that he'd been unconscious for days. *And court figures live and move in their own insular world,* she remembered. It wasn't like the Dominion High Council had its business covered by broadcast media, or made public appearances outside the Anshar's Palace. As part of the diplomatic community for a year she'd probably seen more of the Anshar's high advisors than the average Tzoru did in a lifetime. That left only one question, really. "Sir, why are you here?"

Zrinan gave a Tzoru shrug. "After the Emuqq-Mamit arranged my removal from the High Council, I saw the need to confer discreetly with certain offworld friends. My aides and I attempted to slip into the Thousand Worlds ward. Unfortunately we stumbled into a *warumzi agu* mob. I am afraid I remember little more than that, but Scholar Radi tells me I have been unconscious for most of the last two weeks."

"I tended him for days without recognizing him," Sabub said. "It was only this morning that he became coherent enough to tell me who he is."

"Thank you for summoning me, Sabub," said Lara. On closer inspection she could see that Sapwu Zrinan did not look anywhere near healthy; his face was gray, or at least grayer than normal, and he'd lost a shocking amount of weight. But he was alive, and obviously not quite as retired as everyone supposed. Her mind raced with the implications—too many to easily sort through.

She decided to begin with something simple. "What happened at the High Council?" she asked Zrinan. "No one in the diplomatic community knows exactly why you were replaced."

"Shimatum," Sapwu said weakly. "The agreement provoked a serious crisis within the council. The Zabar decided they preferred the position of the Emuqq-Mamit and changed their allegiance."

Lara grimaced. So the Zabar, formerly a pillar of the Manzanensi, or Monarchist, faction, had switched sides and joined the Militarists. That explained quite a lot. No one in the Commonwealth had any idea that the Shimatum agreement—the single most notable success of Aquilan diplomacy in the Tzoru Dominion in the last generation—had provoked anything more than ordinary grumbling from the more xenophobic factions in the Tzoru government, but apparently it was the straw that broke the camel's back. *So Sapwu fell, and this whole thing began to snowball out of control.*

"Do you think—?" She started to ask another question of the former minister, only to realize that in the time she'd been considering his previous answer he'd drifted off again. "Oh, damn. I think he's unconscious again."

Sabub leaned close to check him, and nodded. "He has been like this all day. I think he is improving, but he still needs better care than I can provide."

"Let's summon the doctor, then." She stood and looked around for the nearest medical professional.

Sabub put a cautioning hand on her arm. "Be careful, friend Lara. If the Hish or the *warumzi agu* find out he is here, there is no telling what might happen."

Lara thought things over. Sapwu Zrinan's presence offered the first real possibility of breaking the deadlock in the Thousand Worlds ward that she'd seen in weeks. "You're right, of course," she said to Sabub. "Stay here and look after him. I'll go get help . . . and then maybe we'll see if we can do something about finally changing this narrative."

13

CSS *Exeter*, Warp Transit

Sikander didn't even realize that he was about to be thrown until he struck the gym mat hard enough to see stars.

He shook his head and scrambled to his feet, ignoring the shock of the whole-body impact and forcing himself to re-engage before his lungs could properly signal that he'd just had the breath knocked out of him. Darvesh Reza merely frowned in disapproval, and shifted his feet slightly to ready himself for the next attack. The two Kashmiris had one of *Exeter*'s gym partitions all to themselves; it was the middle of the afternoon by ship's time, and even during warp transit Aquilan warships observed standard working hours. Almost everyone else on board the flagship had watches to stand, equipment maintenance to tend to, tactical simulations to run, or standard-issue Navy paperwork in need of attention. Sikander, on the other hand, had all the free time in the world. An hour of working out with Darvesh offered at least some way to punctuate the tedium, and physically fight back against the anger and humiliation that stewed in his belly.

"That was rash, Nawabzada," Darvesh told him. In his workout trunks, the gray-haired manservant seemed as gaunt and unassuming as a weathered fencepost, but he'd spent a lifetime studying hand-to-hand combat with almost any weapon imaginable, or none at all. He was one of the most dangerous unarmed combatants Sikander had ever met, a master of Kashmiri *bhuja-yuddha* who'd personally instructed the Norths in self-defense for two generations. "In your eagerness to attack you lost your balance. A hard throw was only one of many options at my disposal when you placed yourself in my power."

Sikander said nothing in reply. He advanced straight in, counting on his superior strength and momentum to bring him to grips with the older man. Darvesh could be as wily and slippery as a snake in a grapple, but even he couldn't discount Sikander's twenty-kilo advantage in muscle. He disguised his approach with a flurry of jabs and slaps with the striking pads on his hands, trying to lure Darvesh into standing his ground and getting caught up in a block-and-strike exchange . . . but somehow Darvesh managed to stay just out of Sikander's reach, and scored with jarring slaps of his own that slithered past Sikander's guard. Sikander shrugged off the stinging hits and pushed forward more aggressively, clutching desperately for some hold, any hold, on the lanky bodyguard's lean frame. Then Darvesh suddenly turned to offense and broke Sikander to the ground with a knee to the hip and a quick pull of Sikander's opposite shoulder. A hard slap to the back of the head as Sikander went down left Sikander's ears ringing.

Sikander bounced back up again, furious at being handled so easily. But Darvesh took several steps back and raised his hands. "I think that is enough, Nawabzada," he said. "One should practice *bhuja-yuddha* when one is in control of one's emotions, not the other way around. There is no point in continuing now."

"Defend yourself, Darvesh," Sikander snapped. "I'm not done for the day!"

"You are welcome to run at the wall a few times if you feel the need to punish yourself, sir, but I do not have to be a part of it."

"Damn it, I'm in no mood for this. I said defend yourself!"

Darvesh studied Sikander, then shook his head. "No, sir. By my account I believe I have accrued seven weeks of unused leave. If you insist on continuing, I shall simply take the afternoon off and perhaps catch up on *Each Day Rises But Once*. I confess that I am anxious to learn whether Chuni accepts Tej's proposal or that of Harbir."

Sikander held his fighting stance for a moment while Darvesh simply waited. Then he sighed and straightened up. "God knows what you see in that drivel, Darvesh, but I suppose you're right. My problems at the moment are not the sort that I can punch my way out of."

"Drivel is an ungenerous word, sir. I find that *Each Day* reminds me of home."

"Love triangles? Twins separated at birth? Mistaken identities? Amnesia striking major characters at least once a season? Honestly, Darvesh."

"The cinematography is exquisite," Darvesh replied. He gave a small shrug. "I can see that you are troubled, Sikander. I know that exercise can be a good way to work out one's frustrations. But I truly do not understand why you blame yourself."

"I don't blame myself! What I find intolerable in this situation is the fact that my friends and colleagues are in need of my help, and here I've been told that I am to do nothing about it."

"Administration is not a prominent role, but it is a necessary one. Your father would expect you to perform any duties assigned to you to the best of your ability, and take pride in doing so."

"Which occupies about an hour of my day," Sikander said with a note of disgust. It hadn't taken long for him to realize that the squadron's Admin Section needed an extra manager about as much as he needed an ingrown toenail. In four days of transit back to Kahnar-Sag he'd spent most of his time in his cabin, since Abernathy and Reyes had no need for him in their operational planning and the admin specialists didn't need him sitting around to watch them work. Perhaps that might change when they arrived in Kahnar-Sag and Helix Squadron got down to the business of juggling personnel assignments and allocating repair resources to address the losses and battle damage suffered in Tamabuqq, but Sikander doubted that he'd be given much opportunity to make a contribution even then. General administrative assignments were Navy code for *we just need a place to put you until we can get rid of you*—hospice care for once-promising careers that hadn't quite finished dying.

And, ultimately, *that* was the situation he'd been trying to punch out in his sparring session, wasn't it? Making his way as a Kashmiri officer in a service dominated by Aquilans who took it for granted that Kashmiris were janitors or mess specialists challenged him at times, but Sikander liked what he did, and in some ways he enjoyed the challenge. He was *good* at it, and he knew that in his four years at the Academy and his ten years of fleet duty since, he'd managed to change some minds about the relationship between the Commonwealth of Aquila and the Khanate of Kashmir, the jewel in its colonial crown. He felt that he still had more to do; he didn't want to end his career in the Aquilan navy, not just yet. Besides, Jaipur had plenty of Norths to look after affairs at home.

Darvesh read the direction of Sikander's thoughts with the expertise one might expect of a man who'd served the North family as a household soldier, trainer, secretary, and bodyguard for the entirety of Sikander's life. "You can appeal the circumstances of your relief to the Bureau of Personnel," he pointed out. "You very well may be vindicated."

"Or I might succeed in turning a private reprimand into a public spectacle, and embarrassing the family more than I already have," Sikander replied. He shook his head. "I always knew the day would come when it would be time for me to go home. But I intended to pick the day, Darvesh."

"Vindication may come in surprising forms, sir. If you find that your superiors are not willing to give you work of value, then perhaps you should give yourself work you can find value in."

"You sound like my father," Sikander grumbled. A tired Kashmiri platitude was not what he wanted to hear at the moment. He had no idea what sort of duties he could assign himself or whether anyone would even notice.

"That does not mean I am wrong, sir."

"No, I suppose it doesn't." Perhaps Darvesh was right about finding something to occupy his mind; anything would be better than hiding in his cabin and staring at the walls until transfer or separation orders came through. He clapped Darvesh on the shoulder. "Until tomorrow, then. I promise I will be in a better frame of mind."

After he got back to his cabin and showered off, Sikander used the squadron's info-assistant program to retrieve years of Foreign Ministry background documents, political analysis, and economic assessments on the Tzoru Dominion, and began reading. If Abernathy and Reyes felt that political intelligence had been overlooked in Helix Squadron's preparations over the last few months, then he'd use his spare time to fill himself in on what Aquila's diplomats knew about the *sebetu* that controlled the Dominion. It was normally work that a military commander would expect his diplomatic colleagues to provide for him, but at the moment, Aquila's diplomats were hardly in a position to advise Commodore Abernathy. *Someone* needed to devote some time and attention to civilian sources, so Sikander decided to appoint himself to the job. Besides, it gave him something to do.

On the last day of *Exeter*'s warp transit back to Kahnar-Sag, Sikander allowed himself a fifteen-minute coffee break in the ship's wardroom. He was tired and he had a headache after close to twenty hours of reading in two days, and caffeine was the best way to fix those problems. *It's why they pay us so well,* he told himself as he poured a mug from the freshly perked urn secured in a small station to one side of the officers' mess, and smiled. He had no idea what became of the salary he earned as an O-4 in the Commonwealth

Navy. His portion of the North family fortune amounted to tens of millions of credits, rendering his actual pay irrelevant.

Mason Barnes came in as Sikander stirred creamer into his coffee. The lieutenant took one look at Sikander, and winced in sympathy. "Haven't seen you around much in the last few days. How are you doing?"

"I've been keeping myself busy—a little extra time in the gym, and a lot of reading up on Foreign Ministry papers about the Tzoru. No one on the squadron staff's got the time for it, and political intelligence isn't really their thing anyway." Sikander shrugged. "Who knows, maybe it'll prove useful."

Mason glanced around the wardroom; the two of them had the room to themselves, but he lowered his voice anyway. "You ought to know that most of us feel you got the short end of the stick, Sikay. It wasn't right for Abernathy to let Reyes cashier you because we all underestimated the Tzoru. And it's not fair to expect you to anticipate trouble that no one else in five different squadrons or ten different embassies saw coming."

"Fair has nothing to do with it. I'm afraid she was gunning for me from the day she rotated into Helix Station." Sikander sighed. "Under Commodore Morse Reyes had to play things straight, but Abernathy's new. He wasn't going to rein her in until he had a chance to observe the staff for himself. That gave her a window in which to work, and the situation speaks for itself."

"Yeah, I guess so," said Mason. He poured himself a mug from the coffee service. "You'd think the Bureau of Personnel would watch out for things like your trouble with her cousin and try not to assign officers with that kind of history on the same duty station."

Sikander shrugged. "It wasn't anything I couldn't manage until the last few weeks." He couldn't very well expect the Personnel bureau to protect him from officers disposed to dislike him before they'd ever served alongside him. On the contrary, the Navy expected its officers to get past any old animosities or personality conflicts that might exist, regardless of who might have been at fault. But that didn't mean it always worked out that way.

"Have you told Abernathy?"

"Told him what, exactly?"

"That Reyes—no, that she's got—" The Hibernian stopped, frowned, and gave up with a shrug. Commanding officers generally didn't have much sympathy for subordinates who complained about immediate superiors being tough on them. And whatever small weight that complaint might have carried certainly wouldn't be enough to reverse a decision to relieve an officer from duty. "Okay, I see your point. Maybe you can take it to the Admiralty when you get home."

"Maybe," Sikander said. He still doubted he could convince Abernathy's superiors to reverse the commodore's decision and reinstate him, and was far from sure that it would be a good idea to try. He drained the rest of his coffee. "Speaking of which, I should let you get back to work. We might be unbubbling in another battle in a few hours, after all. My troubles with Reyes pale in comparison."

Mason gave him a thin smile. "Hang in there, Sikay. You've still got friends here. We'll make sure your side of the story comes out, one way or another."

No new enemies awaited Commodore Abernathy's task force in Kahnar-Sag. The remnants of the Shining Resolve Fleet were long gone, having been chased out of the system by the Nyeiran squadron's aggressive patrolling with a little help from Magdalena Juarez's *Vendaval* and a Montréalais corvette. In fact, they found significant reinforcements on hand—*Exeter*'s sister ship *Brigadoon,* the Californian destroyer *Franklin Bryce,* and a Montréalais light cruiser, *Gloire.* William Abernathy dispersed the damaged ships of the multinational force to the various shipyards and repair facilities of Magan Kahnar with orders to begin critical repairs immediately, and then summoned the senior officers of every ship and detachment in his force to a fleet conference hosted by the Helix Squadron staff in an auditorium aboard the sprawling space station.

Sikander was not invited.

In an effort to distract himself from the ruins of his career, he looked for more make-work in the Admin Section. The commodore's yeomen and personnel specialists had to compile casualty lists and battle reports, but coordinating the use of local repair facilities and drawing up contracts with private shipyards added quite a bit of paperwork to their normal routine. Sikander had no special training for that, but he certainly had an idea or two about how repairs ought to be prioritized between the various damaged ships and which might restore the most combat capability in the least amount of time. He spent hours each day corresponding with the chief engineers of a dozen different warships to create recommendations for Abernathy to review and approve. He also found that most of the other Helix Squadron officers seemed to be avoiding him. Whether they felt awkward about encountering him in his diminished role or feared drawing the attention of Deputy Commodore Reyes by showing too much support for him in public Sikander couldn't say, but he found that he didn't mind being ostracized for a few days. He certainly had no wish to discuss his relief from duty with his colleagues.

Three days after the fleet discussions concluded, Sikander's comm unit interrupted him in the middle of a visit to a foreign-owned Magan Kahnar shipyard that had suddenly decided to triple its quoted rate for temporary repairs to the destroyer *Jackal*. He excused himself from the manager's office, and tapped the unit to answer. "Lieutenant Commander North."

To his surprise, William Abernathy's face appeared in the tiny screen. "Mr. North, where are you right now?"

"The Francoeur Helix yards, sir. I'm trying to straighten

out the contract dispute over *Jackal*'s emergency repair work."

"Damned Canucks. Don't they know there are hundreds of their countrymen waiting for that ship to be patched up?" Abernathy shook his head. "All right, that can wait for now. I need you back on *Exeter* right away. Let Admin Section sort that out later."

"Aye, sir," Sikander replied, wondering what in the world had come up. "I'm on my way."

He left the Francoeur manager with a vague promise about coming back later and expecting a different answer, hurried back to the station's shuttle terminal, and commandeered the next orbiter to return to the flagship. Sikander couldn't imagine what sort of administrative duties required his personal attention with any serious urgency, but it marked the first time Abernathy had bothered to speak to him professionally since the retreat from Tamabuqq. Besides, when a flag officer said *right away* it was generally a good idea to proceed without delay. *Exeter* held station five thousand kilometers above Magan Kahnar, since she had no damage serious enough to warrant yard time; Sikander managed to make the trip in less than forty minutes.

At Abernathy's flag cabin, he paused for a moment to adjust his working service whites—more appropriate for a business visit ashore than the standard shipboard jumpsuit—then knocked and went on in. "You wished to see me, sir?" he asked.

"Ah, there you are, Mr. North." Abernathy, *Exeter*'s Captain Howard, Mason Barnes, and Senior Chief Lin sat around the small conference table in the commodore's office, studying vid footage of the Thousand Worlds ward. It looked much the same as the last time Sikander had seen it just before the retreating multinational fleet had activated their warp generators in Tamabuqq, although he noted a fresh dusting of snow on the rooftops. "Have a seat."

"Thank you, sir." Sikander joined the others at the table, glancing at the screen—aerial footage from a drone, or so he guessed. "That must be new. There wasn't any snow when we left."

"You're correct, Mr. North," Abernathy said. "Mr. Barnes?"

"We received a comm package from Bagal-Dindir this morning," Mason told Sikander. "A Qushabba-clan freighter brought us new message traffic from our embassy. It appears the Dremish managed to keep a channel open through a friendly noble clan. They had to save it for something important—once you send off your only courier you can't very well send any more messages. These were dispatched five days after we left Tamabuqq."

"I see," said Sikander. "What's important enough to use up the Dremish communication channel?"

"The siege continues, as you can see," said Abernathy. "But there's an unexpected development on the political front. Senior Chief Lin tells me that you've got more experience with Tzoru politics than anybody on her team and that you've spent the last week reading up even more. Watch this, and tell me what you think." He pointed a remote at the display and pulled up a new vid.

Ambassador Norman Hart and Lara Dunstan sat at the table in Hart's office. The room looked oddly dim; Sikander realized that the windows were boarded over, and both Hart and Lara wore warm coats as they recorded their message. "Hello, Commodore Abernathy," Hart began. "I'm recording this message on the sixteenth. I understand it should reach you by the twenty-fourth, so keep in mind this news is at least a week old by the time you watch this video. We're still holding out and we expect that we can do so until the tenth of next month—the thirty days you requested in your parting message—but supplies are running short, and I can't promise much more. You know all that already, so let me get to the point of this communication: First Councillor Sapwu Zrinan is here in the Thousand Worlds ward. He was on his way to meet with us before the siege began, but was caught up in local riots and seriously injured. No one recognized him until he regained consciousness. Dr. Dunstan?"

Lara leaned toward the camera. "Councillor Sapwu has provided quite a few insights about the maneuverings at the Anshar's court over the last few months," she said. "Essentially, the Monarchists lost power because one of their major clans, the Zabar, defected to the Militarist faction. The Militarists are sympathetic to the *warumzi agu,* so they let the leader of the movement—a jailed philosopher by the name of Tzem Ebneghirz—stir up his followers with a series of provocative missives from prison. Naturally *warumzi* agitation causes all kinds of trouble for clans in the Mercantilist faction like the Baltzu, who are deeply engaged in trade with the human powers."

"To put it another way, the Hish undermined the Sapwu by turning the Zabar, then set the *warumzi agu* loose on the Baltzu, their real target," said Hart. "Sapwu Zrinan believes that the Hish are hoping that the *warumzi agu* manage to make such a mess—or provoke enough of an overreaction from either the Baltzu or us—that the Anshar will have no choice but to turn to the Militarists to restore order. This is all about bringing a military dictatorship into power under the pretext of suppressing the revolutionaries or protecting Tzoru territorial integrity if we move directly against the *warumzi agu.*"

Sikander grimaced as the scope of the situation became clearer. The Militarist move was quite clever in its way; the Hish stood an excellent chance of securing leadership of the High Council while rolling back the foreign positions in the Dominion and seriously damaging the influence of human-friendly clans such as the Baltzu. It struck Sikander as a very uncharacteristic gamble for the conservative Tzoru clans . . . but maybe the Commonwealth and the Dremish and the Montréalais had all managed to push the Militarists into a corner by taking advantage of the Dominion while it was weak. *We made this their least-bad option,* he realized.

He returned his full attention to the vid; Lara spoke again. "While those are both poor outcomes for us and the other Coalition powers here in the Dominion, it's important to remember that the Militarists represent only one faction. They are currently ascendant at the Anshar's court since the Mercantilists are compromised by their relations with foreign powers and the Monarchists no longer hold the moderating position they did before, but ultimately the major Tzoru clans do *not* want to fight one another. This is a contest of influence and proxies. If we can help the other noble *sebetu* to align against the Militarists, they'll have to back down."

Ambassador Hart nodded as Lara spoke. "Given that, we think the Sapwu and the other Monarchist clans could be the key to resolving this crisis," he continued. "Sapwu Zrinan is not necessarily our friend, but he doesn't want to see the Militarists under General Hish seize control of the Dominion High Council and he knows that the Dominion will suffer terribly if the Militarists provoke an open-ended war against all the great powers. He believes that he can persuade the leaders of all the other major factions in the Anshar's court to unite against the Militarists and force them out of power, at which point loyal troops can put an end to the *warumzi agu* uprising and restore some semblance of order. The difficulty, of course, is that Sapwu Zrinan is here in the Thousand Worlds ward when he is currently believed to be in religious seclusion."

"If the Hish become aware of his presence, we believe they'll have no choice but to move against us," said Lara. "They might even claim that Sapwu Zrinan is under duress and that nothing he says can be trusted—whatever it takes to make sure the first councillor doesn't have the chance to align the rest of the high clans against them before they force the confrontation they're after."

"So far, we have kept Sapwu Zrinan incommunicado," Ambassador Hart concluded. "He's still recovering from his injuries, but as you can imagine we're hesitant to let him reveal his presence by contacting the other clans if that might bring down the major attack we fear." The white-haired diplomat gave a helpless shrug, and gazed directly into the vidcam. "I wish I knew what course of action to advise, Commodore. It's my hope that this report provides you something you can use to break this impasse without escalating the conflict any more. Can we allow Sapwu Zrinan to reach out to the other clans? Or is it more militarily advantageous to maintain the status quo until you return?

"Major Dalton tells me that you can dispatch a light ship to make a quick transit to Tamabuqq and transmit your reply within four or five days of your receipt of this message without exposing that ship to excessive risk. So, we will await your answer. Hart, out."

The cabin fell silent; the images of the ambassador and Lara Dunstan remained frozen on the screen, staring at the rest of them.

Abernathy switched the display back to an exterior view; the planet of Kahnar-Sag hovered in the screen, a thick crescent of green and orange. "So that's the news of the day, Mr. North," he said to Sikander. "Needless to say, this should be considered highly classified. I have no idea what might happen if it becomes public knowledge that Sapwu Zrinan is in a hospital bed in the Aquilan embassy. We four—and the deputy commodore—are the only people in Kahnar-Sag who know about Sapwu, and I intend to keep it that way for now."

"I understand, sir," Sikander said.

"Good. Now, Mr. North . . . what does this *mean*? And how do we use it to our advantage?"

Sikander gazed absently at the image of the nearby planet as he thought through his answer. "I think this is our best chance to avoid a general war between the Coalition of Humanity and the Tzoru Dominion," he said slowly. "As Ambassador Hart said, Sapwu Zrinan is the key to rallying the court factions against the Militarists and bringing about a realignment in our favor. We need Tzoru allies who will be perceived as acting for the good of the Dominion instead of acting to protect their lucrative trade arrangements with foreign powers. The Baltzu and other Mercantilists support us, yes, but they've used up all their moral authority in the eyes of other Tzoru. The Monarchists, on the other hand, are seen as loyal to the traditions of the Dominion. I can't overstate how helpful it would be if they signaled to the other court factions that they can disapprove of the Militarists' scaremongering and still consider themselves loyal subjects of the Anshar."

"We're at least ten days from being ready to mount a new attack on the Tzoru capital," said Captain Howard. "Which means that if we reply today to the ambassador, we'd still be ten days behind our message. That seems like a long time to leave our people in Bagal-Dindir exposed to a potential attack if the Militarists decide they don't like the new direction of events. I think we'd better tell Mr. Hart to keep Sapwu Zrinan quiet for at least another week."

"With all due respect, Captain, I think that's the wrong way to look at this," said Sikander. "Our objective is not to attack the Tzoru capital—although if that becomes necessary we should do so with all the force and determination at our command." Abernathy frowned in disapproval, but said nothing; Sikander hurried on to finish his point. "Our objective is to safeguard our people in Bagal-Dindir in the short term, and ultimately restore the Dominion to the control of factions friendly to our interests. We can do that much more easily with Sapwu Zrinan's assistance than we can without him."

"You're suggesting that we use Sapwu to liberate the Thousand Worlds ward, instead of liberating the ward so that we can use Sapwu," said Abernathy.

"Yes, sir. That is exactly what I am suggesting."

"But how?" Mason Barnes said. "If he starts rallying opposition to the Militarists from our embassy, General Hish will storm the ward within hours. Hell, he might even call it a rescue mission!"

"I can't say that I disagree, Mr. North," Senior Chief Lin said. "It's too risky."

"Risky?" Sikander allowed himself a roguish smile. The idea taking shape in his mind's eye was simply too audacious, too absolutely counter to everything they'd been thinking for the last two weeks, for him not to savor its effect on Abernathy and the others. "Not in the way you might think, Senior Chief. Not if we get Sapwu Zrinan out of the Thousand Worlds ward first."

"For the record," Commander Magdalena Juarez told Sikander six hours later, "I think this is a terrible idea. You're more likely to get yourself captured and create a whole new sea of troubles for the rest of us, especially if the Foreign Ministry finds out that we let Nawab Dayan North's son participate in this nonsense."

"The very point I attempted to raise with the nawabzada this afternoon," Darvesh Reza added. "He chose not to listen to me, Captain Juarez, but perhaps he will listen to you."

"It's my idea, so I'm rather *expected* to participate," said Sikander. "I know the countryside around the capital better than anyone who isn't currently trapped in the offworld district, and I have some friends among the Tzoru. Besides, I'm an officer without a billet at the moment. Everybody else in the squadron staff is absolutely necessary for planning the return to Tamabuqq and the occupation of Bagal-Dindir, and there are no shipboard officers to spare."

The three of them sat in the cozy confines of Magdalena's cabin aboard *Vendaval*. The captain's quarters served as the commanding officer's private office aboard any Aquilan warship, and even though *Vendaval* was only a corvette, her designers had followed the traditional design. Sikander and Darvesh had transferred over from *Exeter* an hour before, bringing with them a senior pilot, a first-class corpsman with a xeno-rating in Tzoru medicine, Petty Officer Ortiz from Sikander's former team, and a security detail of four marines under Sergeant Wall. The nine-person detachment presented the small warship with some considerable berthing headaches—*Vendaval*'s crew numbered only forty-five under normal circumstances, and the special equipment Sikander had requisitioned took up most of the shuttle bay where the extra bodies might otherwise have been billeted. But even so, Sikander was glad that Commodore Abernathy had decided to entrust his mission to *Vendaval* instead of a larger and more heavily armed warship. Magda Juarez and he had served together aboard *Hector* during the trouble at Gadira, and her heroic efforts in leading the cruiser's damage-control efforts had been just as important to their ultimate victory as anything he'd managed to do on the bridge. She'd *earned* her own command, and it pleased him to see his old shipmate and friend doing well for herself.

Another year or two and I might have a command of my own, he told himself. *Provided, of course, I manage to retrieve my career from the bonfire Francine Reyes so thoughtfully prepared for it, and don't get myself killed in the next few days.*

Magda Juarez looked unconvinced by Sikander's argument. "There's also the part of your plan in which I take my ship and my crew—forty-five men and women with four popgun-sized K-cannons—up against twenty or thirty Tzoru capital ships that are just looking for the opportunity to blow us out of space. It's my neck too, Sikay."

"That's why Abernathy sent me to you. It doesn't matter if we're outgunned because, frankly, we lose if *Vendaval* has to fire a shot. We need something fast and big enough to carry the *Aram* but not so big that the squadron will miss its firepower if we don't return in time. *Vendaval* is the only Aquilan ship in the sector that fits the bill." Sikander nodded at the mission orders on Juarez's dataslate. "It's your call, Magda. The commodore gave you the discretion to decline the mission if you deemed the risks unacceptable. But I like our chances better with you than with anybody else I can think of."

Juarez picked up the dataslate. She held it in her one good

hand; she'd lost almost half of the other during the fight to save *Hector* at Gadira, but her two remaining fingers sufficed for scrolling through the op plan. Sikander waited, watching her skim through the document. Convincing Commodore Abernathy hadn't been easy, either. But ultimately the *Vendaval* plan was the only idea he'd been able to come up with that stood a chance of heading off a Dominion-wide war.

And it just might be the kind of coup de main that could save my career, he reflected. Sikander wasn't so desperate that he felt the need to vindicate himself in either victory or death, but he didn't care for the idea of meekly accepting a career-ending reprimand without making his best effort to show his commanding officer what he could do. Since William Abernathy hadn't offered any other opportunities to make up for Intel Section's so-called failures, Sikander had decided on something more flamboyant even as he'd started to explain his idea for extracting Sapwu Zrinan from the Thousand Worlds ward to the commodore. Abernathy—or more likely Reyes—might have seen Sikander as a convenient scapegoat for the embarrassing retreat at Tamabuqq, but the commodore had an appreciation for bold gestures. When Sikander had insisted that he wanted to personally lead the mission to make amends for earlier setbacks, Abernathy couldn't resist.

"All right," Magda finally said, setting down the dataslate. "I agree that the risk to my command is not unreasonable. But I really do worry about the chances you're intending to take, Sikay. Are you sure you want to do this?"

"I wouldn't be here if I wasn't," he replied. "I worry that General Hish can't afford to let the Thousand Worlds ward surrender peacefully. If Lara is right, then he *needs* the siege to end badly, which means something like twenty thousand lives are at stake . . . including Lara's, I might add. I'm willing to risk some hard time in a Tzoru prison to prevent that outcome, if it comes down to it."

"Far be it from me to get in the way of a romantic gesture," Magda said. "All right, *Vendaval* is yours. I'll call in my command team so you can brief them, and we'll lay in a course for Tamabuqq."

14

All stations manned and ready, Captain," said *Vendaval*'s operations officer. He hardly needed to make the report—the corvette's bridge had only eight control positions, and a crewhand was seated at each one. Sikander himself had to make do with a folding jump seat at the back of the bridge compartment that offered nothing more than the ability to sit down somewhere out of the way and watch *Vendaval*'s warp-transit timer slowly count down to 0:00:00 on the main tactical display.

"Very well," Magda Juarez acknowledged. She keyed the comm panel on her battle couch to activate the ship's general-announcement circuit. "All hands, this is the captain. Make ready for system arrival."

Sikander suppressed the urge to offer any advice or commentary. Magda didn't need any insight of his to run her ship, and she had enough on her mind for the moment. *Vendaval* was coming in hot, having spent hours of additional acceleration in Kahnar-Sag to build up a transit-initiation velocity of almost twelve percent of light speed before activating her warp ring. That slashed more than a day off the warp transit between Kahnar-Sag and Tamabuqq, but it also meant that the instant *Vendaval* cut her warp bubble she'd return to the normal universe with every kilometer per second of that velocity. If Magda's navigation team missed their mark by even a tiny fraction of a percent, *Vendaval* might find herself in all kinds of trouble with very little time to do something about it.

"God, these high-speed arrivals make me nervous," Magda murmured, as if reading Sikander's thoughts. "I know the math says it's not all that much more dangerous than a ten-percent transit, but it just *feels* risky. And every Tzoru in Tamabuqq is going to see our light show when we kill the bubble."

"I'm not too proud to admit that I've been praying with great sincerity for the last few minutes," Sikander replied. Magda smiled at that; faith was something else they shared, in addition to a love of fishing and the comradeship of being a *Hector* survivor. Sikander was a New Sikh and she was a Nicosian Catholic, but Aquilan culture generally ranged from firmly secular to militantly atheist. More than a few officers in Sikander's experience regarded religious beliefs as a sign of mental deficiency.

The countdown timer in the display hit zero, and disappeared. The displays flickered for a moment, and then reset as *Vendaval*'s sensors came on-line. Sometimes the jolt between the ship's best guess at conditions outside the warp bubble and the actuality of arrival could be quite jarring, but this time the displays hardly moved at all. Sikander breathed a sigh of relief and thanked God: that was a good sign for the accuracy of *Vendaval*'s navigation.

"Clear arrival, ma'am," the sensor operator reported. "Nothing within thirty light-seconds."

"Very well," said Magda. "Depower and retract the warp ring."

"I'm reading multiple large contacts near Tamabuqq Prime, Captain," the sensor officer said. "Tzoru military profiles."

"That would be the Golden Banner and Monarch Sword fleets," Sikander said. "It looks like they're not too far from where we left them."

Magda nodded. "Then it seems we're where we wanted to be. Helm, bring us to new course three-two-five, up fifteen, maximum deceleration. We want the closest possible pass behind the third planet and we need to kill some of this velocity before we get there."

"Aye, ma'am!" the helmsman replied. "Course three-two-five up fifteen, full deceleration." The display wheeled as *Vendaval* pivoted to point her main drive plates back in the direction in which she was headed, and a subtle quiver rocked the deck plates; inertial compensators couldn't entirely hide the effect of the powerful induction drives straining to cut down the ship's tremendous velocity.

Sikander unbuckled and moved over to study the sensor readouts over the operator's shoulder. Their best plan required the Militarist forces to be committed to guarding Tamabuqq Prime instead of dispersed in system patrols. *They know they're a lot slower than human ships so they wouldn't want to be caught too far from the planet they're trying to protect,* he told himself. *They have to stay close to home, don't they?* But he still needed to confirm that for himself before making any recommendation to Magda Juarez about how to proceed.

"It looks like they've seen us, sir," the sensor operator—a rather pretty young rating with an air of cool competence—said to Sikander as he looked at her console. She pointed at the nearest concentration of Tzoru warships, a light squadron of torpedo cutters in a lunar orbit near the homeworld. "This formation just lit off their drive plates and started maneuvering."

"That's about what we expected," he said. There was never any real chance the Tzoru wouldn't notice the arrival of a warship on a line from Kahnar-Sag, and Magda had convinced him that they couldn't count on being mistaken for a Tzoru cutter. So instead of trying to make their arrival stealthy or pass themselves off as a Tzoru ship, the two of them had settled on the idea of allowing the Tzoru to see exactly what they might expect to see—a single scout ship executing a high-speed pass to collect information about the Golden Banner and Monarch Sword dispositions. The brilliant arrival burst of a high-speed transit shouted to every sensor operator in the system that *Vendaval* was here, she was alone, and she was moving fast; Sikander felt pretty confident the Tzoru commanders would draw the right conclusions from the evidence at hand.

"Any chance that patrol squadron is going to get in your way?" Juarez asked Sikander.

He studied the display a little longer, and shook his head. "I doubt it. They're going to be chasing *Vendaval,* not that they'll catch you. You might need to kick up your velocity again after we part ways, though."

"So noted. I sort of hope they try, though—I'd love to draw off some Ziltus for a few days." The captain examined her displays for a moment, tapping in a few projections. "Looks like two hours or so to deployment."

"With your permission, I'll join my team in the hangar bay and make sure we're ready to go," said Sikander. "We wouldn't want to miss our exit, after all."

Juarez chuckled. "No, that wouldn't do. Good luck, Sikay. We'll be waiting for you."

Sikander let himself out of the bridge, and headed aft through *Vendaval*'s cramped passageways. The shuttle bay was only fifty meters behind the bridge; he ducked through the heavy hatch and sealed it behind him.

The *Aram* filled the entirety of the bay, secured in hastily improvised docking clamps. A battered old Tzoru-built cargo boat designed for in-system operations, it looked very out of place in *Vendaval*'s hangar. Helix Squadron's Logistics Section had scoured Kahnar-Sag for the better part of a day to find a workboat small enough to fit inside *Vendaval*'s hangar, let alone one that was in sound operating condition. Ideally the squadron's engineers would have upgraded the drive and sensor systems and perhaps installed a little bit of armament, but there'd been no time to do anything more than test the power plant to make sure *Aram* was ready for potentially hard use and load a Standard Anglic control module so that an Aquilan crew could handle the tiny ship.

Sikander squeezed around one of the more awkwardly placed cradle struts, and climbed up the workboat's open loading ramp. Thousands of similar vessels could be found in any highly developed star system, filling the role of light transport, tug, equipment tender, and supply boat. Most were designed to support two to four crew and a dozen or so passengers for a short interplanetary hop; Sikander had spent plenty of time in equivalent human craft. He found the four *Exeter* marines busy double-checking cases of ammo and provisions stowed in the cargo bay. Darvesh Reza, dressed in camouflage fatigues, helped.

"How does it look, Mr. North?" asked Sergeant Wall.

"Clear so far," he told the marines. "We're going to deploy as we planned. Everything in order?"

"Aye, sir," Wall replied. The marines had had several days to work on *Aram* while *Vendaval* had been in transit; Sikander didn't really expect any other answer. He took ten minutes to examine his own satchel and equipment, then went forward to the cockpit to confer with Petty Officer Ortiz and Pilot First Class Andrews, another *Exeter* volunteer. Sikander was a trained small-craft pilot—it was a standard requirement for Aquilan line officers—but Andrews was the expert. She'd fly the workboat, while Ortiz routed them around any inconvenient patrols or traffic-control patterns. The three of them updated the workboat's nav systems with live sensor data from *Vendaval*'s bridge, then ran through several simulated deployments and maneuvers to make sure they were ready.

Sikander managed to so thoroughly occupy himself in the sims and preflight systems checks that the warning from Captain Juarez caught him by surprise. "Five-minute warning, Sikay," she said over his personal comm. "Your exit's coming up."

"Five minutes, aye," he replied. He checked the hangar

bay status lights. "We're all sealed up. Open the door and release the clamps whenever you're ready."

"Here we go," Pilot Andrews muttered under her breath.

"Just like the simulations," Sikander told her. "Sergeant Wall, time to strap in!"

"We're ready, sir," said the marine.

Darvesh ducked through the cockpit hatch and took the jump seat. Sikander glanced back at him; the Kashmiri gave him a small nod. Darvesh was a twenty-year veteran of the Jaipur Dragoons and more or less the equivalent of a master sergeant. He'd quietly double-checked the workboat's cargo and personnel arrangements for himself.

Andrews kept her eye on a timer in the display. "Activating deployment program in five . . . four . . . three . . . two . . . one . . . deploy!"

On the signal, *Aram*'s maneuvering plates rumbled to life and kicked the small ship sideways out of *Vendaval*'s hangar. The two vessels shared the same velocity and now proceeded on parallel courses—but just ahead of them loomed the great ocher crescent of Nekelmu, a huge titanian world smothered in thick methane fog. In almost twenty thousand years of space travel, the Tzoru had found no great use for the third planet in their home system; it was uninhabited, home only to a few automated hydrocarbon-processing plants. It also served as an excellent bit of cover to conceal the workboat's detachment from *Vendaval*. The instant the two ships passed into the planet's shadow, Andrews shoved *Aram* down into the upper reaches of the atmosphere and began decelerating at maximum power, while *Vendaval* accelerated up and away from them.

The workboat rattled and shook horribly, the high-pitched wail of tenuous atmosphere suddenly encasing the hull. Something in the outer structure broke loose with a startling *bang!* that put Sikander's heart in his throat. But their simulations proved accurate—*Aram* stood up to the punishment and fell into a slingshot half orbit just above the cloud tops. By the time the vessel shot away from Nekelmu three minutes later, Sikander and his team were thousands of kilometers away from *Vendaval* and heading in an entirely different direction at a much slower speed.

Andrews breathed a sigh of relief. "That was a little more than I bargained for. Did it work?"

"I think so," said Ortiz. He had a rapid-fire Sevillan accent even denser than Magdalena Juarez's, but was careful to stick to Standard Anglic while on duty. "No one that I can see was close enough to get a good look at us."

"We'll know soon enough," Sikander replied. "Kill the engines and coast for a bit. Let's give Captain Juarez time to draw any hostile attention in her direction." As far as any Tzoru monitoring *Vendaval*'s passage were concerned, the corvette had briefly disappeared behind the planet and continued on her way with no change . . . and with just a little luck, they wouldn't pay any attention to a very ordinary-looking system workboat beating a hasty retreat from the vicinity of the human warship.

Ninety minutes later, they warmed up *Aram*'s drive plates and made a lazy turn toward the Tzoru homeworld.

The hop from Nekelmu to Tamabuqq Prime took the better part of a day. If Sikander had been willing to use *Aram*'s full power and set a direct course, they could have made the trip in half the time, but the whole point was to quietly blend in with the local traffic. System workboats like the one they'd appropriated didn't go racing around on beeline courses at maximum power; that simply wouldn't look right, and even the most incurious Tzoru traffic dispatcher would sit up and take note. So Sikander and his team ambled along, trying hard to pass themselves off as a tired old workboat going about its perfectly routine business.

After they established their course for the homeworld, Petty Officer Ortiz went outside and mounted a powerful Aquilan vid imaging system on the boat's stubby airfoil—a bit of preparation they couldn't carry out until after they'd finished the atmospheric pass at Nekelmu. They had to wait half a day for Bagal-Dindir to rotate into view as night fell in the Tzoru capital, but they soon determined that the siege continued with little change at the Thousand Worlds ward. More buildings appeared to be damaged, but the park spaces were still crowded with refugee shelters and the surrounding streets still seemed to be barricaded. That was no small relief to Sikander; after all, their last update on the capital situation was now nine days old, and there'd been a real possibility that unexpected events might have forced the capitulation of the offworlder district.

"Everything seems to be where we left it," Sikander told Darvesh after studying the new imagery. "It looks like we're still on."

The valet and bodyguard nodded in agreement as he watched the vid feed. "I see that the cold weather persists," he observed. "I am not sure whether that is advantageous or not."

"Remember, Tzoru dislike the cold even more than we do," said Sikander. "I think it's going to work in our favor."

"Unless it's too cold for cloud cover," Darvesh warned.

A few hours before they reached Tamabuqq's orbitals, they passed by the station held by the Hish-controlled Monarch Sword Fleet. Ortiz surreptitiously turned their new vid system on the Tzoru warships, making a careful record of the ships that were present and the various degrees of battle damage they'd suffered from their earlier encounter with the multinational force. No doubt Captain Juarez and *Vendaval* had already collected plenty of the same information from their high-speed pass a couple of light-minutes out, but at a range of fifteen thousand kilometers Ortiz's vidcams could resolve imagery down to a few centimeters. None of the Tzoru ships seemed to pay any special attention to the local traffic.

"I can't believe they aren't challenging anything that comes near their capital," Petty Officer Andrews observed. "Aren't they worried about the possibility of covert ops just like this one?"

"It's the first rule of infiltration," Ortiz told her. "People—humans or Tzoru—see what they expect to see."

Sikander nodded in agreement. "The Militarist clans *know* Commodore Abernathy is out there with a fleet that might arrive at any moment. They saw *Vendaval* making a high-speed recon pass, just like they might expect a scout for a larger force to do. And they don't have any reason to suspect that we might want to do something other than add or remove a large number of people from the Bagal-Dindir situation, which our little cargo boat is clearly not about to do."

"But fly like everybody else is flying anyway," Ortiz added.

"I'll try," said Andrews. "I'm right where I ought to be in the orbital traffic lanes. But I really wish we had a Tzoru along to answer the comm circuit if someone starts asking questions."

"We didn't know if we could find the right guy in time," Sikander admitted. They would have needed a qualified skiff pilot from an absolutely reliable clan, but asking around in Kahnar-Sag for help in finding a Tzoru with those qualifications would have certainly raised questions. Fortunately Intel Section had studied the Tzoru small-craft traffic systems near Tamabuqq Prime for years, just in case they ever needed to do something along the lines of what he and his team were engaged in at this very moment. Given the volume of traffic and the inefficiency of the Dominion bureaucracy, the Tzoru systems were perfunctory at best; approaching ships simply transmitted a flight path and interacted with controllers only if something unexpected came up. If challenged, they had a good Tzoru voice-sim module and could probably pass. *Probably*, Sikander told himself, and tried not to dwell on the possibility. "Any response to our flight plan?"

"As far as I can tell they took it, sir," Andrews replied.

"We've got to queue up here"—she pointed at a high orbital path—"for one orbit, and then we're cleared to deorbit and make our approach for Ispuram."

"Good," said Sikander. He looked over the navigational displays one more time, and nodded. "Looks like we have a few hours, then. I'm going to try to get some rest before we hit atmosphere. Darvesh, you should too."

To his surprise, he actually managed to fall asleep for several hours. And, also to his surprise, *Aram*'s approach continued unchallenged. Five hours after his conversation with the pilot, Sikander rose, ate a protein bar, and made his way to the cargo deck to begin suiting up for the mission.

He donned a heavy-duty flight suit of black nanofiber tough enough to stand up to full vacuum at need. Then he strapped on light battle armor, a helmet with a tactical display, a mag pistol in a shoulder holster, a carefully loaded cargo pack, and a personal wing. Darvesh dressed beside him, adding a heavy carbine to his loadout. By the time they finished, the workboat bumped and jostled its way through Tamabuqq Prime's upper atmosphere—a much slower and more routine passage than their violent separation from *Vendaval*.

Sergeant Wall checked Sikander and Darvesh from head to toe. "You're both good to go, sir," the sergeant said. "I'm going to get out of here and crack the hatch for you. Good luck!"

"Thanks, Wall." Sikander switched on his helmet's display, and selected the nav view. The urban sprawl of Bagal-Dindir covered half the screen. The Tzoru didn't permit overflights of the capital, but he'd carefully selected a plausible destination that would allow *Aram* to pass just a few kilometers to one side of the banned airspace as it deorbited. He and Darvesh seized the handholds the marines had welded in place for their use as the sergeant retreated from the cargo deck—and then the boat's rear ramp slowly opened, filling the cargo bay with the deafening windblast. At thirty kilometers' altitude, the sky was black as pitch, and the atmosphere appeared to be a thin greenish haze over the curvature of the planet.

"Coming up on insertion point," Andrews reported in his ear. "Three . . . two . . . one . . . go, go, go!"

Sikander and Darvesh released their handholds and threw themselves out the back hatch, tucking into cannonball-like shapes. The airstream was still powerful enough to slap Sikander like the fist of a giant, knocking him almost senseless as the horizon spun and tumbled wildly. He closed his eyes to keep from getting sick, and let himself fall for the better part of a minute. The workboat continued on its way as the two Kashmiris fell away from it. In fifteen minutes or so, Andrews would drop out of the Ispuram traffic pattern and put *Aram* down in the high mountains forty kilometers north of Durzinzer, where the Aquilans would wait for Sikander's call.

When his timer indicated that he'd fallen far enough, Sikander carefully opened up his posture and began to orient himself visually. It was the middle of the night in Bagal-Dindir, and the lights of the city glowed beneath him through a layer of thin icy clouds. He arrested his tumbling spin with a few economical motions of his hands, and then deployed his personal wing. For the moment he left its engine off—as far as the Aquilan navy knew the Tzoru didn't have any ground-based sensors capable of resolving a stealthy target such as a falling body with airfoils made of a nearly EM-transparent composite—but all the same he meant to minimize their time in actual powered flight. Instead he glanced around, and spotted Darvesh plummeting groundward a few hundred meters away, likewise ready with his personal wing in place.

Sikander nosed over and gradually changed his near-vertical fall into a steep, fast glide. Despite himself, he grinned with excitement. He loved skydiving, and he simply never seemed to find the opportunity to indulge himself. Of course it would have been better in daylight with a view stretching to hundreds of kilometers, but there was something exhilarating about falling in darkness, plunging past wisps of cloud that seemed as solid as battlements until the moment he pierced them. Darvesh, on the other hand, hated the very idea of jumping out of a perfectly good flyer; Sikander knew that as much as he enjoyed this part of the mission, Darvesh was praying for it to end.

He passed through the last veil of cloud, and locked in on the Thousand Worlds ward—a blacked-out polygon in the middle of the otherwise well-lit Tzoru city. A gentle bank and a slight addition of thrust from his wing's induction motor aligned him with his goal. "Here's hoping we're right about their lack of good sky-observation systems," he murmured to himself, and nosed down again to arrow steeply toward the center of the dark patch below. Low-light goggles revealed the tangled sprawl of buildings and narrow alleyways winding through the ancient district, but he banked again to settle on the expansive gardens of the Aquilan embassy. Then, abruptly, the walls and rooftops raced past just underneath his wing. Sikander pulled up sharply and hit a powerful braking blast with his wing's drive unit—and then he hit the ground, a sudden semicontrolled drop and roll in a thin layer of cold snow.

He stood up, his legs trembling from the sheer exhilaration, and unharnessed his wing as Darvesh piloted in to a skidding, awkward landing a few meters away. "Touchdown," he signaled on *Aram*'s comm channel. Then he removed his helmet, taking a deep breath of Bagal-Dindir's icy air.

Several Aquilan marines advanced out of the shadows, Major Constanza Dalton trotting out ahead of them. "You have a talent for dramatic entrances, Mr. North," said Major Dalton. She wore a baggy white smock over her combat armor, but even in the dim light of the embassy garden Sikander could see that she looked thin and tired. "I have to say, it's nice to see a friendly face. What brings you to Bagal-Dindir?"

"I hear you've got a special guest staying with you," Sikander replied. "I thought I'd drop by and visit as long as he's here."

Dalton gave him a weary smile. "I thought that might be it. I've already sent word of your arrival to Ambassador Hart and Dr. Dunstan. This way, if you please."

Sikander and Darvesh followed the marine officer to the embassy's comm center. Cots and makeshift pallets for both humans and Tzoru crowded the building's working spaces and hallways; the embassy had been pressed into service as an emergency shelter. She showed them to a secure conference room just off the communications center, and stepped out to send for coffee. Sikander took the opportunity to shuck his backpack and weapon harness; Darvesh followed suit.

"Sikander!" Lara Dunstan hurried into the room. He had just enough time to register the fact that she too looked noticeably thinner and more tired than she'd been the last time he'd seen her before she caught him in a fierce hug. Taken aback for a moment, he raised his arms to encircle her and return her embrace. She nestled into his arms; she'd always been just the right height for him to brush his face against her golden hair when she held him close. Then to his surprise she lifted her face up to his and kissed him soundly.

"Hello, Lara," he managed when she pulled away. "What was that for?"

"I've been worried sick about you," she said. "In case you've forgotten, there was a naval battle in Tamabuqq a few weeks ago. I had no idea if *Exeter* was damaged or if you were hurt." She glared at him a moment and punched him on his shoulder. "That's for making me worry about you!"

"Thanks, and ow!" Sikander rubbed at his shoulder. "You should know I've been worried about you, too. I'm glad to see that you're all right." He realized that he meant it quite seriously. He'd done his best to occupy himself with his duties—assigned or self-imposed—ever since he'd learned about the *warumzi agu* siege of the Thousand Worlds ward, but concern for Lara had never been far from his mind. In fact, it was hard not to grin with giddy relief now that he knew that she was well and that he was with her.

"Me, too," she said. "It's good to see you, Sikander. Now what in the world are you doing here?"

"Hopefully bringing this situation to a conclusion we can all live with. But it depends on Sapwu Zrinan."

"I see that you received our message, then. I assume you have a proposal for him."

"Of sorts," said Sikander. "I'd like to discuss it with you and Ambassador Hart before we bring it to the first councillor. I've been told it's a terrible idea."

"Exactly what kind of terrible idea?" Lara asked in a skeptical tone.

Sikander allowed himself a small smile. "We're going to sneak Sapwu Zrinan out of the Thousand Worlds ward and take him home."

An hour before sunrise Sikander, Lara, and Ambassador Hart met with the ambassadors of the Empire of Dremark, the Montréalais Republic, and the Nyeiran Star Empire. Sikander knew Erika Popov and Jerome Hamel—in passing, anyway—but this was his first encounter with Honored Speaker Chau-Drak-Zeid. The Nyeirans naturally didn't participate in the same social functions that the representatives of the human powers did, and tended to keep to themselves within the diplomatic community. Sikander regarded himself as a reasonably open-minded individual and worked hard to avoid judging anyone, alien or human, by appearance alone, but Nyeirans combined some of the more unsettling features of crabs and cuttlefish in a spiky carapace. Fortunately Speaker Chau carried himherself with a serene calm and minimized hisher gestures, speaking in even tones with a surprisingly human-sounding voice. Sikander had heard from various xenologists over the years that despite their different appearance Nyeirans acted and thought quite a lot like humans did, with many of the same ambitions and drives. On a mere hour's acquaintance he couldn't say if that was true or not, but he'd already learned that the only reason the Ward of a Thousand Worlds remained unconquered was that two hundred brave and competent Nyeirans were co-operating fully in the defense of the offworld district.

"So, that's the situation," Sikander said, concluding a hasty briefing on the disposition of Abernathy's forces and the plan to retrieve the former first councillor from within the besieged district. "Our equipment allows us to bring out the first councillor and one other person. Commodore Abernathy suggests that should be Ambassador Hart—a senior diplomat may be needed in Kahnar-Sag or Latzari, and this is an Aquilan mission, after all. But he also notes that in the current crisis the Commonwealth is willing to do its utmost to look after the interests of all the powers accredited at the Anshar's court. If there are specific instructions or messages you would like to have conveyed to your forces outside Tamabuqq, we shall be happy to do so."

"I fail to see why you made provisions for only one additional traveler," Erika Popov grumbled. "It seems to me that this Tzoru skiff you have hidden nearby could carry representatives from several powers."

"That is true, but we didn't dare attempt a landing in the Thousand Worlds ward," Sikander told her. "The *warumzi agu* might not have weaponry that can threaten aircraft or ships leaving the district, but the Militarist clans do, and we simply can't be sure whether they'd be inclined to open fire on a vessel attempting to escape. We thought it safer to plan a different sort of extraction."

"I think that an overt escape attempt might also provoke direct action from the Hish or their allies," Lara added. "It'd be better if the Militarists continue to believe no one can get through the *warumzi agu* barricades."

"Let us assume that it does not matter who else accompanies Councillor Sapwu," Speaker Chau said. "I think the better question is whether allowing him to leave is to our benefit or not. Can the Monarchists restrain the Militarists?"

"It hurts nothing to try," Hart pointed out. "The goodwill of the Sapwu might be worth something even if we are forced to capitulate."

"To the Aquilans who smuggle him out to freedom, perhaps," Jerome Hamel said. "The benefit is less obvious to the rest of us."

"My dear colleagues, I am not asking whether Sapwu Zrinan should be permitted to go," Hart told the other ambassadors. "Aquila has the means available to get him away from here to someplace where he may be able to do good for us all. We intend to proceed with the operation."

"Conveniently providing you with the opportunity to escape this dismal siege as well," Popov said.

Hart's mouth tightened and he gave the Dremish ambassador a hard look. It was the first time Sikander had seen the man angry . . . but with the reserve of a trained diplomat, the ambassador held his silence just long enough for the others to appreciate the scope of the insult before responding. "I don't intend to go, Mrs. Popov," he said clearly. "I'm the head of the Aquilan mission to the Tzoru Dominion, and I'm responsible for nearly a hundred diplomatic personnel. It's impossible for me to leave while they remain in danger."

"If that is the case, then who do you think should go?" Hamel asked. "Erika? Myself? Chau?"

"I regret that the equipment needed for our escape cannot accommodate Speaker Chau's anatomy," Sikander quickly said. "I am afraid Nyeirans are simply too different from humans or Tzoru for the gear to fit. My apologies, Speaker."

"None are needed, Lieutenant Commander," Chau replied. "As it so happens, I share the same obligation to my post that Mr. Hart does. I too cannot leave without all of my people."

"Nor I," Jerome Hamel said after a moment. "But it seems wasteful to not make use of the opportunity."

"I agree," said Hart. "So I propose to send Dr. Dunstan in my place. Deputy Ambassador Yeager hasn't yet recovered from the shrapnel wounds he sustained last week, which makes her the most senior Aquilan available to travel. And I have come to greatly depend on her competence and insight. I trust her to speak for me, and I believe she can more than adequately represent your own positions too."

Erika Popov frowned and folded her arms. "If you had already decided on sending Sapwu Zrinan and Dr. Dunstan out of the Thousand Worlds ward, why consult us at all?"

"Professional courtesy, Erika," said Hart. "Like it or not, all our fates are tied together. Commodore Abernathy is coming back . . . and maybe, just maybe, Sapwu Zrinan's support is the key to resolving this crisis without a goddamned *massacre*. This is our best play, and I'm taking it. I suggest that you ride out the roll of the dice with the rest of us."

Sikander had wondered about that too, but now he perceived the danger confronting Hart. *He can't let any of the leaders of the other legations seek separate terms before Abernathy comes back. He has to convince them to stick it out for at least two more weeks.* He held his breath, waiting for the Dremish ambassador's response. If she decided that she'd rather stand down her troops and strike some kind of deal with the Hish instead of allowing Aquila to attempt to resolve matters through Sapwu Zrinan's influence, she could wreck the whole scheme. The multinational force defending the Thousand Worlds ward couldn't survive the defection of even one moderately sized contingent of troops. He glanced at Lara, and saw that she realized the danger of the moment too.

Popov scowled at Hart, then finally snorted and gave a small toss of her head. "Fine," she said. "I don't suppose anyone has spoken with Councillor Sapwu to determine whether he is willing to risk his neck in an escape attempt, or what exactly he expects from us in exchange for his assistance?"

"That's the very next item on my agenda," Hart replied in a dry tone. "I think the message will carry more weight if all four of our nations show support instead of just one. With your kind permission, I'll ask the first councillor to join us now."

15

How is it that a single human warship continues to elude all the fleets at our command?" General Hish Mubirrum asked of his oldest offspring. "Each day that passes while *Vendaval* remains at liberty to spy upon our defenses and report our movements causes more of the *sebetu* allied to us to wonder why the Hish cannot remove one minor nuisance."

Admiral Hish Sudi inclined her head, acknowledging the rebuke. "I understand this, Lord Mubirrum. But catching an enemy ship that is faster than its pursuers is extremely difficult." The two of them stood together in the observatory chamber of the sprawling Hish palace. An ancient orrery suspended from the ceiling served as a rather old-fashioned but still accurate depiction of the Tzoru home system; modern holographic projections displayed the location of naval forces, orbital facilities, and commercial traffic lanes around the gleaming metal spheres representing the planets. A conventional tactical display would have been more practical, but Mubirrum loved the craftsmanship of the thousand-year-old machine . . . and physically pacing the spaces between his system's worlds made them *real* to him, and helped him to grasp the intricacies of naval movements.

"If you need to catch someone faster than you, set a trap,"

Mubirrum said. "Let his speed carry him to you instead of chasing after him."

"We realized that from the first moment the Aquilan arrived in Tamabuqq, and began moving our swiftest forces into blocking positions ahead of *Vendaval*," said Sudi. She activated a command wand and gestured toward the orrery and its holographic enhancements; delicate golden threads appeared, marking the courses of warships. "Unfortunately the time needed to move ships into *Vendaval*'s path and force the humans to accept an engagement is measured in days, not hours. And since the Aquilan is free to maneuver in three dimensions, it requires a disproportionate number of our own lighter ships to cast the net. Our forces are just now reaching their positions."

Mubirrum examined the display, counting no less than six Tzoru vessels moving to englobe the Aquilan's projected position. "So I see. When do you expect contact?"

"Later this evening. But I must caution you that a successful interception is unlikely. *Vendaval* will almost certainly maneuver in such a way that four or five of our vessels will be left completely out of position. Whichever one is left with a chance of catching the Aquilan might get a fleeting shot or two at extreme range . . . or they might not."

"Have we no commanders competent in this sort of exercise?"

Sudi gave a small shrug. "If you define competence as the ability to defy the laws of physics, then no, my lord, we do not."

Mubirrum snorted. Not many of his younger kin or family retainers would have dared to answer his dissatisfaction in such a way. Sudi, on the other hand, respected him without fearing him. He wished more of those who looked to him for leadership could find it in themselves to follow her example. "More ships might do the trick," he said. "Center a globe of six on each of those six points, perhaps?"

"That would probably work, but it would require us to commit almost all of our light warships to the task of catching just one lightly armed enemy scout," said Sudi. "There is a very real possibility that the Aquilans are hoping to draw off our screening squadrons with these maneuvers. If *Vendaval* leads dozens of our ships away from the homeworld and then the rest of the human fleet arrives . . ."

"Disaster ensues. Very well, I can see why it would be foolish to overcommit to the pursuit. So what can we do about *Vendaval*?"

"We can keep it away from key places we don't want it to get too close to. But other than that, I expect we'll have to put up with *Vendaval* until it leaves." Sudi moved beneath the display, turning to face her parent. "It's a scout. Sooner or later it will return to Kahnar-Sag to make its report."

"At which point we'll have perhaps nine or ten days until Abernathy returns with his fleet," Mubirrum said. He didn't have Hish scouts keeping tabs on the human forces in Kahnar-Sag, but he received updates with every Tzoru merchantman or commercial courier that arrived in Tamabuqq. He'd assumed that after being defeated in their first attempt to relieve their embassies, the fractious human powers would give up on the idea of fighting their way back to the skies above Bagal-Dindir and scattering the *warumzi agu*. However, humans—as he saw every day at the Thousand Worlds ward—had an astonishing ability to ignore reality and continue in vain attempts to change the outcome of events that had already been decided.

He studied the orrery with its gleaming globes, imagining how it might look when the human fleet returned. Without looking away from the majestic display, he asked Sudi, "Speak truth, cherished offspring. Can you defeat Abernathy's force again?"

The admiral sighed. "It will be difficult," she admitted. "We have two or three times their number of major warships and we have the heavy battle line of the Golden Banner Fleet, but the human ships are much faster than ours and can attack from far outside our range. We're a feral *alliksisu* fighting an archer riding a *ziniraktu*—he will inflict a hundred wounds from a safe distance, then close to finish us when we are already beaten. If I somehow manage to bring Abernathy to close quarters our numbers and our heavier warships should prevail, but why would he be so reckless as to wander within my reach? I surprised him once by shifting the Monarch Sword Fleet to Tamabuqq and concealing it, but now he knows that it's here. The only advantage I have is that I know where he needs to go. He can't maneuver me away from Tamabuqq Prime."

Mubirrum nodded to himself. That was his understanding, too. "It's a deadlier version of your challenge in cornering *Vendaval*. What if we brought additional fleets into play and moved them into positions so that the humans would have to get close to at least one of them?"

"Are such fleets available?"

"Assume for now that they will be. I may be able to arrange reinforcements from the fleets of nearby systems."

Sudi gave a small shake of surprise; she certainly understood the politics of the High Council well enough, and she knew that most fleets close enough to reach Tamabuqq before the human force were under the control of clans not particularly friendly to the Hish. "None of those formations are as powerful as the Monarch Sword, but still, that would help," she said. "Any force we positioned to intercept Abernathy's advance on the homeworld would, of course, be at risk of being isolated and annihilated at range in turn, but at least the humans would have to peel back our defenses one layer at a time. And if our outlying forces managed to extend the fighting long enough, we might get the close-range battle that favors us."

"I will see what I can do about bringing more forces to bear, then."

"Good," said Sudi. She glanced again at the orrery and the positions of the ships. "It would be optimal if we brought those reinforcements into Tamabuqq after *Vendaval* leaves to make her report. I confess I am surprised that it has not already departed to report on its observations."

"If they already know the day on which they intend to begin their return to Tamabuqq, then *Vendaval*'s commander may have orders to remain here until the last possible moment at which he could return and update Abernathy on our dispositions. We might not be able to wait until it leaves." Mubirrum shook his head. The Aquilans had to know that the Monarch Sword and Golden Banner fleets would rearrange themselves the instant they left the system, and with nine or ten days to alter their dispositions up-to-the-minute intelligence would be sadly out of date. Then again, who could say why a human did anything?

"There is one more possibility," Sudi offered. "*Vendaval* might be a picket like the destroyer that remained behind for a few days after Abernathy retreated. It's here to observe the movements of our fleet, and report if we send a significant force away from Tamabuqq—or if a significant force arrives."

"Ah, that makes sense." Mubirrum had no intention of sending fleets anywhere else at the moment. "In that case *Vendaval* is already providing information to Abernathy by remaining on its station; he knows we have not sent any forces away from Bagal-Dindir and nothing of note has arrived. Well, do what you can to encourage it to leave without overcommitting our faster ships. I see that it is a more difficult challenge than I thought."

The admiral bowed in gratitude; Mubirrum returned the gesture, and left her to handle her fleets. She was certainly better acquainted with the considerations of starship maneuvers than he, after all. But the presence of the lone human ship troubled him. He couldn't rid himself of the uneasy feeling that the humans were up to something more underhanded than simply observing his forces, especially since the multinational task force obviously intended to return soon.

An archer on a zeniraktu, he reflected as he paced through the ornately decorated halls of the sprawling Hish palace. In the far mists of history his *sebet* had faced that threat once before, a nomadic horde ravaging the southern continent where the Hish had risen to power. The Nabbar-Ke had conquered a dozen kingdoms with armies of mounted archers, a tactical innovation the warlords of that age had found nearly impossible to counter. The steep mountains and fierce warriors of the Hish homeland had proved too daunting for even the Nabbar-Ke to swallow up—a victory, he now recalled, that signaled the beginning of the Hish rise to preeminence among the warrior *sebetu* of Tamabuqq Prime. He decided to take Sudi's metaphor as an auspicious sign, and read up on the details of how the Nabbar-Ke were eventually defeated. Perhaps it might offer some guidance in his current predicament.

When he returned to his working office, he found his young kinsman Hish Pazril waiting for him. "Yes?" Mubirrum asked. "What is it?"

"My lord, Ebabbar Simtum requests a private audience. He showed up unannounced not twenty minutes ago."

"Ebabbar is here?" Mubirrum smiled in satisfaction. He'd been expecting a visit from the court chamberlain for days now, although he'd thought that Ebabbar would make it an official call and observe all the formalities. The aristocratic male had been steeped in courtly tradition for the entirety of his life; the fact that he'd simply turned up at the Hish palace suggested that something unusual was afoot. *One standoff at least might be resolved today,* he decided. "Interesting. I will see him; ask him to join us."

"Of course, Lord Mubirrum." Pazril bowed and left; Mubirrum occupied himself by skimming over the documents that had accumulated at his desk while he conferred with Admiral Sudi. A few moments later, the tall warrior returned with a corpulent older male in tow. Ebabbar Simtum looked dull and careworn without his customary regalia; Mubirrum could have easily mistaken him for a rather worried-looking house servant instead of the chief spokesman for the Anshar. At Mubirrum's nod, Pazril withdrew from the room and left the two older Tzoru alone.

"Welcome, Simtum," Mubirrum said. "I am not accustomed to seeing you away from the Anshar's palace. What brings you here today?"

"Mubirrum, I thank you for seeing me." Ebabbar bowed stiffly. "It is my hope that you might be persuaded to return to the High Council and help us restore consensus among the Heavenly Monarch's chief servants. Urgent business of the Dominion goes unheeded because you are not present."

"Because I refuse to turn the guns of the Magnificent Victory Army against Tzoru whose love for their Dominion has left them no other choice but to take to the streets and follow the call of their conscience, you mean. I am afraid my position remains unchanged."

Ebabbar winced. "I understand that you have some sympathy for the complaints articulated by Tzem Ebneghirz and his *warumzi agu,* but it is unprecedented for any one *sebet* to put a stop to the government's workings by withholding their support for the consensus. Revolution and war threaten the Dominion. I beg you, consider the greater good, and help us to meet these dire challenges."

Despite himself, Mubirrum wavered. He was Tzoru, and an appeal to the greater good of the Dominion had the power to move him deeply. The sheer earnestness of Ebabbar Simtum—his dermal patterns bare of paint and unadorned, his robes plain, his round face gray and weary—demanded a better answer than Mubirrum had to give him. But he reminded himself of the stakes, and steeled his resolve. "No, Chamberlain. I cannot agree. The Dominion High Council is broken beyond repair. Different leadership is called for in these troubled times."

"Different leadership?" Ebabbar stared at Mubirrum, struggling to understand what he suggested. "Do you speak against the Heavenly Monarch? That is treason!"

"I serve the Anshar loyally, just as I have served her every day of my life. I shall of course do whatever she commands me to do. But I can no longer allow the cowardice and venality of the council's corrupt elements to sway me from the clear course of my duty to our monarch. If I must stand aside to deprive less honorable *sebetu* of the support they need to complete our destruction, then so be it."

"Our destruction cannot be averted unless we empower the council to act."

"No, it cannot be averted if we do not empower *someone* to act," Mubirrum replied.

Ebabbar frowned, and gazed at Mubirrum through narrowed eyes. "And that someone should be you."

Mubirrum shrugged. "I can think of some others who might serve as well as me. But yes, that is what I meant."

"What is it you want? To be appointed first councillor? If that is the price of your cooperation, Mubirrum, then you shall have it." In theory the chamberlain held no such power, of course, but Ebabbar Simtum stood at the head of the palace's ancient bureaucracy and could bring great influence to bear in such matters. The other clans on the council might very well decide that submitting to Hish leadership represented a necessary evil to preserve their own positions.

"Perhaps I have not been entirely clear," said Mubirrum. "I will consent to serve, but not as part of a council riddled with corruption and incompetence. If the Heavenly Monarch has need of my services, she may appoint me as Sharur-Tal and bestow upon me the powers I require to save her Dominion."

"Sharur-Tal? You must be mad!" Ebabbar literally gaped in astonishment. "There has been no Sharur-Tal in five thousand years. Why, the very concept is a throwback to the time of clan wars and never-ending vendettas."

"A time of great disorder, in other words. Tell me, Simtum, what are we living in if not another such time?"

"There may be some truth in that," the chamberlain admitted. He fell silent, considering the consequences of Mubirrum's bold proposal. After a long moment, he slowly shook his head and said, "Still, what you ask is impossible. The other *sebetu* of the Dominion High Council will never agree to subject themselves to autocracy."

"Then I suggest that you do not put the matter to their vote. If I am not mistaken, the Anshar retains the power to appoint such servants as she requires to wield power on her behalf. A properly worded imperial instrument could create the necessary position and appoint someone worthy to fill it."

"No such instrument has been issued in centuries. Political meddling is beneath the dignity of the Heavenly Monarch," Ebabbar replied, defaulting to the customary position of the Anshar's high officials. While it was true enough that the Anshar herself did not deign to take sides in the squabbles of the high clans, in Mubirrum's experience her officials had no compunctions about doing so behind the scenes. "That is not the customary use of her imperial mandate."

"But once upon a time it was. As you noted not a moment ago, it used to be customary for the Anshar to appoint a Sharur-Tal to protect the realm, until the time came that it was custom no longer," Mubirrum pointed out. "In this case we merely restore a custom that was allowed to fall by the wayside. Need I convince you that the Dominion itself teeters on the brink of destruction? It seems to me that the dissolution of our realm and the ignominious collapse of the monarchy are likewise not customary uses of the Anshar's mandate."

"And you say you can prevent that catastrophe if only we entrust you with supreme power."

"No, Chamberlain. I say only that I will try with all my might to preserve the Anshar's Dominion, and this is the only way I see any hope of success." Mubirrum slowly got to his feet and leaned over his desk, putting the force of conviction behind every word. "An alien fleet gathers in Kahnar-Sag even as we speak. Within two weeks, perhaps three, they will attack Tamabuqq again and impose whatever punishments and humiliations they like upon us. Only by combining the strength of all the high *sebetu* under a single commander can we prevent their complete victory. Nothing less will avail."

Ebabbar Simtum measured Mubirrum for a long moment . . . and then he submitted, inclining his head. "So be it, then. I shall inform the Heavenly Monarch that you stand ready to serve at her command. An imperial instrument naming you Sharur-Tal will be issued at noon tomorrow."

"I am honored by the responsibility with which the Anshar charges me," said Mubirrum. He bowed graciously to the chamberlain, spreading his hands in acknowledgment. As supreme warlord, he would have all the fleets and armies of the Dominion at his command . . . in theory. Whether the lords and administrators who governed distant worlds or whose clans believed in peace at any cost would follow his orders remained to be seen. *The Nineteenth Prophecy tells us that victory breeds loyalty,* he reminded himself. If he showed that he wielded strength enough to deal with the threat of Abernathy's return—and, perhaps, finally put the Mercantilists in their place—clans all over the Dominion's one hundred and twenty-two worlds would eagerly join his banner. And if he did not prove strong enough, well, perhaps he would join the philosopher Ebneghirz in retiring to Kadingir Temple while a dynasty tens of thousands years old collapsed around him.

He returned his attention to the chamberlain. "We will speak again later today, but for now we both have much to do. You must prepare the instrument and inform the key officials of the change. And I must prepare orders for all the forces that can be summoned in time to meet the humans' attack. Every hour counts."

"I can see that," Ebabbar admitted. "If we do this—if we confer this authority upon you—what will you do about the *warumzi agu*?"

Mubirrum glanced out the chamber's windows in the direction of the Thousand Worlds ward, miles away on the far side of Bagal-Dindir. An hour ago he would have said that he'd simply commit Hish troops and arms to the task of reducing the offworlders' stronghold and be done with it, but something Admiral Sudi had said came to his mind.

Why would Abernathy be so reckless as to wander inside our reach? he asked himself. And he realized that he just might have the answer to the question.

He looked back to the chamberlain. "For the moment, nothing at all," he told Ebabbar. "I find that the *warumzi agu* are exactly where we need them to be."

16

Bagal-Dindir, Tamabuqq Prime

Two hours after midnight, Sikander tested the ice at the shores of Lake Gishtil. Weeks of cold weather had left a three-centimeter sheet over the dark water, extending several hundred meters out into the lake. Another week or so and the lake might freeze over entirely, which would present the defenders of the Thousand Worlds ward with an entirely new problem. At the moment, the two-kilometer-wide artificial lake effectively blocked the *warumzi agu* from attacking the east side of the walled district; Tzoru were strong swimmers but they could not endure cold water. If the lake froze hard enough for troops on foot to cross *over* the ice, however . . .

"Things seem quiet on the far shore," said Major Dalton, scanning the promenade and museum buildings on the other side of Lake Gishtil with a powerful pair of digital binoculars. "No one is moving around. I think they're hunkered down for the night."

"As we should be, too," Sapwu Zrinan said. The former council leader shivered as he looked at the icy lake. "I have grave misgivings about this plan. It is not clear to me whether we will freeze or drown first. Surely there must be another way to slip out of the Thousand Worlds ward."

"Your dry suit will keep you warm except for a little contact around the periphery of your mask, sir," Sikander told him. "And the mask draws oxygen from the water so you will not run out of air before the mask runs out of power, which it won't for thirty hours or more. I promise you, we will not freeze, and we will not drown."

"It's still . . . *unnatural*," Sapwu said. "I am far too old to engage in this sort of nonsense."

Sikander glanced at Darvesh in the shadows. He'd worried about this part of the plan. Tzoru simply didn't go in for even the mildest of action sports. They did not get anything like the sense of excitement or physical exhilaration that humans did from risky or challenging activities. They were certainly capable of athletic feats equivalent to human performance—any Tzoru could swim circles around a human, after all—and recognized the value of keeping in shape with regular exercise, but they didn't do it for *fun*. Worse yet, Tzoru had a deep-rooted aversion to cold water nearly as strong as a human claustrophobe's fear of tiny spaces. Despite some elements of their appearance, Tzoru weren't really anything like Earth's amphibians or reptiles—they were warm-blooded, for one thing—but cold temperatures could cause Tzoru to slip into a torpor-like state more easily than humans suffered hypothermia, and in water that spelled near-certain death. They barely tolerated cold air, and even then they bundled up in layer after layer of heavy robes. If Sapwu Zrinan proved unable to master his natural aversion, Sikander was prepared to sedate him . . . but he had to imagine that step of the process would be at least a little traumatic for all involved.

Fortunately, Lara came to his rescue. "I haven't ever done this either, Lord Zrinan, but I have complete confidence in Mr. North and our equipment. The reason this will work is that no reasonable Tzoru could possibly expect anyone to attempt this crossing in this sort of weather. Tens of thousands of *warumzi agu* surround the other sides of the Ward of a Thousand Worlds, but over there"—she pointed across the ice—"no one is keeping watch."

"I suppose," Zrinan muttered. Reluctantly he began to pull on the dry suit laid out for him; Major Dalton and two Tzoru servants from the embassy staff assisted him.

Sikander took the opportunity to don his own dry suit—it could fit over the wearer's street clothing, although winter coats and shoes would need to be towed along in a waterproof case—and check over his gear one more time. In addition to winter clothing, weapons, and comm gear for the second stage of their journey, he also carried a satchel filled with encrypted dispatches from various embassies and missions in the district, including one from Chau-Drak-Zeid for the commander of the Nyeiran squadron in Kahnar-Sag. He didn't know exactly what the speaker had recorded for hisher people, but Chau had made him swear that he would not permit the message to fall into any other hands.

Lara finished sealing her dry suit about the time he finished with his. It was quite baggy on her, since Sikander had been forced to bring a one-size-fits-all suit. "Does this look right?" she asked.

He checked the fit of the cuffs and gloves, and made sure her seals were secured. "I think you've got it," he told her. "Not exactly fashionable beachwear, but it'll do."

"Good." Lara tugged at the suit. The two of them stood a short distance from Major Dalton's marines and the small crew engaged in helping Sapwu Zrinan dress; they had a moment of privacy. "You know, I'm surprised that your commanding officer selected you for this mission. Sending the Nawabzada of Ishar to go sneaking around on a planet full of hostile aliens with just one bodyguard seems like the sort of thing the Navy would try to avoid."

"Well, it *was* my idea. And I had a personal stake in the situation."

Lara studied him in the shadows. "I don't know whether to feel flattered or guilty. You knew that Norman would never leave his post, didn't you?"

"I suspected that he wouldn't, although to be honest I

thought I'd have a hard time convincing the ambassador to send you instead of Mr. Yeager. Is he hurt badly, by the way?"

"He's got a leg full of shrapnel and he can't walk on it, but you're avoiding the question. How in the world did you convince Abernathy to let you do this?"

Sikander hesitated. "I told him that I wanted the chance to earn his confidence again," he finally said. "After we were forced to retreat from Tamabuqq three weeks ago, the commodore relieved me of my staff duties. I had to come up with something if I wanted to save my career."

Lara's eyes flashed. "Dear God, you're kidding me. He sacked *you* because he drove his task force into a Hish ambush?"

"That's the Navy. Abernathy certainly wasn't going to sack himself. Captain Reyes convinced him that I was the right scapegoat for the whole fiasco—I'm afraid she's had it in for me for a long time."

"In other words, your superiors agreed to let you risk life and limb on the most audacious mission you could think up so that you could atone for them relieving you?" Lara shook her head. "I don't know whether I'm angrier at the Navy for putting you in this position, or you for buying into it. Who is this Captain Reyes, by the way? And what did you ever do to her?"

"She's the deputy commodore, and a friend of Peter Chatburn," Sikander replied. Lara was well acquainted with the trouble Chatburn had caused Sikander after the Gadira incident. They'd begun dating during the board of inquiry and investigations following his return to the New Perth Fleet Base, and more than once she'd heard him rail about the proceedings. *That was my second offense against Reyes,* he reminded himself. He hadn't ever told Lara about the first, since he'd promised to keep the whole business confidential. But that didn't stop his mind from returning to the confrontation in the Greene Hall museum again. He remembered Victor Gray snarling in his face—

—standing so close that a little fleck of spittle strikes Sikan-der's cheek. "Down on the deck, Snottie!" Gray screams. "Give me fifty, you worthless piece of Kashmiri shit."

Midshipmen Marshall, Fonseca, and Burke snicker among themselves, enjoying the show. "That ought to improve his attitude a bit," Marshall says to Gray. "But I don't think it's going to make him any less stupid."

Sikander throws his cleaner and his rags to the ground and drops into the push-up position. He can do push-ups all day long in High Albion's gravity, and throwing his body up and down against the floor is exactly what he needs to keep from punching Victor Gray in his mouth. "One, sir! Two, sir! Three, sir! Four—"

That's when Victor Gray kicks Sikander's left hand out from under him. Sikander hits the floor hard enough to see stars, and before he can even process a single thought, he bounces up and takes Victor Gray to the ground.

Everything he's been holding back for the last three months of hazing and harassment breaks free in a blinding white fury. He throws wild, angry punches until the other upperclassmen pull him off Gray, then yanks himself free and tackles the bloodied upperclassman again, shrugging off kicks and punches from the three older midshipmen until he's once again dragged off Gray.

"Midshipman North! Enough!" A familiar voice finally sinks in through Sikander's rage. He looks around and finds Midshipman-Commander Farrell, the senior in charge of his company, restraining Gray's companions. Mason Barnes stands beside him, eyes wide as saucers, and Sikander realizes that he must have gone for help when Gray threw him out—

"That's not all there is to the story, is it?" Lara asked. "Is it?"

Sikander shook his head, returning his attention to the bitterly cold lakeshore. "Sorry—old memories," he said. "In addition to the usual trouble I seem to have with High Albion's best and brightest, I'm afraid I crossed her family back in my Academy days. I went up against a cousin of hers in a disciplinary committee hearing."

"You never mentioned that before."

"It was a long time ago. And I promised to keep the whole business quiet."

Lara studied him for a moment. "That's a really stupid reason to risk your life on a crazy idea like this."

"Perhaps, but I really do hope that the first councillor can help avert an all-out war between the Coalition powers and the Dominion. It seems like our best chance, anyway."

"Councillor Sapwu is dressed, sir," Darvesh called softly from the shore. "If Dr. Dunstan is ready, I believe we can proceed."

"Very good," Sikander answered him. He gave Lara a quick smile, and the two of them rejoined the others. He checked Sapwu's fittings for himself; the Tzoru breathing crest didn't really fit in a mask made for humans, so some modifications had been necessary. Then, while he briefed Lara and Zrinan on the use of the rebreather system in the mask and the handheld swim motors, Darvesh and a pair of marines used fire axes to clear a lane through the lake shallows to a point where they could submerge.

"I should also warn you that it will be very dark in the water," Sikander told Lara and Zrinan when he finished. "We don't want to use any bright lights under the ice just in case someone happens to notice, so we'll tether up and use chemlights to mark our positions. Leave the navigation to Darvesh and me—we won't let you get lost."

"We're ready, sir," Darvesh reported from the lake.

Sikander nodded. "Then it's time for us to go. Mr. Hart, Major Dalton, thank you for your help. God willing, we'll see you again soon."

"Good luck, Mr. North," Norman Hart said. "And you, too, First Councillor. Let us hope that your efforts over the next few days help to bring an end to this chaos."

"That prospect is the only thing I can imagine that might compel me to undergo this ridiculous and terrifying experience," Sapwu said, encompassing the dry suit and the lake with a single sweeping gesture. "I am as ready as I can be."

Sikander led Lara and Zrinan out into the lake, wading deeper through the icy water. He felt the cold pressure squeezing in around the suit's legs and torso, but he stayed dry, and the cold was . . . tolerable. He took a moment to fix Sapwu's mask, and then Lara's; she gave him a quick wink as she pulled it over her face, and submerged immediately. Then he donned his own, and gently drew Sapwu down into the water.

"*Cold!*" the Tzoru hissed. The comm gear in the mask picked up his strangled cry and transmitted it to all four of the divers. "I can feel it on my face!"

"That's normal, sir," Sikander told him, floating close by and watching his face. He made eye contact with Zrinan, and kept a hand on his shoulder. "There's a little exposed skin around the perimeter of the mask, and yes, that does get cold. But you'll notice that your limbs and torso are dry and warm, and you're breathing just fine."

"I—I am, aren't I?" Zrinan let out a small sound of relief. "All right. I see that I won't die, but I would like this to be finished as soon as possible."

"Perfectly understandable. Lara, how are you doing?"

"A little water in the mask but I'm fine. I've dived before, just never in a dry suit." Lara floated comfortably, looking around. "It's *really* dark. Are you sure you know which way to go?"

"Check your swim motors. There's a nav panel right in front of your face when you hold it in front of you. It shows our course." Sikander waited while Lara and Zrinan lifted the handheld motors into place, and oriented themselves. "Darvesh, are you ready?" The valet had the waterproof cases with most of their gear; he'd tow them while Sikander shepherded Zrinan and Lara as needed.

"I am already under way, sir," Darvesh replied. "You may see my chemlight ahead of you."

"So I do. Okay, nice and slow now, gently squeeze the handles of your swim motors . . . good, just like that. You steer it like a bicycle."

"A what?" Sapwu Zrinan asked.

Of course an aristocratic Tzoru would have no idea about bicycles, Sikander thought. "Um, you steer by pushing one hand ahead and pulling the other back. Try it a little bit, sir, and you'll see how it works."

"Ah, I see. This is a very clever device!"

"We'll gradually increase speed as we get comfortable," Sikander told him. "Let the motor do the work, it's a very long swim otherwise."

He watched carefully as the old Tzoru settled on the glowing course line and drove ahead through the darkness. The ice formed a pale shadow overhead; it was a moonless night, but the lights from the surrounding city colored the sky a dim greenish-golden hue. His swim unit's depth finder showed the lake bottom only six or seven meters beneath him, but he could make out nothing but inky blackness below—a rather unnerving sensation even for an experienced diver. Fortunately, Sapwu Zrinan seemed quite occupied with his motor and its nav display, working earnestly to avoid even the tiniest deviation from the course line.

A few minutes into their dark voyage they passed beneath the stretch of open water that still remained unfrozen in the middle of the lake. Sikander had to quickly correct Zrinan before the councillor surfaced; chances were that nobody on the shore would be looking, but he didn't want to test that with a lot of unnecessary splashing. Then they passed under the shadow of the ice again. It was difficult to keep track of time or distance in the dark; Sikander could not quite shake the impression that he wasn't really moving, only hovering in the cold water while meaningless numbers counted down on his motor's display panel. But finally the distance counted down to zero, and he found Darvesh motionless in the water ahead of him. Here the bottom came into view, shoaling up swiftly so that the four of them floated in a band of water only a meter wide between the muddy bottom and the covering ice.

Sikander collected the swim motors from the others and sank them; they didn't need to take them along. While he did that, Darvesh produced a laser knife and carefully cut a ragged square panel from the ice above. When the valet finished, he gathered his legs beneath him and slowly shouldered the ice up and out of the way, sliding it aside like a manhole cover. He paused for a long moment, crouched low in the water, and then straightened up. "All clear, sir," he reported.

"Very well," said Sikander. "Everybody follow Darvesh—try not to splash too much, please."

He waited while Zrinan and Lara clambered up onto the lakeshore. They stood on a sloping, grassy bank in the shadow of a monument of some kind, screened by frozen treeferns. Darvesh dragged his cases into a sort of bower screened by dense shrubs. Then they quickly doffed their dry suits and dressed in the Tzoru-style winter clothing they'd brought with them. No human could pass for Tzoru at close range, but they might not appear too suspicious if someone only caught a glimpse from forty or fifty meters. Just in case, though, Sikander and Darvesh armed themselves with mag pistols in shoulder holsters beneath their robes and caps.

"What now?" Zrinan asked quietly.

"We walk," Sikander replied. He nodded at the monument. "This is the end of Waqbu Promenade. We'll find our ride near the fountain circle, a couple of kilometers down the boulevard."

"No one's going to be in the park at this hour. We'll look pretty suspicious, won't we?" Lara asked.

"Only if there's anybody around to see us. That's why we chose this route—there's good cover and it should be pretty much empty in the middle of a cold winter night."

They sank the waterproof cases and the dry suits with the swim motors before sliding the ice panel back in place to conceal the fact that someone had been there, and set out at the best hiking pace Sapwu Zrinan could manage. Waqbu Promenade was essentially a hundred-meter-wide strip of parkland that ran through the city from the lakeshore to the High Waqbu Platform five kilometers away. By day the personal carriages of Bagal-Dindir's aristocrats frequented its winding roadways, but now the parklike promenade and the surrounding city were eerily quiet. Without motor vehicles or loud nightlife, Bagal-Dindir might as well have been some long-abandoned ruin in a winter wilderness. Twice Sikander and his companions saw Tzoru out and about despite the hour and bitter cold—a utility crew working to repair part of the city's buried power grid, and a gang of militia in green armbands emplacing a barricade and antivehicular weapons in front of one of the city's ancient armories. Both times the small party slipped past unnoticed by staying well back in the trees on the far side of the wide boulevard.

Sapwu Zrinan kept up well enough at first, but as two kilometers stretched out to three, the old Tzoru's steps began to slow. The combination of his recent recovery, the icy swim, and finally a long walk in a frigid night seemed to be taking its toll. Darvesh glanced back at Sikander as their pace slowed; Sikander nodded and dropped back to lend Zrinan his arm. "Just a little farther, sir," he told the councillor. "We're almost there."

"Good," said Zrinan. He clutched Sikander's arm, leaning heavily. "I fear that I am not as recovered from my injuries as I had thought."

"Nawabzada, there is a complication," Darvesh said softly from his position at the head of their little procession. He pointed through a gap in the treeferns; the silent fountain stood in its wide circular plaza fifty meters ahead of them, sheathed in glittering ice. Beneath the shadows at the edge of the circle stood an *alliksisu* yoked to a light transport wagon. The draft beast steamed and shifted beneath a winter blanket. No one was in sight—and then three *warumzi agu* dressed in heavy robes appeared from behind the carriage, talking excitedly among themselves as they examined the conveyance.

"Damn," Sikander murmured. He hurriedly drew Sapwu and Lara back under the shadows.

"What's the trouble?" Lara asked.

"That's our ride, but it looks like we've got some unexpected guests." Sikander keyed his comm unit and spoke softly. "Wall, where are you? We're on the west side of the fountain, over."

The Aquilan sergeant's reply came back as a whisper. "Sorry, sir. A patrol came along so my driver and I decided to duck out of sight. We're behind the food stand on the north side of the circle, over."

Sikander glanced to his left and spotted the shuttered booth at the edge of the circle. He couldn't fault the sergeant for choosing to hide. A wagon without a driver might be a suspicious sight in a deserted park in the middle of the night, but a wagon *with* a driver would invite questions that might be difficult to answer. "I see your position," he told Wall. "Stay put while we figure this out."

"I'm pretty sure I can take them, sir. But I was hoping they'd get bored and move on."

"It's clear and still, sir," Darvesh warned. "The sound of gunfire will carry a long way."

Sikander nodded. That had occurred to him, too. "Do you have a better idea?" he asked Darvesh.

"I believe I can lure them away. Give me three minutes."

"Very well, go ahead." Sikander keyed his mic again. "Hold your fire, Sergeant. We're working on something."

Darvesh moved off into the darkness behind them. Sikander kept his eyes on the three *warumzi agu* by the wagon. They were too far away for him to make out their discussion, but he had to imagine they were wondering whether they should look around for a driver. *Or just take the wagon and bring it to their commander,* he told himself. He couldn't let the *warumzi* do that—he needed the transport to get out of Bagal-Dindir. Noisy or not, gunfire might become necessary. Quietly he drew his mag pistol from under his coat, and steadied himself against the trunk of a tree.

A distant strain of music from the forest off to his right caught Sikander's attention. He recognized the opening theme of *Each Day Rises But Once,* coming from the dense shadows beneath a stand of large treeferns in the woods southwest of the fountain.

The three *warumzi agu* heard it too. They turned together and moved away from the wagon to investigate, plunging into the forest. A moment later, Darvesh rejoined their group. "I think that should occupy their attention for a few minutes, sir," he told Sikander. "I suggest that we use this opportunity to be on our way."

"What did you do?" Sikander asked.

"I buried my personal vid viewer underneath a shrub and turned it on. It will not be easy to find."

"It seems to me that inflicting that horrible show on those unsuspecting revolutionaries ought to be against the rules of war," Sikander said, and grinned. He tapped his comm unit. "Sergeant Wall, we're moving. Meet you at the wagon."

Wall simply clicked his mic once in reply. Sikander ushered Lara and Sapwu Zrinan out of their cover, and hurried toward the waiting *alliksisu* and transport. Unlike the open carriages favored for passenger use, this was a working wagon, not unlike a light truck. Sikander approved of the choice—it seemed like the sort of vehicle that might be out and about for early-morning cargo deliveries. He opened the door and helped the old Tzoru into the covered truck bed; then Lara, Darvesh, and he clambered inside as well. Darvesh took up a position at one of the small windows with his mag carbine, watching to make sure the *warumzi agu* did not return.

Sergeant Wall and a Tzoru bundled up from head to toe emerged from the brush behind the food stand and climbed up into the driver's compartment. With a soft hiss and a tap of his goad the driver prodded the *alliksisu* into motion, and the beast plodded quietly away from the fountain circle. Sikander hadn't realized before just how quiet a Tzoru transport was; the *alliksisu* had thick, soft pads on its feet instead of hard hooves, and the maglev suspension eliminated any creaking or clattering wheels. The party simply drove away along the curving roadway until the fountain and the *warumzi agu* thrashing through the brush disappeared into the darkness behind them.

"That was a little more exciting than I'd hoped," Sikander said when he finally relaxed his vigilance. "Good to see you, Sergeant Wall."

"Likewise, sir," Wall replied. "Any trouble getting out of the Thousand Worlds?"

"A cold night for a swim, but we managed. Who's your companion?"

The Tzoru driver twisted around to look back into the main cabin. "I am Gidru Numen, honored friend. I am pleased to be of service this evening."

"The Gidru are friends of ours," Wall explained. "Ortiz contacted them after we put the *Aram* down, and they were kind enough to arrange the wagon for us."

Sikander was gratified to see that part of the plan had worked out; he'd been worried that the team he'd left behind on *Aram* might find it difficult or dangerous to reach out to Tzoru clans that were on good terms with Aquila. He'd been surprised when Petty Officer Ortiz had signaled that he'd arranged transport just a few hours after landing. In a pinch the marines had planned to simply commandeer a wagon and do their best to avoid being noticed by bundling up in Tzoru robes and sticking to deserted streets.

"Thank you, Numen," Sikander said to the driver. "I am Mr. North; this is Chief Reza, Dr. Dunstan, and our friend Tumh Isar." That was a Tzoru name about as common as *John Smith* in Anglic-speaking worlds. Gidru Numen might be a friend, but he didn't need to know exactly who he had in his wagon this morning.

"You might as well make yourselves comfortable," Wall told them. "It's two hours to the rendezvous point, or more if we need to avoid patrols."

"What happens if we do run into a patrol?" Lara asked.

The marine smiled and showed her a dataslate hidden under his robe. The small screen showed an aerial image of Waqbu Promenade slowly drifting by underneath. "We'll steer around them, ma'am. I've got a couple of Dragonfly recon drones overhead to help us avoid that sort of trouble. They shouldn't draw any attention."

"Good work, Sergeant," said Sikander.

"Sir, you can tell me that when we're back on the *Aram,*" said Wall. He returned his attention to operating the recon drones, while Gidru Numen urged the *alliksisu* into a shambling trot.

Sikander positioned himself to keep watch out the right side and rear door of the wagon, while Darvesh watched to the left and ahead. Gidru soon turned off Waqbu Promenade, choosing a route through the industrial districts and suburbs that dotted the eastern half of the capital. From time to time, Wall murmured to the driver and directed him to turn down one alleyway or another, avoiding other traffic or diverting around barricades. The wagon's main compartment slowly warmed up under the influence of an underpowered heating element and the proximity of four passengers, but Sikander made sure to keep the windows cracked open; he wanted to be able to hear trouble coming if Wall failed to spot it from overhead.

Bagal-Dindir passed slowly by: kilometer after kilometer of wide boulevards, stands of alien forest, old courtyard-style homes of commoner *sebetu* and the beetling castle-like holds of the great *sebetu,* workshops and storefronts illuminated by dim golden streetlights. A heavy frost formed on the treeferns and the slick walkways, glittering white beneath the dark sky. *We picked a good night for this,* Sikander decided. No Tzoru wanted to be out in the cold weather, and those few who were seemed so miserable and self-absorbed they couldn't care less about one lonely wagon making its way through the streets.

"I'm beginning to think we just may get away with this," Lara murmured, peering out the window beside him. "I never realized how empty the streets are at night. Everything seems so *peaceful* here. You'd never know that there are thousands of people pointing guns at each other just a few kilometers behind us."

"The weather helps a great deal," Sikander replied, keeping his eyes on the streets behind them. He kept his voice down, too. Sapwu Zrinan dozed in one corner of the wagon, and he did not want to distract Darvesh or Sergeant Wall from their own vigils. "And I'll note for the record that we are not quite out of danger yet."

"So noted," said Lara. She remained silent for a time, then squeezed his hand. "I'm sorry for whatever trouble you got into with your superiors, Sikander. I know that they make it harder on you than they would for an Aquilan of the right family, and it infuriates me. But I'm glad you're here now, and I'm grateful for the chance to do something about the Thousand Worlds situation instead of hiding inside the walls and hoping for the best. Thank you for coming to get me."

He shrugged awkwardly in the shadows and squeezed her hand back, unable to think of any better reply. Then Sergeant Wall spoke from his seat beside Gidru. "We're here, Mr. North."

Sikander got up and moved to the front of the cargo compartment to look over the front bench. A frost-coated cargo station sprawled beside the road, dim and gray beneath the approaching dawn. Scores of similar facilities ringed the outskirts of Bagal-Dindir, marking the edges of the capital's restricted airspace and serving as transshipment points where regional ground transports or orbital lighters could drop off goods for distribution via maglev wagon. Several lighters were parked in docking cradles around the building, dark and buttoned-up against the cold weather. A few hundred meters to one side, *Aram* squatted on an auxiliary landing pad, warm light spilling from its cockpit windows and its open hatch.

"Never thought I would be so happy to see a beat-up old Tzoru barge," Sikander said aloud.

"Me neither, sir," said the marine. He glanced again at his drone controls. "Looks clear for now."

"Then let's be on our way," Sikander replied. He roused Sapwu Zrinan with a gentle touch to the shoulder, and began to gather up his gear.

Ten minutes later, *Aram* lifted off and started its long climb up into orbit. And twenty hours after that, *Vendaval* looped back into Tamabuqq's inner system and decelerated just long enough for a high-speed rendezvous with the cargo boat before racing away from the pursuing Monarch Sword torpedo cutters trying to intercept her.

17

Sikander spent most of the first day of *Vendaval*'s transit to Latzari sleeping in the tiny cabin set aside for his use. He hadn't realized how tired he felt, but after the nerve-racking journey to Tamabuqq Prime, the hectic hours of discussion and preparation in the Aquilan embassy, the escape from the Ward of a Thousand Worlds, and finally the technically difficult rendezvous with Magdalena Juarez's speeding warship, he was simply exhausted. He slept for fourteen hours straight, and got up only because he was so hungry he couldn't stand another hour in his bunk without getting something to eat.

Magda joined him in the wardroom as Sikander busied himself at the cold-cut tray the mess stewards typically left out between meals. "I see you're finally awake," she said. "I was beginning to wonder when I'd see you."

"Thirty-six hours without sleep and a cold-water dive caught up to me, I'm afraid," Sikander answered. "Did I miss anything while I was out?"

The captain shook her head. "Not really. Once we started boosting on our transit course nothing in Tamabuqq could catch us, and no one's going to beat *Vendaval* to Latzari. I think we got away with it, Sikay."

"I suppose we did." He indulged himself with an enormous

bite of the roast beef sandwich he'd just made, and chewed a moment before continuing. Some New Sikhs chose to commit to a vegetarian diet, but nothing in the Guru Granth Sahib mandated that, and Sikander was far from ready to give up eating meat in any event. "Still, there's no way the Hish didn't see the *Aram* rendezvous with *Vendaval* on your way out of the system. Now that they know you were waiting for us, they'll be able to backtrack their orbital traffic records and figure out where we came from. It won't look much like an innocent bit of reconnaissance when the Militarists piece it all together."

"That was never really the objective, was it?"

"I know, but I would have liked to keep the hostile clans in the dark a little longer. I worry that we might have disturbed the status quo by making them wonder who we picked up in Bagal-Dindir and why we sent *Vendaval* to get him."

"That can't be helped now. Besides, our reconnaissance wasn't really all that innocent. My ops team has been looking at the imagery your intel specialist recorded from *Aram*. I think you captured some important material there."

"We did?" Sikander took another bite of his sandwich and followed Magda as she took a seat at the wardroom table and pulled out her dataslate. A few quick taps on the screen slaved the wardroom's large vid display to the smaller device, then she pulled up footage of the Tzoru battleships orbiting above Tamabuqq Prime. She quickly zoomed in on several frames, arranging them on the screen.

"That's heavy damage from K-cannon hits," Sikander said, setting down his sandwich to study the images. He had a little training in battle-damage assessment from his coursework at the Navy's intelligence school; he'd attended a short term there immediately prior to his Helix Squadron assignment. "Repairs are under way . . . but they're not very far along, are they? This footage was taken thirteen days after the battle, and they still haven't welded armor patches over the hull breaches. I would have imagined they'd be in more of a hurry, given the fact that Helix Squadron could return at any time."

"That's what I thought, too. Of course, Tzoru shipyards aren't all that efficient to begin with."

"No kidding," Sikander said, recalling his brief exposure to Tzoru shipyards in Magan Kahnar. "On the other hand, maybe the *sebetu* that run the yards aren't very interested in helping the Militarists. Or maybe *warumzi agu* trouble elsewhere in the Dominion is interfering with the delivery of repair materials to the capital and slowing things down."

"A lack of materials might explain something that's been bothering me." Magda pointed at several of the images, one after the other. "What do you see here, and here?"

"The drive plates are cracked. Those ships aren't going anywhere soon, are they?"

"None of the Tzoru heavies with drive-plate damage are," Magda said. "I noticed that earlier today when I was looking over the imagery—I guess it's the engineer in me. I couldn't find *any* Tzoru ships getting work done on their drive plates. Sikay, I don't think they have any replacement plates on hand."

Sikander gave a low whistle. "In which case, the Golden Banner isn't a battle fleet anymore—it's an orbital battery. Isn't that interesting?"

"Make sure you include that with your report to the commodore," said Magda. "It seems to me that opens up a lot of possibilities for our return engagement."

"I will," he promised. "Thank you, Magda!"

When he finished his sandwich, Sikander decided to check on Sapwu Zrinan before he dove into serious image analysis on *Aram*'s footage. As useful as it would be to bring William Abernathy an update on the Militarists' fleet strength and the *warumzi agu* positions around the Thousand Worlds ward, it would be even more helpful to be able to tell the commodore his impression of Sapwu Zrinan's outlook or what kind of deal Lara Dunstan might be able to strike with the Monarchists. He'd have several days to work on the battle-damage assessment after *Vendaval* delivered Sapwu Zrinan to his homeworld, but his opportunities to speak with Sapwu—*or Lara,* he told himself—dwindled by the hour as the corvette raced toward the Latzari system.

He stopped by Sapwu's quarters first, only to learn from *Vendaval*'s doctor that the Tzoru aristocrat was still resting. The combination of age and a recent recovery from serious injury had left the old Tzoru exhausted, so Sikander decided to leave him alone and headed down to Lara's cabin instead. By time-honored tradition, *Vendaval* had made room for civilian guests by bumping senior officers out of their quarters, who in turn dislodged more junior officers; Lara stayed in a stateroom that normally belonged to the corvette's gunnery officer.

Sikander paused at the door and knocked. "Lara? It's me," he called. "Are you awake?"

"Just a moment!" she replied. He waited for a minute or two, and then she opened the door for him. She wore a long white bathrobe, and her hair was wet.

"Oh, I'm sorry," he said. "I see I caught you getting out of the shower. I'll come back later."

"No, it's fine," she said. "I'm decent. Please, come in. What's on your mind?"

"Well, as you wish." Sikander stepped inside. "I wanted to check on you and make sure you were all right. I know it's been a difficult few weeks and I was worried that you were . . . that is, that you might be feeling . . ."

"A stiff dose of survivor's guilt?" Lara finished for him. She sighed, and sat down on the edge of her bed. Sikander took the desk chair beside the bed; the cabin was so small their knees almost touched. "I confess this is the second shower I've taken since we came aboard. Hot water's been in short supply lately; it's the first time in a month that I've actually felt *warm.* But yes, I hated myself a little bit for enjoying it so much."

"I'm sorry. I wish you hadn't been caught up in this whole thing."

She gave him a small smile. "It's the job, I guess. Sometimes you wind up serving in places where no one wants to go at the exact moment no one wants to be there."

"Is it anything you want to talk about?" he asked.

"No, not yet. Or—I don't know." She reached for a towel; Sikander handed one to her and waited as she wrung out her long hair. "I hated feeling like there was nothing I could do. The *warumzi agu* had no interest in talking to us, and the high clans that might have been inclined to help out simply couldn't intervene. I had to find some way to keep myself busy, so I tried to help out in food distribution. Ten years of postgraduate studies and Foreign Ministry work, and the best way I could contribute was to organize soup kitchens."

"Someone had to do it, and I'd bet that you handled it better than a lot of others might have. You saw a place where you could help and you did your best—there's no shame in that." Sikander took her hand in his. "Besides, you're in a position to make a real difference now. If you can find the right lever to engage the Sapwu in resolving this whole mess, you might save a lot of lives."

Lara nodded, but a flicker of uncertainty crossed her face. "Maybe, but I wish I had an idea what that lever might be. Everything I thought I'd learned over the last year about how things work in the Dominion went out the window a month ago. So much is riding on me! I'm an analyst, not a negotiator. What if I mess this up?"

"You won't," he told her, and he realized that he meant it. "You're one of the smartest women I've ever met. You know more about the Tzoru than they know about themselves. Be confident; trust your experience and your intuition. They won't lead you wrong."

"I understand what you're trying to say, and I appreciate the effort," she said. "But that doesn't mean I *believe* it. I wish you were coming with me."

"I'm afraid I can't. There isn't anything I can tell the

Sapwu that you can't explain better. I'll do more good at Helix Squadron."

She gave him a bitter smile. "Which means that while I'm trying to get the Sapwu to take a stand, you'll be sailing into another battle—a battle that everyone knows is coming but nobody knows how to stop."

He gave a helpless shrug. "As you said a moment ago—it's the job. This time we know a lot more about what will be waiting for us. And I promise I'll be as careful as I can."

"That doesn't mean I won't worry." She raised his hand to her cheek, and squeezed his fingers. Then she leaned close and kissed him firmly. The delicate scent of her damp hair filled his nostrils.

"Once again: What was that for?" he said when she finally pulled away.

"You saved my life at Durzinzer. You may have saved me again at the Thousand Worlds ward. And now it seems to me that I have no idea when or if I'll see you again. So what do you think that's for?"

"Lara, I'm not sure," Sikander replied, trying to talk over the hammering of his heart. Part of him was very, very sure, but he didn't want to dive into the sort of entanglement that hadn't worked out so well before—at least, not without being certain that he knew what he was doing. That didn't stop his arms from circling around her waist. "I don't know where I'll be or where you'll be—"

"Then let's just agree this is my idea." She leaned in and kissed him again, and this time Sikander's hand seemed to slip of its own accord within the soft hem of her robe. She sighed and rocked forward a little bit, until his fingers found her and teased her. "Oh, please," she whispered, and moved against him more urgently.

Sikander lowered his mouth to kiss her neck, then moved lower to nuzzle at her small breasts while she cradled his head in her arms. Impatiently he drew back and wriggled out of his uniform, while she stood and undid her robe. Then he pulled her down onto him as she straddled him in the chair; they moved together with her damp hair cowling his face and her firm body writhing against him. He clenched her tightly and lost himself in the moment.

Later, when they lay together in the cabin's single small bunk, she sighed softly and reached up to caress her fingers across his chest. "Are you sure now?" she asked.

He smiled and stroked her hair, still damp from the shower. "Well, we still have two days before we reach Latzari," he said. "Perhaps I'll figure it out." Then he reached for her again.

The day before *Vendaval* reached Latzari, Sikander and Lara heard from the ship's medical officer that Sapwu Zrinan was ready to receive visitors.

Zrinan had been given the captain's cabin, the largest and most comfortable quarters available; Magda Juarez instead occupied her executive officer's stateroom for the short voyage. Sikander and Lara found Zrinan seated at the cabin's conference table, reading through a Tzoru-language version of the *Helix Daily Post*. The wide vidscreen on the room's outer bulkhead showed the stars sliding past as *Vendaval* sped through the interstellar gulfs. The image was a complete fabrication, since a warp bubble completely isolated a starship within its own miniature universe during transit, but Sikander had always enjoyed the projection nonetheless.

"Good morning, Lord Zrinan," Lara said. "May we join you?"

"Please do," the old Tzoru said. "I would enjoy the company."

Lara took a seat opposite Zrinan; Sikander busied himself at the coffee service, filling two cups. "I came by to make sure you were comfortable and hopefully recovering from our long night out," said Lara. "How are you doing?"

Zrinan set down the dataslate and gave a small Tzoru shrug. "I feel stronger every day, although I must admit that it is . . . unsettling . . . to be the only Tzoru aboard. I usually make this trip aboard a Sapwu argosy with a large retinue."

"You won't be alone for much longer, sir," Sikander said, setting a cup of coffee in front of Lara and keeping one for himself. "*Vendaval* accelerated aggressively before initiating our warp. We're making excellent time."

"It is no great matter," Sapwu said. "I am enjoying the opportunity to be with my own thoughts, and the speed of your vessel is making the voyage substantially shorter than my customary trip."

"I see you're reading the *Daily Post*," said Lara, nodding at the dataslate. "I wasn't aware you followed human news agencies."

"I do not. In truth, this is the first time I have ever read a human-published news digest. Before today I did not even know that there was such a thing within the Tzoru Dominion."

"There are three or four human news outlets operating in the Dominion now," Lara told him. "The *Helix Daily Post* is the best of them, though. They employ a number of Tzoru journalists and local sources, while the others focus on delivering news from human space to the expatriate community. When I want to know what's going on in the Dominion, the first thing I do is check the *Post*."

"I suppose I must take your word for it, Dr. Dunstan. The Dominion described in these articles is not the Dominion with which I am familiar." Sapwu shook his head. "I don't recognize my own nation anymore. Humans have brought more change to worlds such as Shimatum or Kahnar-Sag in the last fifty years than my people managed to accumulate over the last five thousand. Now it seems those changes have reached Tamabuqq, too. We Tzoru are not good at change, I fear. That is a human trait."

"Lord Zrinan, *nobody* is good at the sort of change your people are dealing with," Sikander said. "My home is a system called Kashmir. We fell under the influence of the Commonwealth of Aquila more than a hundred years ago. Our society was very traditional in many ways—not as much as a Tzoru world, of course, but unusually so for humans. We lost our independence, many of our institutions vanished, whole sectors of our economy came under the control of Aquilan businesses." He allowed himself a grim smile. "Trust me, in some ways the Dominion is bearing up better than my people did; Tzoru aren't going to war with each other, for example."

"I do not find that reassuring."

"I didn't intend to reassure you. I am only pointing out that it's a familiar pattern: Rich states with more advanced technology and stronger governments bring difficult changes to their less developed neighbors, sometimes without even knowing it."

"Familiar for you, perhaps. The Tzoru have been unified long enough to forget such axioms of power, if indeed we ever knew them." Zrinan studied Sikander for a moment with a sidelong glance. "How did the humans of Kashmir survive the changes brought by the Aquilans?"

"Some changes were for the better, even if many were not. We are one nation today instead of a collection of warring states, and Aquilan commerce now connects Kashmir to the rest of humanity's worlds." Sikander shifted uneasily in his seat, thinking of Alberto Reyes's Starburst of Valor in its glass case at the Academy. Peace and prosperity, such as they were in Kashmir, had come at a bitter price. "Those changes should have been ours to choose, not Aquila's to impose. But I believe that Kashmir will emerge stronger from this relationship when we finally outgrow it. I couldn't wear this uniform if I did not."

"Do you not fear that you have lost what is Kashmir in becoming Aquilan subjects?" Sapwu asked.

"Of course we do. But my family has always felt, and I agree, that we're not trying to become Aquilan. Instead we like to think that we're taking what is best from Aquila and making it our own. Kashmir in years to come will be a proud and powerful system—and it will still be Kashmir, if not exactly the Kashmir it would have been otherwise. I believe that might turn out to be true for your people, too."

"Mercantilists like the Baltzu certainly seem to hope so for the Tzoru. I am not sure, though. I see something like this"—Sapwu picked up the dataslate with the news publication still centered in its display—"and I wonder if we have not already been conquered and swallowed up by the powers in the Coalition of Humanity. If the result of peace is the same as the consequences of losing a war, then perhaps the *warumzi agu* and their Militarist sympathizers are right to resist."

"If you truly believed that, I think you wouldn't have come to the Thousand Worlds ward when the *warumzi agu* uprising broke out in Bagal-Dindir," Lara said.

"No, I suppose not." Sapwu Zrinan got up from the table, and paced away to gaze at the starfield in the wide display. He moved slowly, but his posture seemed straighter than it had a day or two ago, and he did not grimace or limp as he walked. "I went to the Thousand Worlds ward to beg your ambassadors to find some way to convince your people to stop provoking the intolerant forces within the Dominion. It was the only thing I could think of to avert catastrophe, even if fate doomed my efforts to failure."

"Fate might have something different in mind now," said Lara. "Who knows? The delay caused by your injuries may have provided just the right amount of time for the Mercantilists and the Militarists and the *warumzi agu* and the commanders of our own fleets to all see the consequences of their actions. Maybe people are ready to listen now."

Zrinan gave a snort of amusement. "If there is one thing I cannot understand about humans, it's your childlike optimism. I think sometimes that if your houses burned down you'd be happy for the opportunity to rebuild them."

"Depending on the house and what was in it, some humans would probably agree with you," said Sikander. "Still, I think Dr. Dunstan makes a good point: Now that everyone's had a taste of the *ninka* they've been brewing, they might be ready to throw out the kettle."

"That is a Tzoru expression!" said Zrinan.

"I've picked up a few things since I've been on Helix Station," Sikander told him. "You're never too old to learn something new, after all."

"Perhaps." Sapwu inclined his head to Sikander, acknowledging the point. Then he turned back to Lara. "I fear that is exactly what I will have to do if I am to turn events to a new course, Dr. Dunstan. I know that you expect me to rally the neutral court factions—the Manzanensi, the Kishpuzinir, all the rest—against the Hish and the Emuqq-Mamit, and assert the council's authority against those who are seeking to incite open war. But even if I believe that is the only rational course of action, there will be many among my former allies who find the Militarists' arguments more persuasive than mine. If I am to convince them to break with the Militarists, I must be able to show them that they can get what they want through peace, not war."

"I can see that," said Lara. "What is it that you think they want?"

"For things to go back to the way they were before humans came to the Dominion, of course. Everything else is simply a matter of detail."

Lara nodded thoughtfully, but Sikander rubbed at his jaw and frowned. "I don't know if anyone can make that happen, Lord Zrinan," he said. "We can't promise to remove tens of thousands of Aquilan citizens and businesspeople from Tzoru territory, let alone Dremish or Montréalais or any of the others that aren't actually our citizens. Time doesn't run backwards, after all."

"I did not say that the conservative factions in our society would only be satisfied by the complete removal of your kind," Sapwu replied. "I said that they would be satisfied if things were like the way they were before humans came here. That is not the same thing."

Lara and Sikander exchanged looks, and Lara raised an eyebrow. "I think the first councillor has a point, Sikander."

"Maybe, but I'm not sure I can see a difference," said Sikander.

"The *warumzi agu* and the conservative clans who are unwilling to suppress them don't object to *humans*," Lara said. "They object to what humans represent: *change*. We're dealing with reactionary forces in Tzoru society, forces that we've empowered by frankly being pushy and insensitive on questions like opening markets and basing rights and establishing our own sovereignty. Those are specific grievances that can be addressed."

"Transforming a colonial relationship into a more equitable partnership, in other words." Sikander grimaced; as he'd just observed a few minutes ago, Kashmiris were intimately familiar with the challenges presented by that process. "That might placate the conservative Tzoru, but what's in it for the human powers benefiting from those advantageous agreements? Especially since we're talking about half a dozen different nations who are going to insist that somebody else should be the one to give back their base or amend their trade deal? Just because the great powers are cooperating in the face of an immediate threat to their diplomats and civilians doesn't mean that they're capable of jointly renegotiating their existing deals. The Dremish, the Cygnans—even our own Commonwealth, I fear—will never agree."

"Likewise, the Baltzu, the Gisumi, and other *sebetu* you think of as Mercantilists have little reason to seek new terms," said Zrinan. "They have been greatly enriched by various agreements."

"Which also means that they have the most to lose if the current situation continues to deteriorate," Lara pointed out. "That's what we need to make everyone understand: A general war means that everybody loses. The Coalition powers and the Mercantilist *sebetu* can have half a cake, or they can have none."

The room fell silent as Sikander and Zrinan considered Lara's point; stars quietly drifted past in the viewscreen on the bulkhead. Then Zrinan shifted in his seat. "What is a cake?" he asked.

Vendaval did not spend much time in Latzari. The corvette killed its warp bubble just long enough to decelerate and signal a Sapwu-clan pinnace to rendezvous for passenger transfer. Sikander and Magda said their good-byes to Sapwu Zrinan and Lara at the midships airlock, along with the four-man marine detachment; in theory, Lara would be quite safe as a diplomatic guest of the Sapwu, but Sikander was not inclined to take any chances. He knew he'd feel a lot better knowing that a security detail of Aquilan marines guarded her. Magda agreed with him and exercised her authority to issue Sergeant Wall and his squad the necessary orders.

"Mr. North, Captain Juarez, I thank you for your assistance," Sapwu Zrinan said as they stood by the hatch. "I will do what I can to advocate a peaceful resolution to the crisis, but we have lost a lot of time."

"We can ask no more than that, Lord Zrinan," Magda Juarez said. She exchanged bows with Zrinan, who then made his way through the docking passage to the waiting Tzoru pinnace.

Sikander turned to Lara. Her eyes sparkled with mischief as she held out her hand for a proper handshake between a public servant and a serving officer. "Good luck," he said. "My part of the job was easy compared to what's ahead for you."

"Convincing a Tzoru clan that hasn't had a new idea in five thousand years to throw in with the uncouth alien barbarians invading their holy dominion?" Lara smiled. "I'll think of something, I guess. Take care of yourself, Sikander."

"You, too," he said. She stepped close to brush her lips against his before she made her way down the passage, following her marine detail. Sikander gazed after her until the airlock sealed and two heavy mechanical thumps signaled the retraction of the docking passage.

Magda raised an eyebrow. "You've got it bad, haven't you?"

"I don't know what you're talking about. Besides, we broke up years ago. Anything serious between Lara and me is ancient history at this point."

"You certainly spent a lot of time in her cabin if that's the case," said Magda. "Well, I'd better get us turned around. Time is of the essence, or so my orders say."

Sikander felt his cheeks flush. He drew himself up with as much dignity as he could muster and retreated to the safety of the somewhat-delayed analysis work on the fleet observations Magda's crew had recorded during their stay at Tamabuqq.

The transit to Kahnar-Sag was another short one, only three days. When *Vendaval* reached Kahnar-Sag, Magda Juarez headed straight for *Exeter;* with the Tzoru workboat filling the shuttle bay, *Vendaval* had no launches of her own available to shuttle Sikander and Darvesh back to the flagship. Magda personally conned the corvette's delicate docking maneuver as she came alongside the heavy cruiser and married the docking tube to *Exeter*'s airlock. After the two ships were locked together, she walked Sikander down to the airlock. "I'll be along as soon as I get this Tzoru piece of junk out of my hangar," she told him. "Give the commodore my respects. And good luck, Sikay."

"Thanks, Magda," he said, and crossed over to the flagship. At *Exeter*'s quarterdeck, Sikander found that Abernathy had left word for him to report to the commodore's flag cabin as soon as he came aboard.

He hurried up to the flag cabin. William Abernathy and Francine Reyes were seated at the commodore's conference table when he entered the room, studying ship schematics on the cabin's largest display—repair requests, or so Sikander guessed. "Reporting as ordered, sir," he announced. "I'm back from Tamabuqq."

"Welcome back, Mr. North." Abernathy got up from his seat and came around the table to shake Sikander's hand. After a moment, Reyes stood as well, although she did not bother to greet him otherwise. "I was just beginning to worry about *Vendaval* and whether you'd encountered some unexpected trouble. Tell me—how did it go?"

"We were successful, sir. Chief Reza and I jumped into the Thousand Worlds ward while our team found a landing spot for the light transport we borrowed, and we extracted Sapwu Zrinan the next night. Captain Juarez delivered him to Latzari and then we proceeded here." Sikander handed Abernathy a datachip. "This is a complete mission report, plus a battle-damage assessment on the Tzoru fleets orbiting Tamabuqq Prime. We got a close look at the Golden Banner during our approach and departure."

"And Ambassador Hart?"

"He decided to remain in Bagal-Dindir, sir. He sent Lara Dunstan to Latzari in his place."

Reyes frowned. "So you decided to smuggle your girl-friend out of the siege instead of a diplomat with the pleni-potentiary powers to make whatever agreement we need to make with the Sapwu?"

Sikander met her eyes with an icy chill. "Mr. Hart felt that he had a responsibility to the personnel at the embassy, one that he could not abandon. Since Deputy Ambassador Yeager could not travel due to injuries he'd sustained during the siege, the senator selected the next-most-senior choice to represent the Commonwealth's interests. That happened to be Dr. Dunstan."

Reyes scowled at Sikander's tone, but she said nothing. Abernathy cleared his throat, and motioned to the confer-ence table. "I see," he said. "Have a seat, and tell us what we need to know. What are conditions like in the Thousand Worlds ward? Can they hold out until we return?"

"They're bad, sir," Sikander replied, taking the seat indi-cated by the commodore. "Food stores are running out, the cold weather is a real hardship, and the *warumzi agu* have been shelling the district with a handful of old museum-piece artillery tubes—that's how Mr. Yeager was wounded. There are a lot of sick and injured people within the old walls. On the other hand, the cold weather has been the only thing stopping the revolutionaries from storming the place. Major Dalton told me that she fears the first good thaw might give the *warumzi* the break they need to gain a foothold inside the walls, and once that happens, it's all over. And that assumes the Hish or some other Militarist *sebet* don't decide to end things sooner by committing their troops. I don't think we can afford to delay our return at all."

"Attacking before we were ready proved costly just a few weeks ago," Reyes observed. "We've received reinforcements, yes, but barely more than we needed to make up our losses from the first attack."

"I can't tell you for certain that you have enough firepower to blast your way through the Golden Banner and Monarch Sword fleets and any other formations the Militarists get into place over the next few days," said Sikander. "All I can say is that we can't wait much longer to make the attempt, because the Thousand Worlds ward is going to have to capitulate in another ten days—or less if the weather turns against us."

"I guess we'll have to go with what we've got here on hand, damn it all," said Abernathy. "What about Sapwu? Can we count on his fleet? Will he be able to stand down the Militarists?"

"If the Supernal Glory Fleet moves on Tamabuqq you shouldn't assume they'll join a fight against the Golden Banner or Monarch Sword, sir. Open fighting between the high clans is simply unthinkable to the Tzoru—it's completely outside the norms of their civilization. But Sapwu Zrinan is strongly in favor of a peaceful resolution to the current troubles, and he can exert a good deal of pressure on the neutral clans to withdraw their support from the Militarists."

"I'd hoped for something more concrete after committing

a warship for ten days to pluck him out of Bagal-Dindir and ferry him to Latzari," Abernathy said, scowling.

"We need something more than a purely military solution, sir," Sikander said. "Sapwu Zrinan represents an answer to the political challenges facing us. If we can solve those, the military situation clears up quite a bit."

"On the other hand, I have a feeling that if we solve the military challenges, then the political situation might become a lot more manageable," Reyes observed. "One's within our control, and the other isn't. I think we should stick to the things we can be certain of, Commodore."

"You might have a point there, Francine," Abernathy said. "I don't have the patience for any more damned surprises, that's for sure."

"I'm not quite finished, sir," Sikander said. "I have two more items to report. First, I can tell you that you hurt the Tzoru warships badly in our first attack. Our battle-damage assessment shows that most of the Golden Banner Fleet is virtually immobilized by drive damage. Captain Juarez suspects that the yards in Tamabuqq might not have replacement drive plates to repair them."

"Really?" Abernathy leaned back in his chair and tugged at his stiff mustache. "That's interesting. They'd still be in the way because we can't land troops in Bagal-Dindir without going through them, but it's certainly helpful. What's the other thing?"

Sikander produced the sealed envelope Speaker Chau had given him. "I have orders for Fleet Commander Teirhun of the Nyeiran squadron here in Kahnar-Sag. The Nyeiran ambassador told me that in hisher view the situation now requires Teirhun to cooperate fully with the relief of the Thousand Worlds ward. Chau said that Teirhun will act upon these instructions and accept the orders of the combined fleet commander to resolve the crisis."

Abernathy let out a sharp bark of laughter and slapped the table. "I suppose the prospect of starvation and lynch mobs helped this Chau character to reconsider the limits of his or her authority. All right, then. That's a battle cruiser, a light cruiser, and four more destroyers we can add to the force. I think I like our chances, D-Com!"

Reyes allowed herself a thin smile. "So do I, Commodore. If we can get there in time."

"If we can get there in time," Abernathy agreed. "Mr. North, you'd better take those orders on over to the Nyeiran commander. Heshe doesn't know it yet, but they're going to be getting under way before the end of the day."

"Yes, sir," Sikander replied. He didn't relish the idea of paying a visit to a whole shipful of Nyeirans and could only imagine what the interior spaces must look like. They were unsettling creatures, although that was no fault of their own. On the other hand, Speaker Chau had struck him as a very reasonable entity and seemed to possess a reassuring demeanor. If that was typical of Nyeirans, he'd be fine. "I'll see to it at once."

"Very good," Abernathy said. "Oh, and one more thing. As of this moment I'm tearing up your letter of relief—you are officially reinstated. Good work, Mr. North."

18

Night on Latzari lasted for four days. Lara Dunstan knew that was not really the right way to look at it, but the human circadian rhythm demanded something close to four eight-hour sleep periods and four sixteen-hour wakeful periods during Latzari's ninety-nine hours of darkness. Tzoru had similar body clocks, since they'd evolved on Tamabuqq Prime, a world whose day was about the same length as Earth's. When they'd colonized Latzari, thousands of years ago, they'd adapted to the world's characteristics by building cities bathed in golden light to help fool the natural cycles of the body into staying awake for a workday that regularly began and ended in the hours of darkness—and sleeping chambers with impenetrable blinds to simulate night during the ninety-nine-hour day.

At least Latzari made up for its orbital peculiarities with some of the most spectacular skygazing Lara had ever encountered. The domain of the Sapwu clan was a large moon orbiting Sagkal-Ama, a gas giant with magnificent cloud bands of purple and gold. Like many such bodies, Latzari was tidally locked, with one face forever turned toward its primary; the huge planet never moved from its dominating position in the sky above the Sapwu stronghold of Muqur-Ba. To add to the celestial scenery, Latzari enjoyed three-quarters standard gravity, which meant that the mountains towering around the capital were some of the steepest and tallest Lara had ever seen. It reminded her of pictures she'd seen of Machu Picchu on Terra, except the vertical jungle clinging to the mountainsides around her guesthouse gleamed with bioluminescent flora and the golden lanterns of Tzoru platform-homes built into the sides of sheer cliffs.

Lara stood on the balcony of her suite, lost in the scenery for a time. It was surprisingly warm; she and her small entourage had arrived in Muqur-Ba shortly after sunset, and it would take thirty or forty hours before the chill of the night really began to set in. *How does anybody not know about this?* she wondered. Human tour operators or resort builders would make a killing in Latzari, but as far as she knew no one had ever considered establishing a tourism industry in this system. No doubt the standoffish ways of Sebet Sapwu had a lot to do with that, but it did make her wonder what other marvels might be hiding in the other hundred and twenty-one worlds of the Dominion and whether they'd ever been seen by human eyes.

Perhaps they shouldn't be, she decided. Nothing would make Muqur-Ba more ordinary than busloads of human tourists filling up the same big chain resort hotels found anywhere in the Coalition of Humanity. *Maybe the Sapwu know exactly what they're doing by keeping human commercialism away from places like Latzari.*

"Dr. Dunstan?" Sergeant Wall appeared on the balcony. "Ma'am, the Sapwu transport is here."

"Thank you, Sergeant," she replied, tearing herself away from the view. "Let's not keep them waiting."

She followed Wall back into the sprawling guest suite—the city did not have hotels per se, but it did have luxurious guesthouses operated by commoner *sebetu* that made up a reasonable approximation of a human hospitality industry—and then out to the adjacent landing pad, where a Tzoru open-top flyer waited. The sergeant opened the door for her, then climbed in. Lara doubted that she'd need a bodyguard to go speak with the Sapwu clan elders, but Petty Officer Ortiz had reminded her that appearances mattered quite a bit to the Tzoru. She'd also accepted half a day's delay between arriving on Latzari and meeting with Zrinan and the other Sapwu leaders, for the same reason. Regardless of her mission's urgency, she couldn't push too aggressively for a decision; aristocratic Tzoru would regard that as a sign of desperation or immaturity. While Zrinan might be favorably disposed toward her after the escape from Bagal-Dindir, he'd made it clear to Lara during their short ride from *Vendaval* to Latzari that it was just as important to build consensus within the clan as it was in the dealings of the Dominion High Council.

The flyer lifted off gracefully and steered through the warm glow of streetlamps and Sagkal-light for the Sapwu palace at the heart of Muqur-Ba. Lara noted no prohibition against overflights here; that courtesy belonged to the Anshar alone, and no other noble *sebet* dared to assert such a requirement on their own worlds, even one dozens of light-years from Bagal-Dindir. The Tzoru pilot said nothing as they flew up to the palace's expansive landing pad, several kilometers from the guesthouse and nearly a thousand meters higher up the mountainside. When they alighted, a chamberlain in Sapwu livery met them on the landing pad. "This way, honored guests," she said, and led Lara and Sergeant Wall through the palace to a veranda overlooking the city below.

Three Tzoru waited at a large wooden table illuminated by glowing lanterns: Sapwu Zrinan, a tall male of middle years, and a female so old her dermal patterns were white as snow on her wattled hide. Lara leaned over to whisper, "You might as well find a place to make yourself comfortable, Sergeant. This could take a while."

"Thank you, ma'am. I'm just a shout away if you need me for anything." The sergeant peeled off to wait with the chamberlain while Lara advanced out to meet the waiting Tzoru.

"Welcome to our home, Lara Dunstan," Zrinan said, bowing. "May I introduce two of the elders of my *sebet*? This is Sapwu Kezzum"—he motioned to the taller male—"and this is Sapwu Garba, who happens to be my honored parent."

"I am pleased to meet you both, gracious hosts," Lara said in Tzoqabu, bowing with what she hoped was the proper degree of gratitude. "I thank you for agreeing to see me so swiftly."

"It is nothing," said Kezzum, acknowledging her with a nod. Zrinan's mother remained silent.

"We do not represent all of the Sapwu who would normally take part in this sort of discussion, but we understand that time is pressing," Zrinan said. "The three of us can speak for our absent brothers and sisters. If we develop a consensus about how our *sebet* should act, the rest will support us."

"I understand," Lara said, and hoped that she actually did. She had plenty of experience with how Tzoru clans acted in concert with each other and in speaking with individuals representing their clan's views, but she'd never really been present at the internal deliberations of an aristocratic clan. Tzoru didn't speak much to outsiders about things that happened inside their homes, and they certainly didn't record them in historical texts.

"Just a few hours ago, we received news from Tamabuqq," Zrinan continued. Lara's heart leaped in her chest. *Did the Thousand Worlds ward fall?* she wondered, not daring to ask the question for fear she might make it true. Zrinan, however, ignored her stricken look and kept speaking. "Something has happened in the capital that has not happened in several thousand years: The Anshar named a Sharur-Tal to serve as her supreme warlord. General Hish Mubirrum accepted the honor a few hours after we left the homeworld."

"There is a Sharur-Tal?" Lara frowned, searching her memory. She knew the term well; during the long span of Tzoru history there were several eras in which reigning

Anshars chose to appoint a single autocrat to serve as their high minister and military commander, not unlike the shoguns of ancient Japan. No doubt more than a few of those Sharur-Tals had appointed themselves to supreme power, relegating their monarchs to the role of revered figurehead while they went about the work of governing the Dominion as they saw fit. The institution had fallen out of use dozens of centuries ago, undermined by the resentments and jealousies of other aristocratic clans who grew tired of ceding power to one of their own. "I had no idea that the old title could still be assumed. It hasn't been used in centuries, has it?"

Sapwu Garba let her mouth fall open in laughter. "Well, it seems this human knows a little bit about our history. I thought for certain that you would have to explain that to her, Zrinan."

"Only what I've read in a couple of textbooks," Lara said. "I know the title, but I don't know exactly what this *means*. I seem to recall that the powers of the Sharur-Tal varied quite a bit over the centuries. What can General Hish do now that he couldn't do before through his effective control of the council?"

"For one thing, start a war," said Sapwu Kezzum. "Compel all the high *sebetu* to fight alongside him, for another. And, should a *sebet* fail to contribute to the effort as he directs, he could declare them all traitors and destroy them."

"So there's nothing to stop General Hish from moving against the Thousand Worlds ward?" Lara asked.

"That remains to be seen," Zrinan said. "The courier who brought us this news reported that he has not done so yet. It may suit his purposes to allow things to remain as they are."

"Or he may be unwilling to test his strength yet," Garba observed. "There is a difference between authority and consensus. Hish Mubirrum may have one, but he does not yet have the other."

"And that is the point to which we must now speak, I think," said Zrinan. "Dr. Dunstan, I have apprised Kezzum and Garba of our discussions aboard *Vendaval*. I explained that the Commonwealth of Aquila wishes the Sapwu to challenge the Militarists who now control the Dominion High Council in order to quell the *warumzi agu* and restore normal relations between the Dominion and the various human powers. While we are far from content with the current disorders, we are not convinced that what you propose is in our best interests."

"Surely peace is in everybody's best interests," Lara replied. "Aquila is not in favor of wars of conquest, but I have to warn you that some of the other human powers are. If we fail to find a way to stop this conflict, you'll be playing right into their hands."

"Is peace in our interests?" Kezzum asked. "Your people have all but conquered worlds such as Kahnar-Sag or Shimatum. Your warships orbit our worlds, your corporations crush any of our merchant *sebetu* that do not surrender their markets, your citizens defy the authority and laws of the Anshar in a hundred different offworlder concessions. There are whole cities on Tzoru worlds where our people live only as laborers and menials under human overlords. Perhaps Tzem Ebneghirz and his followers have a point."

Lara almost wilted under Kezzum's vehemence. She'd figured that the other Sapwu leaders would share Zrinan's outlook, but it seemed that was not the case. *Is he a* warumzi agu? she wondered. *He certainly speaks like one!* Her first instinct was to apologize for offending Kezzum, her second to argue with him and point out the benefits of those treaties . . . but she had to guard her words. What she said now might set expectations that Ambassador Hart or other Aquilan diplomats would have to live with for years. She composed her answer with care, and met Kezzum's gaze evenly before she spoke. "Lord Kezzum, I can't speak to agreements made by other powers or negotiated years ago," she said. "But I do know that talking is better than fighting. Help us to work around the hard-liners in the Dominion High Council, and we'll have a chance to give your concerns the consideration they deserve."

"An empty promise!" Kezzum snapped.

"No, a simple statement of fact," said Lara. "As long as the Militarists of the Emuqq-Mamit control the council, your ability to look after your clan's interests or shape the Dominion's policies as you deem best is severely limited. General Hish isn't returning our calls, Lord Kezzum. No one's complaints can be addressed until we have someone we can negotiate with."

"It seems our guest is not so easy to bully as you thought, Kezzum," said Garba. "Stop your blustering and use your ears. I want to hear what she has to say."

Kezzum settled back into his seat, his expression unreadable. Lara turned to the elderly female. "It seems to me that the Dominion would be better off with the Sapwu speaking for the Anshar instead of the Hish. The combined squadrons of the Coalition powers are on their way back to the Thousand Worlds ward—the crisis is coming within a matter of days. Send the Supernal Glory Fleet to Tamabuqq Prime. If the Sapwu show up in force, you'll have a say in how events play out. And we'll have someone we can talk to if General Hish refuses to speak with us."

"Young student, you understand much about us, but you miss much too," Garba said. "Consensus brought the Hish and the other Militarists to power. It's not our place to defy that consensus because we do not like the results. There is no precedent, no place in our traditions, for Zrinan to return to the Anshar's court and seek to reverse the decisions that have been made."

"There isn't much recent precedent for refusing to suppress revolutionaries or seeking the title of Sharur-Tal, but that didn't seem to stop General Hish," Lara replied. "With all due respect, Lady Garba, traditions stay traditions only until someone decides they're not useful anymore."

"Spoken like a human," Kezzum muttered.

"Which does not mean she is not correct," Zrinan said to the other male.

"Yes, but *when does it stop*?" Kezzum demanded. "Which

Tzoru worlds are safe from their hunger? How much is enough for their fleets and their corporations? Even if we do as they ask, what is to stop Aquila or Dremark or the Nyeirans from demanding yet another city on yet another world as soon as we have brought down the Hish for them?"

Lara couldn't muster an answer for a long moment. "I don't know what to tell you," she finally admitted to Kezzum. "I can discuss Aquilan agreements, if that would help. Ambassador Hart will stand by whatever adjustments I deem necessary."

"That's a question for the Baltzu—Shimatum is their world, not ours," said Garba. The old female shook her head slowly. "I simply don't see how we can involve ourselves in any of these issues now."

Kezzum folded his arms and gazed off into the shadows of the lamplit garden. Zrinan looked to the other two Sapwu leaders in turn, then stood and faced Lara. "You have given us much to consider," he told her. "Let us think about what you have said and discuss this among ourselves. We will speak again soon, Dr. Dunstan."

Lara started to protest, and barely managed to stop herself. *We don't have the time for this!* she fumed silently. Unfortunately, she knew Tzoru well enough to know that pushing for an immediate decision would not help her at all. A dismissal was a dismissal . . . and if both Kezzum and Garba were unused to dealing directly with humans, Zrinan might do a better job of advocating cooperation without her around. She decided to make the best of it, and be a gracious guest. "Of course," she said. "I thank you for this conversation, and I look forward to our next meeting."

She stood, bowed, and oriented herself on the imposing figure of Sergeant Wall, waiting patiently twenty meters distant by the doorway through which they'd entered. The walk through the Sapwu palace back to the landing pad passed by in a fog as Lara tried to assess what had just happened. She'd assumed that Zrinan had the authority to commit his *sebet* to whatever positions he deemed appropriate, but it seemed that clan leadership was not quite as clear-cut as she'd believed.

She took no interest in the magnificent view as the Sapwu pilot flew her and Sergeant Wall back to the guesthouse. Instead she chewed at her lip as she replayed the conversation in her mind. *Did I miss anything? What else I could have said to get the Sapwu to commit?* She was more than a little tempted to tell the driver to turn around and take her back to the palace so that she could make an appeal based on simple emotion and urgency; she simply didn't have the luxury of waiting for Sapwu Kezzum and Sapwu Garba to come around on their own, not if she had any hope of convincing them to intervene at the Thousand Worlds ward in time to prevent the outbreak of open warfare between the Tzoru Dominion and the great powers in the Coalition of Humanity.

"Is it something you'd care to talk about, ma'am?" Sergeant Wall asked her.

Lara gave herself a small shake, realizing that she had no idea what the marine was referring to. "I beg your pardon, Sergeant?"

"Whatever it is that you're stewing over, Dr. Dunstan. You're staring a hole in the back of the front seat. Doesn't take a fancy degree for me to see that you're not happy with how things went."

"No, I guess it doesn't," Lara admitted. She gave a small shrug. "I did my best, and I just don't know if I made any impression on them."

"Ma'am, I'm just a dumb grunt, but I know that if you did your best you don't have anything to regret. Sometimes the other team's got something to say about how the game goes."

"Yes, but so much is riding on getting this right. They said they'd think it over. That could mean *anything.*"

"From a human, sure. But you know the Tzoru—they're careful not to say things they don't mean. My guess is that if the Sapwu told you they'd think it over, they're really going to think it over."

"Hmm. You're right." Lara looked at the big sergeant in surprise. She hadn't expected that he'd be able to tell her something about the Tzoru that she'd overlooked, but he had. "Why is it that the guys who tell you that they're just dumb grunts usually aren't?"

Wall grinned. "You never saw my math grades, ma'am."

The flyer slowed and drifted down to alight on the landing pad by their guesthouse. Lara allowed herself one more moment of self-pity, then marched inside and immediately got to work on her dataslate. She started by transcribing as much of the conversation as she could, doing her best to capture every turn of phrase—standard Foreign Ministry practice for a discussion with representatives of another power. Then she moved on to creating new files on Sapwu Kezzum and Sapwu Garba, jotting down her impressions of what they wanted and what role they played in clan decisions. One meeting wasn't much to go on, but it was a place to start. *And it might help some other Foreign Ministry rookie when he or she runs into these Tzoru again,* she told herself.

The work absorbed her attention for several hours; she hardly even noticed when one of the marines brought her a sandwich and a soda for her midday meal, such as it was in Latzari's long night. She took two bites and went right back to her writing.

That was when she heard the gunshots.

A few months ago, she wouldn't have recognized the sounds for what they were; modern magnetic weapons made a sort of shrill chirping sound when they fired, and old-fashioned firearms were museum pieces on most Aquilan worlds. But six weeks within the walls of the Thousand Worlds ward had taught her what gunshots sounded like, since the ill-equipped *warumzi agu* militias had to make do with antiquated weapons. Lara stared at the doorway leading into the suite's common room for only a moment before her recently honed reflexes kicked in. She dove under her desk.

"Gun! Gun!" human voices shouted from the common room.

"Death to the alien defilers!" screamed a Tzoru. More Tzoru echoed the cry. "Death!"

"Get down! Get down!" one of the other marines barked. Lara only caught a glimpse of motion through the open door, a marine running past with his mag carbine raised, Tzoru figures darting from one side to the other, and then a whole fusillade of mag-weapon fire and explosive gunshots rocked the guesthouse. She heard high hissing Tzoru wails, human grunts of pain and shock, smashing furniture . . . and then silence.

Cautiously she poked her head around the side of her desk. "Sergeant Wall?" she called. "Ortiz?"

No one answered—and then a big Tzoru male wearing a green cap appeared in the doorway to her room. He carried a wicked-looking hatchet of some kind in his hand, and he bled freely from wounds in his side and his arm. But as soon as he caught sight of Lara, he bared his serrated teeth in a predatory snarl and started toward her, raising his weapon.

Lara scrambled back, eyes fixed on the gleaming edge of the hatchet as she groped for something she could use as a weapon. She found a slender lamp fixed in a sconce on the wall, and with desperate strength yanked it free, turning to meet the Tzoru with the hatchet. But just as the raging *warumzi* rushed at her, a mag weapon chirped from the doorway behind him. The lethal dart blew a four-centimeter hole through the center of his chest. The Tzoru fanatic staggered one more step toward Lara before collapsing to the floor.

Sergeant Wall leaned against the doorway, mag pistol in his hand, the front of his uniform soaked in his own blood. Somehow he managed to smile for Lara. Then he slumped to the floor, dead on his feet.

"Dear God," Lara murmured, beyond shock. She stood frozen for a long moment, trying to understand what had just happened. Then some hidden survival instinct kicked in. She stepped over the dead Tzoru and hurried to Wall's side. There was nothing she could do for the sergeant, but she took the pistol from his massive hand and peered cautiously out into the room beyond.

Five green-clad Tzoru lay sprawled on the floor, along with another marine—Davis, she thought. Petty Officer Ortiz stood at the other side of the room, staring in amazement at a Tzoru carving knife embedded in his forearm. And the remaining two marines, Corporal Harris and Private McKenna, stood by the guesthouse door, mag carbines cradled in their arms.

"Dear God," Lara repeated, trying to take in the scene. "Where did these Tzoru come from?"

Corporal Harris turned at the sound of her voice. She was a tall, big-boned young woman, the squad's medic. She towered over Lara in her battle-dress uniform. "Dr. Dunstan, are you okay?" she asked.

"I'm not hurt," Lara said. "But Sergeant Wall . . ."

Harris grimaced. "I know. I saw him get hit."

"What happened?"

"One of these guys"—Harris toed a Tzoru lying motionless on the floor—"came up to the front door and said he was a messenger. When we opened up to let him in, the whole group was waiting just around the corner. They shot the sergeant and rushed the door."

"But Latzari is supposed to be safe!" Lara said.

"I guess Tzem Ebneghirz has followers everywhere," Petty Officer Ortiz said. He looked over to Corporal Harris, cradling his arm. "Um, I don't want to be a crybaby about this, but there's a knife in my arm and I really don't want it there anymore. Corporal, can you do something about it?"

"Yeah, of course, in just a second." Harris looked around, examining the windows and doors. Only after she satisfied herself that no immediate threats were about to materialize did she return her attention to the intel specialist. "Ortiz, you're senior man now, but I think we ought to get out of here and relocate to the next house over until we figure out what we need to do. There might be more bad guys on the way expecting to find us here."

Ortiz looked pale, but he nodded. "Makes sense to me. Dr. Dunstan, that okay by you?"

"I agree," said Lara. "Let's get out of here."

She allowed Harris and McKenna to escort her away from the bloody scene. No more Tzoru waited for them outside, but she felt better when they were inside the adjacent building and the door was secured behind them. She even managed to find a washroom and close the door behind her before the uncontrollable trembling and gasping sobs completely overwhelmed her.

By the time she rejoined her reduced entourage fifteen minutes later, McKenna and Harris had relocated the squad's gear from their original quarters as well as Lara's own scanty travel kit. The marine medic sat by Ortiz at the dining room table, bandaging the petty officer's arm, while Private McKenna stood watch at the front door, mag carbine at the ready.

Lara looked at Ortiz's arm, then glanced over to Harris. "How is he?" she asked the medic.

"Should be fine—the knife missed the big blood vessels," Harris replied. "I think the tendon's going to need some work, though. I can give it a try, but he'd be better off with a real surgeon."

"I think I'll wait, thanks," said Ortiz. "And, for the record, it hurts like hell."

"There's a whole bunch of Tzoru soldiers coming," McKenna suddenly said from his post by the door. "What should I do?"

"Hold on!" Lara said immediately. She hurried over to peer out the marine's window to see for herself. "Those are Sapwu house troops. Let them in."

McKenna gave her a dubious look. "You sure about that, ma'am?"

"If the Sapwu want us dead there's nothing we can do about it," said Lara. "These guys are the closest we'll find to

Tzoru police. Open the door." Then she squared her shoulders and made herself stand still and breathe slowly to meet the Sapwu soldiers.

As Lara had suspected, the Tzoru soldiers had little idea of how to investigate the scene or even what sort of questions to ask. Once she finally got them to understand that the *warumzi agu* had attacked her little delegation in the guesthouse, they did a good job of sweeping the area for any other fanatics and securing the scene. Then they reported to their superiors, who showed up half an hour later and repeated the process. Just as Lara finished the second round of explanations, the golden lights of an ornately decorated Tzoru skybarge appeared outside the room's canyon-facing windows. The craft settled down on the landing pad by the guesthouses; moments later, Sapwu Zrinan emerged and hurried toward the house.

Lara excused herself from the Sapwu captain questioning her, taking a deep breath and smoothing her skirt suit. The last thing in the world she wanted to do was think about any kind of diplomatic fencing with the Sapwu elders, but she couldn't let them know that. So instead she made herself wait patiently as Sapwu Zrinan entered the room.

"Dr. Dunstan, my *sebet* is so sorry," he began, offering a bow of acute apology. "Nothing like this has happened on Latzari in centuries. I am ashamed and appalled."

"I know it was no fault of yours, First Councillor," Lara said gravely.

"I praise the Sixty-Four that you were not personally injured." Zrinan's hands fluttered as he spoke, a sign of deep agitation among most Tzoru. "Truly, I had no idea that you and your escorts were in any danger here. With your permission, we will post a detachment of Sapwu house guards around your quarters to prevent any more attacks. Or, if you prefer, we will place any ship in this system at your disposal and take you wherever you want to go."

"I thank you for that." Lara decided that Sapwu Zrinan either meant what he was saying from the bottom of his three-chambered heart, or he was the most masterful actor she had ever encountered among the Tzoru. "I take it you've seen the other building?"

"Yes, I did. Simply terrible. Again, I am so sorry."

"Who attacked us?" Lara asked. "Do your security people know any of them?"

Zrinan nodded wearily, and moved away from the others in the room, leading Lara out onto the room's balcony to seek a little more privacy for their conversation. "I deeply regret to inform you that they are known to us," he said as Lara joined him outside. "They are retainers in the service of Sapwu Kezzum. We believe that he made arrangements to assassinate you soon after you arrived. After your visit, he instructed his agents to carry out the attack."

"Wait. *Sapwu Kezzum* ordered my death?" Lara demanded. "Where is he now?"

"He is confined," Zrinan told her. "Trusted Tzoru are rooting out the *warumzi agu* sympathizers among our retainers even as we speak. I shall of course keep you informed of the investigations."

"Of course," said Lara. "Yes, please do."

The Tzoru aristocrat remained silent for a long time, regarding Lara with his black eyes until she began to wonder if he expected her to say something else. Then he bobbed his head in another awkward gesture of apology. "Sapwu Garba and I are in agreement," he said. "Our *sebet* cannot challenge the existing consensus in the Anshar's court. The *warumzi agu* must be suppressed, but attempting to impose our will on events in a time of so much bitterness and uncertainty would only exacerbate the disorders that now beset the Dominion. If all choices lead to disaster, then it is better to do nothing at all and accept what is fated to be."

"But if you choose not to intervene, then you allow the revolutionaries and the militarists to make your choices for you!" Lara protested. She groped for an argument that might sway the former first councillor. "Doesn't the Seventh

Prophecy teach Tzoru that to do nothing in the face of injustice is to participate in it?"

"And the Ninth reminds us that when you strike a blow, it is impossible to foresee on whom it will eventually fall." Zrinan gestured from the balcony in the direction of the guesthouse Lara and her guards had vacated; Tzoru dressed in the somber blue gowns of a mortician *sebet* silently carried out a shrouded form—human or Tzoru, she could not tell. "I am afraid that humans bring out the worst in us, Lara Dunstan. In the fifty centuries my *sebet* has governed this world, never have we raised our hands against an honored guest. It would be better for us both if we had nothing to do with your kind."

Fifty centuries? Every time Lara thought she'd finally accustomed herself to the sheer span of time embodied in Tzoru culture, some new evidence of the Dominion's awesome antiquity rose up to shake her. *The Sapwu have ruled Latzari since the time of Egypt's Middle Kingdom,* she realized, and then pressed on with her point. "That may be true, Lord Zrinan, but our fates are entangled already. As my friend Sikander said a few days ago, time doesn't run backwards—"

She stopped herself in midsentence, struck by a sudden insight. *Time,* that was the key! If she'd learned one thing in years of studying the history of the Tzoru Dominion, it was the fact that Tzoru saw time entirely differently than humans did. She turned away from Zrinan, staring at the spectacular orb of Sagkal-Ama in the night sky as she developed her thought. Zrinan started to answer, but she held up her hand, thinking hard; the old councillor fell silent, waiting for her.

"Time doesn't run backwards," Lara repeated, turning back to him. "The future comes whether we want it to or not, doesn't it? Especially here in the Dominion. We think that things are always going to be like they are now, but the future never turns out to be what we expect it to be."

"There is truth in your observation, but what does it have to do with the *warumzi agu* and the troubles that now beset us?" Zrinan asked.

"Everything, I hope," said Lara. "Lord Zrinan, Tzoru can *outwait* humans—that's how we craft our appeal to the other *sebetu*. I think I know how everybody can have a whole cake, if Tzoru are as patient and humans are as short-sighted as I think they are."

The old Tzoru twisted his head to study her with one skeptical eye. "The cake is a metaphor?"

"The cake is a metaphor," Lara agreed, and allowed herself a small smile. Then she told Sapwu Zrinan exactly what she had in mind.

19

Clear arrival, sir!" Giselle Dacey announced from her station by the flag bridge tactical display as *Exeter* shut off her warp ring in Tamabuqq. The cruiser's sensor systems blinked to life, rapidly updating with new scans of the Tzoru capital system. "Several units are executing minor navigational corrections, but no major transit dispersion to report."

"Very well," Commodore Abernathy replied. Like all the other personnel in the squadron's command team, he wore his battle armor over his shipboard uniform, but he left his helmet sitting on the arm of his acceleration couch. Whether he'd intended it as a gesture of confidence or preferred the simple convenience of not trying to watch and listen to the activity of the flag bridge through an opened visor Sikander couldn't say, but everyone else in the compartment wore their full armor. "Are the Tzoru fleets still hugging Tamabuqq Prime?"

The ops officer studied her display for a moment before answering. "Yes, sir. They shifted their positions a bit from *Vendaval*'s last report, but they're all within half a million klicks of the planet."

"As we thought, Commodore," Francine Reyes observed

from the battle couch beside Abernathy's. "They don't want to risk being caught out of position."

"They're also showing us what we expect to see, and most traps begin with bait just like that," said Abernathy. He frowned under his stiff mustache, taking a moment to think before he spoke again. "Ms. Dacey, looks like it's going to be Plan Alpha. Pass the word to everyone, if you please. And keep your eyes open for surprises, they've had weeks to get ready for us."

"Yes, sir!" the ops officer replied. Her fingers flew over her console as she relayed the order to implement the combined fleet's first battle-plan option via the tactical network.

"Mr. Barnes, broadcast on all frequencies, both civilian and military: This is Commodore William Abernathy, officer in command of the allied fleet now arriving in Tamabuqq. Civilian craft now operating near Tamabuqq Prime are hereby advised to leave the area immediately or proceed to port. All vessels, civilian or military, remaining within one million kilometers of Tamabuqq Prime three hours from now will be assumed to be hostile or serving as cover for hostile units and will be fired upon. This is your one and only warning. Abernathy, out."

Sikander winced at the commodore's tone, but made no other protest. *The high-ranking clans aren't going to like that very much,* he reflected. Ordering every civilian ship around another nation's capital world to flee or face destruction was not a conciliatory gesture, but then again William Abernathy had good reason to be suspicious of Tzoru merchant shipping venturing too close to his fleet. He wasn't sure if the commodore would really fire without warning on a Tzoru merchant ship that didn't get out of the area in time, but the stern wording of Abernathy's warning might prevent that scenario from arising. *If I were a Tzoru transport skipper I'd power up my drive and head for safer space after I received that message, anyway.*

Abernathy turned to Sikander next. "Mr. North, any sign of the Sapwu or their Supernal Glory Fleet?"

"No, sir," Sikander reported, trying not to look at Francine Reyes as he did so. "We're still correlating contacts in-system. If they arrived recently and they're any distance away—"

"—we might not have seen them yet," the commodore finished. Any naval officer understood that a ship that appeared from a warp bubble twenty light-minutes distant would not be observable for twenty minutes; warp transits might cheat the speed of light, but few other things in the universe did. "Very good. Let me know when they show up."

"Yes, sir." Sikander checked his display again, then keyed the Intel Section internal circuit, keeping his voice down to avoid interfering with the business of the flag bridge. "Senior Chief, any sign of the Sapwu? They might be on the ground somewhere."

"No, sir, not yet," Senior Chief Lin answered from her post in the squadron's intelligence center. "We're looking for them, and we're catching up on in-system chatter in case any of the Tzoru official news outlets are talking about the Dominion High Council."

"Keep me posted." Sikander would have given a lot to know how Lara Dunstan's mission to Latzari had gone, but it seemed he'd have to wait along with everyone else for that news. He moved on to the tactical situation instead. "How does the Tzoru unit count compare to *Vendaval*'s imagery? Can we account for everybody we saw last time we were here?"

"We're double-checking to make sure, sir, but I think the answer is yes," said Senior Chief Lin. "I'm pretty sure the Monarch Sword and Golden Banner fleets are still here, even if they are jumbled up a little bit."

"Very well," Sikander said. "Keep looking—I wouldn't be surprised if the Hish tried to bring in another regional fleet to meet us or improvised a minefield of some kind. And let me know the second you get good imagery on Bagal-Dindir."

"Aye, Mr. North," the intelligence specialist replied. "You'll be the first to know."

Sikander left his team to do their work, watching as the ships of the multinational fleet shifted into their preplanned positions and turned together toward Tamabuqq Prime, only three light-minutes distant. Most commanders chose to terminate warp transits at a conservative distance from the busier inner regions of a star system in order to minimize collision dangers and make sure that the dangerous radiation bursts of collapsing warp bubbles were kept well away from any inhabited planets. Today William Abernathy sliced that safety margin drastically, hoping to reduce the amount of maneuvering it would take to bring his fleet into battle and giving the Tzoru commanders less time to react to his fleet's arrival. Sikander knew Abernathy had wanted to aim for a warp emergence point only one light-minute out from Tamabuqq Prime, but as long as the fleet included captains from navies that weren't quite up to Aquilan standards, he simply couldn't take the risk.

It's probably for the best, Sikander decided. Reinforced by the powerful Nyeiran squadron and a handful of additional units that had collected at Kahnar-Sag over the last three weeks, the combined squadrons would need some time to arrange their screening elements and form up battle lines before engaging. The heavy hitters now included the cruisers *Exeter, Brigadoon, Hawkins,* and the hastily repaired *Burton,* as well as the Montréalais *Dupleix* and *Gloire,* the Dremish *Prinz Oskar* and *Kassel,* the Nyeiran *Dreik Jol,* and the powerful Nyeiran battle cruiser *Tauk Ze Yur,* the largest warship in the force. Abernathy's Plan Alpha arranged the cruisers into two open-order columns, with *Exeter* at the head of the first column. The Aquilan and Nyeiran destroyers made up the formation's port-side screen, which faced the strongest Tzoru concentrations; Magdalena Juarez's *Vendaval* was there, although as one of the lighter ships present, she was assigned the trailing position. The starboard screen belonged to the lighter units of the Montréalais, Dremish, and Californian squadrons. More important, the combined fleet now escorted a landing force of nearly three thousand

Aquilan, Dremish, Californian, and Nyeiran troops scraped together from garrisons all across the Dominion. None of the great power squadrons included any assault transports, so the troops had to embark on a motley collection of freighters commandeered in Kahnar-Sag. And, as promised, Abernathy had left the Cygnan *Cagliari* behind in Kahnar-Sag, ostensibly to stand guard over Magan Kahnar while the rest of the fleet was gone.

Even though Sikander had had the better part of a week to take it all in, he was still impressed now that he saw Abernathy's formation taking shape. He wasn't the only one; beside him Mason Barnes let out a low whistle. "Twenty-five warships in five different navies," he said. "No one's seen anything like this in generations."

Sikander nodded. "I became curious yesterday and did a little research. It's the largest human fleet to offer battle anywhere since the Dremish Unification wars fifty years ago." As a one-star flag officer, William Abernathy was not really senior enough to be in charge of such a large force, but none of the other Helix Station squadron commanders from the other nations outranked him . . . although Sikander wondered if the Nyeiran Teirhun actually did but chose not to press the point, since human warships in the international fleet outnumbered Nyeiran warships five to one.

"That's quite a sight," Francine Reyes said to Abernathy, unconsciously echoing Mason's line of thought. "If only they were all Aquilan, I'd say we were ready for anything."

"We work with the tools we've got, D-Com," Abernathy said. "Still, they seem sharp enough. The damned Nyeirans are keeping station better than our own ships at the moment."

"I think they're anxious to impress us," Reyes said.

Abernathy snorted. "It seems so. Ms. Dacey, signal battle acceleration, if you please. Now that we're here there's no sense putting things off any longer."

"Battle acceleration, aye," Giselle Dacey replied.

The allied ships spun together in their formations, pointing their main drive plates in the same direction and quickly increasing power to begin adjusting the fleet's course. Even with the close-approach warp arrival, it would still take a couple of hours of near-maximum thrust to bring the fleet within engagement range of the Tzoru warships guarding Tamabuqq Prime. That was the nature of most space battles: hours or sometimes even days of laborious maneuvers to get within weapon range of the enemy, followed by a blistering barrage of fire that might be over in a fraction of the time spent on initial maneuvers. Under standard tactical doctrine, Sikander's own experience of battles breaking out suddenly at close range should have been the exception, not the rule.

He settled in to wait out the approach, trying to busy himself in the Intel Section work of assessing the movements, observable damage, and suspected command arrangements of the Monarch Sword and Golden Banner fleets. Lin and Macklin soon identified several ships in the Militarist formations that appeared to have been hastily repaired during the twelve days since *Vendaval* had departed. Nothing was important enough to report to Commodore Abernathy, so Sikander simply made note of their findings in the tactical systems. But then Mason Barnes spoke up from his position by the comm specialists' consoles. "Commodore, signal from the Californian destroyer *Bryce*," he said. "They've detected a Tzoru formation in the sensor shadow of Zalasa. The tactical systems are updating now."

"Looks like the Hish managed to sneak some reinforcements in when we weren't looking," Abernathy remarked. "Very well, Mr. Barnes. My compliments to *Bryce*'s captain, good work."

"They hid on the second moon last time we were here," Reyes said. "I guess they figured we'd be looking for that today and decided to try the first one instead." Abernathy only nodded in reply.

Sikander shifted his attention to the new formation. He could see at a glance that *Bryce*, at the head of the starboard-side screen, happened to be the ship closest to Tamabuqq

Prime's first moon; no wonder she'd spotted the new Tzoru ships before anyone else. He keyed his team's internal circuit. "Senior Chief, you've got the new contacts?"

"Yes, sir. Just a moment . . . okay, we've got them. That's the Resounding Triumph Fleet from Ingurra, under the control of a minor clan allied with the Hish. How do the Tzoru come up with these fleet names? Anyway, it looks like three armored cruisers, two light cruisers, and six or seven obsolete torpedo boats."

Sikander allowed himself a small smile in response, even though the circuit was voice only. He'd been wondering about the grandiose names himself. *I'll have to look into how the tradition got started . . . but not right now,* he told himself. He forwarded the information to the tactical systems. "Commodore, we've got an identification on the new formation. It's a small provincial fleet from Ingurra, under the control of Hish allies. No modern warships in their order of battle."

"Very good. We'll ignore them as long as they stay out of our way," said Abernathy. "Let's come left a bit and make the Militarists work a bit to bring their units to bear, Ms. Dacey."

Mason Barnes glanced at Sikander. "That makes three Tzoru fleets as I count 'em," he said quietly. "Looks like today's the day that Reyes gets that war she's been hoping for."

"Let's hope we see one more. The Sapwu might be able to talk some sense into the Hish."

"You sure they won't line up for the other side if they do show?"

Sikander gave him a look. "I have faith in Lara. She'll find a way to persuade them to do something about the Hish."

"I hope you're right, or the d-com'll make your life miserable all over again," Mason observed.

Sikander shrugged and returned his attention to his work. The distance between the Tzoru fleets and the allied squadrons steadily dropped as minutes crawled by; Intel Section studied and identified one Tzoru warship after another, evaluated signal traffic, and ensured that the commercial traffic complied with Abernathy's demand. He was glad that he had something to occupy his attention. Throughout the fleet, officers and crews manning weapons consoles and tactical displays and damage-control centers could only sit or stand by their posts and wait for the battle to start.

Abernathy ordered another course change, forcing the Militarist forces to realign again to meet his new line of advance—and then twenty minutes later altered it again, and after that a third time, as the Monarch Sword Fleet jumbled up in its efforts to quickly adjust position and the Resounding Triumph belatedly broke out from behind the moon Zalasa in an attempt to reach a position where they might be relevant to the coming fight. The Golden Banner Fleet shifted slightly, but held its position close to Tamabuqq Prime; either they intended to make a stand as the last line of defense, or they knew it was hopeless to try to match Abernathy's maneuvers.

It still came as a surprise to Sikander when the engagement began. "Sir, Fleet Commander Teirhun requests permission to open fire," Mason Barnes reported from the communications center. "He says the Monarch Sword battle line is well within *Tauk Ze Yur*'s range."

"Ours, too," Reyes said to Abernathy.

The commodore nodded. "Let's begin, then. Ms. Dacey, pass the word to all units: Fire according to Fire Plan Alpha. Screen commanders, maneuver as needed to intercept Tzoru light units."

"Aye, sir!" Giselle replied. A moment later, *Exeter*'s kinetic cannons thundered to life, shaking the ship with their powerful blasts.

Fire Plan Alpha was brutally simple: Each ship in each column in the allied formation targeted the corresponding ship of the Militarist formation. Since Abernathy had organized his battle line into two columns, the plan directed the fire of two ships against each Tzoru ship under attack. *Exeter* and *Tauk Ze Yur* opened fire on the Tzoru battle cruiser *Etzu-Kanu* at the head of the Monarch Sword column, while *Brigadoon* and *Prinz Oskar* turned their guns against *Shuha-Daku* in the second position, the third ships engaged their opposite number, and so on. Only the first five Monarch Sword ships came under fire, but the Tzoru ships farther back in line were too far away to reply with effective fire anyway.

Heavy salvos of K-cannon penetrators traveling at thousands of kilometers per second raked the Monarch Sword's battle line. Many of the shots missed; hitting a maneuvering target could be devilishly difficult even on the practice range. But the sheer weight of fire meant that *Etzu-Kanu, Shuha-Daku,* and the ships following after them couldn't dodge every attack. Fierce explosions erupted all over the head of the Monarch Sword column as tungsten rods slammed into armored hulls, instantly transformed into incandescent metallic gas by the unimaginable kinetic energy of each impact. A dense pattern of penetrators from one of *Tauk Ze Yur*'s battleship-weight weapons struck just under the turret ring of *Etzu-Kanu*'s forward mount, and literally blasted the entire turret into space in a spray of white-hot metal. Shots from *Prinz Oskar* and *Brigadoon* riddled *Shuha-Daku*'s central core, wrecking two of her three fusion plants in the blink of an eye.

"Damned good shooting!" Abernathy shouted, teeth bared in a fierce grin. "Keep it up!"

The Monarch Sword heavies answered with volleys of their own. One of the peculiarities of shipboard weaponry was that the targets of enemy fire never actually *saw* any shots coming their way. Sensors could pick up the powerful electromagnetic blooms of kinetic cannons launching their slugs, and radars could spot the inbound penetrators, but unless a K-cannon shot actually *hit* something, it left no visible sign of its passage. *Exeter* lurched and jerked as her helmsman dodged the Tzoru return fire; other human ships did likewise as their own systems detected incoming attacks.

"The Monarch Sword escorts are maneuvering for a torpedo attack on the left flank, sir," Sikander reported, watching his display. "I count five Ziltu-class cutters and a mix of half a dozen other types."

"Open the range, Ms. Dacey," Abernathy ordered. "Let's not allow those little bastards to draw us into another knife fight. And signal Contre-Amiral Verger to intercept the Resounding Triumph Fleet, since they're so anxious to get into the fight. Tell her to stand off and hit them at range—I see no reason to give them a fair shot at us."

"Aye, sir!" Dacey entered the new orders in the tactical link, while Mason Barnes confirmed them by direct communication to the sub-unit commanders.

Commodore Abernathy nodded in return, watching as his orders unfolded in the flag bridge's central tactical display. "Seems almost too easy," he muttered. "I know that two weeks of drilling in Kahnar-Sag didn't make us *that* much more efficient. What's going on here?"

"The Golden Banner Fleet is sitting on their thumbs," Reyes pointed out. "Admiral Hish is fighting us with only half her fleet."

"Right, but the Golden Banner Fleet can hardly maneuver." Abernathy looked over to Sikander. "That's the damage assessment from *Vendaval,* isn't it?"

"Yes, sir," Sikander confirmed.

"I don't get it, D-Com," the commodore continued. "The Militarists divided up their force for us. They've got three fleets—well, two and a half—that can't support each other. We can easily defeat them in detail. What kind of moron is in charge over there?"

"They might not understand modern fleet tactics," Reyes said, shrugging. "Sure, they surprised us last time by hiding their torpedo boats behind freighters. But coordinating the operations of multiple formations might be something that's just beyond their capabilities, and they don't know they shouldn't try it."

"Mr. North, what do we know about the Monarch Sword commander?" Abernathy asked.

"Admiral Hish Sudi, sir. She's a close relative of Hish Mubirrum, but she's supposed to be well-regarded as a commander." Sikander glanced over the notes his team had assembled on the Tzoru senior officers. He couldn't argue with the conduct of the battle so far, or the effect of the poor coordination between the Tzoru fleets, but he was pretty certain that the Tzoru understood the idea of concentrating their forces in the face of a superior enemy. "I can't tell you what Hish Sudi is trying to accomplish right now, but I promise you that she knows she can't win a duel of long-range gunnery against us and she knows we have no intention of letting her get forces into close range again."

"I'm afraid that doesn't help very much," Commodore Abernathy said. He stroked his mustache, eyes locked on the tactical display. "Well, far be it from me to refuse the help of my opponent. If Hish Sudi wants to keep dancing like this, the music suits me just fine."

Soft green light bathed the command deck of the battleship *Ulhumahasu,* dimmed so that the various instruments and displays at Hish Sudi's disposal stood out brightly in comparison. She had the habit of pacing the deck in measured steps, taking in the flow of information to the flagship by silently listening to the reports on the command channels and pausing from time to time to eye the holographic representation of the battle that formed the center of the cavernous compartment. If *Ulhumahasu* came under fire she would take her place in the armored seat reserved for her use, but until that moment she found that her slow pacing helped her to concentrate, and perhaps reassured the battleship's command crew that nothing taking place at the moment struck her as surprising or particularly worrisome. At least part of her studied posture was justified; nothing now taking place surprised her. But, on the other hand, it was terribly, grievously worrisome despite her outward calm.

She grimaced as the voice channel from the battle cruiser *Shuha-Daku* suddenly cut out in midreport. If fate smiled on the other ship, that was a simple power outage from the accumulated damage—or perhaps a communication emitter scrubbed off the hull by a grazing impact—and not a command deck hit, but Sudi doubted *Shuha-Daku* had been so lucky. *The aliens are shooting us to pieces!* she silently fumed. *I warned Mubirrum that we had no hope of forcing a close engagement outside the orbital approaches. We are wasting ships, and wasting lives!*

She paused to study the males and females in the command deck. All were occupied with their duties; if they doubted her orders, they gave no sign of it. Pride of the Monarch Sword Fleet, the battle cruiser *Ulhumahasu* had the acceleration of a light cruiser, a handpicked crew, and a battery of kinetic cannons nearly as heavy as those of the Golden Banner battlewagons. One for one, it was likely a match for any ship in the alien task force except perhaps the Nyeiran battle cruiser or the big Dremish cruiser . . . but it seemed that the human Abernathy had no intention of providing her with the sort of opportunity under which she might commit *Ulhumahasu* to the fight.

She sighed, and turned to the communications array at one side of the compartment. "Contact General Hish," she instructed the technicians there.

Hish Mubirrum must have been waiting for her call; his face appeared in the holographic display as soon as the technicians established contact. "I thought you might call, Admiral," he said. "I am watching the battle. It does not seem to be going well."

"It is not," Sudi agreed. "As I feared, Abernathy has learned caution. He is using his advantage in range and maneuverability to keep his distance and systematically destroy our mobile units."

"What of the Resounding Triumph? Did they not succeed in closing from their position near Zalasa?"

"The humans stayed far enough away that we had no hope of surprising them with the new fleet."

The general frowned, but nodded in understanding. "You

warned me that it would be difficult to bring the Resounding Triumph into battle at the right moment. I see now that you were right. What are your intentions, Admiral?"

"I cannot continue this exchange of fire for much longer. *Etzu-Kanu* and *Shuha-Daku* are already crippled, and we are sustaining serious losses among our lighter forces too. I must fall back to the high orbitals and combine the Monarch Sword with the Golden Banner." Hish Sudi gave a helpless shrug. "Unfortunately, Abernathy is proving more patient than I had hoped. There is nothing to prevent him from standing off and completing our destruction there, but we might be able to inflict at least some damage if we can bring the Golden Banner Fleet into play."

"Then I think we must deprive Abernathy of the luxury of time," Mubirrum replied. "Fall back as you propose, Admiral. I will take action down here to encourage the humans to seek out a closer engagement. Good luck to you, my offspring." The display flickered and went dark.

Hish Sudi turned back to *Ulhumahasu*'s command crew. "Break off the action," she ordered. "We are retreating to high orbit. Let us see how the humans feel about fighting under the guns of the Golden Banner."

"Sir, the Monarch Sword Fleet is withdrawing," Giselle Dacey reported. "They're falling back on the position of the Golden Banner Fleet."

"Continue firing," Commodore Abernathy ordered. "Give me a pursuit course that keeps us at least forty thousand kilometers from the Tzoru battlewagons. We'll stand off and hammer them until they decide they've had enough."

"I'm surprised they didn't just take up this position right from the start," Reyes murmured. "Keeping the Monarch Sword and Golden Banner together doubles their firepower, not that it helps them much in this situation."

"Admiral Hish is making the best play she could with a bad hand, D-Com. Her best chance was to maneuver in such a way that we'd be drawn into range for a surprise flank attack from the Resounding Triumph Fleet." The commodore pointed at the tactical display as he spoke, sketching out the fleet maneuvers that might have unfolded. "She couldn't keep the Golden Banner battleships with her because they're just too slow-footed to draw us into any kind of positional tactics. Besides, I wouldn't be surprised if she has serious political concerns about leaving the sky empty over Bagal-Dindir."

"I see that, but she couldn't have seriously expected those old rust buckets in the Resounding Triumph to overpower us," said Reyes.

"As I said, it was a bad hand—not that I'm complaining, mind you." Abernathy glanced over to Sikander. "Mr. North, any sign of the Sapwu yet?"

"No, sir."

"Is there any point to offering terms to this Admiral Hish? Do the Tzoru have any kind of tradition of striking their colors when they're beaten?"

"They do, sir," Sikander replied. He was a little surprised that Abernathy would be willing to extend any such offer; after all, the commodore had been humiliated in the First Battle of Tamabuqq, and a lot of men would have taken grim pleasure in completely annihilating an enemy that had embarrassed them. But William Abernathy was proving to be a cannier and more patient commander than Sikander would have guessed from the vicissitudes of their first few weeks together on Helix Station. *Admiral Hish isn't the only one who's had to make the best of a bad hand lately,* he reflected. "You have to look back in their history quite a ways to find examples of serious conflict, but everything I've read about Tzoru warfare suggests that they tend to fight just long enough to see who's got the upper hand. Then they head to the bargaining table to hammer out peace terms that reflect the new facts on the ground, so to speak. They're proud, but they're pragmatic."

"Thank you, Mr. North." Abernathy shifted in his seat

and rubbed his jaw absently as he stared at the tactical map and thought over the situation. "D-Com, what do you think?"

"The Tzoru commanders might believe we're extending the offer from a position of weakness, sir. It might reinforce their resolve if we extend the offer before they ask for terms. I think I'd wait for them to reach out to us."

"I thought so, too. Very well, let's help this Hish Sudi character to see the light sooner rather than later." Abernathy tapped a few commands into his own console, adding a new set of vectors to the tactical display. "Mr. Barnes, get me Contre-Amiral Verger, please."

"Aye, sir," said Barnes. "She's on your screen, sir."

The severe visage of Sabine Verger appeared in the personal comm display near Abernathy's battle couch. "Commodore Abernathy," she said with a small nod. "What can I do for you, sir?"

"I think it's time to chase off the Resounding Triumph Fleet," said Abernathy. "Please take the units of our starboard-side screen and deal with them. I'll detach . . . *Dupleix* and *Gloire* for support. I don't think you'll need them, but I'd rather not send your light units in against armored cruisers, obsolete or not, without some firepower backing them up. Can you do it?"

"Yes, Commodore," Verger replied. "And I will be happy to have our cruisers with us. What are you going to do?"

"Stand off at long range from Tamabuqq Prime and kill Tzoru battleships one by one until they tell me they've had enough," Abernathy told her. "Rejoin the main body once you've dealt with the Resounding Triumph. Good hunting, Sabine."

"*Oui*. And you as well, William." Verger cut the connection; a moment later, Sikander saw the mixed destroyers guarding the right-hand side of the allied fleet turn toward Zalasa, while the two Montréalais cruisers fell out of the battle line and followed the lighter ships.

The main body of the international fleet continued in

pursuit of the Monarch Sword Fleet, firing steadily at the withdrawing ships. The Militarists returned fire as best they could, with occasional extreme-range salvos from the Golden Banner battleships peppering the advancing human ships. A golden-hulled Hish cruiser—Sikander didn't see which one—blew up in a brilliant sphere of light as *Prinz Oskar*'s K-cannons found a fusion-bomb magazine and touched off one of the devices. *Helena Aldrich's work,* Sikander noted. *I shouldn't be surprised—God knows I've seen her gunnery before!* Then a grazing hit scored *Exeter,* knocking out a pair of point-defense lasers and leaving a six-centimeter-deep gash of white-hot vaporized metal along the cruiser's flank, while the ill-starred light cruiser *Burton* lost one of her main-battery turrets to another lucky hit from the retreating Tzoru cruisers. Damage signals, mostly minor, trickled in from a number of allied ships; inevitably, at least some of the Militarists' fusillades found their marks. On the port flank, the Aquilan and Nyeiran destroyers swept through the Monarch Sword's light units virtually unscathed, while first one and then another of the Monarch Sword heavies lost power and fell out of line. And above the barren, cratered surface of the moon Zalasa, Sabine Verger's little task force fell upon the Resounding Triumph fleet and raked it savagely with a coordinated torpedo attack.

"I think we've got this," Mason Barnes murmured to Sikander.

"I think you may be right," Sikander agreed. Outnumbered and outgunned—on paper, anyway—the human and Nyeiran warships were more than a match for the best the Militarist *sebetu* could throw at them, now that William Abernathy knew what he was up against. *Maybe we didn't need the help of the Sapwu after all. Well, we didn't know that at the time, did we?*

"Mr. North!" Petty Officer Macklin's voice crackled over the Intel Section circuit, bringing Sikander back to full alertness. "The offworld district in the capital is under attack, sir! Looks like armor and assault flyers from the Militarist clans are moving in!"

"Damn!" Sikander swore. He activated the feed from the powerful vidcam trained on the Tzoru capital. *Exeter* and the rest of the multinational fleet were still half a million kilometers from Tamabuqq Prime, so the imagery was not the best, but he could easily recognize the Tzoru war machines moving into position. He looked up at Commodore Abernathy, absorbed in the task of wrecking the Tzoru battle line with long-range K-cannon fire.

"Commodore, urgent developments on the ground!" he reported. "Heavy formations are moving in Bagal-Dindir. The Hish are launching an all-out assault on the Thousand Worlds ward!"

20

William Abernathy stood with his hands on the console and glared at the remote imagery from Tamabuqq Prime, ignoring the regulations that directed every hand from junior rating to the captain of the ship to remain strapped in during combat maneuvers. The situation had finally overwhelmed his ability to resist his own natural restlessness. "So close!" he snarled. "Damn it all, if only we'd gotten here just a few hours earlier . . ."

"Sir, they've given us no choice," Francine Reyes said. She'd followed Abernathy's example, getting up to study the aerial view of the Tzoru capital. "We've got to get our ships into position to fire on the columns advancing against the Thousand Worlds ward and we've got to get our troops on the ground. Like it or not, we have to press the engagement."

"We can't do that unless we push on down to low orbit, which means that we'd be sailing into point-blank range for what's left of the Monarch Sword and Golden Banner fleets," Abernathy said. "And I remind you that we've got a couple thousand Aquilan and Dremish and Californian troops sitting in civilian freight carriers, not naval assault transports. They can't take a hit."

"We screen them as best we can. It might not be pretty, but we'll win that fight."

"Maybe," Abernathy said, but he seemed unconvinced. "Mr. North, what's your assessment?"

Sikander studied the imagery for a moment, collecting his thoughts. Something nagged at him, a sense that perhaps he was missing some piece of the puzzle. "Hish Mubirrum could have ordered this assault at any time in the last five weeks, sir. He waited for you to get here before launching this attack."

"If that's true, then *why?*" Reyes demanded. "Why wait until we're close enough to potentially intervene before moving against our embassies? If he'd attacked just a few days ago we couldn't possibly have stopped him!"

"Because he's baiting a trap," Abernathy answered for Sikander. "The Tzoru knew they'd have to find a way to make us come to them. Moving against the Thousand Worlds ward now guarantees that I'll have to fight the battle on their terms. They know I can't sit here a half-million kilometers away and let their ground forces overrun our people in Bagal-Dindir."

"Sir, that's certainly true for the Militarists," Sikander said. The idea nagging at him stubbornly refused to come into focus; he tried to capture it as he spoke, and couldn't quite do so. "But I have to point out that the Tzoru hold a deep reverence for the prestige and person of the Anshar. I seriously doubt that most of the high clans would be willing to invite a battle immediately over their capital, no matter what tactical advantage they see in it. If that's General Hish's plan, it's his alone."

"What exactly are you getting at, Mr. North?"

"We're dealing with one aggressive faction, sir. There are other factions on the ground, clans that aren't on board with whatever Hish Mubirrum is up to."

Abernathy frowned. "Perhaps, but it doesn't matter. General Hish is right about one thing—we *have* to intervene to protect the civilians in the offworld district. Whether I'm playing into his hands or not, we're going to fight our way down to the planet and clear out any Tzoru warships that get in our way."

Sikander tried again. "Sir, the Sapwu—"

"*Are not here,*" Francine Reyes said, interrupting him. She directed a cold look at Sikander. "Perhaps we'd be better off basing our assessments of Tzoru intentions on what we can prove, rather than what we believe to be true. We haven't done well lately by counting on the Tzoru to behave as we expect them to."

Commodore Abernathy gazed at the live feed of Bagal-Dindir a moment longer, then made a brusque gesture of dismissal and returned to his battle couch. "Give me the tactical display, Ms. Dacey. Mr. Barnes, general command circuit, if you please."

"Aye, sir," Barnes replied. He made a quick selection on his panel. "You're on, Commodore."

"All units, this is Commodore Abernathy," the commodore said, facing his small comm screen. "We have detected a major assault against the Thousand Worlds ward. Our embassies in Bagal-Dindir are in imminent danger of being overrun. We need to take station over the capital and get our troops down to the ground, or all of this will have been for nothing. I am now implementing Plan Foxtrot. We're going to go in and protect our people, and we're not going to let anyone get in our way. Good luck to you—Abernathy, out."

Sikander grimaced. Plan F was the worst-case scenario the squadron operations team had worked up in their planning over the last couple of weeks—an immediate and heavily opposed landing. When Giselle Dacey's specialists had gamed it out in the tactical simulations, the results had been uncertain and more than a little bloody . . . but it had worked most of the time. *Better a bad plan than none at all,* he decided.

Dacey and Barnes immediately began passing along new positioning orders, reshaping the combined task force. They summoned Contre-Amiral Verger's detached units back from their pursuit of the Resounding Triumph Fleet, and directed the cruiser columns to form a tight escort around the half-dozen requisitioned transports carrying the fleet's landing force. In every other op plan, the freighters carrying the landing force stayed well back from any ship-to-ship fighting, waiting for Abernathy's warships to destroy or drive off any opposing forces in orbit around Tamabuqq Prime. The new plan nestled the transports in the center of the task force and escorted them all the way to the landing zone, guarding them with the hulls of the formation's cruisers and destroyers . . . which meant that no warship was permitted to evade fire that might otherwise jeopardize the vulnerable ships they protected. *God, let this work,* Sikander silently prayed.

He glanced up from his displays, and found Francine Reyes watching him with an icy expression. They locked eyes for a moment before some development in the tactical display caught her attention. *Now what in hell was that about?* Sikander wondered. It was hard to miss the fact that Reyes had argued against the mission to extract Sapwu Zrinan, then argued that it hadn't yielded any real benefit for the effort and risk, and now seemed all too ready to tell William Abernathy *I told you so* because the Sapwu had not come to Tamabuqq. Having once convinced the commodore to destroy Sikander's career, was she already plotting to reverse Abernathy's rehabilitation of him? Was it simply a matter of laying the foundation for blaming unexpectedly high losses on another so-called intelligence failure? *Or maybe she's worried that a political solution might still be possible. Why would she want to fight it out if there's a chance that we might somehow contain this situation?*

"Because she *wants* a war," he murmured, answering himself. Oh, Deputy Commodore Francine Reyes certainly had no use for one Lieutenant Commander Sikander North; she'd made that plain enough during his time with Helix Squadron. But she'd also made it clear that she found merit in the grim old Navy toast *To a bloody war and quick promotion!* Before the previous battle in Tamabuqq, she'd observed to Sikander and the other staff officers that an ambitious officer could reap real benefit from some actual battle experience in her service jacket; a general war against the decrepit

Tzoru Dominion would offer plenty of opportunities. If that was true for Sikander, Mason Barnes, and Giselle Dacey, it was true for Francine Reyes as well. *Was she envious of my experience at Gadira this whole time? Could it be that her antagonism toward me wasn't about Victor Gray?*

He glanced over at William Abernathy, and found himself remembering again the day they'd met. Powell Hall, the Disciplinary Committee hearing—

—erupts in confusion behind Abernathy and Sikander as they exit the room. Commander Abernathy takes Sikander by the arm and physically pulls him through the doorway of an empty classroom just down the hall. The winter sunlight is dim and gray; trees with snow-covered branches droop like tired sentries outside the windows. "Damn it all, North," he snarls angrily. "What do you think you're doing?"

"Telling the truth, sir," Sikander answers, still shaking with anger from the sudden confrontation with Victor Gray in the hearing room.

"Didn't anyone tell you to keep your mouth shut? When you get hauled before the committee you don't argue about it—you take what they give you." Abernathy throws up his arms in a gesture of disgust. "Hell, I knew that much when I was a snottie!"

"Gray struck me first," Sikander says. "I'll state it under a polygraph if I have to. Better yet, put him in the polygraph and ask him who hit who."

"We don't put gentlemen under a polygraph. We take them at their word. If a man's character and actions are so questionable he can't be cleared without a damned lie detector, then maybe he isn't the kind of material the Commonwealth Navy needs."

"So you say, sir. Am I supposed to let a bigot and a sadist like Gray kick my ass because he doesn't like the way my Anglic sounds or the sound of my name? Is that the kind of

material the Commonwealth Navy needs? For that matter, if I let him treat me that way, am I?"

Abernathy grimaces, his mouth tight under his stiff mustache, but his fierce expression softens slightly. "Don't you get it?" he asks Sikander. "Gray wasn't trying to kick your ass, although I'm sure he would have been grateful for the opportunity. Gray was trying to provoke you. He wanted you to take a swing at him just so we could put on this little song and dance today, and run you out of the Academy. You gave him exactly what he wanted."

"Then I'll make sure everyone knows what he did before I go, sir," Sikander snarls. "I am not going to stand in front of the Disciplinary Committee and beg their forgiveness for defending myself! My father raised me to stand up to bullies, no matter what the cost."

"And Gray's father is the Senator Tarminghay, who happens to chair the Appropriations Committee and has something to say about how the Navy conducts its business," Abernathy replies. "So you are going to go back to that hearing, tell them that the statements that have been given are truthful— because they are, even if they aren't complete—and you're going to say you're sorry for losing your temper that day in the museum. You are not going to slander Victor Gray. If you toe the line, I'll see to it that you aren't expelled."

"And what about Gray? Does he go unpunished?" Sikander asks.

"Leave Gray to me," Abernathy replies with a sour look. "There's a missing datacard from the security cam in the museum. I've got a guess about where it is."

Sikander studies the older officer for a long moment, wondering whether he can trust him. Finally he nods. "Very well, Commander Abernathy. I'll do as you ask."

Thirty minutes later, Sikander stands mute as the Disciplinary Committee sentences him to extra duty tours for the remainder of the year, docks him a month's living stipend, and puts him on a two-year probation. And three weeks *after the hearing, Victor Gray quietly resigns his appointment and leaves the Academy.*

"Mr. North, you look like you have something on your mind," Abernathy said suddenly.

Sikander gave himself a small shake, bringing himself back to *Exeter*'s flag bridge; the commodore waited for him to speak. "You once told me not to give my enemy what he wants, sir," he told Abernathy. "I think I understand what General Hish is trying to do."

"What do you mean?"

"This attack on the Thousand Worlds ward isn't about forcing you to fight on Militarist terms, sir, although Hish Mubirrum is happy to give that a try. It's about forcing you to attack the Tzoru homeworld and defy the Anshar's authority for all to see. General Hish thinks that the only way he can save the Dominion from us is to convince Tzoru everywhere that we're dangerous and barbaric. He's hoping we'll take this opportunity to prove him right, even if that means losing a battle for Bagal-Dindir."

Abernathy shifted in his seat, scowling behind his mustache. "Even if that's the case, Mr. North, what other choice do I have? We can't stand by and let our people be massacred on the ground. He's forcing my hand."

"He isn't giving you many options," Sikander admitted. "But I think we can still attempt to limit the hostilities, sir. Concentrate our fire on Monarch Sword units, and leave the Golden Banner Fleet out of things as much as we can—don't return fire against them unless we absolutely have to. And we should avoid any direct attack or landing on the Anshar's Palace. Keep our troops in the offworld district for now, and fire only on enemy formations that directly threaten the Thousand Worlds ward."

Reyes gave Sikander a sharp look. "This is not the time to exercise restraint, Mr. North. You're asking the commodore to place Tzoru sensibilities above the lives and safety of our own personnel."

Sikander ignored the deputy commodore, and kept his eyes locked on Abernathy's face. "Sir, Hish Mubirrum wants you to start a general war. Maybe that can't be avoided now— but maybe it *can*. Your restraint may be the very thing that ensures the fighting ends today, here, instead of spreading across the entire Dominion. Don't give the Militarists the crisis they need to stay in power indefinitely."

Abernathy hesitated a moment longer . . . and then he gave Sikander a curt nod. "All right, Mr. North, we'll try it your way. Ms. Dacey, amend the firing plans. Target the Monarch Sword units first, and leave the Golden Banner alone for now. If we have to, we can deal with them after we handle the Hish fleet."

Giselle Dacey looked dubious, perhaps wondering about the wisdom of leaving powerful targets unengaged if they were potentially hostile, but nodded. "Yes, sir. We're amending the firing plan now."

"Good. Bring us into low orbit above Tamabuqq Prime, if you please."

A gentle nudge pushed Sikander back against his seat as *Exeter* changed course and picked up speed; even with artificial gravity, the acceleration of a modern warship's powerful drives couldn't be completely masked by compensators. The international force swept past the drifting hulks of the Hish cruisers *Etzu-Kanu* and *Shuha-Daku*. Behind *Exeter,* the remainder of the Resounding Triumph Fleet reversed course near Zalasa and pressed after the combined squadrons, now boosting hard for the orbital approaches of the Tzoru homeworld. The old armored cruisers operating near the first moon had little chance of catching up to Abernathy's force in time to influence the fighting above Tamabuqq Prime . . . and even if they did, Sabine Verger's formation was in good position to chase them away again.

Exeter shook and shuddered again as Captain Howard resumed fire. Hundreds of heavy penetrators blasted through the vacuum, raking the Militarist line of battle. The old battleship *Aqqru*—a beautiful vessel whose hull was decorated by dragon bas-reliefs fifty meters long—tumbled out of control toward the atmosphere of the planet below, her drive plates knocked out while she attempted to dodge incoming fire. A salvo from the Nyeiran *Dreik Jol* stitched no less than five hits through the bow of the Monarch Sword cruiser *Nisi-Karmi,* triggering secondary explosions that gutted the hull almost from stem to stern. She, too, began the long and fatal plunge down through the green haze of Tamabuqq's high atmosphere. But the Tzoru warships did not die alone. In a furious skirmish along the port-side formation screen, the hastily repaired *Jackal* lost her main drive at the exact moment a pair of Ziltu-type torpedo cutters attacked, and was hammered to a drifting wreck by two close-aboard fusion detonations. *Dreik Jol* lurched out of formation when a shot from the Monarch Sword battleship *Ulhumahasu* wrecked one of her drive rooms, and a ragged salvo from another Tzoru cruiser clawed *Burton*'s midships turret into molten tatters. Then *Exeter* shuddered again, and the power in the flag bridge flickered out for a half second before returning.

"We took a hit somewhere," Abernathy observed, wincing.

"The lights came back on, so it can't have been too bad," said Reyes. "All the same, I'd prefer to avoid more of those if we can help it."

The internal circuit by Abernathy's seat beeped, and Captain Howard's voice crackled over the speaker. "Commodore, my gunnery officer just pointed out that we've now got Tamabuqq Prime backstopping our fire against some of the Tzoru ships in lower orbits. We'd better be careful about downrange misses."

"Damn, but you're right! Thank you, Quentin, I missed that entirely." Abernathy looked over to the comm section. "Mr. Barnes, urgent warning to all units: Check your fire if the planet is directly behind your target! If we fire on ground targets we'll take care to do so when we mean it, not because we missed something else. Moderate maneuvers to clear your lines of fire as needed are authorized."

"That might expose the transports, sir," Reyes said, keeping her voice low.

"I know that," Abernathy said. "But there's a lot of metal flying around out there today, and I want to silence those guns as fast as we can."

"Sir, new contacts!" Giselle Dacey suddenly announced. "Distance thirty-five light-seconds, bearing zero-three-five down ten. It's a formation—eight heavy ships, fifteen screening units."

"Where did they come from?" Reyes asked. "They didn't unbubble that close in, did they?"

"They were partially screened behind Tamabuqq Prime, ma'am. And there is a good deal of merchant traffic scattering out in that direction."

"Now what?" Abernathy growled. "Did the Militarists scrape up another provincial fleet for us to deal with?"

Sikander brought the new group to the center of his display and started to run his recognition programs on the distant contact, but his team in the intel center beat him to the punch—the answer arrived on his console before he finished running his own analysis. He couldn't help himself; he stood up out of his seat, leaning over his displays. "Identification on the new force, Commodore! It's the Sapwu Supernal Glory Fleet, or at least a big part of it. They're heading for Tamabuqq Prime at their best speed."

"They took their bloody time," Abernathy said. "Very well, I suppose it's better late than never."

"Signal for the task force commander from the Sapwu fleet, sir," said Mason Barnes. "I'm sending it to your comm panel."

The image of Lara Dunstan standing beside Sapwu Zrinan on the bridge of a Tzoru warship appeared by Abernathy's screen. Zrinan wore the elaborate formal robes of a high official in the Anshar's court, but the Tzoru behind him were dressed in the heavy golden battle armor of a high-status clan. Lara wore a borrowed set of marine working fatigues and carried a helmet under one arm; like the standard Navy jumpsuits, marine fatigues could serve as vacuum suits at need. "Commodore Abernathy, I greet you," Sapwu Zrinan said. "My technicians tell me that there will be a noticeable delay in our signals at this distance, so I will not attempt to hold a conversation with you while you are engaged in battle. Please advise your warships to avoid firing on the Supernal Glory Fleet—we will not impede your advance or interfere with your actions so long as you refrain from firing on the Anshar's Palace. I wish also to inform you that I am in communication with Zabar Wuqq of the Golden Banner Fleet. I believe they may be convinced to cease hostilities too."

"The situation in the palace seems confused," Lara added. "The Sapwu are talking to the other high *sebetu* even as we speak. If you can give us a little time, I think we can convince everybody but the Militarists to stand down. We'll be in orbit in—" She glanced aside, checking with someone off-camera before looking back. "—thirty minutes, give or take."

The transmission ended. Abernathy glanced at the tactical display and the imagery from the ground. "Time is the one thing I can't give Dr. Dunstan and her Sapwu friends at the moment," he said, thinking aloud. "Not while the Militarists and the *warumzi agu* are making a push to overrun the Thousand Worlds ward. Mr. North, get on the channel with the Sapwu and tell Dr. Dunstan and Sapwu Zrinan that we're pushing ahead to get our troops on the ground. We won't fire on the palace or the Golden Banner Fleet so long as they don't fire on us, but we're going to protect our people on the ground and we're going to blast our way through anyone that gets in our way."

"Aye, sir," Sikander replied. He cleared his console of his intel reports, and replaced them with a comm window; he'd leave the battle-damage assessments to his team down in the intel center for now.

"And see if you can find out what the hell is happening on

the ground, and whether the Sapwu can do anything about that," Abernathy added. He looked back to Giselle Dacey at the tactical console. "Ms. Dacey, you heard the news. The Golden Banner Fleet is standing down, so blow a great bloody big hole through anybody else who's standing in our way and get our fleet to Bagal-Dindir."

The battleship *Ulhumahasu* shuddered with another hard hit somewhere aft of the command deck. The thin scream of escaping air momentarily filled the compartment, and Hish Sudi's hands flew to her breathe mask to ensure that it fit properly over her face before the reassuring clang of armored doors sealing shut ended the threat of complete depressurization. *We are only delaying the inevitable,* she thought, face expressionless beneath her mask. The human and Nyeiran fire was simply too heavy and too accurate for even *Ulhumahasu* to endure for long, and as one Monarch Sword ship after another was blown apart, more and more enemy ships shifted their fire to the few Hish vessels that remained in the fight.

She was not afraid of dying, but the prospect of dying in a futile action without a chance of victory galled her. It would have been better to refuse the battle altogether, and preserve the Monarch Sword for another fight on another day, but Hish Mubirrum's orders were explicit. The Sharur-Tal required the fleet to exert its utmost effort to damage or delay the invaders. In the face of such a command, any true daughter of Sebet Hish could only stand her ground and die proudly in the Anshar's service.

The battle is hopeless, but not the war, Sudi told herself. If she inflicted enough losses on the humans here today, perhaps another provincial fleet could move on their base at Kahnar-Sag. And if the humans lost Magan Kahnar, then their next-closest fleet base was at least two months' warp transit distant. Not even a powerful empire such as Aquila or Dremark could wage war successfully across such vast distances. In fact, she should make that recommendation to Hish Mubirrum before—

"Admiral Hish!" Sudi's chief tactical assistant wailed in alarm. "The Golden Banner Fleet is withdrawing!"

Hish Sudi whirled around, her resignation shattered by the unexpected news. "I gave no such order!" she barked. "What do the Zabar think they're doing?"

The tactical assistant waved his hands in confusion. "I cannot answer that question, Admiral, but they have ceased firing on the alien task force and are breaking orbit. And I think the human squadrons are no longer firing on them, either."

Hish Sudi stared at the display in consternation. There was no doubt of it—the Golden Banner Fleet was retreating from the battle. Most of the old battlewagons could barely maneuver after years of neglect and the damage from the first battle against the alien invaders, but they retained enough drive power to move ponderously out of the line of fire. "The faithless cowards!" she snarled as she watched the Zabar battleships turn away. For a moment she was tempted to order *Ulhumahasu*'s batteries turned against the Golden Banner to punish them for their shameful retreat . . . but aristocratic *sebetu* did not fight one another, and such an action could only make an already disastrous day worse. Besides, she had more than enough opponents in front of her already.

"Admiral, what do we do?" the tactical assistant asked.

What can we do? she wanted to reply, but she held her silence. Clearly the Sapwu had made the Zabar an offer, and the thrice-cursed Zabar had decided to return to their original allegiance. And that meant the Manzanensi likely had enough of the Dominion High Council to reassert control. *But there is a Sharur-Tal now. Mubirrum could dissolve the council if he wished—he will deal with the Zabar, and the Sapwu too. The best way I can help him is to save something of our forces, while making sure all the high* sebetu *know who our true enemy is.*

"Admiral, your orders?" the tactical assistant repeated.

"Instruct our escorts to withdraw to Badibira," she told him. They might—*might*—have enough speed to escape Tamabuqq if she could give them enough cover. As for the battle line of the Monarch Sword, there would be no escape for them. "Signal the rest of the fleet to follow *Ulhumahasu*. We will destroy as many of the Anshar's enemies as we can before we are overcome."

Ten minutes later, a K-cannon penetrator fired from the Nyeiran battle cruiser *Tauk Ze Yur* vaporized *Ulhumahasu*'s flag bridge. Hish Sudi was killed instantly.

A sudden chorus of cheers in the flag bridge drew Sikander's attention from his comm link to Lara Dunstan. He looked at the tactical display, and saw the Monarch Sword flagship—the most modern and powerful warship to be found in any Tzoru fleet in the Dominion—break in half under the staggering weight of K-cannon salvos from multiple warships.

"What is it? What happened?" Lara asked him, a few seconds later. The Supernal Glory Fleet had not yet closed enough distance to completely eliminate the time lag in their transmissions. It was strange to be so close to her again after their paths had divided them by dozens of light-years, yet still be no closer than a face on a screen. The brief and torrid resumption of their romance was the last thing he should have been thinking about, but in the ten days they'd been apart he simply hadn't had a moment to examine his feelings about what had happened. Now events had brought them together again—or at least within a million or two kilometers of each other, anyway.

"*Ulhumahasu* is out of the fight," he told her. "That's the Militarist flagship. It looks like what's left of the Monarch Sword Fleet is scattering."

"So does that mean we've won?" she asked.

"The first part of the battle, anyway. We've got control of the orbital approaches above Tamabuqq Prime. But there's still the question of getting our soldiers down to the ground, and making sure all the side switching is done with for today." Sikander glanced at the vid feed of the Thousand Worlds ward. Bursts of smoke peppered the ancient district and pocked the old stone walls, grim evidence of Militarist heavy artillery pounding the offworld enclave. *We've got to silence those batteries or there will be nothing left to protect,* he decided. "Speaking of which, there are some Karsu artillery batteries that are firing indiscriminately on the Thousand Worlds ward. Sapwu Zrinan's got about five minutes to convince the Karsu to stand down, or those batteries are going to be erased by orbital fire."

Lara grimaced. "The Karsu aren't answering Lord Zrinan's signals. They seem determined to ride it out with the Hish and the other Militarists. But please make sure Commodore Abernathy knows that he needs to keep the collateral damage to an absolute minimum."

"He understands the political implications," Sikander told her. "Keep me posted if the Sapwu get anyone else to stand down; we'll try to limit our fire to military formations that are actually firing on us or on our people in the Thousand Worlds ward."

"I will," Lara promised. "But you need to understand that we're asking the noble *sebetu* to reevaluate allegiances they've held for generations in some cases. I'm trying to help them see that Hish Mubirrum broke with tradition first by not suppressing the *warumzi agu,* but it's difficult for them. We're lucky the Zabar agreed to stand aside, to be honest."

"I know you're doing your best."

"Can you reach Ambassador Hart? I've been trying but I get no answer."

Sikander shook his head. "Mason's got intermittent contact with Major Dalton, but the major isn't at the embassy building and she can't spare anyone to try to get the ambassador on the line. I'll let you know if we get through. And keep me posted on the Karsu negotiations."

"Such as they are," Lara replied, scowling with frustration. "God, what a mess. Are all battles like this?"

He remembered molten steel splashing across *Hector*'s bridge, Captain Elise Markham dying in front of his eyes, and grimaced. "No—some are worse," he told her. "Some are a *lot* worse."

He turned his attention back to the fleet operations as Lara put him on hold to relay his message about the Karsu batteries, and tried to anticipate the next point of contention. Now that the Militarist fleets no longer posed a threat to the combined task force, Giselle Dacey's Ops Section shifted to coordinating ground bombardment from the warships of five different navies, doing their best to check and double-check the targets in and around Bagal-Dindir before assigning fire missions. Some captains chose not to wait for orders from the flagship, engaging targets when they spotted them. The Dremish cruisers systematically hammered military bases and emplacements that were hundreds of kilometers from the capital in some cases, evidently determined to root out any center of Militarist fighting power they could reach. At the same time, the improvised landing force on the task force's civilian transports busily disembarked in a mismatched collection of borrowed orbiters and assault landers from the hangar bays of the larger warships, reinforced by dozens of Tzoru workboats pressed into duty as makeshift landing craft.

"We're losing control of things," Reyes observed. A taut frown of disapproval creased her face.

"I'll say," Commodore Abernathy growled. "It's a damned five-way race to the ground, apparently. Ms. Dacey, see if you can at least keep the troop carriers from flying through active bombardment lanes, if you please."

"I'll do my best, sir," she said.

Sikander held his breath as a battered workboat full of Californian rangers cut the corner of *Prinz Oskar*'s firing lane. Fortunately the Dremish gunners managed to check their fire, although a torrent of angry and profane Nebeldeutsch erupted over the command channel. The troops making up the landing force had been drawn from scores of outposts, stations, and ship's companies near Kahnar-Sag—a Dremish battalion here, a Californian company there, a Nyeiran regiment hurriedly rushed in from the nearest Imperial base. The Aquilan contingent consisted of a short regiment drawn from the new base at Shimatum: two infantry battalions with an air assault battalion in support under the command of a Colonel Iverson, whom Sikander had yet to meet. The ground troops had had even less time to drill alongside their counterparts from other powers than the warship crews; Sikander was not surprised by the chaos of the landing operation.

"First assault wave away, more or less," Giselle Dacey announced. "Ground fire is sporadic and inaccurate, sir. I don't think the Tzoru ground-based defenses pose much of a threat to our assault transports and orbiters."

"We should take them out anyway, sir," Reyes said to Abernathy. "Frankly, I'd suggest dropping a kinetic strike on any ground-based batteries within a hundred kilometers of Bagal-Dindir and make sure no one down there even *thinks* about taking a shot at our landing forces. I wouldn't put it past the Tzoru clans to claim neutrality until they see a good chance to open up on our landers."

Sikander looked up from his console. "Sir, I advise against that. Dr. Dunstan just reminded us that we need to be careful about the collateral damage."

"We won't have to worry about collateral damage if we eliminate any possible Tzoru resistance. For that matter, I suggest we detach our destroyers to pursue what's left of the Monarch Sword Fleet and make sure they don't cause any trouble for us down the road." Reyes leaned forward, emphasizing her point. "This is our opportunity to make a clean sweep of things and teach the Tzoru a lesson they'll never forget. They're in no position to stop us."

"And that's why we *shouldn't* do it, sir," Sikander said to Abernathy. He ignored the venomous look Reyes shot in his direction. "Showing an enemy that you're strong enough to let him live is a lesson, too."

"Sir—" Reyes began.

"*Enough,* Francine. I get it, you want to punish the Tzoru. But I think we've got enough enemies here already." Commodore Abernathy raised a hand to forestall any more protest from his deputy, watching the mismatched group of unarmed landers and military assault craft drop away from the transports in the center of the allied formation; a second wave began forming up almost at once. Then he keyed his intercom to *Exeter*'s bridge. "Captain Howard?"

Howard answered immediately. "Yes, Commodore? How can I help you?"

"Captain, I am turning over tactical command of Helix Squadron to you," Abernathy said. "By my reckoning Contre-Amiral Verger is the senior officer of the allied force remaining aloft, so comply with her orders to the best of your ability unless you think she's asking you to do something that is clearly not in the interests of the Commonwealth."

"Of course, Commodore," Quentin Howard replied. "Where are you going to be, sir?"

"I'm heading for the hangar bay. Whatever happens next is happening on the ground." Abernathy stood and tucked his helmet under one arm. "I'm not sure that Ambassador Hart is in any position to speak for the Commonwealth at the moment, which means that I may now be the senior representative of our government in this system. I have to assume that it falls on me to straighten things out as best I can. If anything comes up, the deputy commodore will be here with most of the staff to advise you on how to proceed."

Francine Reyes's eyes flashed, but she gave no other sign of her disapproval. Customarily, the deputy commodore took over for the squadron commander in situations like this one. Quentin Howard was technically senior to her, though . . . and it appeared that was enough for William Abernathy to sideline her for the rest of the day. Captain Howard raised his brows since he understood that as well as Reyes did, but he recovered quickly. "Very good, sir," he said.

Sikander quickly returned his attention to his console, making a conscious effort to keep his face impassive. *About time she was put in her place,* he decided. *Good for Abernathy!* He noticed that more than a few of the other watchstanders and officers in the compartment had also developed a sudden and intense interest in their posts.

"Mr. Barnes, get me a personal audio link to Contre-Amiral Verger," Abernathy continued. "I'll brief her on the way down to the hangar bay and make sure she's ready to take over. And Mr. North, have someone from Intel Section come up and relieve you here. You're with me."

21

The sky burned above Bagal-Dindir.

General Hish Mubirrum had no desire to watch the spectacle. In the first place, he had no time to spare for gawking at battles that were no longer in his hands, but more importantly he knew exactly what the fireballs and their smoky trails meant: *defeat*. The sight filled his mouth with a bitter taste, but even so he could not bring himself to look away. The funeral pyres of hundreds, perhaps thousands, of brave Tzoru warriors scarred the sky; it was fitting that he should bear witness.

"Which one is it?" he asked Hish Pazril, who stood behind him on the mountainside terrace and likewise gazed up into the winter sky. The air was clear and cold, but not as bitterly cold as it had been over the last month. A dusting of snow clung to the mountaintops, but little frost remained in the lowlands.

"That is *Aqqru,* Lord Mubirrum. She hit the atmosphere out of control and broke apart on reentry. *Nisi-Karmi* burned up over the southern continent, far out of our line of sight."

"Is there any danger on the ground?"

"A piece of *Nisi-Karmi* struck the outskirts of Muma-sikk and caused a moderate impact with a small number of deaths," said Pazril. He gestured at the smoke trails far overhead. "*Aqqru* will hit out over the sea. No one else will be hurt."

"May their stories be remembered in the final unfolding of the Sixty-Four Prophecies," Mubirrum said. He turned away from the fiery spectacle and went back inside his fortress. A sprawling bunker-like complex, Eningu-Luz dated back to the days when atomic warfare between rival *sebetu* remained a serious threat to the power of the Anshar. Over many centuries it had become a secluded retreat for the high officials of the court, its original military purpose forgotten. But when Mubirrum had first claimed his seat on the Dominion High Council decades ago, he'd made the modernization of the old complex a pet project of his, manning the facility with Hish troops and provisioning it for an hour exactly like this one. His engineers assured him that the facilities buried beneath Mount Eningu could withstand most orbital bombardments, and any kinetic strike powerful enough to eliminate the stronghold would necessarily destroy much of Bagal-Dindir—a price Mubirrum believed that not even the most uncultured humans would be willing to pay. Still, all communications to and from Eningu-Luz were routed via buried cables to remote transmitters just in case.

An armored lift brought Mubirrum and Pazril to the primary command room, crowded with sensor displays and tactical representations of the Tamabuqq system, the surface of Tamabuqq Prime, and the environs of Bagal-Dindir. Mubirrum first directed his attention to the representation of the planet and its orbital approaches. The bright icons representing the Golden Banner Fleet hovered together in a distant geosynchronous orbit, ceding the closer orbital paths above the capital to the combined fleets of the hostile powers.

Traitors! Mubirrum fumed silently. By ancient tradition the Golden Banner Fleet served as the Anshar's personal shield, sworn to ensure that no enemy ever defiled the skies of the homeworld. For centuries the command of the Golden Banner had been one of the most prestigious and fought-over sinecures that the court could bestow on a noble *sebet*.

The Zabar had held control of the Golden Banner all of Mubirrum's long life . . . but now that the test had finally come, they'd abdicated their sworn duty. *I should have installed some Hish as Golden Banner commanders. They would have remembered their duty, and if some of the battleships refused to abandon their posts, others might have found it impossible to leave.* But of course the Zabar would have protested furiously against the removal of any of their captains, and he'd had to keep them happy with their new place in the Emuqq-Mamit faction or risk their defection back to the Sapwu and their Manzanensi.

But they defected anyway, so I might as well have seized their battleships when I had the chance. Mubirrum scowled at the display, fighting down the rage he felt roiling inside him. At least the Monarch Sword Fleet had fought hard, but most of the bright purple icons representing Hish Sudi's fleet now wore the diamond-shaped icon that marked a destroyed or disabled ship no longer capable of continuing the fight. A number of light ships and a small remnant of the battle line fought on near one flank of the human fleet, but they'd been pushed far from the sky above Bagal-Dindir and seemed powerless to interfere with the scores of landing craft and small transports now ferrying troops from the invading fleet down to the Dominion capital.

"Why are we not firing on the landing craft with our ground batteries?" Mubirrum asked Pazril. "Surely we must be able to eliminate some of them before their troops reach the ground!"

"We are engaging them, General," said Pazril. "But they are more difficult targets than we anticipated, and orbital fire hammers any ground battery that reveals itself by firing on a landing vessel. We destroyed several in the first wave, but lost most of our emplacements to retaliatory strikes. We're now redeploying additional air-defense assets to the landing zones, but as more human and Nyeiran troops land, the potential benefit of exposing those weapons systems diminishes."

"Do it anyway," Mubirrum told him. Sustaining a ground attack would require a continuous stream of orbiters and light transports ferrying additional supplies and equipment to the planet's surface; he wanted to interfere with that process in any way possible. Unfortunately, the best tool for that job was a fleet in orbit, and the Monarch Sword Fleet was no longer in position—"Wait a moment. Where is *Ulhuma-hasu*? I don't see it in the orbital view. Why is Hish Sudi withdrawing without orders?"

"I have terrible news to report, my lord," Pazril said with a stricken expression. "We just received word that *Ulhuma-hasu* has been destroyed. There are no survivors."

"Our most powerful warship," Mubirrum murmured. "And our most capable admiral, as well." He closed his eyes, struggling to master his grief. As a warrior he honored Hish Sudi's death in battle, but as leader of the Dominion's forces he knew that he'd asked her to stand against an enemy she had little hope of defeating . . . and as a proud parent the thought that he'd never see his eldest offspring again wounded him in a way he'd never been wounded before. It was not the Tzoru way to dote on children who'd grown to adulthood, not the way humans did with their offspring, but Mubirrum had dreams and aspirations for Sudi—dreams that now seemed bitter and futile indeed. *One of those fiery streaks in the sky might be Sudi,* he realized. *But then we are all shooting stars, aren't we? The only question is what sort of trail we leave across the sky in the moment that is given to us.*

Pazril waited in respectful silence for a long moment, then moved closer and lowered his voice. "General, we have lost control of the planetary approaches and we cannot prevent the enemy from landing. What are your orders, my lord?"

"In other words, should we request terms?" Mubirrum understood what Pazril really meant. He did his best to set aside the tragedy of Sudi's death and weigh the decision. Since powerful spacegoing warships had first appeared, the question of whether it was possible to resist planetary invasion had troubled strategists and commanders. In most cases control of the orbital approaches meant control of the sky and the ability to land attacking troops at any point on a planet's surface. On the other hand, anyone defending a developed world could easily muster millions of soldiers to defend it, far outnumbering any conceivable attacking force. Given the disparity of numbers, conquering and occupying a planet with defenders determined to resist was frankly impossible—but an attacker *could* seize limited objectives on the ground, strategic targets he wanted to capture intact instead of demolishing with orbital bombardment. Once an attacking force gained a foothold on the ground, their control of the sky made it extremely difficult for defenders to pry them out of position, especially since if the defenders *did* succeed in forcing the attackers to retreat, the attackers might decide to simply destroy what they couldn't hold on the ground. In the long-ago days of the Dominion's interplanetary wars, most invasions were settled once the attacker demonstrated the will and ability to seize a capital or center of production, at which point negotiations for the terms of capitulation ensued. The invader received the benefit of capturing some strategic center of gravity intact, while the defender saved his world from widespread devastation and perhaps restrained the invader's gains by negotiating what exactly would be surrendered.

In the current situation, the stakes seemed clear enough. The humans and their Nyeiran allies had little interest in anything on Tamabuqq Prime outside of Bagal-Dindir, but they could not risk an indiscriminate bombardment of the city without endangering their own embassies and expatriate population. Mubirrum had the perfect opportunity to stand his ground without fear of being outmaneuvered from above or simply erased by overwhelming bombardment, and he suspected that Commodore Abernathy didn't have more than a few thousand troops available for his assault. He saw no reason to surrender those advantages.

"We have fifty thousand soldiers in and around Bagal-Dindir, plus five or six times that number of *warumzi agu* in armed formations," he told Pazril. "I am not ready to concede the capital yet, not when we are about to seize the Thousand Worlds ward. I choose to negotiate when Abernathy asks me the terms for the release of the offworlders we'll have in our hands by the end of the day."

"Yes, General," said Pazril in reply.

Mubirrum glanced once more at the orbital display, his gaze lingering on the place where *Ulhumahasu* should have been. Then he strode over to the city representation, a large table with a holographic surface showing the vast sweep of Bagal-Dindir and its surrounding lakes and highlands, along with glowing icons marking the location of the forces engaged in the fighting. Wide gaps now marred the walls of the Thousand Worlds ward, breaches blasted through the ancient fortifications by Hish and Karsu artillery. Mobs of *warumzi agu* militia streamed toward the gaps, only to meet a stubborn resistance just inside the walls where the denizens of the ward had improvised rubble barricades to block the streets and turned the sturdier buildings into fortified strongpoints. Militarist advisors and observers reported the obstacles as the revolutionaries encountered them and called in additional artillery strikes—but one by one, the enemy ships overhead destroyed batteries that continued to fire on the offworlders' defensive positions. An early effort to overwhelm the defenses with an air assault by armed troop-carrying skybarges had faltered when the humans—Dremish troops, or so Mubirrum had been told—revealed an unsuspected cache of antiair rockets they'd saved for just such a moment. Now any Tzoru military vehicle in the air had to contend with armed assault craft from the orbiting fleet as well as surprisingly heavy ground fire within the ancient walls.

Pazril noted the direction of his gaze and pointed at one of the gaps in the wall. "The *warumzi agu* should break through here at any moment, General," he said. "The offworlders don't have enough defenders to stop them, not even with their troops now reaching the ground."

"Good," Mubirrum said. What the *warumzi agu* would do once they found no defenders in front of them he could not say . . . but then again, perhaps he didn't care. While he'd allowed himself to hope that he might be able to ambush Abernathy's fleet in orbit and he remained at least a little optimistic about his prospects for repelling an invasion of the capital, those were only tactical objectives. The whole point of the Thousand Worlds siege, the dismantling of the Dominion High Council, and the determination to resist Abernathy's careful attack was not to defeat the enemy powers here and today—although Mubirrum would certainly have accepted victory if William Abernathy had foolishly found a way to offer it to him. No, the point was to set the Dominion on a course to resist alien aggression at any cost, to ignite a wider war and perhaps finally awaken the sleeping giant that was the Tzoru Dominion. Mubirrum might personally regret *warumzi agu* atrocities against offworlders who fell into their power, but if Tzem Ebneghirz's followers managed to convince the humans they could not be placated, they'd only help him in his own effort to establish a policy of confrontation over concession.

No single human power holds one hundred and twenty-two worlds, he reflected. *And not all the armies of all the human realms can subdue even a quarter of our Dominion. We will lose worlds and fleets, but we will win in the end. There is no other way to preserve our way of life.*

"General Mubirrum, there is a call for you from the palace," a young technician told him. The female motioned toward a private communications booth screened off from the rest of the command center. "The chamberlain's office reports that human orbiters are overflying Bagal-Dindir and demands an explanation."

"It seems I must reassure the bureaucrats that we are aware of the obvious," Mubirrum remarked to Pazril. "I shall return in a moment. Redouble our efforts to assist the *warumzi agu* militias in their attack against the Thousand Worlds ward. There is no more reason to allow the offworlder resistance to continue."

"Of course, Lord Mubirrum," Pazril answered. He turned to his subordinate commanders, and began issuing orders.

Mubirrum followed the technician to the communications booth, and found himself facing the holographic image of Ebabbar Simtum, not a minor functionary as he'd expected. "Chamberlain," he said, nodding his head in greeting. "I have much to occupy my attention at the moment. What do you need?"

Ebabbar wore his customary robes of office, but his expression was drawn and worried. "General Hish, our military experts tell me that they no longer believe the offworlder attack can be repelled. They fear for the safety of the Anshar, and so do I. This entire situation is an unmitigated disaster!"

Mubirrum responded with a curt gesture of annoyance. "I do not agree with your so-called experts, Chamberlain. The humans mounted this attack by committing almost every soldier and warship they currently have within the borders of our Dominion. They may succeed in temporarily occupying part of the capital, but they simply do not have the numbers they need to hold their gains for long, and they cannot keep their fleets here indefinitely. We can outlast them if we remain resolute."

"And if the humans send their troops to secure the Anshar's Palace?" Ebabbar asked. "Can we outlast them if a human mag pistol is pointed at the Heavenly Monarch's head?"

Mubirrum hesitated a moment. He believed that even the humans understood the Anshar's role in Tzoru society and respected it, but perhaps he'd been too quick to make that assumption. "For that reason I was about to recommend the evacuation of the Anshar to a place of safety," he told Ebabbar, temporizing. "It may be an excess of caution, but of course there is no such thing when it comes to her personal security."

"A precaution that has not been necessary at any point in the last five thousand years," Ebabbar said with a frown, his eyes hard as black flint. "Sapwu Zrinan makes a persuasive case that the only way to ensure the Heavenly Monarch's safety and to salvage something out of today's many disasters is to sue for peace. This is no time to run risks such as moving the Anshar through a city under attack, General Hish."

"Sapwu Zrinan?" Mubirrum said, unable to conceal his surprise. "He has no business at the palace! He retired to religious study."

"We have broken with many other traditions lately, so I suppose Lord Zrinan's decision to unretire is hardly worth noting at this point," Ebabbar replied. "Regardless of the proprieties of his return, I am inclined to believe that he is right. Hish Mubirrum, the Anshar requires the presence of her Sharur-Tal for urgent consultations at the palace—*immediately.*"

"Impossible!" Mubirrum spluttered. "We have no time for discussion and debate today, Chamberlain. I am Sharur-Tal, and I alone will determine how to meet the enemies now threatening Bagal-Dindir." He almost added that it would be foolish in the extreme to risk moving the Dominion's supreme military commander under the threat of enemy air attack, but stopped himself when he remembered that he'd just suggested that course of action for the Heavenly Monarch herself. Ebabbar Simtum might be a vacillating bureaucrat, but he was not stupid enough to let a slip like that pass by unremarked.

"And the Anshar alone will determine whether her Sharur-Tal is capable of honoring the oath he swore to defend her dominion," said Ebabbar. "She demands your presence, Lord Mubirrum. I would comply, if I were you." Then the chamberlain cut off his link, leaving Mubirrum facing a blank screen.

"This is madness," Mubirrum growled. No force in creation could return events to the course they'd been diverted from weeks ago; even Ebabbar had to see that. He glared at the blank display for a long moment as he brought his emotions under control, and when he'd mastered himself again, he considered the situation with the cold and simple pragmatism by which he'd tried to help guide his people through the unfortunate times in which he'd happened to live.

Hish Sudi warned me that our first victory over Abernathy's fleet would be difficult to repeat. A month ago the humans underestimated us; now I have underestimated them. One way or another, I will not see another day in power. He had little concern for his own life—he was old, and he had no wish to see what might be coming in the next few years. No, in these last few hours in which the freedom to act remained in his hands, he had to take steps to set the Dominion's course in such a way that it would not matter that he was no longer in power. They were hard decisions, hard and merciless, and untold death and destruction would flow from them. But Hish Mubirrum saw no other way to preserve the Dominion. *It is the warrior's burden,* he told himself. *We harden our hearts and do what must be done.*

He straightened his back, settling his heavy armor over his shoulders, and returned to the command chamber. Hish Pazril and his subcommanders waited for him. "What did the chamberlain want?" Pazril asked.

"I have been summoned to the palace," Mubirrum told his younger kinsman. "Make ready my skybarge and arrange the heaviest possible escort. I would be derelict in my duty if I neglected to take every necessary step to ensure my safe arrival."

"The palace!" Pazril's eyes widened in astonishment. "Does the chamberlain not see that we are fighting a battle at the moment? He must wait!"

"I would be happy to keep Ebabbar Simtum waiting until the sun died. However, it is the Heavenly Monarch who requests my presence. I must go."

The younger warrior stood in silence for a moment. "Of

course," he finally said. "I will arrange it at once, General. We can be ready in a quarter-hour."

"Not you, Pazril." Mubirrum shook his head. "I have another task for you, a task of great importance. Let your subordinates see to escorting me to the palace. Nothing else we do today is as important as what I now entrust to you, and I must know that you will carry it out no matter what develops over the next few hours."

"My lord?" Pazril said, a flicker of confusion in his eyes.

Mubirrum dismissed all the others nearby with a gesture, ensuring privacy for what he had to say next. He lowered his voice anyway, drawing Pazril close. "The time has come for the Peerless Swords of Scarlet to carry out the special duty for which we assigned them to Kadingir Temple. Tzem Ebneghirz must die—and it must be clear to all that he died at human hands."

22

Bagal-Dindir, Tamabuqq Prime

Dear God, what a disaster," Sikander murmured in his native High Panjabi, peering through the armored viewport by his seat in the passenger compartment of *Exeter*'s armed orbiter. Fires burned across Bagal-Dindir, ignited by dozens of pinpoint kinetic strikes from the fleet overhead. Attack craft screamed across the sky in no pattern or order that he could discern, strafing *warumzi agu* street barricades or dropping guided ordnance on the better-protected fighting vehicles and strongpoints of Militarist units. Tzoru shock cannons fired intermittently, hurling lightning-like bolts into the sky, while rockets lanced up from batteries hidden in the city below, vainly chasing after the human assault transports and leaving great daggerlike exhaust plumes that gleamed gold and white in the afternoon light. Everywhere Sikander looked, mobs surged through the streets, some racing toward the Thousand Worlds ward, others seething and roiling their way toward some other objective they deemed important. "This is worse than Tanjeer!"

"I doubt that, Nawabzada," Darvesh Reza replied in the same language, but he craned around in his seat to peer out of his own viewport. Regardless of the fact that Commodore Abernathy's personal command group intended to go nowhere near any kind of ground fighting, there was not a chance in the world that the Kashmiri sergeant would allow Sikander to go knowingly into a battle zone unescorted. As a result, Sikander's own personal bodyguard accompanied a dozen Aquilan marines assigned to the job of keeping William Abernathy's small command group safe. "Tanjeer was insanely dangerous. However, I note for the record that your father would disapprove. This is hardly Kashmir's fight."

"I'm exactly where my duties require me to be. And I'll point out that this time I didn't volunteer for anything—the commodore required my presence."

"And therefore mine as well," said Darvesh. He turned his attention to his mag carbine and battle armor.

"What's all that, North?" Abernathy asked from across the narrow aisle.

"I seem to have developed a habit of visiting exotic planets in the middle of pitched battles," Sikander told him. "Chief Reza does not approve."

The commodore gave them both a fierce grin, and thumped his own borrowed battle armor. "It does a man good to hear the sound of the guns once in a while and find out that he's got what it takes to head in the direction he needs to go. Invigorating, you might say."

Spoken like a man who wasn't at Tanjeer four years ago or Durzinzer last month, noted Sikander. He chose to keep that observation to himself. Now that he'd found his way back to Abernathy's good side, he was in no hurry to find a new way to antagonize the squadron commander.

The orbiter streaked low over the streets of the Tzoru capital. Sikander caught a glimpse of the wrecked barricades marking the siege lines surrounding the Thousand Worlds ward, and then the wide boulevard just outside the walls. Half a dozen burning wrecks—armored vehicles and light Tzoru skybarges—littered the area, surrounded by disorderly crowds of Tzoru. Whether they were firefighters, citizens with some idea of rescuing soldiers injured in the wreckage, or *warumzi agu* scavengers hoping to salvage the vehicles' armament, he had no idea. A moment later he lost sight of them as the shuttle cleared the old city wall and dropped down toward the ground. The pilot threw the large orbiter into one last aggressive turn that pushed Sikander deep into his seat, then flared sharply and set down in the gardens of the Aquilan embassy. The door-ramp at the back of the passenger compartment dropped open with a hiss of equalizing pressure, followed by a wave of damp, chilled air. The smell of smoke filled his nostrils.

Abernathy popped up out of his seat at once, but Mason Barnes moved to intercept him. "Hang on just half a minute, sir," the Hibernian lieutenant drawled. "We ought to let the marines disembark first and clear the area."

The commodore scowled impatiently, but recovered quickly. "Quite right, Mr. Barnes. Good thinking."

Sikander unstrapped and stood as well. He recognized the sounds of distant strife at once—the high chirping of heavy mag-rifle fire not too far off, the *pop-pop-pop* of old-style Tzoru firearms, and above it all the raucous tumult of angry crowds, strangely like the roar one might hear from a large stadium just out of sight. He waited in the passenger bay with Abernathy and Barnes while the marine contingent deployed, then followed Abernathy out when the marines gave them the clear sign.

He looked about to get his bearings . . . and found the Aquilan embassy in ruins.

"Damn," Abernathy muttered, taking in the sight. Several of the buildings in the compound had been reduced to rubble, including the dormitory building and the garage. The main residence still stood, but it had lost most of its front wall, now a jumble of broken masonry spilling out into the street. Holes two and three meters across pockmarked the side of the building facing directly into the garden. Scores of Aquilan civilians—junior diplomats and support staff—crowded around a wing that had collapsed entirely, digging furiously in the rubble alongside a number of the embassy's Tzoru servants. "What happened here?"

"It must've been the Militarist artillery, sir," Barnes observed. "I guess they've had lots of time to zero in on specific targets in the ward."

"A threat that could strike again at any time," Darvesh murmured softly to Sikander. "We should not remain in the open any longer than we must, sir."

Sikander nodded in reply. The fleet overhead had already destroyed a number of Militarist emplacements, but it was unlikely they'd found all the threatening weapons. Then again, if he were a Hish artillery commander, he'd probably scratch the Aquilan embassy off his target list and move on to the next one. The building hadn't been altogether flattened, but clearly the Militarists had knocked it out as a command facility.

The commodore dismissed *Exeter*'s Cormorant with a curt nod to the pilot—armed assault craft were in very short supply among the combined squadrons, and it was needed more elsewhere—then strode over to a knot of diplomatic personnel standing by a garden gazebo, shivering under blankets. "Ambassador Hart!" he called out.

"Commodore Abernathy," Hart replied. His arm was in a sling and a thick layer of dust caked his shoulders and hair, but he smiled broadly as he caught sight of the Helix Squadron commander. "You've returned in the very nick of time."

"Not for the embassy itself, it seems," Abernathy said. "When did that happen?"

"A little more than an hour ago. I think the Militarists decided to exact some retribution when they realized they couldn't stop your fleet." Hart shrugged, and immediately winced in pain. "Speaking of which, what's the situation in orbit? We lost track of events when we lost the command center."

"We smashed up the Militarist battle line. Then the Golden Banner Fleet stood down and moved off, so we've got control of the Tamabuqq system."

"The Zabar reconsidered their support for the Militarists," Sikander added. "Sapwu Zrinan is here with the Supernal

Glory Fleet from Latzari. He's talking to the other *sebetu* of the High Council to see if they can leverage General Hish out of power. Lara Dunstan is with him, but I'm sure she's anxious to speak to you."

"The Sapwu are here?" said Hart. "Good. I'm pleased to hear that your clandestine visit bore fruit, Mr. North."

Sikander gestured at the surrounding district with a sweep of his hand. "I think that remains to be seen, sir. Let's secure the rest of the ward before we declare victory."

"Of course," Hart said. "Major Dalton relocated to—"

"Friend Sikander!" Sikander glanced around, and found Radi Sabub hurrying up. Abernathy's marines immediately raised their weapons, alarmed to find a Tzoru rushing toward the commodore and ambassador. Half a dozen mag rifles suddenly sighted in on the Tzoru scholar; Radi Sabub froze in midstep, gaping in surprise.

"Hold your fire!" Sikander shouted. "Hold your fire! He's friendly."

"Yes, please—hold your fire," Hart confirmed. "Commodore, many of the Tzoru here in the Thousand Worlds ward are not our enemies. Make sure your people know not to fire on unarmed Tzoru."

"What about the *warumzi*?" Abernathy asked. "There are a lot of them inside the walls already, aren't there?"

"There are," said Hart. "The general rule of thumb is that Tzoru shooting at you are probably *warumzi agu,* and Tzoru who aren't shooting at you or waving swords in the air are probably on our side. Also, watch out for Tzoru wearing green. None of our friends wear green."

Radi Sabub carefully indicated the white armband on his left arm. "As Mr. Hart says," he said, eyes fixed on the mag rifles covering him. "Many of us are serving as medics and in rescue teams. White bands are good!"

"All right, then." Abernathy nodded to Barnes. "Lieutenant, please get the word to Colonel Iverson and the troop detachments of the other powers. No sense allowing something tragic to take place."

"Yes, sir." Mason Barnes keyed his comm unit, and began issuing instructions to his team aboard *Exeter*.

Sikander moved over to Radi Sabub as *Exeter*'s marines lowered their weapons. "I'm glad to see you, Sabub," he said. "How are you?"

"Extremely frightened," the scholar said. "That will pass soon. Today is a terrible day, but I hope that perhaps it is the end of the madness that has gripped my people. A troubled and confusing peace must be better than what we have all lived through for these last forty days."

"A statesman of ancient Earth once said that there was never a good war or a bad peace."

"How very Tzoru-like. Tell me, is friend Lara safe too? I worried about both of you after you left."

"She is," said Sikander. He glanced up at the sky. "In fact, she isn't far away. She's with Sapwu Zrinan and the Sapwu fleet. I expect she'll join us down here just as soon as the shooting stops and the talking begins again."

"The sooner, the better," Radi Sabub replied. "It seems to me that there is a great need for her insight and advice today."

Sikander smiled, then noticed Commodore Abernathy listening to his comm device and signaling to his escorts. "Colonel Iverson has a command post set up at the Montréalais embassy," Abernathy said to the small team. "Seeing as our own embassy isn't going to be terribly useful in that regard, we're going to relocate. Mr. Hart, I understand that Major Dalton and some of your peers are already there."

The ambassador nodded. "I've been out of touch with things for the better part of an hour. I'm with you, Commodore. It's just three blocks east of here."

"Then let's go," Abernathy said. The small party set out on foot down the rubble-strewn street; *Exeter*'s marine contingent formed a moving cordon around the commodore and the ambassador.

"Stay close by, if you don't mind," Sikander told Sabub. "We might need a Tzoru for interpretation or cultural explanations." He'd also feel better if he knew that the scholar was under the protection of Aquilan marines, and therefore somewhat less likely to be mistaken for a *warumzi agu* by some overly enthusiastic Dremish or Californian trooper and shot dead on the street.

"Of course," said Sabub.

Sikander glanced at Darvesh to make sure Darvesh understood that he meant to keep Sabub safe, and then the three of them fell into Abernathy's small procession. This part of the Thousand Worlds ward had been badly damaged by the same artillery barrage that hit the Aquilan embassy; dozens of rowhomes and small shops lining the street showed damage, while billowing smoke from others hinted at fires raging within. Parties of common Tzoru did their best to shift rubble aside or fight the fires with bucket brigades; Sikander guessed that with the water mains shut off from outside the district, they had no other alternative. Bursts of mag-rifle fire or crackling Tzoru shock guns echoed through the streets, but the work parties ignored them—and, in fact, paid little attention to the Aquilan group hurrying down the street.

They passed another building that was nothing but a heap of rubble, and Sikander winced when he realized the place had been one of his favorite restaurants in the Thousand Worlds ward. Across the street, a lovely little park with a stand of treeferns several centuries old had been reduced to a tumbled ruin of trunks stripped bare or upended altogether. *Our orbital fire, or Militarist rockets?* he wondered. Whatever else happened in Bagal-Dindir in the future, the Thousand Worlds ward would never be the same. He hoped that didn't prove to be a metaphor for the Tzoru Dominion in general.

He turned away from the wreckage of the city park—and at that moment the bright white bolt of a Tzoru shock rifle lanced out of the ruined building beside the park, burning down one of the marines on that side of the street. *"Contact right!"* several marines shouted at once.

Several more shock bolts less accurate than the first followed, although one passed close enough to Sikander to fill his nose with the acrid odor of ozone and make his skin tingle with static. He threw himself down on the street, and as an afterthought reached up to pull down Radi Sabub as well. The Aquilan marines responded by turning their mag rifles on the building shell—an old guildhall, or so Sikander thought—and letting loose with a ferocious barrage, smashing the windows and masonry with a hail of hypervelocity penetrators.

Sikander drew his own mag pistol, and rolled over onto his side to scan the street behind them. It was all too easy to get caught up in looking at what everyone else was looking at, but *Exeter*'s marines had more than enough eyes on the guildhall already; he wanted to make sure no one else threatened them from a different direction. Darvesh did the same, but he watched their left flank. *At least he's got a longarm,* Sikander thought. All of Abernathy's officers wore pistols, but they'd left the battle arms to their marine escorts. Shooting their way through the Thousand Worlds ward wasn't what they'd landed for.

"It seems this part of the district is not as secure as we'd believed," Abernathy remarked. He propped himself up behind a mound of rubble and took aim with his pistol, peppering the building from which the shot had come. "Mr. Barnes, see if you can update Major Dalton on our situation."

"Yes, sir!" said Barnes. He ducked down and pulled out his comm unit.

No more shock bolts came from the guildhall, and the harsh chirping of mag-rifle fire gradually slackened. "Did we get 'em?" Abernathy asked the marines nearby.

"Maybe, sir," one replied. He rose to a crouch, ready to investigate. But at that moment dozens of green-clad figures burst out of the bullet-pocked doorways or bounded through the broken windows, hissing fierce Tzoru war cries. Sikander spun around to face the old guildhall again, caught up in the shouts of alarm and sudden eruption of firing. Marine rifle fire cut down six or seven of the *warumzi agu* within the blink of an eye, blasting them into bloody ruin the instant they broke cover. But other radicals returned fire with old-style firearms or fumbled with Tzoru military-class shock weapons, and a ragged wave of *warumzi* in the front rushed the Aquilans, armed with spears and ancient Tzoru swords.

"Holy crap!" swore the marine nearest to Sikander. She dropped three of the sword-armed Tzoru with three quick shots, but then a bullet from an old-style firearm found the hip seam in her body armor. She crumpled to the street, biting back on a scream as another *warumzi* with a spear leaped for her. Sikander slewed his heavy pistol around and dropped the spearman with a clean shot in the middle of the chest, blasting the Tzoru into a limp tangle of nerveless limbs.

William Abernathy fired wildly, and managed to stop another attacker with a lucky shot that blew apart the Tzoru's knee. Then the commodore dropped his pistol, swearing viciously as he shook his hand—a *warumzi agu* bullet had found his wrist. Ambassador Hart pulled him down behind the same rubble pile he sheltered behind.

Darvesh sighted and fired in the opposite direction. "Behind us, Nawabzada," he said calmly.

Sikander rolled over again and looked back down the street. Another group of *warumzi agu* darted toward the group of Aquilans. "Oh, shit," he muttered. Bracing his pistol, he fired, and fired again, knocking down another of the new attackers while Darvesh coldly and efficiently dropped the hostiles one by one. For a moment Sikander feared that it would not be enough, and they'd be overrun by sword-wielding fanatics . . . until a vicious hail of fire erupted from an alleyway to one side, cutting down the attacking *warumzi agu* from behind. Human soldiers dressed in stippled black and gray camouflage appeared in the street behind the Aquilan group, breaking up the attack from that quarter.

"Those are Dremish battle uniforms, if I am not mistaken," Darvesh observed. "Today I must confess I am happy to see them."

"Me, too." Sikander looked back to the guildhall and the fighting in that direction, but it was over—*Exeter*'s marines had cut down all the *warumzi agu* in the initial rush. At least fifteen bodies littered the street. Cautiously he got to his feet.

"Anybody hurt?" Abernathy called.

"You are, sir," said Barnes. "Better let me have a look at that hand." The lieutenant trotted over to examine Abernathy's wounded wrist.

Since it appeared that the commodore was being looked after, Sikander hurried over to the marine who'd been hit near him. "Hang on there, marine," he told her.

"Thank you, sir," the wounded trooper replied. She grimaced in pain. "What in the hell hit me?"

"Rifle shot, I think. It certainly looks like a bullet wound." Sikander peered at the injury, fumbling for his medical kit. He didn't think the bullet had hit any vital organs, but he had to imagine that she had a cracked or broken hip bone.

"Some warmie took me out with a fucking antique? You've got to be kidding me."

"I guess he got lucky," Sikander told her. He found a wound-dressing pack and pressed it over the injury, looking around for the squad medic. "This marine needs some help!" he called.

"I'm here, sir!" Another of the marines moved up to kneel beside the wounded woman. "I've got her."

Sikander clapped the injured marine on the helmet, and stood up to let the medic do his job. He found the Dremish soldiers trotting up to join *Exeter*'s marine contingent—and, at the head of the detachment, a familiar face. Kapitan-Leutnant Helena Aldrich wore Imperial battle dress and heavy composite plate armor over her torso, and she carried a short-barreled Gerst autorifle just like the troopers around her. *At least she had the good sense to dress for the occasion,* he decided.

"We meet again on a battlefield, Mr. North," Aldrich said with a hard smile. "But it seems that today we are on the same side."

"Ms. Aldrich," Sikander replied, nodding. "You showed up at just the right time."

"I happened to be on hand with *Prinz Oskar*'s detachment when your Mr. Barnes advised us of your difficulty. Since we were the nearest body of troops we were sent to help." Aldrich shifted her autorifle and glanced around, frowning. "I fear that today's fighting is turning into a hundred small skirmishes just like this one. We've broken up all the large *warumzi* formations nearby, but there are disorganized bands of fanatics holed up here and there all over the Thousand Worlds ward."

"So I see," Sikander said. "We certainly didn't expect to run into these fellows only a block from the embassy." He'd hoped that breaking up the Militarist assaults with air strikes and orbital fire would more or less settle the ground fighting in the offworlder district, but it seemed that dealing with the revolutionary militias would require some sort of methodical sweep. The ground-troop commanders probably knew that already, but he made a mental note to check for himself when they reached the command post.

It took a few minutes to arrange stretcher teams for the wounded marines and the few *warumzi agu* who could be helped. Abernathy's injury proved to be minor, although he had a broken bone in his wrist. He refused any systemic pain reliever for fear of "getting all fogged up," as he put it, but he allowed the squad's medic to apply a local pain agent for some temporary relief. Then they set out again, making their way out of the area that had been hammered by Militarist artillery. The transition surprised him—one moment buildings with missing windows and shattered masonry surrounded him, and the next he turned the corner on a street that appeared to be completely unscathed. Only the regimental command post parked on the lawn of the Montréalais embassy and the weapon emplacements set up on nearby rooftops indicated that this was not a typical day in the Thousand Worlds ward.

Abernathy and Hart headed straight into the command post; Sikander and the other Helix Squadron staff officers followed. A tall, dark-haired woman in Aquilan field armor—Colonel Iverson, or so Sikander guessed—met Abernathy at the entrance to the post. "Welcome to Bagal-Dindir, Commodore," she said, taking Abernathy's good hand. "Sorry for your trouble on the way over. Our perimeter is one part confusion and one part wishful thinking."

"I know you're doing your best, Colonel," Abernathy replied. "Bring me up to date, if you please. What do I need to know?"

"We've got troops sweeping the Thousand Worlds ward for more pockets of *warumzi agu* resistance like the one you ran into, but it's mostly a mop-up operation at this point." Colonel Iverson pointed at several blue and green icons in the tactical projection—Aquilan detachments and allied units on the move in the offworlder district—and then widened the display to include the entire city. "We've taken out most of the actively hostile Militarist armor and artillery with air strikes and orbital bombardment."

"Good," said the commodore. "What are these white icons over here?"

"Those are formations under the control of high clans from other factions that remain unengaged." Iverson shrugged. "We're getting local signals that they plan to sit out the fighting."

"Nothing like watching someone else take a first-rate drubbing to help you figure out which side you want to be on." Abernathy grinned at the display.

"Speaking of which, we've got some news from the Supernal Glory command ship, sir," said Mason Barnes. He held one hand up to his ear, concentrating on his comm device. "Sapwu Zrinan's asking us to refrain from engaging the forces of the Ninazzu, Abnu, and Maruz clans. He's convinced them to remain neutral today. The Ninazzu, Abnu, and Maruz are not, I repeat not, belligerents today."

"Finally, some common sense," Abernathy observed. "I can't imagine that clans like the Ninazzu or the Maruz are in a big hurry to support the Militarists right now."

"My guess is that General Hish is finding out today that he has fewer friends than he thought he did," said Hart. "We just might manage to keep the lid on this whole situation after all."

"In which case, Mr. North deserves the lion's share of the credit. It was his idea to convince the Sapwu to intervene against the Militarists. He argued for it at every turn, even when the rest of us insisted on trying to solve this situation with K-cannons and orbital strikes." Commodore Abernathy turned to Sikander and clapped him on the shoulder with his good hand. "A lot of people owe you an apology, Lieutenant Commander. Well done!"

"Thank you, sir," Sikander replied. He allowed himself a smile of satisfaction; over the last few weeks he'd learned that William Abernathy saved his praise for moments when he meant it sincerely. If nothing else, it felt good—*very* good—to finally be proved right about something on Helix Station, and perhaps save a lot of lives in the process. "Dr. Dunstan did the hard part, though. I merely provided the necessary transportation."

"New report, Commodore," Barnes said. "The Karsu are throwing in the towel. They just told the Sapwu that they'll stand down if we stop hitting their formations."

"Good," Abernathy said. "They're the clan that sent the Shining Resolve Fleet against us in Kahnar-Sag, correct?"

"They are," Norman Hart said, nodding. "They're staunch Militarists. If they've had enough, then the Hish are almost completely isolated, which means it's about time for me to get to work again. Excuse me, please." The ambassador broke away from the military personnel, heading toward a small conference area at one side of the post where the Dremish ambassador Popov and the Montréalais Hamel stood engaged in conversation.

Sikander was more than a little curious about how the

Commonwealth of Aquila, the Empire of Dremark, the Republic of Montréal, the California Union, the Kingdom of Cygnus, and the Nyeiran Star Empire intended to carry out any joint negotiations with the Dominion High Council or any other Tzoru authority, but that was not his job today. *Probably just as well,* he thought. *Once they've figured out they are no longer in any collective danger, they'll be back to the usual game of trying to get ahead of one another in no time at all.*

Iverson and Abernathy fell into a discussion about how to coordinate the sweeps searching out pockets of *warumzi agu* resistance. Sikander followed along attentively until his own comm device pinged—a call from the Intel Section aboard *Exeter*. He moved a few steps away from the others so that his conversation wouldn't interfere with theirs, and answered. "Lieutenant Commander North."

"This is Senior Chief Lin, sir. We've picked up some unusual movement on the ground. We think we might have a lead on the Militarist command center."

"Really?" Sikander focused his attention on the chief's report. "Okay, Senior Chief, I'm listening. What have you found?"

"We spotted a heavily escorted skybarge lifting off from a place called Eningu-Luz a few minutes ago. The flight's on its way to the Anshar's Palace."

"Hang on, I'm looking at the map." Sikander scrutinized the tactical display in the regimental command post. "Where is this place again?"

"Northeast of town, maybe forty kilometers from the palace. It's an old fortification that originally served as a stronghold for the Anshar's household troops in the days when the Anshars had their own armies," said Lin. "To tell the truth, we thought the place wasn't in use anymore. There are a bunch of sites like it all around Bagal-Dindir. We never would have given it a second look if it hadn't been for the unusual flight activity."

Sikander found the icon on the tactical display. "I can see

it's a little out of the way," he said. "Do you have any idea who's on that flight? Do we have anything in position to intercept?"

"Sort of and not really, sir," said Lin. "My guess is that we're looking at a very high-ranking Hish because the flight assets all appear to be Hish combat aircraft. As far as intercepting the flight, they're already halfway to the palace, and all our armed orbiters and assault shuttles are busy around the Thousand Worlds ward. By the time we get approval—"

"Our big shot will already be at the palace, and we don't want to hit the palace," Sikander finished for his deputy. "Any other unusual movements to report, Senior Chief?"

"Most of it's already on the tactical repeater, sir. But there's one more flight from Eningu-Luz: a pair of skybarge troop transports. They took off just before the big group, and they're now landing at Kadingir."

"Kadingir?" Sikander asked. "The mountain temple?"

"Yes, sir. Tzoru troops are deploying there, and it looks like they're off-loading some heavy equipment."

"Why are troops moving to occupy a remote shrine?" Sikander mused aloud. He would have imagined that the Hish had more than enough on their plate with the fighting in Bagal-Dindir. *Are they setting up a refuge or strongpoint of some kind?* He remembered his visit to the place months ago: rugged terrain, old stone walls, and difficult, winding stairs. The place could be defended for a long time against a ground assault, but of course the Militarists knew perfectly well that troops with air transport would hardly need to fight their way up the stairs.

"No idea, sir," Lin replied. "It's a mountain, so it's got good line of sight. Some kind of communication relay or sensor array, maybe?"

"I suppose so," said Sikander. "All right, Senior Chief. Keep me posted on any new developments. I'll brief the commodore on the airlifts. North, out."

He headed for the corner of the command post where Abernathy and Iverson continued their conversation. The commodore held his injured hand under the opposite arm, but his attention remained fixed on the colonel's report. Sikander braced himself to interrupt, but then his eye fell on Radi Sabub, standing by the entrance to the post as if he were not sure whether he should follow Sikander inside. *Maybe Sabub would know why the Hish care about the temple.*

"I apologize, Scholar Radi," Sikander said to the Tzoru. "I let myself get caught up in everything that's going on, and I forgot that I'd asked you to stay close by."

"Perfectly understandable," the scholar replied. "I can see that this is a day of extraordinary disorder. It's a wonder that anybody can manage anything at all in this sort of situation."

"I have a question for you: What's at Kadingir Temple? Is there anything there that General Hish would take a special interest in? Relics or holy items he might want to protect, perhaps?"

Sabub thought for a moment. "Kadingir houses an exquisite set of bronze drums recording the Sixty-Four Prophecies. They are quite authoritative, and many scholars retire to Kadingir to study them at first—" The Tzoru stopped, his eyes widening a little with a sudden thought. "No, that is not it, friend Sikander! Kadingir is the place where the philosopher Tzem Ebneghirz chose to enter religious seclusion earlier this year. His teachings form the foundation of the *warumzi agu* movement."

Sikander remembered that name, all right—his early encounters with the *warumzi agu* had fixed it in his mind. "Ebneghirz, *the* Ebneghirz, is at Kadingir? You're certain of that?"

"Yes, friend Sikander. It was the subject of a good deal of discussion among my people, since everyone knew he was forced into seclusion by the Baltzu and the other Mercantilist *sebetu*." Sabub cocked his head to one side. "Why, what is happening at Kadingir?"

"Nothing good, I fear. Thank you, Sabub—this might be very important," said Sikander, and then hurried back to Commodore Abernathy.

23

Kadingir, Tamabuqq Prime

The last rays of sunset painted the mountaintops a spectacular green-gold as the VO-8 Cormorant raced northward. Pilot First Class Andrews deftly skirted rocky crags and followed the winding valleys that scored the rugged range, keeping to the gloom below the ridgelines. Sikander sat in the boat's command seat, but he left the flying to Andrews. He had other things to think about, such as the Dremish Falke-type assault shuttle leading the way just half a kilometer ahead of *Exeter*'s orbiter.

I never imagined that I'd be going into a fight alongside Dremish soldiers! For two generations of Aquilan naval officers, the Empire of Dremark served as the hypothetical enemy in any number of exercises and strategic plans. Nine out of ten of Sikander's colleagues expected to fight a war against Dremark at some point in their careers—and at Gadira Sikander had come closer to that reality than anybody on Helix Station except Magdalena Juarez or Karsen Reno. He no longer hoped for the opportunity to prove himself against the Navy's traditional rival, but neither did he expect to see the two great powers ever join forces against some other foe. It came down to the fact that the Tzoru Dominion was a *long* way from home for Aquilans and Dremish . . . and the dumb luck that had left contingents of Commonwealth marines and Imperial soldiers close by Commodore Abernathy's command post when he'd learned about the Hish clan's sudden interest in Kadingir Temple.

"Five klicks out, sir," Andrews said. She kept her attention fixed on the terrain imager in the center of the console. "Better tell everyone to strap in. We're running out of valley and I'm going to have to break cover in just a second."

"Very well," Sikander replied. He felt reasonably certain that every one of the twenty-four Aquilan marines in the orbiter's passenger bay was already strapped down. *Exeter* didn't carry a true assault lander like the Dremish *Falke*, but the VO-8 Cormorant could serve as one in a pinch. It carried a light automag cannon in a chin turret and enough armor to stand up to small-arms fire or light crew-served weapons, and the big stern ramp made it easy for heavily armed marines to disembark in a hurry.

Major Constanza Dalton occupied the third seat in the orbiter's cramped cockpit. She keyed her intercom and announced, "Thirty seconds, everybody. Hang on, we're coming within line of sight of the target." She was junior to Sikander by a couple of months, which meant that he commanded the Aquilan component of the raid, not her. But just as he wouldn't interfere with Andrews's piloting, Sikander had no intention of trying to tell a marine officer how to command her troops in a ground action. *Exeter* marines made up one squad in the back of the orbiter, but the other squad came from the embassy garrison who'd been fighting Tzoru under her command for the last five weeks; Dalton and her veterans had a great deal of bitter and hard-won experience relevant to the mission at hand. And Darvesh Reza rode in the back, too, armed just as heavily as any of the marines.

"Got the chin gun, sir?" Andrews asked Sikander.

"I've got it," Sikander affirmed. He kept his hands loose on the Cormorant's weapon and countermeasure controls, and watched the valley beneath them shallow rapidly as it climbed up to meet the mountain's shoulder. The Dremish pilots had picked an approach that would keep the two landers hidden from any hostile forces on top of Kadingir for as long as possible, just in case the Hish warriors had managed to set up any antiair systems. It made for a bumpy, bonejarring ride, but that seemed far preferable to dodging rockets or shock-cannon bolts. Nobody had ever come up with a good way to shoot through mountainsides, after all.

The two shuttles popped up over the ridgeline into the last golden gleam of sunset—and there stood the ancient shrine of Kadingir, clinging to its mountaintop. Andrews slalomed sharply around several knife-edged natural buttresses, doing her best to get to the temple as fast as possible without clipping a hillside on the way in. For an instant Sikander thought that perhaps they'd caught the Hish soldiers sleeping, but then he spotted a Tzoru skybarge hovering over the ancient structure. An instant later, a shock cannon spat a bolt of crackling white lightning at the VO-8 from an emplacement atop the temple ramparts. Other weapons opened up on the two human landers.

"Shit!" Andrews yelped, yanking at the control yoke to dodge. "Taking fire!"

Sikander hunched lower in his seat, unable to keep himself from flinching at the eye-searing bolts streaking past the armored viewports. Andrews and Dalton likewise ducked in their seats—the urge was difficult to resist. "So much for surprise," he said.

"Arrow Two, this is Arrow One," the comm unit crackled. Sikander recognized Helena Aldrich's voice; the Kapitan-Leutnant outranked him, so she held nominal command of their hastily organized strike force. "We are engaging the enemy flyer. Suppress the ground fire, over."

"Arrow One, Arrow Two. We're on it, over," Sikander replied. He activated the orbiter's automag cannon and tracked in on the origin of the shock bolts, slashing the weapon's power as he did so. Even a light mag cannon could easily punch through several feet of brick, and he might accidentally shoot clear through the shrine if he didn't exercise a little caution. Since he didn't want to kill anybody but Militarist soldiers, he couldn't take that chance. Cutting the chin cannon's muzzle velocity in half wouldn't change its accuracy in the least, and it would still be enough to wreck anything short of a grav tank that got in the way of its magnetically accelerated penetrators.

He zeroed in on the origin of the shock bolts and let loose with a couple of short bursts; the gun whined and thumped under his feet, lashing the shrine's south-facing walls with a hail of fire. Puffs of shattered brickwork and dust walked back and forth across the ancient battlements. Andrews slewed the orbiter sideways, doing her best to use the rocky spires for cover. At the range of two kilometers he couldn't quite make out whether his rounds were hitting the shock-cannon emplacement or not . . . but then a bright blue-white flare erupted in the shadows of the temple's south terrace as the shock cannon's capacitor suddenly exploded.

"Good shooting!" Dalton said, clapping a hand on Sikander's shoulder. "Walk some bursts over to the left, we're taking some small-arms fire from that side. Must be some fighting positions down in those rocks."

Sikander turned the Cormorant's gun in the direction Major Dalton suggested. He spotted the boulder patch she pointed at, but he couldn't make out any Tzoru warriors in the area. Figuring that she might have seen something while he was focusing on the shock cannon, he hosed down the general area with a long burst.

Ahead of them, the Dremish assault shuttle peeled away, turning toward the Militarist skybarge—a heavily armed combat flyer that fell somewhere between an assault lander and a grav tank. A barrage of shock-cannon bolts and guided rockets erupted from the skybarge's weapons stations; Aldrich's pilots replied with an automag cannon even heavier than the one on the Aquilan shuttle. One shock bolt blew a meter-wide hole through the Falke's starboard-side stabilizer, but the rugged craft shrugged off the hit. Bright tracers from the Dremish guns stitched across the flanks of the skybarge in return, blasting pieces of armor off the Tzoru craft. The skybarge wasn't fast, but it was surprisingly nimble, spinning and bobbing among the crags while the Dremish assault craft dodged its rockets and tried to line up a clear shot. One of the Tzoru rockets streaked past the Falke and detonated against the rocky slope behind it, but then the Dremish gunners succeeded in knocking out one of the skybarge lift plates. The barge suddenly sagged onto its side, suspended only by the opposite engine; Tzoru warriors tumbled from its deck, tiny fluttering shapes falling to their deaths hundreds of meters below. Then the whole skybarge dropped precipitously until its side hit the sloping hillside and it tumbled into a fatal crash.

The Dremish shuttle curved back around, heading back toward the shrine—only to suddenly turn sharply and head off again. "Arrow Two, this is Arrow One," Helena Aldrich coolly reported. "There is another skybarge approaching from the east. We will deal with it. Proceed with your deployment if you've cleared your landing zone, over."

"Arrow One, Arrow Two. Acknowledged. We're landing our marines, over," said Sikander. He leaned forward and pointed out one of the shrine's larger buildings to Andrews and Dalton. "There, that's the main temple. There's a big courtyard just inside. Does that suit you, Major?"

"Good enough," said Dalton. "The faster we're on the ground the better I'll like it. I always feel like a sitting duck when we're in the air."

"Andrews, put us down," Sikander said.

"Yes, sir," the pilot replied. She dropped the nose of the orbiter and goosed the throttle, darting in to close the last kilometer or two of range. Sikander glimpsed a few Tzoru in dark armor sprawled motionless on the temple terrace or dashing for new positions under cover, but he had no time to engage them; Andrews gave him only a few seconds before she roared over the temple rooftop and dropped down into the courtyard. Several Tzoru scholars dressed in yellow robes scattered in panic, fleeing into the temple interior, but then the VO-8's belly skids thumped onto the ground and the stern door dropped open with the high-pitched whine of hydraulic motors.

"Watch for the civilians," Sikander told Dalton. "Remember, one of them might be Tzem Ebneghirz."

"We'll do our best," said the major, unstrapping from her seat. She hurried aft through the short companionway linking the cockpit and the passenger bay, while her marines stormed down the stern ramp and fanned out into the courtyard.

Sikander waited a moment for the marines to deploy, then unstrapped and stood up. "I'm debarking," he told Andrews. "It's your shuttle. Take station a kilometer or two off and stand by for fire support, if we need it. And watch out for any other Militarist flyers that might be around."

"Got it, sir," the pilot replied. "I'll be standing by. Be careful out there."

Darvesh waited for him in the passenger bay with a helmet and a mag carbine. The two Kashmiris wore Navy battledress uniforms with armored vests, but Major Dalton's marines had the benefit of heavy combat armor and full-sized mag rifles; Sikander knew it was his job to stay out of the way and let the marines do their work without worrying about keeping him safe. Burst after burst of mag-weapon fire echoed through the stone corridors of the temple, interspersed with the crackle of Tzoru shock rifles and shouts in both Anglic and Tzoqabu.

They hurried down the ramp and found a quiet corner of the courtyard to shelter in while Andrews lifted off again in *Exeter*'s orbiter. The pilot circled the temple complex once, then moved off a short distance, disappearing behind the rooftops. "Best to wait here a moment, Nawabzada," Darvesh told Sikander. "Your mother will have my head if I allow you to be shot today."

"It seems to me that I'd be pretty upset with you, too," Sikander told Darvesh, and smiled. "I promise that after today we'll steer clear of uprisings, revolutions, and other public disorders for a while. I signed on to be a dashing starship captain, not a ground pounder with a rifle."

"Conflicts rarely permit the opportunity to keep one's hands clean, regardless of where one fights," Darvesh replied. "I have found—"

BOOM! A powerful explosion rocked the ancient temple complex, reverberating from the surrounding mountainsides. Sikander actually felt the force of the blast like a slap in the damp air and a shiver in the flagstones under his feet. He ducked against the stone wall in pure reflex before straightening up again, ears ringing. "What in the hell was that?" he demanded.

"It sounded like a conventional explosive," said Darvesh, peering down the nearest corridor. "I do not believe we have any ordnance of that sort, nor the Dremish. It must be Tzoru."

"Did they mine the place?" Sikander wondered aloud. He keyed his comm device. "Major Dalton, what's going on in there?"

"We've got a problem, sir," said Dalton. "You'd better come see this. We're at the eastern end of the building."

Sikander glanced around to make sure of his bearings. "On my way," he told Dalton. Then he set off into the temple interior, Darvesh at his shoulder. Intricate tilework thousands of years old covered the walls and floors; softly glowing lamps in ancient stone sconces provided a dim greenish illumination. Each chamber inside the temple held great bronze cylinders or drums mounted on thick vertical posts, displaying long scrolls of metal foil covered in stamped lettering—ancient depictions of the Sixty-Four Prophecies that formed the basis of Tzoru religious philosophy. Two old Tzoru priests lay dead on the floor, their yellow robes scorched with charred black patches. *Shock-gun bolts,* Sikander realized. He was glad to see they hadn't been killed by mag rifles. *They must have been caught in a cross fire, the poor bastards.*

In the next chamber they found a dead Tzoru warrior in ornate black armor crumpled against a wall pocked with mag-rifle impacts. The warrior's bullet-riddled breastplate featured a winged-sword design executed in bright red. "The Peerless Swords of Scarlet," Sikander observed.

"What was that, Nawabzada?" Darvesh asked. He did not look at Sikander, instead covering the room's other entrances with his weapon and watching out for any unexpected threat.

"The Peerless Swords. They're one of the legions or regiments traditionally charged with protecting Bagal-Dindir—we try to keep track of prominent military formations around the capital. If I recall correctly, the Peerless Swords are an order or brotherhood dominated by the Hish clan." Sikander wasn't surprised to see them here; the Peerless Swords were likely to be entrusted with any task Hish Mubirrum deemed important. "They'll also be some of the best Tzoru soldiers you can find."

Darvesh acknowledged the warning with a silent nod, and led the way into the next room. Here they found two more dead Peerless Swords, and two of Major Dalton's marines—one of them a medic—kneeling by a third marine unconscious on the floor. A smoking black char mark in the fallen marine's torso armor spoke to the violence of the firefight. Since there was little they could do that the medic wasn't already doing, they moved on to the large gallery that marked the end of the eastern arm of the Kadingir Temple. Major Dalton, her master sergeant, and a comm specialist all waited in this last chamber. Sikander also noted another dead Peerless Sword at the feet of the three marines, and several more yellow-robed priests burned down by shock-gun bolts. *Once might be an accident, but three in the same room? What's going on here?*

"Mr. North," Dalton said. She noticed the direction of Sikander's gaze and nodded at the dead Tzoru civilians. "That's interesting in a gruesome sort of way, but it's not actually what I called you over to see."

"It isn't?" Sikander asked. "All right, Major, what have you got?"

"This," Dalton said. She pointed at the dead Tzoru with the muzzle of her rifle. The Peerless Sword had evidently been engaged in setting some kind of charge at the base of one of the room's columns when he'd been killed. A green tube encircled the base of the pillar just below the great bronze drum inscribed with ancient Tzoqabu markings; the warrior still clutched a small black device with suspicious-looking wires in his bloody hand. "We found this fellow connecting the wires in that device to the tube at the base of the pillar. The civilians were dead already when we entered the room."

"That looks like some kind of demolition charge," Sikander said. None of the wires had been plugged in yet; if the black device was a detonator, then it wasn't yet connected to the main charge.

"Tzoru military explosive. My people have found more Tzoru soldiers carrying the explosive tubes. We haven't found any set charges, but this place is big and there's a lot of ground to cover. I can't promise that there aren't some that are already in place."

"I don't understand. The Militarists are rigging the temple for destruction? Why in the world would they do that?" That certainly explained the explosion Sikander had heard a few minutes ago—a charge carried by one of the Tzoru soldiers must have been detonated when struck by a mag-rifle round.

Major Dalton shrugged. "Beats me, but I'd guess that the Hish soldiers wanted to make sure none of the temple priests interfered with the operation. My marines are report-ing shock-burned civilians all over the place."

"An act of deliberate cruelty," Darvesh said softly. "What kind of soldier kills his own people and destroys the places he holds sacred?"

"A very obedient or desperate one," Sikander replied. Tzoru had such a powerful reverence for their history and culture that it seemed impossible that any of them, even Hish Mubirrum, could contemplate such wanton destruction. *Some sort of plot to cover up Tzem Ebneghirz's presence here, or conceal the fact that they spirited him away? Or do the Hish think they need to destroy Kadingir for some other reason altogether?* He couldn't imagine what that might be, but Tzoru sometimes did things that humans wouldn't do, and vice versa. They were aliens, after all. He looked back to Dalton. "What's the status of your sweep?"

The major glanced at a tactical map display built into the back of her left gauntlet, studying the layout of the complex. "We've cleared the main temple. There's some contact just outside the western entrance—it looks like the Tzoru soldiers are holed up in this building here, and this one here. They're in between us and the Dremish."

"The dormitory and the library," said Sikander, leaning close to look at Dalton's display. "I remember those from my visit last year. I'd say keep moving, and meet the Dremish in the middle."

"Arrow Two, Arrow One." Helena Aldrich's voice sounded in Sikander's ear. "We have deployed on the western end of the complex and are sweeping the structures there. Make sure your marines exercise good fire discipline, over."

"Acknowledged, Arrow One," Sikander told Aldrich. "Same for your soldiers—we're exiting the main temple building and we're moving your way. Also, be advised that the Militarists are rigging demolition charges. They're planning to level this place, over."

"Demolitions?" Aldrich fell silent for a moment, perhaps just as surprised as he'd been. "Understood. I am warning my people. Arrow One, out."

"One more thing, Mr. North," said Major Dalton. Another burst of fire echoed outside, a little more distant now—the fighting seemed to be moving away from them. "I'd like to evac Howe, if it's okay by you. He's shot up pretty bad and I don't want my medics treating him here."

"Go ahead," Sikander told her. "And tell your people to keep their eyes open for any more charges or remotes. If General Hish thinks it's important to destroy this place, I figure we should try to stop him."

"Point taken, but let's be clear: We bug out the second we find one of these charges armed. No Tzoru shrine is worth my marines' lives." Dalton turned and hurried off through the chamber's great doorway, heading toward the sound of the firefight and barking orders over her troop command circuit.

Sikander followed more cautiously, keeping his weapon trained in front of him. When it came down to it, two squads of marines were not all that many troops to sweep a building the size of Kadingir's main temple, and they didn't know how many Peerless Swords might be present. He and Darvesh moved through several small chambers, finding more signs of recent fighting—ancient mosaics charred by shock bolts or pitted with mag rounds—but no more bodies. Then a fresh barrage of shots echoed outside, followed by angry human shouts and guttural Tzoqabu replies.

"Major Dalton does not waste time," Darvesh said quietly.

"Marines," said Sikander, and shrugged. He'd known quite a few during his service, and one thing he'd learned was that they were not procrastinators. He followed after Dalton's command group, hurrying toward the temple's main entrance. Great bronze cylinders, unthinkably ancient by human standards, gleamed in the shadows to either side of the main passageway, each inscribed with a priceless religious text. He simply couldn't believe that any Tzoru would choose to destroy Kadingir . . . in fact, it flew in the face of everything he thought he understood about the conservative *sebetu*.

He glanced back at his companion. "Darvesh, if you were the Hish, why would you plan to destroy a site like this?"

"To keep it from falling into enemy hands?" Darvesh answered. "To conceal something else that I did not want discovered? Or perhaps to send a message of some kind, although I could not say what that might be."

"That's about what I came up with, too," Sikander replied. He could easily imagine that General Hish had some idea of using Tzem Ebneghirz to coordinate a wider campaign of *warumzi agu* resistance against the foreign powers that had defeated his fleets. But even so, how did destroying Kadingir further that plan?

He started to say more, but then a flicker of movement caught his eye. A Tzoru dressed in a yellow robe crept out of a shadowed alcove ten meters ahead of the two Kashmiris, looking down the hall in the direction of the gunfire and shouts from the main entrance. *A civilian waiting for the fighting to move outside,* Sikander realized. The fellow hadn't realized that somebody might be trailing after Dalton and her command team; he didn't even look in Sikander and Darvesh's direction.

"Stop right there and turn around slowly!" Sikander called, covering the Tzoru with his weapon just in case. "We don't want to hurt you."

The Tzoru—a stoop-shouldered, slightly built male in his middle years—froze in midstep. He twisted his head around to look back down the hallway behind him, and slowly raised one hand; the other he cradled to his torso. "I am unarmed," the Tzoru said in Tzoqabu; Sikander's translation device fed the interpretation into his earpiece. "I only wish to get to safety."

"Show your other hand!" Sikander ordered. He and Darvesh advanced on the fellow, weapons trained. His finger tensed on the trigger as he waited for some sort of weapon or explosive to appear. The old Tzoru turned around . . . and Sikander spotted the ragged, black-edged char mark of a shock-bolt injury high on the priest's shoulder. He exhaled slowly, lowering his weapon, then halted in surprise.

The Tzoru in front of his mag carbine was none other than Tzem Ebneghirz.

The philosopher lacked his customary dermal decoration and the green robes associated with the *warumzi agu* movement, but Sikander had spent a lot of time studying the dossier prepared by his intelligence team. Tzoru could be difficult to tell apart, but the age and build were right . . .

and the fellow's voice was a dead match for the recordings in the diplomatic intelligence summaries he'd studied a few weeks ago.

"Check him for weapons and bind him," Sikander told Darvesh. "It's Tzem Ebneghirz."

A flicker of resignation crossed the Tzoru's face as he heard his name; Sikander guessed that Ebneghirz had hoped to be taken for one of the temple attendants. Darvesh slung his weapon and moved up to pat down the philosopher while Sikander kept him covered. "I told you that I am not armed!" he protested, this time in excellent Standard Anglic.

"A routine precaution," Sikander told him. "We've had a lot of *warumzi agu* shooting at us today."

Darvesh finished his search, and drew a set of restraints from his battle uniform's utility pocket. He cuffed Tzem's hands together. "Be careful, Tzoru are very flexible," Sikander warned him. Darvesh nodded, and examined the bindings again.

Ebneghirz bared his sharp teeth in pain. "Is this necessary? I am wounded."

"So I see, sir," Sikander said. "Who shot you?"

"One of the Hish soldiers." Ebneghirz tested his restraints and grimaced. "They began to execute the priests when they detected your aircraft approaching."

"In God's name, why? What could the Hish possibly want with their deaths?"

"Ask the Peerless Swords," Ebneghirz snapped. "I have been wondering the same thing, and the soldiers did not choose to explain themselves when they opened fire on my companions. I only survived because your attack interrupted them at their work."

"The burn is not too deep. I will treat it when we reach a safe place to do so," said Darvesh, inspecting the philosopher's injury. "You are fortunate that we arrived when we did."

"That remains to be seen." Ebneghirz straightened up and looked Sikander in the eye. "Now that I am your prisoner, human, might I ask into whose hands I have fallen? Which of your barbaric empires shall decide my fate?"

"I am Lieutenant Commander North, serving in the Aquilan Commonwealth Navy."

"And what does Aquila intend to do with me?"

"We won't shoot you, but beyond that it's not really up to me. You've stirred up a great deal of trouble, Tzem Ebneghirz. I don't know who you will answer to or what the charges might be, but I'm sure that someone in authority is going to want to talk to you."

"I do not recognize the authority of any human power over a Tzoru on a Tzoru world."

"I'll let the diplomats and the lawyers sort that out later." Sikander keyed his comm device again. "Arrow One, this is Arrow Two. We have secured Tzem Ebneghirz. He's alive with minor injuries, over."

"Acknowledged," said Helena Aldrich. A sudden outbreak of chirping mag-weapon reports and crackling Tzoru shock bolts echoed through the stone corridors. "We're dealing with some stubborn resistance near the ceremonial gate. Request that your marines set up a firing position on the high terrace to the southeast, over."

A concussion grenade detonated outside, bringing a fine rain of dust down from the ancient rafters overhead. Ebneghirz winced at the new fusillade of shots. "Your soldiers are destroying a temple that was ancient before your kind mastered the art of making clay pots," the philosopher said. "This is no place for a battle!"

"I regret the necessity—truly, I do," Sikander told him. "But you should know that the Peerless Swords of Scarlet were in the process of setting demolition charges when we arrived. Your own Militarists planned to blow Kadingir completely off this mountaintop."

Ebneghirz hissed in shock. "That cannot be true! I do not believe you!"

"Believe what you like," Sikander replied. He activated the command channel. "Major Dalton, did you copy all that?"

"Roger that," said Constanza Dalton. "I'm positioning a fire team on that terrace for Ms. Aldrich. The western entrance to the temple is clear."

"Got it. We're just behind you." Sikander nodded to Darvesh, who took a firm grip on the Tzoru's arm. He wanted to question Ebneghirz at greater length and find out what the Hish soldiers were up to; the philosopher seemed angry about the attempt on his own life, but he'd clearly been appalled at the idea of wrecking Kadingir, let alone murdering its priests and scholars. *But first, let's get out of the building that may or may not be wired with additional charges before we interrogate anybody,* he decided.

They came to the temple's main entrance, and Sikander was surprised to see how dark it had become in the short time he'd been inside. A thin band of gold lingered over the mountains to the west, turning the ancient stone buildings of Kadingir into deep black silhouettes. The Dremish Falke and the Aquilan Cormorant orbited the site a few hundred meters off, visible only as ominous shadows overhead. Mag rifles hummed and chirped intermittently from the temple's outbuildings as the human soldiers slowly worked their way through the buildings. The Tzoru defensive fire seemed to have mostly died away.

The two Kashmiris led their prisoner over to a stone bench a safe distance from the temple, and sat Ebneghirz down while Darvesh applied a salve and healing spray to his injured shoulder. The Tzoru endured the treatment without complaint. "A thought occurs to me, Nawabzada," Darvesh said as he worked. "When you asked me earlier why someone would want to destroy a site like this, I told you that it might be to keep something hidden. It seems to me that concealing the circumstances of a murder—or an assassination—might be something to hide in such a way."

Sikander stared at Darvesh, and glanced back at the

Kadingir Temple. "It's not about Kadingir, is it?" he said slowly. "The Hish planned to make a martyr of Ebneghirz. And if the temple was destroyed by demolition charges, it might even look like humans bombed the place." *A desperate play for Hish Mubirrum,* he realized. *Killing Ebneghirz would amount to surrendering his hold on the* warumzi agu *movement. No wonder he hesitated to arrange this until it was clear he could not prevent the combined powers from taking Bagal-Dindir.*

"Or, at the very least, it would not be clear what happened or who was responsible. How would the *warumzi agu* respond if they believed that humans had killed the founder of their movement?" Darvesh asked.

"With outrage, I suspect." Sikander had to imagine that a dead philosopher buried in the rubble of a sacred temple would mark the end of any hope that the xenophobic *warumzi agu* might willingly lay down their arms. Months, maybe years of unrest or outright guerrilla warfare could follow here in Tamabuqq, perhaps throughout the Dominion. He studied the Tzoru philosopher. "Is that what the Hish planned for your followers?"

"So it would seem," Ebneghirz said with a wry shrug. "On reflection, I see a certain merit in Lord Mubirrum's design. It might have been better if I had not flinched from the soldiers' shock rifles." He fell silent, keeping any further thoughts to himself.

"Arrow Two, this is Arrow One," Aldrich commed. "We have cleared the library. Where are you, over?"

"On my way," Sikander replied. He motioned to Darvesh. They stood up Ebneghirz and escorted him away from the plaza outside the temple entrance. A flagstone path with wide, shallow steps led down a few meters to the next-lowest terrace of the complex; here they found Major Dalton's command group, as well as a small party of Dremish soldiers—Helena Aldrich and her own command team. The two groups sheltered behind a thick stone wall, which offered good cover against any fire coming from the complex's dormitory building.

"Ah, there you, Mr. North," Aldrich said. She smiled humorlessly. "And I see you've made a catch. I seem to recall you are an enthusiastic angler."

"Ms. Aldrich, Major Dalton," Sikander said in reply, nodding instead of saluting. "How are we doing?"

"All clear except for the last building," said Dalton. "Some number of Militarist soldiers are barricaded in the upper floors. We were just debating whether we should drop some troops onto the roof to pry them out from above, blast them out with fire from the landers, or just let them sit tight for now."

"They may have more demolition charges," Aldrich pointed out. "Best to eliminate them immediately. I will have our lander open fire."

"There may be civilians in that building," Dalton said. "We have no idea who we'd be hitting."

"That did not stop the Hish from shelling our people in the Thousand Worlds ward," Aldrich replied. "Besides, the Militarist soldiers already addressed that consideration when they rounded up the temple attendants and began executing them. I see no reason to exercise restraint now."

"Only a building of historic significance," Ebneghirz said in a bitter tone.

"Which does not concern me," said Aldrich. She keyed her comm unit. "*Oberleutnant, feuer.*"

A blinding rain of tracers erupted from the black shadow of the Dremish assault lander, blasting the upper floor of the large dormitory on the next-lower terrace. Sikander realized that the Dremish pilots must have had their fingers on the trigger, just waiting for the order to fire. He peeked over the wall, watching as mag-cannon rounds lanced clear through the target in a lethal sleet. The Dremish gunner didn't care what might have been behind the target; he fired at full power, carving through the old building with abandon. In fact, quite a few of the rounds carried hundreds of meters past the dormitory to lash the ancient gateway arch known as the Eningurra. Stone and mortar exploded like dry cereal under the furious pounding, rocking the whole structure.

"Holy crap!" Constanza Dalton swore. "How about a little warning next time? I've got people just a floor below!"

"Stop, stop!" Sikander shouted. "You're hitting the monument downrange!" He took an angry step toward Aldrich and grabbed her by the shoulder, turning her to look down to the right where the rounds pounded into the Eningurra.

The nearest Dremish trooper snarled something in Nebeldeutsch and grabbed at Sikander to pull him away from the Kapitan-Leutnant, at which point Darvesh appeared like magic to lock his arm through the soldier's. The lanky Kashmiri pried the fellow off Sikander with one efficient twisting motion. A sudden scuffle ensued, as other troopers surged up to grab Darvesh, and Aldrich angrily yanked herself away from Sikander's grip—but she looked in the direction Sikander pointed, and she winced. "*Feuer einstellen,*" she ordered.

The murderous rain of mag-cannon fire ceased at once. Sikander blinked away the white streaks in his vision, while the shrill buzzing reports echoed back and forth from the mountainsides. The scuffling between Aquilans and Dremish came to a halt as everyone looked at the target of the attack.

Smoke and dust billowed from the cannon-raked building. And, two hundred meters downrange, the Eningurra gave a single sharp cracking sound, then collapsed into a heap of rubble.

"Well, *shit,*" Major Dalton snarled. "Nice shooting. Not a chance at all we'll be reading about that in tomorrow's newsfeed."

Sikander gave Aldrich a stern look, but said nothing more. He turned to apologize to Ebneghirz . . . but the Tzoru philosopher was gone.

"Damn it!" he snarled. "Where's Ebneghirz?" But before

anyone answered, he caught sight of the philosopher in his yellow robes, hurrying back up the steps of Kadingir's main temple. Without a moment's hesitation, Sikander darted away in pursuit. He took the old stone steps of the path three at a time, chasing after the Tzoru.

"Nawabzada! The charges!" Darvesh shouted in alarm. The Kashmiri sergeant hurried after him.

Sikander ignored him and ran after Ebneghirz into the gloom of the temple. He was not a bad sprinter, but even injured with his hands bound together, the old Tzoru bounded along with surprising speed. *Damn, I forgot how quick Tzoru can be when they put their minds to it!* he thought. *The mob at Durzinzer should have fixed that lesson in my head.*

"Ebneghirz, stop!" he shouted. "We're not going to hurt you!"

The philosopher did not answer. Sikander paused to listen, and thought he caught a soft rustle of footfalls off to his left. He turned and sprinted in that direction, and in the gloom almost ran right into one of the Sixty-Four Prophecies on its great bronze drum. A strange tone near his foot caught his attention. He glanced down—and saw that a green tube wrapped the bottom of the bronze drum's pillar. A single blue light blinked on the small black device wired to the charge.

"Mr. North!" Constanza Dalton's voice hissed over his comm link. "My team in the dormitory just found a detonator on the body of the Hish commander! It's counting down—get out of there!"

"You've got to be kidding me," Sikander muttered. He heard Darvesh storm into the temple's main entrance hall, calling for him—and he also heard footfalls coming from the passage to his right. He ran to the right, plunging deeper into the temple. "Ebneghirz, the demolition charges have been set!" he shouted. "We've got to get out of here!"

"Then I suggest you save yourself at once, Mr. North," the philosopher called back from the gloom. His voice echoed from the cold tiled walls, but Sikander couldn't tell where it came from. "I have been thinking about Hish Mubirrum's plans for me, and it seems to me that he is right. If I must die to become the symbol my people need to fight on, then I accept my fate."

"Nawabzada, where are you?" Darvesh shouted from somewhere in the chambers behind Sikander. "We must go!"

Sikander ran down the passage to the next chamber, but Ebneghirz was not there. *It's the stone and tile,* he realized. Sound just bounced around in the old temple. Ebneghirz could stay a room or two ahead of him for at least a few minutes . . . which he might not have. "Ebneghirz, listen to me! This is not the answer—you can't allow General Hish to use you like this. If your *warumzi* fight on against all the great powers at once, it will be a disaster for the entire Dominion! Thousands—*millions*—could die!"

"There is no dishonor in dying for the right cause." Now the old Tzoru's voice echoed from a different passage to Sikander's left.

"What about dying for a lie? For one Tzoru's ambitions?"

"That prospect dismays me, of course. But if my people are to be swept away by history and forgotten, let us die fighting as Tzoru and not as slaves to barbarians. I choose to play my part in Hish Mubirrum's clumsy scheme since that is what I must do for my people. No true subject of the Heavenly Monarch could do otherwise." Ebneghirz paused. "I see that the indicator on the demolition charge is blinking faster, Mr. North. I bear you no personal malice, so I repeat my earlier advice: Save yourself."

Sikander stood at a branch of two stone passageways, not sure where Ebneghirz's voice came from. He grimaced in frustration and turned in place, looking one way and then another as Darvesh shouted for him from elsewhere in the temple, and both Dalton and Aldrich stepped all over each other's transmissions in an attempt to urge him to leave. There was nothing but darkness down the left-hand passage, but to the right he saw a glimmer of dusk—the gallery at the eastern end of the temple where Major Dalton had found the first charge.

"The detonator," he murmured to himself. *Ebneghirz is watching a detonator blink!*

"Darvesh, the eastern gallery!" Sikander shouted over his shoulder. Then he darted down the right-hand passage to the large room that made up the eastern end of the temple building. Carved wooden shutters lined the walls on three sides, with glints of the evening light shining through. The charge was still fixed to the bottom of the pillar in the middle of the room . . . and the indicator light on the detonator in the dead soldier's hand strobed rapidly, accelerating even as Sikander watched it.

Tzem Ebneghirz stood calmly a few meters away, his hands still bound before him. He shook his head sadly. "I will not come with you," he said to Sikander. "You may shoot me if you like, but I doubt that will help you very much."

"No, it won't," Sikander agreed. He dropped his mag carbine and covered the distance to Ebneghirz in one single bound, catching hold of the philosopher before he could flee again. Ebneghirz tried to twist away from Sikander, but Sikander punched him in the midsection, hard enough to drive the air from his lungs in an audible gasp. Then as Ebneghirz sagged, Sikander dragged him across the room in three more steps and threw both himself and the Tzoru philosopher through the wooden shutters at the end of the room.

It was a three-meter fall onto the steep mountainside outside. Sikander landed heavily on one leg, jarring himself so hard that he chipped a tooth when his jaw slammed shut. But he reached out and seized Ebneghirz with one hand before the philosopher rolled down the slope, then caught himself by seizing the thick stem of a shrub as he slid by. "I've got Ebneghirz!" he gasped. "Darvesh, get out of there!"

For a long moment, there was no reply. Then Darvesh dove out the same window Sikander had used, hitting the ground awkwardly and sliding into the tangle of Sikander and Ebneghirz. Sikander lost his grip on the shrub—but Darvesh caught it as he slid past, and reached out to catch Sikander's flailing hand.

Approximately four seconds later, the charges in the temple went off with a deafening roar. Blocks of stone and masonry weighing hundreds of kilos soared over Sikander's precarious perch and tumbled down the mountainside . . . and the ancient temple, nearly twenty thousand years old, collapsed into a heap of dust and rubble that washed over them like an avalanche of stone.

24

Bagal-Dindir, Tamabuqq Prime

It felt strange to be surrounded by humans again after two weeks among the Sapwu. It felt even stranger to ride comfortably in the bright sunlight of a balmy winter morning instead of scurrying from cover to cover in the Thousand Worlds ward and waiting for the next shell to fall. Yet the thing that felt strangest of all to Lara Dunstan was the fact that the ornate skybarge on which she rode actually *flew* along the Avenue of Memory as it sedately approached the Anshar's Palace. Only the most important Tzoru customarily approached the palace in the air, but today defied all precedent for Bagal-Dindir's diplomatic corps. After the collapse of Militarist resistance in Bagal-Dindir and the suppression of the *warumzi agu* mobs thronging the capital, the Anshar's servants had hurried to invite each foreign legation in the Thousand Worlds ward to the palace. Lara shared her unusual travel arrangements with no less than eleven ambassadors and at least forty personal assistants, translators, and bodyguards, while hundreds of additional troops accompanied them in the heavily armed human and Nyeiran shuttles flying escort for the procession.

Lara shook her head in bemusement. Ambassadors normally visited with entourages composed of a few picked assistants and translators, not assault shuttles packed with marines in battle armor. And *normally* the battle-scarred Aquilan cruiser *Exeter,* moored in the shallow waters of Lake Ulpun just three kilometers from the Anshar's Palace, wasn't part of the city's skyline. That had taken more than a little negotiation among the representatives of the great powers whose warships had won the Second Battle of Tamabuqq. The Dremish, the Montréalais, and even the Nyei-rans had all argued vociferously for the right to ground their own warships in the Tzoru capital, too. But Lake Ulpun simply couldn't accommodate four or five major warships, so they'd grudgingly agreed to allow Commodore Aberna-thy's flagship to represent them all, at least for today. Lara understood there was some kind of rotation scheme being worked out so that the other victors could each have a turn menacing Bagal-Dindir with one of their own warships.

It always comes down to the biggest guns, doesn't it? Lara gazed at the distant cruiser, and sighed. *The Tzoru are beaten and everyone knows it, so what does it matter who's got their finger on the trigger?*

Ambassador Hart caught her small frown of disapproval. He moved away from the other diplomats gathered at the prow of the skybarge to join her at the starboard-side rail. "Something on your mind, Lara?" he asked.

"Mr. Hart," she replied, acknowledging his question. "It's nothing, really, but . . . I can't help wondering if this is the right way to go about this." She nodded at the armed shuttles escorting the slow procession of borrowed skybarges past the monuments of ancient Anshars. "Tzoru have very long memories. They won't forget the day humans rode in tri-umph over the grounds of the Heavenly Monarch's palace. We should have helped the Dominion's high councillors to save face."

"Perhaps," Hart allowed. "I agree it's a somewhat vulgar display. But, as you say, Tzoru have long memories, and it's important that they remember today for a very long time. If we expect them to see us as victors, then we must act as their traditions tell them victors should act. To do anything less is to invite new misunderstandings."

"I think you needn't worry on that account, Ambassador. The noble *sebetu* will understand this very well, that I can promise you."

Hart shrugged. "Believe me, Lara, they should count themselves lucky that we're ready to listen to them. Popov wanted to flatten every square meter of the palace and its monuments with systematic orbital strikes before we took any calls. For a while the debate focused on whether we should give them one hour's warning or two until I prevailed upon my peers to save that sort of demonstration until we were sure nothing less would do."

Lara didn't bother to hide the distaste in her expression. "Parts of this complex are five times older than the Pyramids of Giza. It would be a crime against humanity—well, a crime against history—to do something like that out of simple spite."

"Simple spite? No, I'd say it's carefully calculated spite, my dear. But even so it's a tactic with some usefulness in situations like this." Hart tugged at the lapels of his coat, adjusting its fit on his shoulders. Like everyone else who'd endured the siege of the Thousand Worlds, he'd lost a good deal of weight in the last couple of months. "Look, we're here. This spectacle is almost over."

The skybarge landed in the center of the magnificent plaza that stood before the palace's main entrance. The ziggurat-like building towered overhead, its sides sheathed in gold leaf that gleamed brightly in the morning sunshine. Palace attendants and minor officials stood in orderly ranks by the open doors, resplendent in their ceremonial costumes, while scores of Tzoru guards in decorative armor waited behind them, their flame lances festooned with colorful pennants. None moved a muscle as two of the assault shuttles escorting the ambassadors' vessel alighted on the plaza beside the skybarge and deployed human and Nyeiran marines in full battle armor. Lara couldn't help but notice that the marines kept their weapons at the ready, if not quite pointed at the palace guards. The heavily armed shuttles and worn battle armor struck her as out of place amid the Tzoru pageantry—a deliberate discourtesy in the place where symbols and gestures mattered more than anywhere else in the Anshar's realm.

She sighed, and followed Ambassador Hart when he debarked. *I tried to tell them,* she consoled herself. Not even the most xenophobic Militarist would entertain the idea of springing some kind of ambush against visitors invited to present themselves to the High Court of the Tzoru Dominion. The marines, the armed shuttles, the guns of *Exeter* trained on the city from a few kilometers away, none of them were necessary. Centuries upon centuries of palace etiquette provided all the protection any human could wish for today.

Norman Hart joined Erika Popov, Jerome Hamel, and Speaker Chau-Drak-Zeid at the foot of the skybarge's gilded ramp. The four senior ambassadors exchanged a few quiet words that Lara missed before the palace chamberlain, old Ebabbar Simtum himself, marched up to genuflect before them. "Welcome, honored friends," the chamberlain proclaimed in a loud voice. "Please, follow me. The High Council of the Dominion is assembled to greet you."

"Of course," Jerome Hamel replied for the group. "We're anxious to speak with them. Please lead the way."

Ebabbar bowed again before escorting the four ambassadors into the palace proper. Lara fell in with the aides, seconds, and military commanders who made up the ambassadors' entourages. As far as she knew, no humans had ever been accorded the honor of a welcome at the palace entrance, or even permitted to set foot in the processional halls set aside for the high ministers of the Anshar's court. It probably wouldn't be the first precedent to fall today, or so she guessed.

She found herself walking side by side with Major Constanza Dalton of the embassy marine detachment. Like her troops, the major wore battle armor, but she didn't bother with a mag rifle, settling instead for a heavy pistol on each hip. "I never thought I'd walk into this place to dictate terms," she murmured to Lara. "Funny, isn't it? Three years in Bagal-Dindir, and this is my first time in the palace."

"Mine, too," Lara admitted. "I wish it were under different circumstances, though. I feel like we don't belong here." The Anshar's officials were very selective about whom they invited into the palace; even the most important ambassadors might go years between visits. The sight of all of them visiting at the same time with full entourages and military escorts was, to the best of her knowledge, unprecedented. *I seem to be using that word a lot today.* She tried to take in everything she saw as they proceeded along the grand hallway leading from the gate to the council chamber without being too obvious about gawking, but she couldn't help herself.

Dalton seemed unimpressed by the magnificence of the hall. "If the Anshar didn't want us to visit, she shouldn't have allowed her subjects to send us such compelling invitations," she said. "I'm here because her people made it clear we had some things to straighten out. I lost too many good marines over the last two months to let this go now."

Trust a marine to reduce a complicated situation to its simplest elements, Lara told herself. She held nothing but the deepest admiration for all the uniformed personnel who'd defended the Thousand Worlds ward, but she couldn't let herself see things in such stark terms. Diplomacy was a game played in shades of gray, after all. She returned her attention to the magnificent hall around them, studying bas-reliefs thousands of years old that covered the walls to either side. She recognized images of dozens of famous figures and holy sites in the artwork . . . including, at one point, a fine image of the Eningurra at Kadingir.

Lara sighed again. She'd seen vid captured by soldiers during the fight at the ancient temple thirty-six hours before, including the Dremish troopers' accidental destruction of the sacred gateway—fifty thousand years erased in one clumsy moment. Then again, she'd also seen imagery of the destruction of the main temple by Hish demolition charges; humans weren't entirely to blame for what had happened at Kadingir. She hoped that those two tales wouldn't prove to be a metaphor for Tzoru civilization in general, but as matters stood that was a bet she didn't think she would take.

The marine noticed the direction of Lara's gaze. "And that's another thing—if the Tzoru didn't want their holy places shot up by mag-cannon fire they shouldn't have made them into high-value targets. Speaking of which: Any idea what they're going to do with Ebneghirz? He caused my marines no small amount of trouble."

"I have no idea," said Lara. "The Dremish want to try him and then execute him. The Nyeirans and the Montréalais want to send him into exile. I think we'd settle for a message of conciliation and disarmament to his *warumzi agu*, followed by a quiet retirement from public affairs." Tzem Ebneghirz was now in a brig aboard one of the warships in orbit, guarded by soldiers from six or seven different nations, each of which had its own idea about how to deal with the inspiration behind the *warumzi agu* movement. She thought Sikander might be taking part in the interviews, since he'd arranged the raid to get Ebneghirz out of the Militarists' hands, but she hadn't seen or spoken with him since the battle. She had a hundred things to look after now that the diplomats of the Thousand Worlds ward had the opportunity to ply their trade again, and she imagined that he had to be busy too.

Dalton snorted. "Good. The sooner we uproot the *warumzi*, the better I'll—*whoa*."

Lara drew in her breath as the procession emerged into one of the most lavishly appointed chambers she'd seen in her life. Luminous globes representing each of the one hundred and twenty-two Tzoru worlds drifted beneath the soaring ceiling, while reliefs covered in copper leaf ringed the walls, depicting the Sixty-Four Prophecies. The sheer age and vastness of the Tzoru Dominion seemed tangible in this room, a weighty presence that momentarily cowed even the confident marine walking at Lara's side. Even though Lara had never been in this room, she recognized it from dozens of different depictions she'd encountered in her studies. "The Hall of Auspicious Judgment," she murmured to Dalton.

The marine merely nodded, unable to bring herself to speak. Lara settled for steering her quietly to one side as more guards and marines and diplomatic functionaries filed in behind them. Hundreds of Tzoru already filled the room in crowds packed closely to the room's walls; around the table in the center of the room stood the full membership of the Dominion High Council. Lara recognized representatives from the Baltzu, Zabar, Maruz, Karsu, Gisumi, Zag, and Ninazzu *sebetu* on sight, and could guess at the *sebet* of a dozen more council members by the costumes and emblems they wore. The Anshar herself did not appear to be present, but she quickly spotted the screened balcony where the Heavenly Monarch was said to sit when she wished to observe the council's deliberations.

Chamberlain Ebabbar murmured something to the four ambassadors representing the combined powers. They nodded and stepped forward as he announced them to the assembled council. "Honored councillors, I present the appointed and accredited representatives of the Empire of Dremark, the Nyeiran Star Empire, the Commonwealth of Aquila, and the Republic of Montréal: Madam Ambassador Erika Popov, Honored Speaker Chau-Drak-Zeid, Ambassador-Plenipotentiary Norman Hart, and Minister Jerome Hamel." The Tzoru ministers bowed collectively as the chamberlain concluded his introduction.

"We thank the High Council for receiving us," said Popov brusquely. She made a show of searching the assembled councillors and ministers with a slow sweep of her eyes. "However, I do not see General Hish Mubirrum among you. Is this body empowered to treat with us in the absence of your Sharur-Tal?"

Sapwu Zrinan stepped forward from the rest of the council members and approached Hart, Popov, Hamel, and Chau, spreading his arms in a courtly Tzoru bow. "It has been brought to the Heavenly Monarch's attention that recent misunderstandings have led to many regrettable developments," he said. "In light of the Anshar's concerns General Hish Mubirrum has chosen to resign from the Heavenly Monarch's service and seek religious seclusion. As the Sharur-Tal's last command, the High Council has been restored to its former function as the Dominion's governing body. I have agreed to accept the responsibility of serving as first councillor until such a time as a more qualified candidate can be found."

"That seems like a very convenient way for General Hish to avoid the necessity of explaining his actions," Jerome Hamel observed with a frown. "We may return to that question later, First Councillor, but for now you may proceed."

"Of course." Zrinan bowed again, his face unreadable. "On behalf of the Heavenly Monarch, I would like to extend the Dominion's sincere apologies for the recent disorders and assure your governments that their interests are our interests. We intend to move at once to bring an end to the demonstrations and incitements that have caused so much trouble. Furthermore, we are directing our military forces throughout the Dominion to cease all operations to head off any more unfortunate escalation. We wish only to put these troubles behind us and resume peaceful relations."

Major Dalton shifted uncomfortably at Lara's side. "Are they kidding us?" she growled softly. "He makes it sound like this all was some sort of stupid accident!"

"It's the way their culture works," Lara whispered back to Dalton. "If you assign responsibility to someone, you risk breaking consensus. It's easier to let failure be an orphan." By Tzoru standards, the abrupt resignation of Hish Mubirrum was a shocking repudiation of the Militarists' policies and about as close to officially assigning blame as the Anshar's court would ever come.

The soft murmurs in the Hall of Auspicious Judgment died away as the assembled Tzoru and foreign officials waited to see how the representatives of the great powers responded. Lara had half an idea about that already, since she'd spent most of the last day carrying unofficial messages back and forth between Sapwu Zrinan and Norman Hart, and she'd also participated in some of the embassy staff's what-if planning sessions leading up to this moment. Popov's rather rude question about Zrinan's authority had surprised her, but little else so far.

"The Commonwealth of Aquila desires peaceful relations, too," Ambassador Hart said to Zrinan. "However, our citizens throughout the Dominion have suffered serious losses as a result of your government's inattention to the actions of its own citizens—namely, the *warumzi agu*—and the hostile actions of Militarist clans that attacked our forces. Some amount of restitution is required."

"The Republic of Montréal has similar concerns and claims," said Jerome Hamel.

"As does the Nyeiran Star Empire," Speaker Chau said. "In addition we require that the individuals responsible for these misunderstandings must answer for the part they played in events. Hish Mubirrum must stand trial for waging a war of aggression against the peace-loving peoples of this region."

"And the Empire of Dremark insists that all Tzoru *sebetu* that fielded military forces against us be disarmed and sternly sanctioned for their actions," said Popov. "In light of the current crisis, we intend to take certain areas of the Dominion under our direct administration until your government demonstrates that it is capable of preserving order and honoring your treaty commitments to Dremark. Apologies are all well and good, First Councillor, but blood has been spilled. As Mr. Hart says, some restitution is required."

"Likewise, the Montréalais Republic must also insist on taking systems of special concern to us under our administration," Jerome Hamel quickly added. "Temporarily, of course—a simple precaution until the rule of law is reestablished throughout the Dominion."

Shocked silence fell over the hall. Tzoru of minor *sebetu* gaped in surprise or quietly fluttered their hands in distress; human diplomats and soldiers exchanged glances that ranged from stern satisfaction to winces of embarrassment. Even though Lara had expected something very much like the Dremish and Montréalais demands, she had to fight down a moment of panic. She'd known that several powers intended to demand Hish Mubirrum's head, but disarming aristocratic Tzoru clans and claiming the right to govern Tzoru worlds represented a sore test for the fragile cease-fire she'd worked so hard to bring about. *It's going to be a feeding frenzy . . . but I think this can still work.*

"Holy crap," Constanza Dalton breathed next to her. "We're going to be shooting at each other again by lunchtime. There's no way the Tzoru can go along with that."

"They will," Lara whispered back. "The council's reached a new consensus to settle this without more fighting. It's hard, but they'll live with it for now."

"How can you be so sure?"

"Because Tzoru can take the long view," Lara said. *And Sapwu Zrinan has a few demands of his own that we're going to accept whether we like it or not.* In fact, the bold demands just presented to the Dominion High Council pretty much made the next step inevitable.

Sapwu Zrinan's shoulders slumped as the ambassadors spoke, but he allowed himself no other sign of displeasure as they listed their demands. "It is the Heavenly Monarch's wish that peace be restored throughout the Dominion," he said in a weary voice. "We are prepared to make reasonable accommodations as needed to bring this situation to a conclusion."

"We are pleased to hear that," said Ambassador Hart. He reached into his suit pocket and withdrew a datacard, which he handed to Sapwu Zrinan. "This document was jointly prepared by all major powers engaged in the recent hostilities, and contains a list of the claims and requirements the Dominion must meet in order to bring all hostilities to an end. You have until sunset tomorrow to review the terms and signal your acceptance. Otherwise, we will have no choice but to see to our own restitution and impose our terms by force."

Sapwu Zrinan accepted the correspondence without expression. "Decisions such as this take some consideration, Mr. Hart. I do not know if we can give you your answer in time."

"That is entirely up to you, First Councillor," said Hart. He gave the old Tzoru a shallow bow, one mirrored by the other three representatives standing at the front of the council. "We will await your reply. Until then, we take our leave."

Hart gave a small nod to the others, and one by one they turned and marched out of the Hall of Auspicious Judgment.

Cold mist blanketed Lake Bel-Irzum. Hish Mubirrum sat on a simple wooden stool in an open-sided pavilion, staring out over the dark waters. The mist hid the opposite shoreline, but steep green mountainsides towered up out of the drifting vapor. He'd been at the lakeshore for most of the morning, listening to the condensation drip steadily from the branches of the great forest around the Irzum-Ishir Monastery and watching the cold moisture bead up on his monastic robes. It seemed to him that there was a lesson hidden in the mist: Things close at hand, like the shore, remained hidden, yet things farther off—the dark peaks looming overhead—were made clearer and more certain by a little distance. *I can see the shape of things that must come to pass,* he told himself. *I simply cannot yet see how they begin.*

He considered that thought at length, ignoring the cold and the damp that perpetually blanketed the ancient monastery on its little island in the mountain lake. Unlike most other ancient sites on this ancient world, Irzum-Ishir was a place of wood, not stone. The deepest and oldest forests on

Tamabuqq Prime surrounded the place; its buildings were made of wood and constantly replenished, rebuilt year after year to the same plan. Even now the scent of the forest and the newly sawn planks filled his nostrils. *How many times will I rebuild this pavilion before I die?* he wondered. He was not young, but he was in good health. He might pass decades yet before his final rest—perhaps long enough to forget what it meant to wield power and govern the affairs of the Dominion.

A soft footfall behind him on the thick carpet of needle-leafs covering the path caught his attention. He straightened and turned his head to see who approached: a young commander dressed in the armor of the Sapwu clan. A whole company of Sapwu warriors guarded Irzum-Ishir to make sure Mubirrum developed no ideas about rethinking his newfound commitment to the monastic life . . . much as he'd once taken similar precautions to make sure Tzem Ebneghirz stayed put in Kadingir until his usefulness came to an end.

"Yes?" Mubirrum asked, rather annoyed at the interruption.

"I have been instructed to bring you a gift and a message," the Sapwu officer said. He set a small wooden box on the bench beside Mubirrum. "Sapwu Zrinan said that you would know its purpose."

Mubirrum picked up the box; it felt heavy. "And the message?"

"Human soldiers are on their way to arrest you. The human powers have demanded the right to hold you answerable under their own laws for war crimes they say you committed against their people. They will be here in less than an hour." The Sapwu did not meet Mubirrum's eyes, instead gazing out over the misty lake for a moment before he turned away. "I take my leave."

Mubirrum stared at the mountain peaks, now slowly disappearing as the mist thickened. The very idea of the Dominion surrendering a prisoner on Tamabuqq Prime to alien justice sickened him, not because of the obvious danger to his own life or the shocking ignorance of Tzoru tradition under which vanquished enemies were allowed to retreat from public life with dignity. No, it was the sheer powerlessness of his people that galled Mubirrum. "Has it really come to this?" he said to the lake.

The dark waters made no reply. With a sigh, Mubirrum opened the small wooden case. Inside lay a shock pistol with a single charge remaining. *Most likely the Sapwu commander's own sidearm,* he decided. *I wonder if he wants it back when I am done with it.* He snorted in bitter amusement and put the case back down on the bench beside him, then returned his attention to the lake and the mists.

He waited until he heard the human shuttle's engines reverberating from the mountainsides before he reached for the pistol.

The Dominion's acceptance of the cease-fire demands ended up taking five days, not two. After Hish Mubirrum's suicide, some of the great-power representatives—Erika Popov of Dremark, specifically—had come close to spoiling the whole deal by calling for additional punitive measures, since someone had clearly helped Mubirrum to deprive the victors of the ability to put him on trial. Ultimately most of the human nations decided they were content with Mubirrum's death regardless of how it had come about, and symbolic trials meant little when compared to trade concessions and basing rights and decades of compensatory payments. It seemed that the scramble for the spoils of empire was back on with redoubled intensity.

A week later, Lara received the call she'd been expecting.

She dressed in her best suit—still a little loose on her—and made her way to the temporary office Ambassador Norman Hart was using while his own underwent repair. "Mr. Hart?" she called, knocking on the door. "You asked to see me, sir?"

"Ah, there you are. Come on in, have a seat." Hart looked up from some document on his dataslate and set down the device, waiting for Lara to take her place before continuing. "I received a very unusual communication from the Anshar's Palace this afternoon—an imperial instrument, no less. To the best of my knowledge it's the first that has ever been addressed to non-Tzoru."

A ball of anxiety churned in Lara's stomach, but she maintained an expression of polite interest. "That's unusual. What does it say?"

"It's a legal notice. The Anshar is exercising her right under a rather obscure clause in our Shimatum agreement with Sebet Baltzu to terminate the Commonwealth's basing rights and exclusive trade arrangement upon the accession of a new Heavenly Monarch." Hart picked up his dataslate and studied its contents with a stern expression before dropping it to the desktop again. "I've been told informally to expect similar documents for Kahnar-Sag, our little corner of the Thousand Worlds ward, and a dozen more Aquilan concessions and agreements throughout the Dominion. From what I understand, every power represented in the Dominion is receiving similar notifications today."

"May I?" Lara asked, nodding at the dataslate.

"Be my guest." Hart pushed the device across the table, and waited while Lara reviewed it. "I find myself wondering where the Tzoru got the idea to exercise an archaic royal prerogative that was buried in boilerplate text common to just about any contract created in the Dominion."

"I told them to."

Norman Hart possessed a trained diplomat's ability to guard his emotions; throughout the long weeks of the Thousand Worlds siege, Lara had never seen him come close to losing his temper until this moment. He half rose from his seat and leaned over his desk, his face reddening. "You *told* them to?"

Lara nodded, steeling herself not to flinch. "I've been studying that Shimatum agreement for months. It's sort of hard to miss that odd bit of phrasing when you spend enough time looking at the text."

"Exactly how does that further the Commonwealth's interests in this sector?" Hart demanded.

"It stopped a *war,* Mr. Hart. These terms freeze the status quo for the lifetime of the Heavenly Monarch. She's seventy-three years old, but that doesn't mean as much to a Tzoru as it does to a human; she'll probably remain on the throne for another eighty or ninety years, maybe more." Lara met the ambassador's eyes evenly. "Tzoru are patient—they can wait a long time to get something they want. In the meantime, we have generations to profit from the deals we've negotiated. But, more important, we now have the motivation and the opportunity to transform our relationship with the Dominion into something fair, something that offers real benefits to both sides. That's the only kind of relationship that can last indefinitely, isn't it?"

Hart sank back into his chair, shaking his head. "Dr. Dunstan, what were you *thinking*?"

"I had to give the Sapwu a way to repair the consensus of the High Council. That meant showing the traditional *sebetu* that didn't like us—the Zabar or Ninazzu, for example— how they could get rid of us with a little patience, and showing the friendlier *sebetu* like the Baltzu or Gisumi that they'd be able to keep doing business with us while working out better terms. There was nothing we could do to reach the Hish, but they broke all kind of precedents of their own, and the other High Council clans came to a consensus that the Hish didn't need to be a part of the consensus." Lara gave a small shrug. "The imperial instrument was Lord Zrinan's idea, to be honest. I had no idea how we could signal the policy change to the *warumzi agu* and other hostile factions since the Tzoru pay no attention to mass media, but it turns out that the Anshar's proclamations are the one thing everybody reads. This should go a long way toward placating Tzem Ebneghirz's followers, too."

Hart turned his chair away from Lara and leaned back,

studying the ceiling for a long moment—considering the implications, or perhaps making sure he had his temper under control before he spoke again. "Okay," he finally said. "I can see that you had to create consensus in order for us to have someone we could talk to. But what's in it for the Commonwealth? You just gave away billions, maybe hundreds of billions, of credits in trade deals and basing rights and Aquilan influence. Some future ambassador's going to have to figure out how to salvage something out of all this."

"In eighty or ninety *years,* Ambassador. And, as I said, the situation that we've established here in the Dominion is unsustainable. We'll be better off fixing it in the long run."

"What about the other powers? I guarantee you the Dremish aren't going to take this lying down, nor will the Nyeirans."

"That part's the hardest," Lara admitted. "But if we signal that we're abiding by the letter of the law and respect the Anshar's proclamation, I think everybody else will pretty much be forced to. Erika Popov might be furious, but she can't tell the Tzoru that Dremark ignores the terms of its existing agreements when we're demonstrating that we honor ours." Of course, the Dremish might settle for imposing their demands with warships in orbit . . . but exactly how many Tzoru systems could the Imperial Navy of Dremark occupy for any extended time? Tearing up a contract and attempting to turn a lease into a conquest might work in the short term, but the other great powers would certainly intervene if the Dremish tried to seize more territory than they already controlled.

Hart nodded slowly, thinking through the same implications that Lara had already considered. "There might be something to that," he allowed. "In fact, I'd better get on the comm unit and point that out to some of my peers before they say or do things they won't be able to back down from. This is quite a little hand grenade you just dropped in my lap, Lara."

"I know." She took a deep breath, and set a datacard down on his desk not unlike the one he'd handed to Sapwu Zrinan a week ago. "My resignation, sir. I'm giving two weeks' notice, but I'll understand if you want me out today."

"Your resignation?" Hart sat up straighter, focusing fully on her. "I'm not sure that I'm inclined to let you off so easily, Dr. Dunstan. You've turned our position here on its ear . . . but I don't know if I have any better answers than the ones you came up with. Give me a day or two to figure out what this all means, and then I'll let you know if I expect you to resign."

"Ambassador, it's not up to you." Lara stood, and smoothed the skirt of her suit. "The Foreign Ministry might want my head or they might not, but when it comes down to it, I fundamentally disagree with the policies that led us to this spot. In his own way, Tzem Ebneghirz was right—the *warumzi agu* had good reason to rise up. I think we've been on the wrong side for a long time here in the Dominion."

Hart remained silent for a long moment. Lara wondered if perhaps she'd managed to truly anger the ambassador and braced herself for an explosion . . . but instead he reclined in his chair again, and merely smiled. "If you really believe that," he said, "then it seems to me that you're not going to bring about many changes in our Tzoru policies by leaving."

"Are you seriously suggesting that you'd want me to stay on after this?"

"I'm old and tired, Lara. I've been due for replacement for years now, and I think it's time to call in those markers." The ambassador shrugged. "This used to be a comfortable little backwater, but now we've had a crisis that will grab headlines all over Coalition space. The Foreign Ministry is full of ambitious young fellows who are going to want to take a crack at the 'Tzoru Problem,' especially since you've introduced a new wrinkle to it. I'm inclined to let one of them have the job. You've got a better grasp of the new facts on the ground than anyone in the ministry, and that means you can do a lot to shape our policy here for decades to come. But first you've got to decide if you've got the stomach for the fight."

Lara stared at Hart, unable to decide if he meant what he said or not. "I don't know if I do," she finally answered.

"If I'm not mistaken, you've got about three weeks before regular passenger service resumes." Hart reached for the datacard with her resignation letter, and swept it into a drawer of his desk. "I'll hold on to this for a little while in case you change your mind before then. Give it some thought, Lara—the Foreign Ministry needs people like you."

Lara shook her head. "I don't see myself changing my mind, sir. But I'll think it over." She took a breath, and headed for the door.

Norman Hart called after her as she left. "For what it's worth, Lara . . . you look like a fighter to me."

25

Three weeks after the Second Battle of Tamabuqq, Sikander and Lara returned to Durzinzer. They debarked from the airship on a sunny early-spring afternoon, the only two humans on a platform full of Tzoru going about their business. They waited for the crowd to disperse, taking in the view of the ancient town and its picturesque highlands. "Look at this," Lara said, shaking her head in astonishment. "Not a thing has changed. All the troubles of the last few months, and Durzinzer was completely untouched."

"So I see." Sikander took in the bucolic scene, and breathed deeply of highland air without a hint of smoke or the acrid ozone left by shock-rifle fire or the faint smell of death from bodies buried in the rubble of collapsed buildings. He thought he could even detect the subtle scent of the *kumudda*-ferns beginning to blossom—as much as anything ever blossomed on this planet—now that the weather had turned. Whole districts of Bagal-Dindir had been flattened in the intense fighting to break the siege of the Thousand Worlds ward, and of course the ward itself was still a mess of rubble-strewn streets and unrepaired buildings. Durzinzer, on the other hand, remained completely untouched by the fighting. Finding the place undamaged cheered him more than he would have thought.

He nudged Lara with his elbow and pointed at the waste receptacle by the ramp. "Except that wastebin, of course. I ruthlessly destroyed the previous one that stood at that spot."

Lara laughed. "Well, I'm glad to see that they managed to rebuild. But of course it will never be the same again, will it?"

They shouldered their overnight bags and made their way to the ramp. Sikander winced as he put his full weight on his left ankle, now encased in a light walking cast. He'd managed to break a small bone when he threw himself and Tzem Ebneghirz out the window of the Kadingir Temple, and he hadn't even noticed it for hours until the persistent ache finally drew his attention. The cast was supposed to come off in three more days. *Not soon enough,* he decided. The damned thing got in the way for all sorts of activities.

Lara noticed his limp, and gave him a measured look. "How about we hire a carriage in the square? You don't really want to walk a couple of kilometers on that, do you?"

"It's nothing," he protested.

"Are you seriously trying to impress me by demonstrating that you're tough enough to walk on a broken ankle instead of paying ten credits for a ride? Seriously?"

"When you put it like that, no, of course not."

"Then let's get a carriage."

Sikander hesitated for just a moment, and then realized that he was waiting for Darvesh to make the arrangements. Unfortunately, the valet and bodyguard was recovering from a much more badly broken leg than Sikander's—a block of masonry from the collapsing temple had tumbled down on top of him while he kept Sikander and Ebneghirz from sliding off the mountain. Darvesh had remained aboard *Exeter* to recover from surgery, but he'd made no secret of his disapproval of the idea of another unescorted venture outside Bagal-Dindir, peace or no peace. *Well, I almost got Darvesh killed,* Sikander reflected. *I deserve to feel guilty!* In response he threw his bag over his shoulder and started down the ramp, letting the sharp little pain in his knitting ankle serve as punishment.

Lara must have sensed the turning of his mood. She followed him down the ramp in silence, and waited while he waved down a driver in the square. Only when they'd both settled into the carriage's narrow bench did she speak again. "Worried about Darvesh?" she finally asked.

"Well, yes," he told her. "I know it wasn't entirely my fault. But do you know I never even stopped to think that he would have to follow me into that temple? I just ran inside without a thought for anyone else."

"Where to, honored friends?" the driver asked in Tzo-qabu. She gave no sign that she'd understood anything of their conversation, and simply regarded them incuriously with her dark Tzoru eyes.

"The Radi residence, please," Lara answered her in her language. "It's near the Library."

"I know it well," the driver said, and tapped the *alliksisu*'s flank with her goad. The beast snorted once and set off at a slow amble, plodding softly through the ancient stone streets.

"When do you ship out?" Lara asked him, nestling closer. Spring or not, the season was still early enough for a deep chill to linger in the shadows.

"Four days," Sikander replied. "Commodore Abernathy decided that it was a good time to rotate out some of the staff, and since I'd been here as long as anybody and I was due for some leave anyway, he told me to start packing." Abernathy had also made a point of tearing up the letter of admonition and the letter of relief in Sikander's service jacket, and informing Sikander that he intended to put him in for a commendation for his actions in the retrieval of Sapwu Zrinan from the Thousand Worlds ward and the raid at Kadingir. Sikander had mixed feelings about the recognition and the early rotation. He suspected that Abernathy was in his own way trying to apologize for not reining in Francine Reyes sooner, but he could hardly argue about his orders.

"Well, I'm glad you were able to take a couple of those days to come back to Durzinzer with me," Lara said. "It was a shame we had to leave so abruptly the last time we were here."

"Not much point in spending liberty time in Bagal-Dindir right now—all of my favorite restaurants in the Thousand Worlds were blown up in the siege." Sikander drew her close, enjoying the feeling of her by his side. "Getting out of town for a little bit seemed like exactly what I needed."

"Me, too." Lara fell silent for a time; they listened to the soft footfalls of the *alliksisu,* and watched the charming old homes and workshops pass by.

"Have you decided whether you'll stay?" he asked her.

Lara nodded. "I have to. I've been thinking it over for days and days, and I've decided that we're going at this"— she waved her hand, somehow encompassing the planet, system, and hundred-and-twenty-two-world Dominion all in one gesture—"all wrong. The aristocratic *sebetu,* the Anshar's court, the trade deals and concessions . . . none of those are going to matter down the road. We need to find ways to be friends to the Tzoru people, not the high *sebetu* of the government. We need to show the *warumzi agu* that we're the foreigners who are going to stand up to the other great powers and fight to preserve the Dominion, not carve off our own little pieces of it. Tzem Ebneghirz isn't wrong about what's been happening here."

Sikander smiled. "I've talked to him quite a lot in the last couple of weeks. He's a fascinating person—and, yes, full of dangerous ideas. He doesn't like humans very much and you probably shouldn't trust him. But he can't resist the temptation to do a little teaching if you convince him that you're sincere about finding out what he thinks and why. If I were you, that's where I would start."

"I think I will." Lara turned her face to him again. "So what happens now?"

"I'll take some time to go home, I think. I haven't spent more than a week at one time in Kashmir in four or five years now. After that, I guess it'll be on to my next billet. I should be due for another shipboard tour."

"That's not quite what I meant," Lara said. "I'm staying here, and you're leaving. It might be years before we're in the same place again."

Sikander took his time before he answered. He noticed that the neighborhood looked familiar; the Library domes peered over the treeferns just a block or two away. The home of the Radi was not far off. "I don't know," he admitted. "I hate to say good-bye, but what else can we say? I care for you, Lara, and I hope that our paths will cross again, perhaps when we don't expect them to. But until then . . ."

"I know. That's how it seems to me, too," Lara replied. She sighed, and straightened up. "Well, I'm still glad you came. There's a lot more of the Library to see, and we had to skip all that the last time we were here. I can't wait to show it to you."

"The home of the Radi, honored friends," the Tzoru driver announced, reining in the *alliksisu*. "Do you require any more assistance?"

"No, thank you," said Sikander. He paid the driver and climbed out of the carriage with a little care, making sure to put his weight on his good ankle first, before he turned to help Lara down—not that she needed it. They picked up their bags and made their way to the house's front gate as the driver and his beast plodded off.

Radi Sabub emerged from the house before Lara even knocked. "Friend Lara! Friend Sikander!" he said, bowing low. "I am so glad that you were able to come back to Durzinzer. After so many troubles, it is good to be able to welcome guests again."

"Honored friends!" Radi Damiq bounced out of the door just behind Sabub. "You're back!" Behind her Radi Shuhad and the rest of the Radi clan crowded up to the door, all bowing in warm welcome. Sikander couldn't help himself; he laughed out loud at Damiq's efforts to bow formally while she capered and bounced all around them. The excited Radi children eagerly took their overnight bags in hand and ushered the two humans into the clan-home, peppering them with questions and well-wishes.

"Thank you, Sabub," Lara told the scholar. "You and your family have been so kind to us. And you have shown us what friendship really means in the last couple of months. I wish there was some way we could repay you for all you've done."

"The pleasure of your company is enough," Sabub said. "Will you be able to stay long?"

"Three days," Sikander replied. "I know it's not much to see all of the Library and the beautiful countryside around Durzinzer, but that's all the time I have."

"Then we must make the most of it, friends," Sabub said. "Your rooms are ready."

Lara glanced at Sikander, and gave him a small smile and shrug. "Actually, Sabub," she said, "I think one room will be just fine."

ACKNOWLEDGMENTS

My good friend Warren Wyman has been a sounding board for many of my stories and projects over the years. We talked through quite a few plot points and bits of world-building in some very interesting phone conversations; every writer needs someone they can just call up and talk at from time to time.

Thanks to my editor, Jen Gunnels, for her guidance and support as this story came together (and especially for helping me to bring the Tzoru to life). Thanks also to Richard Curtis for his sage advice and experience. I'm fortunate to have them both in my corner.

And, last but certainly not least, a very special thank-you to my wife, Kim, for facing a scary situation this year with courage, grace, and humor. She's fine now (thank God), but I'd like to take this opportunity to pass along a public service announcement: Mammograms save lives. Schedule yours if you know you're due, or remind the women in your life to do so.